THE GUARDIAN COLLECTION

"END OF THE SIXTH AGE" BOOK TWO

BILL@BILLBEST.NET

W. Best Publishing
1114 Highway 96
Suite C-1 #120
Kathleen, GA 31047

Copyright © 2015 by Bill Best

All rights reserved. No part of this publication may be reproduced, distributed or transmitted in any form or by any means, without prior written permission.

Col Bill Best
1114 Highway 96
Suite C-1 #120
Kathleen, GA 31047

Bill@BillBest.net

Publisher's Note: This is a work of fiction. Names, characters, places, and incidents are a product of the author's imagination. Locales and public names are sometimes used for atmospheric purposes. Any resemblance to actual people, living or dead, or to businesses, companies, events, institutions, or locales is completely coincidental.

Book Layout © 2016, updated 2019, BookDesignTemplates.com

The Guardian Collection / Col Bill Best – 2nd ed.
ISBN 978-1-7321509-1-1

Dedication:

To my military brethren, on-call 24/7 to defend the United States and our allies. May God bless and protect you and your families.

To police, firemen and women, EMTs, and other first responders who also serve 24/7 to protect us, our property, and our loved ones. You are appreciated! May God bless and protect you and your families. May He grant you wisdom and discernment to correctly and safely do your jobs.

To Christian pastors, along with missionaries and those serving in parachurch ministries. You preach, teach, encourage, lead (by example), and serve in countless ways. Your impact is eternal! May God bless, anoint, strengthen, and protect you, your marriages, and your families. May God provide for you and give you discernment, wisdom, and (yes!) a sense of humor along with loads of grace and peace.

Contents

2020 - The Countdown Begins 1
TRAPPED 1
TRANSITIONS 7
PLANS 11
PREPARATIONS 17
CONFRONTATION 21
TEAM'S END 27
CONSTRAINT? 31
FINAL AFFAIRS 35
RECONSTITUTE 39
"MAN MAKES HIS PLANS" 43
SELAH… 47
Guardian – Mach Ten 49
THE CALL 51
WE'RE GOING OPERATIONAL 55
LAUNCH! 61
PETERSON AIR FORCE BASE 67
IGNITION! 73
HYPERSONIC 77
TARGET LOCK 83
INTERCEPT 87
FALLOUT 91
JASON MATTHEWS 97
RECOVERY 103
A DIFFERENT REALITY 107
Guardian – Altered Reality 113
NOT GOOD 115
SLEEPLESS IN TITUSVILLE 121
SABOTAGE? 125
CONTACT 131
RESPONSE AND SECURE 137
DARK REALITIES 143
SIX MONTHS 149
ALIVE?! 155
CINDY AND TAYLOR AL-AMRIKI 161
RELOCATE 167
ON STATION 173
MAKE THEM SUFFER 179

FINAL REWARD	185
Guardian – System Two	193
THE GAME	195
PAST, PRESENT, AND PURPOSE	201
ALIAS	205
SHE'S ALL THAT	209
FOX	217
ENEMIES, OR…?	221
A PAWN IS LOST	225
A DEEPENING DARKNESS	231
A TIME TO REMEMBER	235
A TIME TO FORGET?	241
TRUTH	247
YOU NEED TO KNOW	253
DILEMMA	258
Guardian – The Reckoning	263
SUNDAY	265
MONDAY: All-Hands-on-Deck	271
GOODBYE	279
FRIDAY EVENING	289
DEEPENING DARKNESS	295
REVELATIONS	301
ATTACK!	307
REACTION	313
CONFRONTATION	319
RESOLUTION	325

2020 - The Countdown Begins

1. TRAPPED

Like a threatened cat, Stacey Townsend backed into a corner. Her dark eyes darted around the room, the floor, the ceiling. Her gaze always returned to the door, the only apparent way in or out of the small storage room.

The svelte woman in her early thirties would have stood to a medium five feet, six inches. But her slight crouch—her knees bent, feet shoulder-width apart with her left foot six inches forward of her right—made her appear shorter. And, gave her a fraction of a second extra time to confuse an attacker who would likely be half again her one hundred, fifty-pound weight and up to a foot taller. And if he were smart, he would not be alone.

Unlike a cat, Stacey would not act on instinct. Her enhanced intellect by now would register well above two hundred if she took the test again. Not good if you're trying to remain inconspicuous, and "fly under the radar." It would be like going on national TV wearing a sign, "Here I am, Jason!"

She again tried her smartphone, and as expected, had no connection to the outside world. *Faraday cage,* she thought. She looked around the room again. *How in the world did they find me this time?*

Stacey didn't beat herself up about it. No point. If she didn't escape, Jason and his team would do far more than beat her up. And many more people would die horrible deaths if their research continued to be unsuccessful. And if successful? Stacey shuddered. More would die. Many more.

The lovely young lady was not afraid. As dozens of scenarios and potential outcomes ran through her genetically enhanced mind, she even absent-mindedly swished a lock of her jet-black hair behind her right ear. She had faced this before and knew the exact rules by which she would live or die. And after all these years, she was prepared for either.

Years before, Stacey resolved not to use her powers for destruction unless not doing so would result in greater destruction. In this case, that exception clearly applied. She knew who would come for her. No, not by specific names, or how many. But she knew their boss. And she would rather die than be a lab animal for Jason Matthews again. And yes, she would kill if forced to do so.

Stacey arguably had the highest IQ of anyone alive in 2020. Occasionally, another unique capability manifested itself. And it was happening now. She began operating with dual streams of consciousness. Not rapidly jumping back and forth between tasks as most would describe multitasking. No, she was able to give full undivided attention to two tasks at once.

Stacey One: *How will they try to subdue me? Most tranquilizers won't work. Stun guns probably won't. If they somehow incapacitate me and bind me with ropes or shackles, I'll probably be able to break them. Hmm. If they've worked up a good profile they'd know, I'd give my life to save someone else like a young child. Would that be their play? How long would I have to interdict before they would harm him or her?*

Stacey Two: *Even my own biometrics equipment can't break my cover. Except…The wedding!* Just two weeks ago she attended a wedding at her church. She remembered holding the door open as the newlyweds ran to their car. Cameras – waving – YouTube – that was it. *Jason's scanning high-def images and videos for fingerprints!*

The two Stacey's came back together. *I've got to finish the new gloves,* she thought as she walked to the door. That gave her the time frame and told her that Jason's team didn't have time to fully prepare their trap.

She had to admit that the setup was clever. They—certainly Jason would send more than just a single person to capture her, likely well equipped and funded—they rented a corner shop. It was right along a strip she often walked by in the morning. The door was propped open and a minivan was parked in front loaded with boxes of supplies. It gave every appearance of being set up to open a new business. As Stacey walked by, suddenly a young girl ran out of the shop and hollered for help, that her mother had passed out in a back room. Jason's people knew from her profile that she had a tender heart and extensive medical training, and would try to help. Stacey followed the girl inside, the two of them followed by an older woman who had been sitting on a bench and reading something on her tablet.

They ran to the back of the small shop, the girl opened the door to a dark room, then she and the older woman—likely her grandmother—pulled it shut and deadbolted it. Quick, simple, away from her apartment neighbors, and early enough that no one was in the adjoining shops.

The door was solid as Stacey expected. They had replaced the regular door with a steel exterior door. If they had any sense, it would withstand a battering ram or a very determined genetically enhanced young woman. And the walls were bare, presenting nothing useful as a weapon.

Stacey nodded slowly. She knew how this would play out. And as much as she hated the thought, the reality was that one or more people would likely die today. Inside the locked room, wearing her red and white running suit to match her black hair and dark eyes, she began gentle stretching exercises…and waited.

+ + +

Jason was ecstatic. You could tell by; well, you really couldn't tell. You knew only what he wanted you to know; no more, no less. That was part of the game he played consistently and exceptionally well.

He shook hands and congratulated the team on the successful installation of the thorium reactor on the International Space Station, just days before the aging facility would have been abandoned due to failing solar panels. He especially thanked Cliff Nesmith for his quick thinking, fabricating a critical wrench to replace one an astronaut carelessly allowed to float away during an extra vehicular activity. Cliff transmitted specs to a new generation high-speed zero-G 3-D printer delivered to the station along with the reactor. Within hours, the reactor was successfully installed using a new wrench.

Jason always remembered key people. He was a master team builder, and he had many teams. He might be able to use someone with Cliff's talents. He made sure an aide copied down Cliff's contact information, and the senator returned to his limo.

Building his teams was important. But he could not have cared less whether the mission succeeded or failed. It would have been fine with Jason if the entire Space Station, at least anything surviving re-entry, had slammed into LA. As a matter of fact, such a calamity might have even furthered his plans.

So, he put on a great show and made everyone—future voters—feel that they were really important. But his main takeaway was identifying another potential team member.

Still, his real excitement went much deeper. And far darker. The text was cryptic as always. He must find a better, secure way to communicate outside of normal channels. Hillary did, at least for a while, but that door slammed shut once her private servers were discovered.

The text was simple:

"Seeing the lady on her walk today. Prepared for pleasant meeting."

Skylar always referred to Karen—regardless of whatever alias she used at the time—as "the lady." They'd meet her away from her residence, and they were prepared and expected a good outcome. At least from their perspective.

Jason's dark complexion lightened slightly, his typical smile seemed a little bit more sincere, and his dark eyes sparkled as he settled into the back seat. He ran a hand through his dark hair blown by the Florida breeze, fastened his seat belt, and anxiously awaited the good report he'd worked so many years to make happen.

Karen Lane Richardson would soon be back in his control, and his personally funded, highly proprietary Five Score and Ten—FSAT—project would continue.

It must continue.

+ + +

Skylar Brown never felt better. The no-nonsense African American carried his two hundred, twenty pounds of lean muscle on a stocky five foot ten-inch frame. If someone visited his small apartment outside the Washington Beltway, they'd find an impressive "I love me" room. It was filled with boxing, wrestling, and Karate trophies to show both his proficiency and enjoyment with conflict of the physical kind. There were almost as many more conquests that would never be talked about, even if the bodies were found.

Skylar was intelligent, resourceful, discreet, and Jason's go-to man since his previous security team leader, Louis "Bull" Thatcher, took that FSAT stuff and went crazy. Skylar wanted to take Karen on. Only his fear and respect of Jason kept him from walking right in and confronting the so-called superwoman alone. So, he kept to the plan.

He paid off the child and her grandmother, recruited through contacts with known drug dealers in the area, and sent them on their way. They'd tell no one and didn't ask any questions. Clyde drove up in the transfer van they had rented and the two men grunted as they pulled the heavy nitrogen tank out of the back and into the shop.

The men had sealed the room's air vents when they replaced the door. There were no windows or other places for ventilation, and the large nitrogen tank would quickly displace the air in the small room. Even "superwoman" wouldn't be at full fighting strength after four minutes of no air. And nitrogen itself isn't toxic, so she'd wake up heavily restrained and might have a headache for a while.

Skylar and Clyde rolled the tank back to the small room.

Stacey—Karen Richardson—could hear them coming.

If Skylar had been required to submit an After-Action Report and had chosen to be brutally honest, his description of the next seconds might have gone something like this:

0740: Clyde and I approached the room carrying the nitrogen tank and the hose to run under the door. A gap at the top of the door would facilitate expelling air as the heavier nitrogen filled the room.

0740, Continued: Subject crashed through the wall approximately 32 inches from the far edge of the door, through two layers of half inch sheetrock.

0740, Continued: Subject dropped to the floor in a crouch. Before Clyde and I dropped the tank to engage, she jumped at him and landed a flying kick with her right foot against the left side of his face. The impact snapped his head back and immediately rendered him unconscious. Summary of injuries included a fractured neck vertebra, broken cheek bone, and a severe concussion.

0740, Continued: I began to engage. She landed on both feet and as I attempted a right boxing kick to her chest, she dodged quicker than any opponent I've ever faced. With a single kick to my left leg, she completely shattered my knee.

0740, Continued: As I collapsed, she picked me up by my right arm and leg. She raised me above her head and threw me half-way through the sheetrock wall on the other side of the door that she had gone through.

0740, Continued: I passed out, awakening later and in excruciating pain in the ER.

Lessons Learned:

Good: The room we locked her in was dark. We should have tripped the circuit breaker to keep her from turning the lights on, finding the wall studs, and then using a nail file to mark them. She ran out right between them.

Better: We should have covered the inside of the walls with floor-to-ceiling plywood, a minimum of ½ inch thickness.

Best: We should have done both and immediately gassed the room with nitrous oxide instead of nitrogen.

And we never should have given her five minutes to plan ahead.

Skylar didn't seem to get around to writing that report. But he never forgot the shattered knee. Or that a much shorter, 150-pound woman took down both him and Clyde. In less than a minute.

2. TRANSITIONS

Karen Lane was furious as she quickly walked out of the store. She hurried back to her apartment, but not so fast as to draw any undue attention.

All her senses were operating at an unimaginable level. She walked facing oncoming traffic, and without any outward sign other than casually looking around, she saw every face in every car that approached her. She even saw the Lexus pass her, occupied by an attractive middle age woman who apparently wasn't, based on a protruding Adam's Apple and facial stubble from not shaving that morning. There were the conversations of workers installing a new underground fiber optic cable fifty yards away, and a couple arguing in a car heading past her, even with the windows shut. The noise from all the gasoline and diesel engines. Even the near-silent whine of electric vehicles. She was almost overwhelmed by radios broadcasting sports, news, and what some people called music.

Fortunately, no one heard the dialog screaming in her head:

I'll kill him. This nightmare has to end. And if I don't take him out who knows how many more will die!

She checked the security apps she developed for her smartphone and verified the all-clear from hidden sensors in and around her apartment. She also quickly walked around her building to make sure all appeared in order. Everything was normal as she expected. Jason would have one hundred percent of his resources focused on her take-down, not spread out between multiple locations.

I can't believe he only sent two men…he'll never make that mistake again. I've got to put him down.

Karen quickly walked into her apartment, went to the bathroom, and for the first time in decades she threw up. She was not by nature a violent woman. The few times she did fight, she literally had to. But running from evil incarnate over the years took its toll, and only a last-minute act of grace kept her from killing the men who attacked her. But Jason Matthews…

Got to focus!

She'd give herself no more than five minutes to clear out of her apartment, and three hours to leave town. She'd never be seen in Nashville as Stacey Townsend again. She executed her well-planned exit. For the many years since Jason started tracking her, she never stayed anywhere more than a year. She always paid the rent in advance, and everything she left behind would be picked up by a charity that she would choose shortly after arriving. Even the car would remain, and she'd mail the keys and title to the charity.

She stepped out the door in four and a half minutes, dressed casual and wearing a stylish backpack. She walked to the corner coffee shop to await the Uber she texted. Minutes later her ride dropped her off at a mall. She went into a restroom, and within minutes emerged with a different appearance and under a different alias. Her backpack and her meager belongings were stuffed inside a duffel bag she had pulled out of the backpack.

Discretely hidden away in a sanitary napkin and placed in the bathroom's sanitary disposal slot were her dark contacts and the chemical packet she'd used to change her appearance. That was one product she developed exclusively for herself with no plans to patent or market. Without using any water or even gloves, in three minutes this particular pouch of chemicals safely changed her hair color and eyebrows from black to strawberry blonde. That product alone would generate a worldwide annual revenue of over eight figures. For Karen, that was just pocket change. But being able to quickly morph from one identity to another? Priceless.

The transformation was very routine, just typically not in such a rush. And never before accompanied by such overwhelming fury.

I'm going to kill that man.

She knew his security was extensive, not only as a senator but more so because of his extra-curricular activities. Even Karen hadn't cracked through all the layers yet, but she suspected international crimes including drug trade and human trafficking. She even speculated that he made his second million by harvesting and selling aborted baby organs. Lord knows—and she faithfully prayed to Him often—how she had tried to expose him, to get him put away where he couldn't hurt others. But in spite of her prayers and years of hard work, she hadn't been able to nail down any evidence that would stick. Of course, she could personally testify against him. But that was absolutely out of the question.

As she walked the five miles to the bus station, she began plotting how to execute a United States senator.

Two hours later, a young woman boarded a Greyhound bus outbound from Nashville. She brushed back her strawberry blonde hair as she sat in an empty row of seats. Her hazel eyes flashed with resolve as she planned her next step.

Lynn Blalock was on a bus to Atlanta, Georgia.

+ + +

Jason was furious. You could tell by; well, as usual, you really couldn't tell. Back in his heavily remodeled, ultra-secure penthouse condominium, he poured his first drink. Even in private he tried to maintain the façade. His goals and his tactics to reach those goals required the utmost personal discipline at all times.

He told his multimedia system to play "normal." His seven-channel, high-def multimedia surround system responded with acid rock and a kaleidoscope of flashes, explosions, lightning, and chaos.

Two of his best men, almost instantaneously devastated by a single older woman!

I told those idiots to take her seriously! Both men in the hospital, facing surgeries and months of rehabilitation. And Clyde will probably never be of use again.

His fury gave way a little as he again thought of the bigger picture. And he always returned to the bigger picture.

He sat back in his recliner, took a deep breath, and turned what he called music up even louder. The tension slowly melted away.

I have got to get that woman back and see what makes her tick!

He remembered some of the other pleasures he had allowed himself to experience at her expense and smiled.

Oh yes. And I'll definitely enjoy some private time with her again. In the meantime?

Jason checked his smartphone calendar to confirm that he had a rare day off tomorrow. He muted his multimedia system, placed a call to a special number, and identified himself by a secure code.

"Yes, Sir? What's your pleasure tonight?" a personable male voice responded.

"Female. Fifteen to seventeen. Hmm…don't care about the race. At my place in an hour; pick her up at 9 am."

It was time to play. The teenager will be delighted to give him anything he desired, as often as he desired, for another hit of the designer narcotic his team perfected just two years earlier.

Jason poured his second drink—he never had more than two—and turned his multimedia system back up, basking in the pandemonium.

His plans would put him exactly where he wanted to be by his mid-sixties.

FSAT would give him forty-five years or more to enjoy it. And no one could stop him.

"No one *will* stop me!" he stated out loud, and took a deep gulp of very expensive Scotch, straight up.

3. PLANS

Lynn had plenty of time to think during the bus ride from Nashville to Atlanta. The three-and-a-half-hour drive became six thanks to several stops along the way. Many pundits expected bus transportation to go the way of the pay phone years earlier, but it still had its place. She found that it provided a good transition between locations when the distances weren't too great.

As she reclined her seat back, she thought forward to her next actions.

She assumed they would never expect her to return to Atlanta. It would take her no more than a week to find and rent a suitable apartment and furnish it. She didn't require much, and always chose furnishings that would eventually go to a worthwhile charity which she'd identify during her second week. She would pay the rent by check from one of her many secure accounts. Her furnishings would be bought using a credit card from another account.

Same with a car; never new, always a different model, and always paid by check.

All of her secure accounts, corporations, aliases, tax reporting, and hundreds of other details would easily require dozens of lawyers, CPAs, financial planners, stockbrokers, and more to manage. Lynn—Karen—did it with an average of one hour's effort each day. And she still took the time to support hundreds of carefully-selected and monitored ministries. Only God knew how many thousands of orphans and elderly she had helped, how many clean water supplies had been provided in Africa and elsewhere. And the hundreds of evangelists and missionaries she supported. As Jesus said, we must work while it is still light.

But her thoughts were not currently on the next medical center she might set up in the Appalachia's.

There were perhaps thousands of ways to eliminate Jason Matthews. She would meticulously consider each one in terms of her safety, the safety of others, and potential second and third order effects of each option. What if an Islamic terrorist group took credit for the execution and it reignited some region in the Middle East? What if someone innocent was arrested, tried, and convicted as a scapegoat? And she certainly could not permit any collateral damage.

Memories flashed back to what he had allowed and even directed during her captivity. It was all so clean, so white-coat, so scientific. So cruel.

While they took countless samples, even liters, of her blood and dozens of bone marrow samples – all without anesthesia – they mercilessly tested the "left and right limits" of her abilities. How long did it take for her to heal from cuts and burns in various locations? Did she scar? How did her body respond to extended fasts or lack of water? How did she cope with polluted and bacterial-laden water? Could she develop antibodies that might be profitably marketed?

The "medical research" team played against each other to win Jason's approval by concocting increasingly bizarre tests, taking her to the ragged edge of death again and again. How well might she survive sub-zero temperatures? Fully nude, of course, and covered with electrodes to better monitor all physiological processes. Same with high temperatures, approaching and exceeding Death Valley in the middle of summer. Rapid ascent in an altitude chamber to 18,000 feet. And far, far more.

Always shackled. Always closely guarded. No privacy. Molested and raped by Jason, usually after one of his test subjects painfully died when FSAT failed to do for them what it had done for her. She would hear the screams of pain as they would insanely beat themselves against the walls of reinforced rooms in their final hours. Their short-gained superhuman strength and intelligence would fail, leaving them curled and whimpering in a fetal position until death mercifully overcame them. Jason would be furious and vent his wrath on her, as if was somehow her fault.

Jason's team would find someone else, maybe a homeless addict, to use as experimental subjects. Physically, Karen would quickly recover from his abuse. But mentally and emotionally from the shame and cruelty?

Karen awoke from her nightmare of remembrance as the bus drove over some rough interstate road construction. Her thoughts turned from a quick, clandestine kill to far more intimate, slow and painful ways of taking him down. She would make sure he knew exactly who his executioner was, how she was going to do it, then complete the kill in the same unemotional, clinical fashion as his team had treated her. Her creative side began to emerge…

"Alright, Mr. Matthews. I have successfully transferred all your personal financial assets to various accounts. I want to assure you that I will personally direct them to support multiple organizations that represent everything that you, yourself, oppose. Now, to make sure I have your full attention and cooperation, I plan to break both of your arms, and then both of your legs.

Next, I will place a sound meter at exactly one meter from your mouth. We'll see how many burns I have to inflict, and where, to obtain the desired reading of, let's say, 128 decibels, 'A' weighted. At least, that's where we'll start. Then for our second day's activities…"

Her thoughts were very dark, indeed. The bus arrived in Atlanta. She checked into a hotel, showered, and went to bed. It didn't occur to her that for the first day in many years she had not spent a single minute reading or meditating on Scripture. And not a moment in prayer.

+ + +

"Good evening, Senator."

Billionaire Stan Bishop stood in Jason's doorway, hand outstretched. He smiled slightly, but his gaze seemed always to be just beyond whoever he was talking to as if he were already planning his next step. Jason would never be so presumptuous to say so to the younger man, but the two of them had been cut from the same bolt of cloth. Jason knew it. Stan? Probably not.

"Good to see you, Stan." Jason returned as he stepped aside to let his long-time acquaintance, in many ways his benefactor, enter. Two hefty bodyguards remained outside. Jason knew the men to be heavily armed. He was just as certain that more guards were scattered around the building; some obvious, others not so much. *Reminds me to beef up my security,* Jason reflected, especially since Skylar and Clyde were taken off his active list the previous day.

Jason rarely entertained company. Typical visitors were security personnel scanning his penthouse for any wireless bugs or other vulnerabilities. Occasionally he allowed in people from his various teams, his security detail, and, of course, the males and females, eight and up, brought there to entertain him.

Stan, of course, was the rare and welcome exception.

They walked quietly into his inner room, and Jason shut the door. No eavesdropping devices made would be able to penetrate the security there, and they could talk openly. Jason poured generous portions of his rare, expensive Scotch for them both.

"Are we making progress?" he asked the billionaire.

Stan took a sip, sat in the elegant recliner, leaned it back and stared at the high vaulted ceiling. He looked over at Jason, or rather through him, pursed his lips and slightly shook his head.

"Not really. Sure, we're always moving in the right direction. But who would have imagined that your Founding Fathers created such a system that it would take decades to bring it down? From international and monetary perspectives, the United States is still surprisingly stable in spite of everything. Your read?"

"Same," Jason replied. "We've left the doors wide open for undocumented immigrants to drain our health and welfare systems. We've facilitated crime, drug traffic, and terrorism. Homegrown 'lone wolves' are shooting up theaters and blowing up high-value targets. We and our media sources keep pounding against guns but we're no closer to disarming civilians than thirty years ago. Much of the country is still pro-Second Amendment. And I'm frustrated that we haven't been able to take down the First Amendment to shut up preachers and religious zealots."

Jason paused, carefully choosing his words. "I'd say we have made little progress beyond Obama's days. We've blurred the lines between the branches of government. We've all but eliminated the checks and balances. Public education is completely on our side – has been for decades. We've gone further with wealth redistribution than anyone would have imagined at the turn of the century. Everything's close to anarchy, and still the U.S. is our biggest hold-out."

"Then Trump came in, totally unexpected, and set us back decades. Ever get the feeling that there's almost a force, a Presence that keeps getting in our way? Like a power that's holding us off from our final takeover? It's like he was raised up by divine intervention." Stan mused.

"I hate to think about it, but my mother was a religious person. She used to talk about some kind of spirit holding things back until the Church is removed. Something superstitious like that," Jason said.

"Hmm. But once the Church is gone that Presence is gone as well? Interesting," Stan replied.

They were silent for a beat, brooding over their drinks. Jason always admired the younger man's decorum. He was always open and to the point, but left you guessing what else was on his mind. *We're cut from the same bolt of cloth,* Jason mused again. He even admired the man's wardrobe, the casual elegance of slacks, shirt, sports coat and shoes that was always appropriate, always stylish and expensive looking, but never extravagant.

He also appreciated Stan's business acumen. The man built a small overseas software company he sold for a huge profit just before the dot-com bubble burst. He took his "lessons learned" and tackled international financing. While Jason didn't know all the details—Stan was almost as secretive as himself—he developed a highly proprietary program. "Overlord," as he called it, monitored international financial, political, environmental and other factors. He continued tweaking the complex algorithms to codify the mantra of buying low and selling high. Timing in the finance world is everything, and Stan's program made predictions and then executed critical buys and sells that came down to critical minutes or moments. No other program—and there were many—came close.

Overlord had made Stan millions. Then those millions made billions, especially during the Great Recession of the first decade of the century. Now the program tracked so many simultaneous variables that it had to run on a supercomputer. If all the hidden accounts ever came to light, Stan was probably the wealthiest man alive. And while he had no political aspirations of his own, he had a plan. He used his money to execute that plan. Overlord would set him up as the Financial Minister of that plan. But while he was a patient man, he wanted it within ten years. He had no interest in studying Forex candle charts and stocks the rest of his life.

Jason also admired Stan's isolation. No marriage, no family, just always surrounded by well-paid people who would give their lives for him if necessary. Or would be brutally murdered if they didn't, Jason speculated. Of course, Stan enjoyed all the physical pleasures imaginable. He was one of the first and continued to be one of the most prolific customers of Jason's little side business.

Stan rarely visited Jason as his normal activities were beyond the borders of the United States. When he did, he typically punctuated it with some directive, some new task.

The silence lingered.

"Jason, I think we need to execute your plan for a vectored crisis. Some inciting incident that will expedite our takeover."

Jason nodded. "Maybe set off a series of interrelated incidents worldwide, leading to a crisis we manipulate to our benefit?"

Stan took another sip and pondered. "If we target well enough in advance...say five or six years...we might even bring about a sudden change in leadership within key countries and plan our transformation at that point. We should be ready by then. Agreed?"

Jason smiled. "I do. I'll work on putting pieces together at this end, send you several scenarios, and you can see what the rest of the team might have ready by then. I think it would be most helpful if I were on the Armed Services Committee. I'd like access to deeply classified programs. And I have something in mind that would help drain the U.S. military budget and also might help our cause."

"Agreed. Consider it done."

Within half an hour, the little-known international financial leader had left. His visits ended within thirty minutes; most lasted less than fifteen.

Jason had received his new direction and immediately tweaked it so it precisely fit into his own plans.

4. PREPARATIONS

Lynn awoke from her customary four hours in bed. It had been a restless night, resulting in under two hours of actual sleep.

She absent-mindedly poured peanuts, walnuts, and almonds into a blender along with raw fruits and vegetables to make her SNS; her super nutrition smoothie as she called it. She poured the blend into a large sixteen-ounce insulated beverage container, opened her sliding glass door, and stepped out onto her third story balcony. An intriguing thought had taken form through the night, now three weeks after her escape.

What if she were to give Jason what he wanted? Let him experience for himself the rush, the power, the clarity of thought that FSAT would give him? Her research had brought it a very long way since she took the last true, original dose. Maybe she would inject it from a safe distance by micro-dart.

The discomfort in the pit of her stomach she always experienced whenever she thought of Jason was now continuous. She was oblivious to the flavors she had perfected over the years as she sipped her SNS. *The man is pure evil,* she would remind herself throughout the day, every day. *He deserves to die.* She shuddered once more as she remembered the unspeakable things he orchestrated against her and others. And the direct personal violations of his own, not based on sexual need or lust, but on a need to exhibit raw power and control.

He deserves to die!

Lynn looked out from her balcony, sipping her breakfast as she gazed down at the people below. Over the years, she always tried to get on the third or fourth floor as it provided a few moments to respond to an attack and a psychological advantage of surprise. In seconds, she could grab her backpack—which was always close at hand--and jump to the ground and take off running at a record-breaking sprint.

Returning to her train of thought, her current bio-modeling suggested that she had slowed the process down about four hundred percent from what she'd experienced. An hour after the injection Jason would start to feel a rush. After eight hours, his strength should double, and his IQ should be twenty points higher. After sixty-four hours, he would be three times stronger and he would experience another twenty-point gain in IQ. At the square of sixty-four hours, just under 171 days, he would have four times his original strength and an increase of around sixty points in IQ. But even with her success in slowing down FSAT, he wouldn't make it to even ten days. It would still kill him, horribly. He just might survive eight days instead of two or three.

She finished her smoothie breakfast and went back inside for her morning cyber ritual. Typically, she conducted her business in the evenings; mornings were her time to snoop. She scanned various news feeds, commentaries, and international business reports. She'd spend a few minutes checking up on her favorite charities and ministries she had started or supported. Then she checked up on Samantha Knowles and Mick Thompson, from back in the original FSAT days in the early nineties. Likewise, she'd follow the whereabouts and status of her friends from 2006, Roger and Cindy Brandon. She hoped one day to get back in touch with all of them without putting their lives in danger.

Like, a day when Jason Matthews was no longer a threat. What a thought! Freedom to go anywhere, do anything, be with anybody as herself; not under one of her dozens of aliases.

She took a deep breath then turned her attention back to her tablet.

After her normal news and social dump, she often dove deeper. As a world-class hacker, she kept tabs on the news behind the news in several key areas. Over the years, she'd collected and anonymously sent enough information to authorities to break up a few international crime syndicates. She'd also exposed more than a few cases of banking and medical fraud. Then there were the dozens of cases of gross fraud and corruption at both state and federal levels. Evil was certainly alive and well on planet Earth, she would often lament.

But Jason Matthews...She tried daily to get something to stick to his Teflon façade, but he undoubtedly had CIA-level cybersecurity support, or even better.

After a few more unsuccessful minutes attempting to find something—anything—to bring him down, she set aside her tablet. She poured a cup of coffee and returned to thoughts of a more direct approach. Injecting Jason with FSAT would be poetic justice that an Edgar Allan Poe or Alfred Hitchcock would appreciate. Give him all the benefits he desires. But also make sure he gets the memo that he'll only have eight days to enjoy them. Lynn smiled at the thought of giving him an eight-day countdown app for his smartphone.

But as with everything, she had learned to consider the law of unintended consequences, those unanticipated or unintended second and third order effects of a single action. So, what about the other issue with FSAT? If it also enhances latent aspects of a person's character, what could that mean for someone already as evil as Jason? That was a characteristic her bio-modeling wasn't able to predict. What damage might he do in that time? How many more would die?

Lynn took a long, deep breath and slowly exhaled. Execution by FSAT was not an option. She would have to find another alternative.

+ + +

Now it was personal. And painful. Skylar never spent a day without an excruciating reminder of his failed takedown of a single woman who left him in agony and with months of rehabilitation ahead. Even then, the doctors couldn't promise a favorable outcome.

If we had her and the formula, Clyde and I would be healed by now, he fumed.

In reality, they still had a part of her. They had collected massive quantities of her blood, tissue samples, and bone marrow. But much of it was already used up. And to Jason's fury, the rest had spoiled from improper storage. Even the small amount that remained was degraded.

He put the TENS unit on his knee and turned it to full power. He wouldn't give up. He'd get her so Matthews could continue his experiments. But now he had his own agenda to do a little "experimentation" of his own to avenge his shattered knee from the morning she escaped.

He popped another narcotic pain pill and turned his attention to his tablet. The rest of the team still knew better than to cross him. They provided him with all the tools he needed to access camera feeds while otherwise incapacitated. Never mind that he was using classified equipment from a bed in a rehabilitation center. They still jumped at his command. But he perceived that hairline cracks were forming and spreading in his organization. He knew there was a buzz about how he and Clyde let a single unarmed woman best them, even cripple them, in a matter of seconds. He had to stay on top of things, show he was still Top Dog.

Something on the tablet made his heart skip a beat.

Really?!

Was this the same elusive target who had evaded him all these years? There she was. Street cameras, security cameras, all tracked her to the mall. No reason for her to hide up to that point. But then he picked up a woman of the same height, manner of walking, *and the exact same clothes* walking from the mall a few minutes later! Sure, her hair color was different, and she carried a duffle bag instead of wearing a backpack. But it was her!

All right, lady, let's see where you're heading to now.

He trailed her as she walked across town, from street camera to street camera. In a few more minutes, he saw her enter a bus from a bus station security camera. And he knew.

Atlanta, Georgia. Really?

He followed her from the Atlanta bus depot to the hotel she stayed at for her first week. Then he contacted local officials using the senator's status and one of the better pictures from a security camera. Within an hour they called him back with a name from hotel management.

"Hello, Lynn Blalock," he whispered with satisfaction.

5. CONFRONTATION

"I agree and approve."

That was all Skylar needed to hear from Jason. He put Randy Craig in charge. "RC" as they called him, had been Skylar's "Second" for twelve years now, having started at thirty after years of interstate truck driving. In spite of the considerable and intimidating tattoos across most of his otherwise pale arms and back, he had a cool, quiet disposition. Then there was the six feet, four inches and two hundred forty-pound frame the tats adorned. He was a study in contrasts, but RC could be tough as nails when needed.

Skylar saw the task as a chance to save face from his own defeat: "RC, you need to know that this genetic modification isn't a trick. This woman can out lift, out run, and out think anyone alive today. Clyde and I had a plan that would have been one hundred percent against any other human. Not her. The boss has given us permission to use enough of a classified gas he's getting for us, that we would be able to knock out an elephant for a full day. You'll have a med tech with you, so if it kills her, we can still get all the blood and other samples we need before it all goes bad."

"So...we don't have to take her alive at all costs?"

"That's correct."

+ + +

By choice and necessity, Lynn lived a quiet and solitary life, at least to the extent possible. Anyone she got close to would be in danger from Jason, either as collateral damage or for him to capture and use as bait to get to her. And few, other than Samantha, Mick, and the Brandon's, could be trusted with her secret. What if the world knew that her body might hold the cures for cancer, viral and bacterial infections, and genetic defects? That the same genetic change could increase IQ, physical strength, and lifespan? Well, there would be thousands of "Jason's." From all over the world, scientists and entrepreneurs would be after her. Governments like the U.S. would fear the final, complete breakdown of the Social Security system as people lived and continued to draw money many decades after their retirement. Armies would want to enhance soldiers. Anything could happen.

So, Lynn quietly continued her own research. Anything she discovered that would be beneficial and not destructive, she would anonymously make available to the public domain. But she would release nothing that might lead to anarchy or that could be weaponized.

So far, after decades of research: Nothing.

Lynn was exhausted. She took a quick shower and decided to skip her normal business activities for the day. She felt drained after the escape from Jason just a few weeks earlier. A lot had changed. Most of her time involved planning how to carry out his execution. She spent less time reading and meditating on Scripture, less time in prayer, and virtually no time to praise and worship the Lord.

That night, she went to bed early.

+ + +

From a car secluded a full hundred yards away, RC used binoculars to observe the front window. Lights had gone out at eight.

Slade reported that Lynn had closed her balcony curtains at seven thirty, and all the lights were off. He was almost two hundred yards away.

The rest of the team—two of Skylar's best—would join once RC gave the word. All communications were old tech…smartphones. Skylar warned them that any NSA-type wireless headsets would be what she'd expect and was likely able to intercept and monitor. They were on a three-way.

"You see any other lights on around her apartment?" RC asked Slade.

"No, it looks like she got the first apartment they opened back up after their renovation. Others look empty."

"Agreed. Kinda quiet. We'll give it another hour or two."

Waiting was hard. But no one wanted a shattered knee or fractured neck. Or worse.

Most nights, the neighborhood was quiet. An occasional car stereo, loud muffler, or open pipe motorcycle could be annoying, vulgar, or in this case, a good cover for the noise of breaking windows. Jerome, the fifth man on RC's team, rode by on an old Harley with open pipes, slow enough to mask the sound of RC and Brandon firing gas canisters through each of the front two windows. Slade and Curtis did the same through the back window and the sliding glass door.

Each canister was on target. Each released its classified, powerful gas. Any canister alone would take down a locker room full of NFL players. Together, the four canisters were deadly inside the confined space of Lynn's apartment.

The four men had waited till they believed no one would see them, and now with no sense of urgency they walked up the stairs. They sent a text to Jerome to ride back on the Harley. As he rode by, they set off the explosive to blow the locks on the apartment door.

One of the unique characteristics of the gas that led to its Secret classification was that it quickly dissipated and became harmless shortly after it was exposed to air. So, they walked right in to collect the body.

But RC took Skylar's warning seriously. The men were each armed with large caliber handguns, which they could use much quicker than rifles. RC and Slade each had two guns, and the one both of them had drawn and cocked was an even higher powered, long barrel version of the Judge. At the close distances inside the apartment, one shot would be devastating no matter how "enhanced" *the lady* was.

RC was surprised at how small the apartment was inside, probably under eight hundred square feet instead of a thousand.

No one could survive four canisters in that small an area.

And he was correct.

As the men entered and spread out to search the kitchen and the bedrooms, the last place they expected to find the body…was behind them.

Again, like a cat, but this time barefoot and like a cat stalking prey, Lynn slid up behind Slade in the living room. With her right hand, she grabbed his gun hand, covering the hammer so it couldn't drop onto a round. Before he could make any noise, she rendered him unconscious for a very long time. She quietly lowered his body to the floor, took his gun, and turned off his light.

In seconds, she was behind Crush as he looked into her master bathroom. His take-down was even smoother, as his handgun didn't have a hammer. She grabbed his wrist in a death grip that had the gun pointing back at him. Even if he could have pulled the trigger with his wrist broken, it would have discharged into his chest. He didn't, and she also lowered his unconscious body to the floor.

The third man was down in a few more seconds.

They had been in the apartment for almost a full minute. His men were meticulous, quiet, and should be through by now. Since no one had said anything, it appeared they had a very, very embarrassing miss-fire. RC was not looking forward to reporting back to Skylar—or even worse, directly to Jason—that they had blown it even worse than Skylar and Clyde.

"OK, guess we screwed up. Grab the canisters and let's get outta here."

Silence.

RC rarely got scared. And he never showed it. Until now. The large man started shaking. He turned off his light, put it in his pocket, grabbed his second gun and cocked it. In a slight crouch, he crept back toward the living room.

Still no sound, and no flashlights. The darkness unnerved him. He wanted to turn the hallway light on, but he didn't dare.

His foot kicked something. He crouched down and felt cold hard steel. A gun?

His eyes grew more accustomed to the dark. A third-quarter moon on a cloudless night along with area streetlights provided just enough light to cast two more small shadows on the floor. The other guns?

His shaking increased and sweat stung his eyes. Was she a witch? A demon? He'd seen as many scary movies as anyone. But this wasn't entertainment. It wasn't on the big screen. And it wasn't about someone else.

What happened next almost made the tough man whimper.

"Stop where you are. Or die."

The voice was strong and confident. Compelling. Terrifying.

"I have the Judge from one of your men. Before you can fire at me once, I can blow off both of your knees and both elbows and leave you here to bleed out. Put both of your weapons down and walk into the living room."

He complied.

"We will talk. If you cooperate, I may let you live. I'll even render you unconscious so you can make excuses to Jason. Sit down."

Again, in spite of all his training, all his close calls, and everything else that made him the man he thought he was, he complied.

She stepped into the middle of the room, ten feet from where he sat. The gun was by her side, not even aimed at him. But she had the casual confidence that assured him that he would never get to her before she could carry out her threat. According to Skylar, she could just as easily grab him and throw him off her balcony, head-first.

"You took long enough to follow my bread crumbs. I expected you last week. Got tired of sleeping on a blow-up in the next apartment."

That revelation took any remaining wind out of RC's sails.

"You...expected us...?" he stammered.

"Jason Matthews is an evil, wicked man. On the slight possibility that any or all of you might be legitimate security, I have let you live. So far. But I have some specific questions, and I want detailed answers. And you need to know that I can break your arms, your legs, and even your neck with my bare hands. I'm also totally pissed about a lot of bad things he did to me and wants to do again. So, talk!"

"Yes, Ma'am!" *Crap, did I really say that?*

6. TEAM'S END

Skylar grew more anxious by the minute. As he popped another narcotic painkiller, he glanced at the clock in the rehab center for the twentieth time in five minutes.

"Should have heard by now. Why am I not hearing something…?" he muttered as he rubbed his sore knee. How he wished that he could pace or was at home where he had a lot more at his disposal than just painkillers.

What in the world would he tell Jason now if something went wrong? He glanced at the clock again, feeling weak and sick. He was out of action for several more months. Clyde would not be rejoining the team. What if he lost the remaining five men? And still didn't get *the lady*?

No, Jason would not be happy at all.

+ + +

Jerome parked his loud motorcycle a half mile away and stepped into a transfer van they had modified. Inside was a large container with enough ice to pack out a large deer. Or a full-grown woman. If she were dead, as they all expected, they had a plan to transfer her body to the van without raising suspicions. He would drain and collect all her blood and put it into cold storage. Then he would chill her body until they could transport it to a prepared facility. Once there he could take his time harvesting marrow, eyes, brain tissues, and everything else on the long shopping list provided by Jason's "medical research" team.

He drove the van to her apartment and backed into a spot across from her stairs. After five minutes of waiting for the expected call, Jerome got out of the van and crept up the stairs to her third-floor open door. He drew his gun; a long barrel 357.

Did he hear a conversation as he approached the door? The surprise gave way to apprehension when he detected a strong woman's voice demanding answers, and a subdued RC giving them. Back against the wall beside the doorway frame, he turned and glanced in, seeing a woman's back as she faced

RC sitting in the shadows. No sign of the rest of the team.

He drew in a long, slow breath and stepped into the doorway, feet spread, and a firm two-hand grip on his revolver for the kill shot. He fired; center mass, just below the lungs to smash her backbone but allow him to harvest her heart.

The well-aimed shot completely missed Lynn, instead slamming into what had been the forehead of RC, sitting behind her.

Certain breeds of dogs might have detected his slow, deep breath as the wind swooshed into his nasal cavities; or the sound of denim against skin as he spun into the doorway. Lynn heard both and stepped aside to avoid the shot. She was fast, but she knew she wasn't fast enough to dodge a second shot. She had already verified from RC that these were not legitimate security personnel. Her decision was instantaneous and final. Her single shot from the Judge spread a pattern right above the gun in Jerome's outstretched arms, above any vest he might be wearing, to his neck and chin. It was immediately fatal.

Lynn stuffed the gun in her backpack of critical items, jumped from her third story balcony, ran a few dozen yards then stepped into the shadows and slipped away into the night. Within a few minutes, she heard sirens. Her car was a quarter of a mile away, on purpose.

Lynn would go away as had Stacey, never to be seen again. Neither would the gun.

Within twenty minutes she was miles away. Her transformation to Anna Drake, brunette, was complete. And Karen – Stacey – Lynn – Anna and all the other aliases she had gone by over the years – was lonelier and more conflicted than ever.

Her ploy had worked. She had learned so much. And so little. At such a cost.

The team that came for her, and all the teams over the years, were mercenaries as she had suspected. That made her feel just a tinge better that no legitimate security personnel were injured or…

That was the next issue. Two men were dead. And she had killed one of them herself. She was queasy, uncomfortable. But she also experienced a rush, a thrill that she had finally taken the offensive, played the tough girl, and made some wicked people suffer for a change. She felt empowered, in control. And those attitudes also bothered her. They just didn't seem right.

Was she doomed to be the smartest, strongest, healthiest, and someday the oldest person on earth, and also the loneliest?

Anna forced herself to focus. *Why was it becoming so difficult?*

Okay. Jason compartmentalizes everything. It's clear that there's no coordination between his various endeavors, teams, organizations, or whatever; whether legitimate or not. There's no Rosetta stone, nothing to tie it all together and bring him down. The man is an absolute genius. He plays all of his hands very close.

Was there any way to pin the attack on him? The dead men. One shot the other who and was himself shot by an unknown party from a gun that would never be recovered. Three other men will wake up soon, in police custody, and with severe headaches. One will have a broken wrist, and none will have any reasonable explanation for why they were there, or for their fingerprints on guns found at the scene.

Five men. Two dead. And theirs will be the only fingerprints found. For her entire stay at the apartment, except when she bathed, she had worn the new prototype, transparent graphene gloves she had developed.

Could the attack be pinned on Jason? *It would take a miracle.*

If the survivors start to talk, Jason will have them lawyered up, released on bail and then conveniently terminated.

He gets off again. At the most, I may have slowed Jason down a little.

I tried. I really tried.

That last thought was both a silent prayer and an excuse.

As she waited for the six thirty morning bus to Valdosta, Georgia, Anna again planned how she would execute Jason Matthews.

Senator, you have two weeks to live.

Soft whispers from Scripture that had been such a part of her life, especially since 2006, were drowned out by the turmoil and planning going on in her mind. Admonitions like, "Trust in the Lord with all your heart, and lean not on your own understanding" and "Vengeance is Mine, I will repay" went unheard and unheeded.

7. CONSTRAINT?

No apartment this time. And no car or change of address, which was always a challenge as every relocation included a new alias.

Anna Drake checked into an extended stay motel. She registered for a month and paid the first week with cash. The motel was close to a large Kroger grocery store with a growing organic food section. Her room had a kitchenette so it would be more like a home than some of the dives she had to stay at in the past.

Anna thought through her simple punch list:

Step One: Order materials from my lab.
Step Two: Monitor Jason's itinerary.
Step Three: Execute.

Based on her brief "interview" with RC, all of Jason's bad guy security should now be neutralized and it would take him a while to reconstitute his team. So, any security would likely be legitimate and must be protected. She would try to target his rare "extra-curricular" activities once she found one.

As she had been for weeks, Anna was engrossed in planning the perfect execution to avoid collateral damage and minimize second and third order effects. She sat deep in thought while eating lunch in the grocery store's deli, hardly tasting the sandwich that used to be her favorite. She was typically much more aware of her surroundings and was startled when a handsome, athletic man somewhere in his early forties interrupted her train of thought.

"You must be military. I haven't seen such intense concentration since I left the Pentagon."

His disarming smile caught her off guard as much as his boldness, standing there in front of her with his tray. Short-cropped black hair along with his strong, high cheekbones and cleft chin; his persona shouted "military and important" or an A-list actor playing that role.

"Excuse me," the handsome stranger continued. "I'm Don Draper. I'm TDY here at Moody, and I may be transferred here or up to Robins soon. May I join you?"

Years of loneliness, anger, and isolation overwhelmed her. For a split second, Anna thought once more of what it might be like to be normal.

"I'm sorry. No. I have some important issues I have to think through. And I'm not from around here. But I wish you well on your…career."

That would have been her normal response, with just the right inflection to be pleasant but final. It was a response she had perfected over the years from hundreds of similar encounters.

She simply said, "No."

The stranger smiled, cocked his head slightly, and started toward a different table by the window.

Why shouldn't I have someone to talk to, like any normal person?

Before she could think it through another dozen times, Anna caught herself saying, "Excuse me. Sure. I was just distracted. I'm not military, and I'm not from around here. But what do you think of Valdosta so far?"

She motioned to the chair in front of her. The man's smile continued as he walked back over and sat down.

"Not military, but very intense. So, what brings you to Valdosta, Ms…?"

"Anna. Anna Drake." She extended her hand, which he shook; and held on perhaps a split second longer than typical.

"I'm between things right now. I may stay here for a while. You?"

"Conference. Heading back to the five-sided square, as we call it—the Pentagon—in a few days. We're evaluating the old A-10s, whether to upgrade or retire and replace, and how we'd reallocate missions. My current tour is up in about six months, so like I say, I may end up down here or up in Warner Robins. You're between jobs? What do you do?

He took a bite of his Philly cheese steak sandwich.

The truth? Oh, I'm a billionaire with over twenty-five patents under almost as many aliases. There's a senator who would sacrifice ten mercenaries—even a hundred—to get his hands back on me. And I know I look around twelve years younger than you, but in reality, I'm at least eight years older. I can complete a full Iron Man Triathlon in under six hours and then go to the gym and easily out-press any Olympic weightlifter. And I'm not referring to the women.

She cleared her throat, suppressing a slight smile, and then answered. "I'm into various areas of research and marketing. And just doing things I enjoy since I lost my husband to cancer." She paused, reminiscing but decided to continue before he could chase that rabbit. "Are you a pilot?"

She took another bite of her sandwich, a chicken club on sourdough, and noticed for the first time that it was very good.

Their back-and-forth continued as they enjoyed a pleasant conversation, discussing world events, favorite sports teams, places they had visited, and a dozen other topics. Anna had to admit that she enjoyed just being able to talk to a real person. The fact that he was an intelligent, articulate, drop dead gorgeous Lieutenant Colonel selectee was quite impressive as well.

His phone alarm interrupted her train of thought.

"Oh, excuse me, Anna. Duty calls." He put his smartphone away, took out his wallet, pulled out an official looking Air Force business card, and handed it to Anna smiling.

"I've enjoyed our chat. Here's my number. No pressure, but after you've done your shopping if you'd like to continue our conversation or take in a movie or something, give me a call?"

Anna responded by taking the card and returning his smile.

"I hope you'll call," he said, smiling, as he walked away.

Don's smile got even wider once he turned his back to her. *Grocery stores work every time. Don't be pushy. Let her think she's in charge. We'll be in her bed or mine by ten.*

As Anna started her shopping, she was smiling too. At least, at first. An uneasiness gnawed at her like she was missing something. The internal dialog made it hard for her to concentrate on her main purpose for being here.

It feels good to have someone show me some attention.

Do you honestly think he's that interested in you as a person? You're beauty-queen gorgeous, just another conquest for his ego.

I've helped hundreds of thousands of people for decades; don't I get a little pleasure in life?

You talked an hour, about what? Do you know anything more about him than he knows about you? And you're a pro at concealing who you are.

The guy's a patriot, conservative, intelligent, and personable; what's wrong with me enjoying being with someone for a few days?

Do you even know if he's married? Kids?

The last piece was a real eye-opener. What about that? She had been faithful to her husband, Ed Richardson, their entire marriage. She had honored God by being celibate since his death. Did that apply to Don? And just what would the outcome be of their few days together?

And if he is my knight in shining armor, what would he think about my planning to execute a sitting U.S. senator? Or would he be willing to move from state to state, country to country to avoid men willing to die to capture me, or according to RC, to kill me?

It isn't fair.

To live again for two or three nights…

Anna took the card back out of her purse and looked at it for a long, long time.

8. FINAL AFFAIRS

Four in the afternoon. Anna still hadn't decided whether to call the man or not. She finished putting away her groceries and went for a walk to clear her head. A surprising thought occurred that she hadn't thought of Jason for at least two hours—a good thing.

Anna decided to indulge in some Rocky Road ice cream at a hangout that was apparently popular with college students and young Airmen. The place was packed. She couldn't help notice that most customers were couples; laughing, smiling, enjoying life. Her loneliness was overwhelming.

She ordered her ice cream, paid, and walked over to a table. But something didn't seem right. There was a guy walking across the parking lot—very intense—wearing more clothes than normal for that time of the year. Young, bearded, hands twitching; she glanced back inside the ice cream shop. There were a lot of military personnel inside.

Anna stood up as he entered the store. There was a clear path between her and the door. As she expected, he pulled out two high caliber handguns. Before he could begin his massacre, Anna picked up the heavy steel table she was sitting at and charged him. Her deep throated roar drowned out his chant to his god of destruction until both of them were drowned out as he emptied his guns into her steel table as fast as he could pull the triggers. The sound was deafening and even worse as patrons screamed and ducked for cover or ran for the rear exit.

The heavy steel table absorbed enough of the impact of eight rounds to prevent ricochet. In only a few steps Anna was already at a full sprint. The table hit him with the force of a runaway car, slamming him backward through the store window, past the sidewalk and into the parking lot. She continued her charge and before he could recover, she slammed the table flat down on him, then threw it aside just missing parked cars. By now his guns were several feet away on either side, he was unconscious, and likely would need significant medical attention to set multiple broken bones. But Anna knew too well that there was another risk.

She ripped open his jacket and sure enough, he was wearing an explosive vest. There was no time to wait for a team. If he regained consciousness for even a second, he could take out everyone within a hundred-foot radius.

The vest was sophisticated; homegrown, lone-wolf terrorists had learned a lot over the previous six years. But Anna disarmed it and removed it in seconds. She looked around and identified a young airman who seemed to have enough focus and courage to do what was needed. He hadn't run away; he was approaching to help.

"You. Take his guns and this explosive vest. It's disarmed. Give them to the police when they arrive. If that man moves, don't let him reach for anything. He may have more guns."

Cell phones were coming out as bystanders came closer to look at the young superwoman who single-handedly stopped a terrorist attack with a heavy table and her bare hands.

She heard sirens in the distance, growing louder.

Anna quickly ran into another shop down the strip and out the back door, then broke into a full sprint. No one could keep up with her on foot, but she knew from human nature that at least a few bystanders would try to track her by car. She ducked in and out of a few more shops, even setting off an exit alarm as she went out a back door, then entered her motel through a side door. She slowed to a normal pace and walked to her room. In moments, she stepped back out, carrying her backpack, and walked back to the side door. Sure enough, there were two young adults running down her hall, looking for a thirty-something brunette in a stylish but comfortable brown and tan jumpsuit and matching shoes.

They wouldn't find her. Redhead Stephanie Craig, with matching eyebrows, a light red shirt, and dark slacks left the hotel and walked away. She followed a path that also avoided security cameras, which she had already identified when she checked into the motel.

Stephanie didn't normally cut her hair as she morphed from one alias to another. But too many people had seen her up close and might see her again. She had practiced her quick cut countless times, and the trim was salon-perfect. She had carefully collected the hair along with her other paraphernalia, including her hair color packet, and would discretely dispose of everything where it wouldn't be found. To further the transformation, she had applied a colorful fake tattoo on her neck and an artificial nose piercing with a diamond stud.

Karen had committed to herself and to God, that she would always try to help others when she could. For whatever reason God gave her the unique qualities that were both a blessing and a curse, she would try to use them to His honor. But this time the cost had been high. Within hours, social media would be saturated with viral videos of her terrorist takedown. Jason's team—any remaining—would again have a fix on her position. And...she was out of aliases. Stephanie was her last one. No matter the cost to her prime goal, she now had to sequester herself for a full month and work on the next set of seven.

Every four years, Karen would break away from whatever she was doing and develop seven aliases besides her current identity. She had never run out before. She needed Social Security numbers, drivers licenses, back-stories, bank accounts with credit cards, business cards; and each set became more difficult. To spoof NSA-level facial recognition software, she needed to make more sophisticated dental appliances, contact lenses, and more recently, long-term prosthetics that would change the appearance of her ears. By the next iteration, she'd also need to develop natural-looking add-ons to her chin and nose. And artificial fingerprints and fingernails for her whisper-thin graphene gloves. She had also considered adding collagen injections. But now?

Jason will have to wait.

+ + +

Don was bewildered. Everything had played out perfectly as it had so many times before. He had expected several phenomenal nights with the gorgeous brunette. Then he'd have to go back to the plain-vanilla marriage, family, and all the other responsibilities he endured for the sake of excursions like this.

He hadn't gotten around to asking, but he knew she had to be a physical trainer or an athlete. When he shook her hand goodbye and gently grasped her forearm—that, along with his smile, had always been a winner—her muscles were like bricks under her smooth, soft skin. She must have noticed his mild surprise but had said nothing.

Why didn't she call? He wondered as he ate breakfast in his motel lobby.

A news story on the motel's eighty-inch television caught his attention, as the reporter described a thwarted terrorist attack the previous afternoon just a few blocks away. The lone wolf jihadist had two handguns and over forty rounds of ammo. His explosive vest could have destroyed a medium church which officials speculated was his final target according to documents found on him.

Don lasered in on the news story as similar attacks were increasing across the nation and were the first or second topic of the daily Pentagon briefings.

What he didn't expect were the eyewitness interviews that followed. A single woman had overpowered the terrorist in a matter of seconds. He was in custody and was in extremely critical condition at the local hospital, under tight security. There were no pictures of the actual take-down. Everyone had been fleeing for their lives…but several pictures and videos showed her disarming and removing the bomb vest, then talking to the Airman before running at an incredible sprint into the other store.

Anna?!

9. RECONSTITUTE

Jason was unaware of the brief reprieve he had received. What he was aware of was conflict. Not the normal external conflict he thrived on. It was a strange internal turmoil he had not experienced in, what? Years?

The evening had gone well enough. Business as usual, then some "entertainment."

He thoroughly enjoyed his "side businesses" as he called them and always had a purpose for each one beyond simple dollars and cents.

The Jackson Longevity Research Center had identified and was perfecting FSAT back in 1991. But the facility was destroyed and key personnel were killed when "Bull" Thatcher went crazy. Then there was Richardson, who had since died, and Karen, who continued to elude him. Without FSAT or any other breakthrough to prolong life, Jason wanted a good source of fresh, healthy transplant organs should he ever need them. Hence, the profitable business of harvesting late term aborted babies and artificially growing them several more months. Which also became a superb revenue stream.

He then learned of the plights of many of the young girls who came to his clinics. Some had few or no family connections and were already emotionally scarred and easy to manipulate. He realized he'd found a gold mine for domestic human trafficking. His designer narcotic, brutally addictive after just one dose, made them easy to control. They would do anything—absolutely anything—for that next hit. Even recruiting their boyfriends into the trade for those who preferred that form of entertainment.

Again, very lucrative. And again, much to Jason's personal benefit.

But this last girl troubled him.

She met all his demands, and he gave her the drug. But rather than falling asleep, she became agitated, weepy. He hadn't expected that, didn't need it with everything else on his mind.

She cried out to Jesus to forgive her, rescue her, deliver her, and set her free.

Jason wanted to slam his fist into her pretty face, or worse. But strange feelings from decades ago welled up. He called his special number for an early pickup, and they recovered her without incident. Only after she left did he admit that at least that evening, her prayer had been partially answered.

Jason thought back to his mother, who died of pneumonia one cold, damp

Chicago winter when he was eight. She used to call on that name. She used to pray for him, her "pretty boy" as she used to call young Jason. Then she was gone.

She wasn't there to protect him from the men who ran over his father. Sometimes because of his long hours, Jason's Dad had to leave him at other homes till late at night, or over extended weekends. Some of those men also referred to Jason as a "pretty boy," but it was not a term of endearment. And it certainly didn't result in a loving outcome.

Jason hadn't thought of his pre-adult years in a decade or more. Far too painful. The loneliness, the hurt, the betrayal. He had grown hard, calculating, and even heartless.

But his mother's prayers?

How many had he killed? How many more deaths was he responsible for? Was forgiveness even possible for him?

Weakness!

No. He was accountable to no one. As a human, he was at the top of a ridiculous series of mindless, random events that occurred over thirteen point seven billion years. And he had earned his way to the pinnacle of the human race. It was all chance, and then hard work. Everyone else was there for his pleasure, to serve him. He would bow to no one, have mercy on no one, and regret nothing.

Jason pulled out his smartphone and made a note: "Never regret, or waste energy on remorse." He needed to come up with a strong, private philosophy statement to memorize and meditate on. No time for emotional nonsense; no time for any form of weakness.

Jason toyed with the idea of having the twelve-year-old girl brought back up to him. He started to dial the number but decided he was too tired. He took a quick shower, had his second and final drink for the night, and went to sleep.

Unknown to him, a Presence departed from his penthouse. It had been around Jason several other times, offering emotional healing, forgiveness, a fulfilling purpose, and eternal peace and joy that would one day far exceed all the hurt of his troubled childhood. But Jason had again rejected the offer. For the last time. Jason had left the door of his heart closed and would never experience that gentle tug at his conscience again.

+ + +

A handshake. A handshake and a heart attack. Or a stroke, or maybe some combination of the two. If it didn't kill him, it would be severe enough to force him into medical retirement.

Stephanie had hacked into Jason's medical records from recent years. She marveled at how insecure the Federal site still was, even after the fiasco with Obamacare. In moments, she had a full summary of his overall health, which was actually quite good. He should live to a strong eighty or older before a gradual decline would slow him down in his early nineties. But if you read carefully enough… a little tug here, a little imbalance there?

She would simply attend one of his social functions. She wasn't able to access his private calendar, but his official schedule was very easy for her to hack. Jason had plenty of "I love me" opportunities where he would get to wave the flag, say "God bless America" and campaign for whatever else he didn't believe in. The thought of him holding or even worse, of him kissing a baby turned her stomach.

Get an invitation, pass through security, shake hands with my right hand, clasp my left hand over his, subcutaneous injection, and death within twenty-four hours.

She would continue to work the details, such as whether to use DMSO or micro-needles at the bottom of a ring. Also, she needed to work out the correct hormones and quantities.

Six months earlier a doctor had prescribed a T-3 hormone for mild hypothyroidism.

So… A very high dose injection to put him in thyrotoxicosis, along with adrenalin and cortisol, to really put him over the edge. All natural, normal, unsuspicious…

One particular event on his calendar caught her eye. He was scheduled to speak at a large job fair in a major city hard-hit by federal sanctions against so-called Sanctuary Cities. His motivational speech would be, "American Exceptionalism through a Strong Middle Class." None of which he actually believed, she noted with sarcasm. She would have been appalled had she known the true extent of his hypocrisy.

Four weeks. Plenty of time to get her spare aliases in order. She could plan the exact concoction and administration that would be natural but lethal to him yet harmless to anyone else, plan her trip, and then decide what to do with her new freedom.

She still had Don Draper's card.

10. "MAN MAKES HIS PLANS"

The weeks ticked by for Stephanie. Materials came to her motel, and she checked them off against her priority list. Just two more weeks.

She continued to check social information and news each morning and manage her businesses after dinner. She'd read the Bible and pray only occasionally.

The next morning, she read the news buzz of an impending solar flare that could be severe. She quickly got into deeper scientific feeds from NASA and learned that Solar Cycle Twenty-Five was starting early. IRIS, the Interface Region Imaging Spectrograph sun watching telescope, indicated that a huge Coronal Mass Ejection appeared to be heading straight to Earth. Some speculated that it could even produce a solar EMP; not the fast-cycle E1 and E2 bursts from a nuclear detonation, but a longer E3 cycle that would be especially problematic for electric power grids.

Stephanie had followed stories of upgrades to the country's electrical grid and other infrastructure. Too, she ususally kept a little extra water, canned tuna, and other miscellaneous items on hand; just in case. She didn't expect the event to have much of an impact on her, personally.

Hours later the event seemed to be a non-issue until the tail end of one news story caught her attention. There was speculation that the storm might have caused a system reset on a drone flying over Savannah as a possible explanation of a mid-air collision.

Stephanie turned the volume up as the story continued, accompanied by pictures of a severely damaged four-seat general aviation aircraft that had attempted to land with a damaged rudder on a runway with a high cross wind.

"The pilot, Roger Brandon…"

"Roger?!" Stephanie exclaimed.

"… is credited with an almost impossible landing under the circumstances, but his wife Cindy was pronounced dead at the scene. His son, Frank, died during transport to the hospital. Roger's daughter Susan is in critical condition, and Roger is in serious but stable condition, with possible paralysis from his lower back and down. The FAA is investigating."

Stephanie broke down into uncontrolled sobs. The tragedy affecting her dear friends suddenly put her own issues in a different perspective. Had she really obsessed over Jason for several months, since the attack on her back in

Nashville? Was she actually planning to murder him?

Roger and Cindy. She met them at a church by chance, the only time Roger shared from a pulpit. His simple but profound message on building foundations was a life-changing challenge and new direction after the loss of her husband. It had guided her relationship with Christ, and indeed her entire life, until that recent morning in Nashville. And Roger just lost Cindy and his son?

She cried, prayed, and paced for hours. It has been said that God cannot truly use a man…or a woman…until that person is broken. His strength is perfected in weakness. As that thought came to her mind, Stephanie clenched her fists. "I'm the strongest person alive!" She drew back to put a fist through the solid panel door to her apartment then let her arms fall limp at her side as she realized what she had just shouted.

Over the years, as she sought to build a strong foundation for her life, she had memorized and meditated on large portions of Scripture. She knew the exact reference: 2 Corinthians 12:10; "… for when I am weak, then I am strong."

The message was clear now. She could either continue to go forward on her own, in her strength. Or she could humble herself, be meek before the Lord, and be strong in His presence.

A flood of other Scriptures and Biblical principles rushed over her. She thought of David refusing to kill Saul, choosing rather to place his trust in God. She thought of how Abigail had approached David and kept him from avenging himself against the fool, Nabal. She remembered the words of Jesus on the cross, asking His Father to forgive those who crucified Him, and of Stephen asking God not to hold the sin against the men who stoned him to death. And finally, the warning from the Bible books of Romans and Hebrews that vengeance is God's, and that it is for Him to repay.

But Jason is so brutal. He's so incredibly wicked. He hurt me so much…

"Pharaoh."

She had remembered God's word about Pharaoh in Exodus 9:16: "… For this reason I have allowed you to remain, in order to show you My power and in order to proclaim My name through all the earth."

And she remembered the outcome of that judgment against Pharaoh. God had a bigger plan concerning Jason. It would bring God glory, and Jason would be dealt with severely.

Roger. He had lost so much, and would probably never walk again. He might also lose his daughter.

Stephanie—Karen—knew that she had received her next assignment. Not to go after Jason, but to go after some supplies. It had been years since she'd taken up a paint brush, but a picture had to be put on canvas. And she had to send it to Roger.

She envisioned Christ in a beautiful heavenly setting. But down here, it was as if she and Roger were on a stark, treacherous mountain in the midst of a raging thunderstorm, trying to hold on. As she kept thinking through how she felt, and what she knew of Scripture, the picture started filling in. Christ was regally dressed in white, standing at the top of the mountain in heaven. His arms were bare and muscular, and He was confidently pulling on a strong rope that extended below the heavenly white clouds, and down through a terrible thunderstorm below. The end of the rope was attached to a mountain climber—her! Roger! The climber was struggling but was secure. To the side of Jesus, the Scripture was written, "All authority has been given to Me in heaven and on earth." Near the rope, up above the clouds: "There is salvation in no one else." Also, beside the rope, but down below in the storm, was written: "Believe in the Lord Jesus, and you shall be saved." Finally, below the struggling mountain climber, the words: "For man is born for trouble, as sparks fly upward."

God would take care of her friend. He would take care of her. And in His way, the Righteous Judge of heaven and earth would certainly take care of Jason.

But if he or any of his people ever threaten me, I will defend myself, she affirmed.

Someday, somehow, maybe she and Roger would meet again, and she would be able to personally thank him. Twice now, God had used him to guide the strongest, healthiest, most intelligent person on the face of the earth back to the firm foundation that Jesus spoke of in Matthew 7:24-27.

God was in control. She would turn back to seek the Lord with her whole heart and walk in His light. He had given her a future and a hope, and she would wait upon Him. She would stay in seclusion—maybe leave the country again—and continue her research. She would continue funding the causes she felt compelled to support trying to make a difference for good while she could.

A sense of calm returned, absent since that fateful morning in Nashville.

One day it would all be clear. She was unique for a reason.

Suddenly, as if she had stepped into a cold wind, Karen shuddered. Deep in her spirit she felt something new, a strange sense of apprehension. Something wasn't right. It's as if something in the spirit world had shifted. Like a countdown had begun. What it would lead to, or when, she had now idea. But it wasn't going to be good.

11. SELAH…

Years pass. Karen continues her research and anonymous support of programs, organizations and ministries helping tens of thousands.

But always looking over her shoulder.

Jason's power and influence grow deeper, more sinister. Plans discussed with Stan continue to progress, even as the United States and other Western countries slowly move toward socialism, bankruptcy and anarchy.

Roger Brandon lost his last remaining family member, his daughter. He also lost the use of his legs and was confined to a wheelchair. Now alone, he accepted one final engineering program before retirement.

Roger was urged by Cliff Nesmith to manage an exorbitantly expensive, ultra-Top-Secret program for a manned, hypersonic aircraft designed to intercept ICBM warheads. It would bypass ill-advised treaties that limited American Anti-Ballistic Missile defenses.

The aircraft's classified code name: **Guardian**. Anticipated top speed: **Mach 10**.

+ + +

The Countdown began in 2020. Finally, in November 2025, everything is ready.

Jason Matthews and others meticulously brought hundreds of people together across multiple continents at a specific time…to instigate a crisis that would usher in One World Peace Now. Jason may not have become America's forty-sixth president, but he will be her first Premier. At least, that would be a good start.

Guardian – Mach Ten

12. THE CALL

The terse message quickly went out over secure channels to key personnel worldwide: "*Instigator* launched. Stand by to implement Phase 2."

Within twenty minutes, the Secret Service raced the president and senior United States leaders to shelters deep under the Washington, D.C. streets. There had not been time to board the unique Boeing 747-8, also known as Air Force One, and head north away from the potential impact zone.

+ + +

Justin Townsend wasn't one to be melodramatic. As an experienced lead software engineer, he dealt in facts. But these facts were brutal. After tonight, things would change. Everything would change.

His apartment was a balmy seventy-four degrees, but he shivered. His hands shook. Justin often knocked out multiple reps of leg presses with a very respectful load of iron, but now his legs felt as sturdy as Jell-O. He hurried to his bedroom, grabbing the door frame with a trembling arm. With the other hand he pushed his Multiphone—his critical lifeline—against his ear, trying to catch every word. It was hard because of the noise at the other end.

A distant memory flashed like a horror movie trailer. There was only one other time he'd felt this scared, this out of control. He was eight, playing sandlot football. His older brother came out of a pile-up of kids with a compound fracture of his left arm. "I think I broke it," his brother had said, cradling his z-shaped forearm. Justin almost passed out at the sight.

But now? Justin wasn't eight. He was only a few years shy of the big "four zero," although the handsome, athletic African American looked years younger. Still, he felt like that helpless child again. For the second time in his life, fear gripped him. Terror.

Justin struggled to focus and respond to what he'd heard. He forced himself to take slow, deep breaths. His usual quick-witted nature? Nowhere to be found.

It wasn't a doctor with a diagnosis of the Big C. No sudden, unexpected death of a loved one. He hadn't lost his job…or his upcoming promotion. No papers were served. But the call from Roger Brandon had shaken him to the core.

"They're getting ready to put me in the cockpit. Stay on the line till we go live through Guardian."

Like I'd just hang up and call back later. There might not be a "later." At least, not until the end of World War Three.

He doubted there would be any cellular smartphone service up to the current 2025 Six-G standards at that point.

He will die. Maybe we'll all die.

+ + +

Less than a day before, Justin had sat in a high-tech cubicle squirreled away in a Sensitive Compartmented Information Facility—SCIF—due to the top secret nature of the program. He monitored the progress and success of Guardian's latest test flight, this time with the low-power solid rocket boosters, or SRBs. The full power version would come later.

Each flight would build upon the earlier. Verify ordinary capabilities, then move on to the extraordinary capabilities that would put Guardian in a unique class of its own.

Now, a cold sweat soaked through his shirt as he considered everything that might go wrong. *Did we miss anything? Is it really ready?*

The questions were no longer academic. This wasn't a Test Readiness Review leading to another round of developmental or qualifications tests. A real-world crisis and all the testing was over. Lives were at stake; possibly millions.

Roger's not a fighter pilot!

They'd known each other for years, and Justin was enjoying once again working for his friend and mentor. He remembered when Cliff Nesmith introduced the new hires at Directed Paradigms, Incorporated—DPI—to the wheelchair-bound program manager and lead engineer. Roger was in his early sixties. After security clearances were verified, they entered the secure facility. Then Roger told them about Guardian.

"The world's first hypersonic plane was the X-15. They dropped it from modified B-52 Stratofortress bombers just under two hundred times between 1959 and 1968. Their record of 4,500 miles per hour—Mach Six Point Seven—still holds the record for any manned aircraft, excluding the Shuttle. A rocket engine powered the aircraft for under two minutes, then it glided to a landing. Total flight time: Eleven minutes or less.

"Our goal for Guardian is over 7,000 miles per hour, level flight, for over an hour."

Justin scrambled to set up an ad hoc workstation in his bedroom as if his life depended on it. Maybe it did.

Roger's old, he's crippled; the dude shakes every time he even talks about his mid-air collision!

Is the bird ready? Yesterday's test flight went well. The low-powered solid rocket boosters pushed the aircraft past the sound barrier. The scram jet and ion drive kicked in and thrust the plane to a steady Mach Two. Leading-edge ion shielding seemed to work okay. Ion vector controls operated as expected. The wingtips drooped down all the way to minus forty degrees, where they would add low-drag compression lift at altitudes above 60,000 feet.

Six months. Even three!

Just a few more months of boring, unspectacular tests. Thousands of man-hours of work wrapped around countless details, trying to keep any thread from unraveling with minor to catastrophic results. Like what happened with the Space Shuttle. Twice. High altitudes and hypersonic speeds are very unforgiving.

Details. Even for flight testing, the micro rail gun had to be partially loaded for proper weight-and-balance.

All of that was now academic.

Justin slowly shook his head as he finished setting up his equipment. *How did we get into this mess?*

He had his opinions. His jaw tightened at what brought them to this crisis.

For years, United States' leadership had pursued popularity instead of statesmanship. In an ill-conceived effort to win over enemies, America had lost not only their respect, but also the trust of friends.

Hostile governments grew and built new-generation nuclear and conventional forces while American politicians negotiated away all but a few hundred land, air, and sea-launched nukes. After decades of fighting terrorism in regional conflicts, the country reduced military forces to save money.

Even with the threat of North Korea and possibly Iran perfecting nuclear warheads and delivery systems, the United States backed off on developing credible antiballistic missile, or ABM capabilities. All that remained were thirty aging missiles between the West Coast and Alaska. Sure, there were some ABM capabilities in the littorals; some near-shore Navy vessels were able to intercept warheads out to a few hundred nautical miles. But none could intercept a high-altitude Intercontinental Ballistic Missile—an ICBM warhead.

Trump had refocused on national defense, including the well-publicized addition of a Space Force. Virtually unknown was the highly classified funding to build a manned interceptor designed to circumvent treaties banning any new unmanned ABM systems.

Has it all been too little, too late?

The Tactical Hypersonic Interceptor/Penetrator program was born. THIP—the name was descriptive, but an acronym only a Congressional subcommittee could devise. Roger Brandon was chosen as the program manager and lead engineer. Some questioned his emotional ability to carry out the responsibilities so soon after his loss. Others, like Justin, knew that the assignment was just what Roger needed. And that he was the exact man for the job.

And now they're trying to lift Roger into that prototype aircraft to attempt the impossible.

Roger, of all people...! Is he ready?

Am I?!

13. WE'RE GOING OPERATIONAL

Justin's focus returned. He stood to his full six-foot-three-inch stature, closed his eyes, and took another slow, deep breath. True, he was a happy-go-lucky player who avoided commitments. Yes, he enjoyed reporting to Roger and not having the older man's "top dog" responsibilities and headaches. Straight up, he enjoyed the challenges. Mostly, he thrived on the dope job with excellent pay and benefits. Still, Justin could get serious when necessary. Now more than ever, he must.

Dude, I'm a programmer, not a weapons officer!

He opened his Multiphone out on his dresser. He had pulled the dresser out from the wall so he could project the phone's high definition laser image onto a large section of the opposite wall. A few seconds to adjust parallax and the image became a perfect rectangle. He began the intricate process of accessing and logging into Guardian's software back door. Roger wasn't able to take his phone into the plane, so Justin had to be ready to communicate with him through the aircraft's communications suite.

World's fastest, most expensive, ultra-top-secret manned interceptor flown by a crippled retirement-aged engineer. First time in a cockpit since losing his family. The dude's gotta be a basket case.

Just minutes before, Justin's phone jarred him away from the nail-biting overtime finale of his long-awaited game between Florida State and Florida. The alert was what he and Roger jokingly called the "Bat Signal." Its real name? The Enigma Codec, a VoIP and ultra-secure datalink they developed and proposed to the Defense Advanced Research Projects Agency, or DARPA. Enigma provided a full 1,024-bit encryption with minimal latency. The National Security Administration couldn't even track that such calls took place, much less record or decipher them. Sure, his apartment wasn't "secure." But the encryption might keep both of them from a doing time in Leavenworth, since even the name "Guardian" carried a security classification well above Top Secret.

God, how was he even thinking about such things now? Justin somberly admitted, now might be a good time to think about that, too…about God. If this didn't work, many people would soon meet Him.

Stay on point!

The VoIP App's encryption will datalink through the company interface, via satellite to the aircraft, as soon as Roger boots up the avionics suite. The software's back door was still open for testing. Once testing was over, they would close it to meet cybersecurity requirements. Of course, he'd never logged in from an unsecure computer. Well, once he logged into Guardian, his Multiphone would never again see the light of day. Classified until destroyed.

Roger. If the call had only come from someone else. Ha, good joke! I've been punked!

No. Roger had a great sense of humor, although not at anyone's expense. He also had an uncanny ability to ease tensions in difficult situations. They'd seen more than their share of those on this project. But this wasn't a joke.

Almost nothing less—maybe a fire or late season hurricane—would have torn him away from the game. And certainly not from the hors d'oeuvres and the last half of the Chardonnay he was sharing with his latest lady.

Tamika Stewart was eight years his junior and had caught every man's eye, single or otherwise, when she joined the company as a graduate student intern. Justin had especially taken a liking to her when she admired his motorcycle. She surprised him when she asked to ride it around the block and further impressed him by handling the beast like a pro. Justin raised the stakes by asking if she wanted to join him for a workout at a parcourse track. Tamika called his bluff and not only agreed but kept up with him. She had sealed the deal when she dropped the comment that she took life easy and wasn't interested in any commitments.

All that led to tonight…and interrupted by Roger. The older man's call and micro-burst of information had left no time for questions or even so much as an explanation to the lovely, trim, athletic African American woman:

"Justin, we have a crisis. We're going operational, right now. There's a nuke coming up from over the South Pole, impacting somewhere up the East Coast. We're climbing to 38,000 feet and launching out the back of the C-17. Nose-down, the turbojet should push it supersonic for the scramjet and ion drive. I'll try to fly it, but I need your help. You're my back-seater. And you've got to take it out of the test and diagnostics mode so we can go full combat ops with the railgun."

Right. The aggressive Flight Test Plan called for a dozen more flights beyond the six already completed. Each flight took a large, experienced Integrated Process Team at least four man-months to prepare.

Now a programmer and a crippled engineer…Really?

\+ + +

The C-17 Globemaster III was already well above its normal cruising altitude and continued to climb. In the cargo bay, Army Lieutenant General Rey Alvarez watched as two Airmen secured the cockpit. At six-feet-two and a solid 220 pounds, the man commanded respect. The subdued patches on his Army Combat Uniform Three included Airborne, Rangers, and several lesser known but even more respected indicators of his thirty-two-year career. The only hint of his age of fifty-four was a slight graying around the temples of his otherwise jet-black hair.

Alvarez watched the Airmen climb down from the hypersonic interceptor secured in the cargo bay. They stepped back and looked into the cockpit at the pudgy, 60-something engineer trying to save the world, and saluted the civilian. Roger nodded humbly, then looked over at the Loadmaster as the sergeant removed all but one final strap holding Guardian into the C-17 cargo bay. Roger and the General locked eyes. Alvarez saluted as well, then leaned over and shouted above the noise to his aide. "If he pulls this off, he'll get a Presidential Medal of Freedom!"

Major Dyson, a short, stocky man with a Japanese ancestry, had almost completed his one-year special assignment as the General's aide. He shouted back as they prepared to strap on quick-don oxygen masks before depressurizing the cargo bay: "It'll have to be posthumous, sir." Seeing that the General hadn't connected the dots, he added: "He can't land it."

Alvarez looked over at the now empty wheelchair, strapped to the wall. His jaw tensed. It takes working legs to handle rudders, brakes, and nose gear steering.

General Alvarez had known Roger for several years in a professional capacity. Roger didn't mention it, but Rey speculated that he hadn't recovered from the loss of his family. There he sat in the aircraft, the one man who might give the world a last chance to prevent Armageddon. Now sixty-four, Roger's hair showed more gray than light brown. His dark eyes and olive complexion contrasted with his khaki pants and extra-large long sleeve blue shirt. Even at this distance, the General saw the man shaking.

The world's most unlikely hero?

The four huge C-17 turbofan engines continued surging at full military power as the flight crew demanded every foot of altitude before opening the cargo doors. A similar airborne launch occurred decades earlier when a massive C-5A Galaxy lowered its ramp at altitude and deployed a Minuteman ICBM in an Air Mobile Feasibility Test. Huge Apollo-style parachutes deployed to slow and stabilize the missile as it descended. Then in what was one of the most unusual tests of the Cold War, the solid-fuel missile ignited and separated from its carriage and parachutes. It proved that an air-launched ICBM could literally "go ballistic."

Now a C-17 had to air-launch a much smaller payload. If it could go supersonic, light the scramjet and ion drive, and pull up before cratering into the Texas landscape, it would climb and maintain an extended high-altitude manned hypersonic flight for the first time in history. Its target: An incoming ICBM warhead. But not just any ICBM—this relic from the Cold War was believed to have been decommissioned decades earlier. The shock of its existence was only matched—at least from an unemotional, intellectual viewpoint—by the amazing fact that it had remained operational for so many years. The General knew something about highly classified "black" programs. He marveled at the secret existence of a massive ICBM, years after the fall of the Soviet Union and multiple leadership transitions in Russian and the former Soviet states. The General's eyes squinted. *Maybe there actually is something legitimate about conspiracy theories.*

This particular fractional orbital bombardment system—the relic from the Soviet ICBM program—was coming around "the long way." The launch brought the warhead from over the South Pole. Despite years of growing tensions, the launch from the Ukraine, now again under Russian rule, was immediately relayed to President Juan Garcia by his Russian counterpart Viktor Savin, as soon as the Russian military detected it. Victor also provided his best-guess targeting estimates, his profuse apologies, and offers to help. But nothing could be done. There were no ABM interceptors in the southern states.

The Loadmaster verified that everyone was on oxygen and had wrapped themselves in coats and blankets for the two or three minutes of minus sixty-five degrees Fahrenheit they would experience at that altitude. The flight crew began depressurizing the aircraft.

+ + +

Roger looked over the cockpit's flat-screen monitors, familiar with every detail from both an engineering perspective and his many hours in the Simulator. Although his legs were useless, he was still very much a "hands-on" manager. He attended each test flight and spent nearly as many hours "flying" the Simulator as the test pilot. He wasn't nervous in the Simulator's cockpit. But now?

Roger grasped the interceptor's control stick with a death grip, his hand trembling. To pilot an aircraft, one last time. He didn't fear death; that wasn't it. But to pilot again...and especially this beast! His shirt was soaked with sweat, and he had to wipe his brow before securing the helmet. Fortunately, the helmet designed for Tim Cason, PDI's test pilot, was a close-enough fit for the few minutes Roger would need it.

Roger struggled to think of something else, anything, other than that last flight with his family...

I'll never have the chance to ask Cheryl out.

The exorbitant hours it took to design, build, program, and prepare the Guardian prototype for testing had left Roger little time to himself. Other than attending church most Sundays, there was no time for even a casual dinner date with Cheryl Brock, the early-sixties widow who joined the church's small group he attended Sunday evenings. Her husband had died in a boating accident a few years earlier. Like Roger, she still seemed overwhelmed by the loss. Romance wasn't on his mind, but friendship was.

Was...

I'm coming home. Cindy, Frank, Susan...one way or another I'll be with you in less than an hour.

14. LAUNCH!

A Navy carrier flight deck is something to behold. Each Sailor understands his or her exact purpose and executes it precisely.

But how do you coordinate sliding a hypersonic interceptor out the tail end of a cargo aircraft? Master Sergeant Alan Drake once again verified that everyone was strapped in, alert, and wearing quick-don masks. The masks with their small tanks would provide adequate oxygen for much longer than they would need. They may have sore joints from nitrogen bubbles in the low pressure, but the pure O_2 would help, and they would quickly re-pressurize once Guardian cleared the ramp and the cargo door closed.

"Roger, you all set?"

Roger scanned his cockpit. All screens were active. Justin should complete his link-up at any moment, but they were running out of time. Guardian had to be far away from the C-17 before they could begin. His response was curt: "Let's launch!"

"Flight deck, ready for level plus fifteen and open hatch," Drake called out. Everyone on board felt the dropping elevator effect of the aircraft leveling to a more sedate angle of attack.

"Plus-one-five degrees," Major Burt Knowles reported. "Opening hatch." He nodded to his co-pilot, Captain Sandra White. She ran through in-flight cargo door opening procedures while Burt maintained both altitude and attitude against the aerodynamic buffeting of the opening cargo door.

As the hatch opened, Roger started Guardian's turbojet engine.

In the cockpit, Sandra nodded back to Burt: "Door open!"

Master Sergeant Drake gave another quick glance at Roger, who swirled his finger in a horizontal "Let's go!" circle.

Tethered to a bulkhead D-ring, Drake stepped the last yard to the final strap holding Guardian to the C-17. He had already detached the D-ring and tied a simple knot; anything dangling at hypersonic speed would rip the plane apart. Now, he opened his razor-sharp utility knife and sliced the knot, standing aside so the loose strap wouldn't as easily cut through him as it snapped back.

Noise in the cargo bay was deafening. Inside the Guardian's cockpit, it was almost enough to drown out Roger's beating heart, now fast and irregular. The intense stress had put him into atrial fibrillation, or AFib.

Oh, great. Just what I need right about now.

It got worse. The sickening feeling of Guardian sliding backward and slamming into a 450-knot headwind was more intense than anything he had imagined.

"Aw, puke!"

Roger's outburst came from the fact that he almost did. Only an intense focus on urgent tasks kept him from violent nausea. He lowered and locked the wingtips, raised the landing gear, and throttled the turbojet to full military power. Through it all, he fought to maintain straight-and-level. The buffeting subsided.

"You okay, man?" Justin's question in Roger's headset verified that he had negotiated the data and VoIP links. It was complex, from hacking through the company's classified server, relaying through the Satellite Tactical Digital Information Link, Joint Link 18, and into Guardian's mainframe and communications.

Roger's grand total of aerobatic maneuvers to that point had been two spin recoveries with his instructor during flight training decades earlier. He'd also been on a few moderate theme-park rides with Frank and Susan. Again, many years ago. Cindy wouldn't go near them, but she'd hold sunglasses, cell phones, and other paraphernalia while from her perspective, her husband and their children risked life and limb.

"Yeah, just don't add that to my list of favorites," Roger responded, his voice shaky. "Let's light this thing." His fear of the cockpit continued. He forced himself to concentrate on the critical intercept—fighting off the life-sucking memories of his last flight as a pilot.

Justin displayed the S-TADIL-J18 telemetry at the top of his Multiphone's wall projection. On the bottom left was the operation's manual checklist, and a programming window on the bottom right. The Multiphone now stood on a stand. He manipulated it with hand motions over a wireless 3-D plate on his desk and made data entries using a wireless keyboard.

"You're sixty percent to superconductive. Probably another forty-five seconds. Can you hold altitude?"

Roger checked his altimeter. Not good. The small turbojet was designed for low altitude maneuvering without the scramjet and ion drive engaged. It also served as a high capacity auxiliary power unit to run dual-cycle compressors to cool the magnets, and to provide electricity to charge them once they became superconductive.

One benefit of the increasing tensions with China was that corporate America had learned to create high gauss magnets without foreign supplies of rare earths like neodymium. The alloys developed over the last few years included one—Cliff Nesmith and PDI held the patent—for relatively high temperature superconductivity at minus fifty-five degrees Celsius. So instead of requiring liquid helium or even liquid nitrogen for cooling, they were cooled by R744 refrigerant: liquid carbon dioxide; CO^2.

"Negative," Roger replied. "Losing 1,000 feet per minute. Can't afford a spin." No stall tests had yet been performed during flight testing, and certainly no spin recoveries.

In Justin's programming window, he set up a spreadsheet and plugged in equations and variables. The data displayed as a graphic with curves on his wall and uploaded to display in Guardian's cockpit. In a straight vertical dive with the 12,000-pound thrust of the turbojet, the aircraft should go supersonic within a 22,000-foot drop. But the lower the altitude, the denser the air. That meant more aerodynamic drag and a higher speed to break through the sound barrier's pressure wave. Worse, Roger would lose another 2,000 feet while lighting the ion drive. Plus several thousand more feet to pull out of the dive without blacking out since there had been no G-suit for him.

And a straight dive wouldn't give the coils time to charge. "Can't wait, can I?"

"No."

In a formal test plan, checklist actions would be completed sequentially. First, establish superconductivity. Second, charge the magnets. Third, bring the magneto-hydrodynamic—MHD—generator online to provide the energy to light the ion drive once a supersonic shockwave slammed through the air intake for the scramjet. The MHD would use very little fuel to become a screaming electrical generator and combine with the shockwave and scramjet to rocket Guardian forward, propelled by a gas plasma torch.

In its intended Concept of Operations—CONOPS—at an alert facility, a pilot would quick-start the turbojet and cool the coil while taxiing for takeoff. He or she would ignite the full-power SRBs after clearing the runway and retracting the landing gear. Climb-out would be at forty-five degrees for greatest gain of altitude and speed. By the time the aircraft passed 10,000 feet, the magnets would be superconductive, and the pilot would begin charging them. That height above buildings and sensitive equipment would give an adequate safety margin from minor inconveniences…like locking up a person's pacemaker.

Once the craft hit Mach Two, systems would be ready for a smooth transition to scramjet and ion drive at 30,000 feet, where the thousands-of-miles-per-hour ion stream wouldn't pose a threat.

In its intended CONOPS.

Justin added more calculations to his spreadsheet. His math skills were considerable, as that was his undergraduate major before following his computer software minor to attain a Master's degree in advanced programming and simulations. One unique requirement of DPI was that, except for the receptionist and cleaning personnel, its employees had to have solid expertise in at least two disciplines. Most had three; a few had even more.

Justin continued: "Go for minus sixty. That will give you more time to charge up and an extra margin of safety. Keep your easterly heading to put you further out from Amarillo when you light off."

Justin had opened another window to show the GPS location of Guardian overlaid on a Google Earth map. The cargo plane had departed from Groom Dry Lake just north of Las Vegas, heading east-southeast. Roger had kept that same basic heading and would have been dangerously near the eastern outskirts of Amarillo, Texas.

Roger nosed over to minus sixty degrees—only thirty degrees' shy of diving straight down. Gravity plus the turbojet caused the airspeed indicator to climb, even as the Mach indicator crept toward the magic "One Point Zero." Glancing away from the instruments, he saw the city lights beneath him and agreed with Justin's recommendation to climb out to the east. *Or make a crater between I-60 and I-40.* He again fought off nausea and looked back at his panels.

"Coil temp dropping fast," Justin reported. "You should be S-C in ten." Superconductive in ten seconds...

Roger slammed the large Main Charge circuit breaker to ON. "Main Charge Breaker on," he reported. Even in a sixth-generation super-interceptor like Guardian, a few actions remained mechanical. Engineers agreed that charging the MHD superconductive coils would be one of them.

The first Charge Status segment turned to a bright green, and he knew current was flowing, building magnetic flux.

"Justin, I need you to open a link to NORAD. General Alvarez should have authorized our datalink by now."

"I'm on it," Justin responded. He'd already retrieved the access codes pre-coordinated for later test flights.

The second of ten Charge Status indicators illuminated: Twenty percent. The perimeter of the charge icon turned solid green. The MHD magnets were now superconductive. In moments, the magnetic gauss would exceed MRI machines, at over sixteen Teslas. Roger remembered his years of wearing eyeglasses, grateful for the successful cataract surgery and lens implants. Not only were ferrous metals a no-no; so were any metals that could act as inductors. Metal eyeglass frames might have burned his face. Even metal implants disqualified a pilot. The aircraft was probably the first one in over a century without a backup magnetic compass.

"Don't forget to pull up…" A slight hint of Justin's humor returned. But his voice remained strained through Roger's piezoelectric headphone transducers. Because of the high gauss field, a unique characteristic of Guardian was that even the headset's microphone and headphones had no magnets. Throughout the aircraft, any ferrous material—and there was precious little—had to be shielded.

There was a compelling reason Roger waited until Guardian flew clear of the C-17 before cooling and powering the magnets. As the seventh Charge Status indicator announced seventy percent charge, Guardian's presence anywhere near the cargo aircraft would have doomed the Globemaster III and everyone on board.

The flatscreen's Mach display showed Zero Point Nine Two.

Nine. Frank was nine when we bought our travel trailer…

Tears mingled with the sweat trickling down Roger's face.

15. PETERSON AIR FORCE BASE

Nicholas Cage. Mel Gibson. John Wayne. Brigadier General Selectee Donald Draper. Four men, several differences. Primarily, the first three may have acted the parts of military heroes; Don was one. He'd earned his Air Force rank with several combat tours, two below-the-zone promotions, and real-world, life-and-death responsibilities.

One thing they had in common, however, is that each one attracted the ladies.

Don had attracted one too many.

"Stay at Peterson. Let Donna finish high school believing that we have some kind of marriage. It'll be easier to play the part if you're there and we stay here." Brenda was his college sweetheart since their freshman year. She was his wife and the mother of their grown-and-gone son Scott, and soon to be off-to-college daughter Donna.

For too long, things hadn't added up for Brenda. So, she logged into his "private" accounts and checked his statements using passwords she knew he'd used in the past. And she knew that the theater tickets, charges to FTD, and a big purchase from Jared's had not been for her benefit. They certainly had nothing to do with his military career. He was back at it. What little trust he'd rebuilt over the last few years had gone down in flames.

As Colonel Draper drove to Petersen Air Force Base, home of the 21st Space Wing, he reflected on the new emotion he'd sensed from Brenda. Her call the night before had caught him off guard. Brenda presented herself as cool and to-the-point as any professional briefer he'd seen at his Pentagon tours. She had exhibited the most damning emotion possible for the future of their marriage: Indifference. Her manic-depressive responses to his promises to reform after each affair—at least those she had learned about—all of that was gone. They say the opposite of love is not hatred; it's indifference. That was Brenda.

"The Bible is a story of reconciliation between God and man. And God wants his people to reconcile. You know I've given you every chance. Your continued infidelity has killed our marriage covenant."

Strangely, her matter-of-fact presentation finally got Don's attention.

I've lost her. I really lost her.

He tried to remember names, faces, events, even the most high-energy, erotic, over-the-top sexual marathons he'd had with several of his flings. But he could only think of Brenda. And he was not the only "looker" in their house. Even after all he'd put her through, she was gorgeous.

What in the world was I doing when I had Brenda at home?

Was Brenda having an affair? She'd become active in her church in Warner Robins during his tour at Robins Air Force Base. Sure, it was a church, and she now claimed to be a Christian, and Christians weren't supposed to do such things. But had she found someone there during his tour at Peterson?

They agreed to let Donna finish school at Houston County High instead of uprooting her again as they'd done so many times during Don's whirlwind career.

Major Withers. That's the guy's name.

Don decided to see if the Chaplain was still assigned to Peterson. Don's official responsibilities had led him to attend a Base Chapel service a year ago. The Chaplain made several points that almost broke through Don's "that's fine for you and the women but not for me" firewall. He had to respect the Major's no-nonsense, in-your-face presentation. He was a straight-shooter. Actions have results; choices have consequences.

Still, Don had been content with his successful career and extracurricular activities, so he just filed the points away to eventually be forgotten.

But now he thought back and remembered a few of the main ones:
- Almost everyone's deceived.
- If you're deceived, by definition, you don't know it.
- Two cures: Either seek or be confronted with the truth. Usually the latter.
- Man-up and admit you've been wrong.

Don remembered the Chaplain explaining that he wasn't being sexist, because typically women were quick to make necessary changes once confronted with the truth. But a man's pride often got in his way. *Ouch.*

The only solid, reliable truth, he'd said, was the Word of God. Anything else led to circular reasoning, changing philosophies, and deeper deception.

There was more, but what Don remembered was enough. He'd find Withers and set up an appointment. The realization surprised him; he would fight for his marriage. He would try to win her back.

Don leaned over in his car just enough to glance in the rear-view mirror—his classic BMW didn't have the newer panoramic rear cameras and monitors.

As he sped past LED street lamps, he could see his short black hair along with his strong, high cheekbones and cleft chin. He knew this task would be the hardest of his life. This enemy was more resourceful, cunning, and determined than any he'd faced in combat. And he was looking right at him. Don was sure that not even his high-stress shift in The Chair would keep his mind off Brenda. Not this time.

He was wrong.

Don entered the base, cleared security, parked, and walked toward the NORAD tracking room. Even as he approached the ultra-secure Command Center, he felt a strange tension. The stern, pale faces of the men and women from all U.S. and Canadian branches of service showed an urgency far beyond exercises and occasional real world cyber-attacks.

Don picked up his pace and hurried into the room. As soon as he stepped inside, his heart rate jumped as if he'd just finished his morning run. On the main screen, a low red arc originated from a location that was not a recognized space or missile launch facility. The solid red track showed that its trajectory was southern, not northern.

FOBS?! Or did the Russians secretly develop the super-ICBM they were threatening?

The semitransparent red oval, predicting the possible impact zone, extended upward along the eastern United States. Down south, the bottom of the oval spanned across both Florida coasts, with Orlando in the center. The northern point spanned from Delaware to the central part of West Virginia. He thought of his wife and daughter in Warner Robins, Georgia. But realistically, it didn't take a lot of imagination to speculate that the intended "ground zero" was much farther north: Washington, D.C.

There was no possible intercept anywhere within the range of that arc. Except for an SLBM—a Submarine Launched Ballistic Missile—no one in recent years had suspected an enemy missile attacking upwards from the south. While tensions were higher with Russia than since the fall of the Soviet Union, they had not reached the point that the U.S. was on the alert against an SLBM attack from the South.

No, this was coming in high and fast. There was nothing to stop it. Hundreds of thousands could die. Eventually, many more. The loss would be incalculable if a full-out nuclear war followed. He confirmed on separate monitors that U.S. strategic forces, for the first time in decades, were raised to a high Defense Condition—DEFCON—readiness. Status lights also changed colors as Air Force bombers and ICBM launch crews reported in at a much higher quick-response Posture status. He knew the president would already be in a deep underground bunker, or aboard Air Force One flying north away from the potential impact zone.

God help us. It's really going to happen.

At the Command Console, Colonel John Nelson hit the speakerphone button. "Don, you won't believe this!" Louder, drawing the attention of everyone in the room: "Everyone listen up! You're about to get an upgraded security clearance!" Back to Don, "Biometrics verified and the voice link is secure. It's Lieutenant General Alvarez via SATCOM-3 from a C-17 over Texas. They've just launched something that has a chance to intercept the 'incoming.' General, you're on speaker."

The General's voice boomed through the room—the cargo door was secure, aircraft engines were back to cruise, and he was wearing a noise-cancelling headset. "That's correct. Listen, Don, I need your team to provide full and immediate datalink access to a Mr. Justin Townsend from DPI—that's Delta Papa India. We have just launched a hypersonic manned interceptor code-named Guardian. Do your jobs and there's an outside chance we'll vaporize that warhead."

Don leaned toward the speakerphone: "General, where did the interceptor launch from?"

"Near Amarillo, Texas. He's about to go hypersonic."

The room sat in stunned silence as each expert contemplated the distance and the speed required to cross multiple states in minutes. Air Force Technical Sergeant "Buck" Owens looked up from his screen: "It's Justin, with secure access codes for datalink to Guardian!"

16. IGNITION!

"Oh no."

Too late, Roger realized that his chances of surviving would have been much higher had he thought to have the Airmen break out a first aid kit. They could have wrapped his feet and legs to keep blood from pooling in his lower extremities. If his spinal cord hadn't lost contact with his lower half, he could tighten those muscles to help some. Instead, it was up to his sixty-plus-year-old heart, now in AFib, to...

An alarm sounded as the Mach display turned green.

"One Point Zero!"

As Roger called out the magic number, he and Justin fixated on the altimeter; Roger on one of his "glass cockpit" displays, Justin on his Multiphone's wall projection. As soon as the scramjet kicked in and the MHD powered up to light the ion drive, Roger would have to pull out of the dive as hard as he could endure. And he had to do so without the benefit of a G-suit or the years of a fighter pilot's acclimation to high Gs. If he started an instant too soon, he would drop to transonic. The mission would be over, there would be a smoking hole in Texas, and a nuclear fireball somewhere on the East Coast.

For a brief moment, Justin wondered if he was sitting on "ground zero." *Maybe Gainesville? Only way Florida won't lose this one*, he reflected darkly. *Jacksonville?* Now that would certainly be a huge target. The Naval Air Station in Jacksonville continued to take on more roles, responsibilities, and personnel. The city, too, had become more of a shipping hub for the southeast. Jacksonville was still the largest city in the "lower forty-eight" of the United States' in terms of square miles and had a population of over one million. While New York had eight times as many, the latest estimates of the warhead's trajectory put The Big Apple well outside the warhead's CEP—the circular error probable.

They saw it at the same time.

Meter readings jumped, remaining ion engine indicators flashed green, and Roger's helmet slammed back into the seat's headrest.

"Pull up! Pull up!" Justin bellowed. The scramjet and ion drive screamed online.

Roger pulled back hard on a joystick that provided tactile feedback movement of only three inches. But the tug on his gut, the difficulty breathing, light-headedness, and tunnel vision verified that Guardian was straining to pull out of the dive.

The ion drive...how can you describe sitting in front of a gas plasma torch? It sounded like the otherworldly scream of a tormented soul, rising above the deep-throated roar of a B-1B Lancer bomber with all four engines in full afterburner.

The graphic user interface—GUI—of the altimeter slowed its downward count. What Roger did not see, trying to focus ahead and maintain consciousness in the high-G pullout, was the devastation the ion blast was having on the Texas landscape. Fortunately, his flight path was not over homes, a busy highway, or a dry forest. For years to come, many a Texan would scratch their head as they looked at the two-foot-deep, ten-foot-wide hard-glazed-earth trench. The trench led up to a major electric trunk off the Pampa Energy Center, one of the few coal-fired generating plants still operating in the United States. Speculation would range from classified airborne military laser testing to something from a UFO.

Intense flashes of man-made lightning lit up the sky behind Roger as the conductive ionized gas hit those power lines. It resembled a massive afternoon thunderstorm off the Florida Gulf Coast, truncated into just four seconds. Then the improved electric grid protection kicked in and isolated what had become a direct three-phase, 165 megawatt short to ground.

Roger missed all of that as his eyelids drooped, his breathing became shallower, and his body began to relax.

"You with us? Stay with us!" While Justin could read the aircraft's telemetry, he had no biometrics on Roger. "Are you okay?"

Everything grew dark. Roger's grip weakened on the stick. He was going home.

The aircraft nose was only a degree or two above the horizon; he was just barely above the few trees along his path. Suddenly Roger shuddered, jerked his head to clear his mind and to refocus. The few seconds of relief brought just enough blood flow to prevent a complete blackout. He forced a deep breath, gripped the stick and pulled hard. The horizon quickly dropped below him. Through a sheer act of will, he forced himself to take more deep breaths and to focus on his rate of ascent. Twenty degrees, thirty, then forty; he let up on the stick to maintain forty degrees nose-up. Although the gorilla continued sitting on his chest, it seemed to have lost a few hundred pounds. Blood flow returned to his head. His sight and senses slowly returned.

"Roger!"

"Wow…something else I never want to do again." He sucked in another deep breath. "Any data for me?"

He heard Justin exhale a sigh of relief as he checked the data channels. "From NORAD. You should see the datalink request in a moment. They want you to squawk a secure transponder code so they can track."

Roger scanned the DLS, his Data Link Screen. He saw and then accepted the incoming link request and accepted the transponder "squawk" code. With Guardian's radar image roughly the size of a bluebird, no radar on earth could track him; he had to "tell" them his location in the three-dimensional airspace. The stealth technology was in case Guardian might also serve as an interceptor against the advanced manned bombers and supersonic drones that potential adversaries were developing. The aircraft even included optical stealth.

Vectors came up and displayed on his target screen. Within moments, he could see a miniature, ultra-high-resolution image of what Colonel Draper and his team viewed on their large overhead screen. Roger manipulated the touch screen to zoom in on the East Coast, between Florida and New York, and studied the colored overlay. Even as he watched, the overlay reduced in size and cleared South Florida and Baltimore, Maryland. Those areas were no longer at risk; at least, not for the direct hit. Other effects of EMP, radioactive fallout, and the breakdown of civil government could devastate much of the country for decades regardless of where the nuke hit.

The possible impact zone further tightened to exclude central Florida and Washington, D.C. The width of the band also narrowed closer to the coast.

Draper brooded over the attacker's intent. Would the warhead detonate at a high altitude to maximize EMP effects? Would it be an air burst to maximize the area of destruction from the blast overpressure? Maybe a devastating ground burst, low enough so the fireball would vaporize earth, buildings, trees, people—which would precipitate back out and scatter as flakes of lethal radioactive fallout? Or, since part of the uncertain path extended into the Atlantic Ocean, would it be a sea burst to maximize damage along the coast by a massive tsunami?

Roger noticed a voice call request on his Data Link Screen. NORAD. He answered, patching Justin in for a three-way.

"This is Guardian."

Three-way calls. *Susan used to three-way her calls.* Painful memories flooded over Roger of the destruction many of those calls brought to Susan, and the crushing hurt to the rest of the family.

He swallowed hard, his fast and irregular AFib heartbeat pounding in his ears.

17. HYPERSONIC

"Guardian, this is NORAD; Colonel Don Draper. Don't know what's lit there behind you, but you'd better crank it up or the mushroom cloud will be gone before you get there!"

Roger looked at his Mach indicator and altimeter. The former was climbing toward two point five; the upper range for most military jets. The latter was climbing through 60,000 feet. High, yes, but again within the range of many military fighters. But the G-forces trying to push his backbone through the tail of the aircraft continued at an uncomfortable three point five Gs. He heard the whine and felt the vibration of the wingtips dipping downward to maximize compression lift for the higher altitudes, like the XB-70 Valkyrie test aircraft from decades before.

Justin wanted to be inside the SKIF at DPI, surrounded by virtual reality displays and his multiple 3-D input pads and wearing his personal Bose noise cancelling headset. But even listening to his Multiphone from his bedroom, he clearly heard the Colonel. Nobody was going to trash-talk his baby.

"Colonel, as soon as he clears 80,000 and cranks it past Mach Eight, you better hope your played-out machines can keep up!"

Roger, always the peacemaker, intervened. "Colonel, stand by. Justin, I need to get the ion shield up and stabilized, or it's going to get very hot in here, fast."

Guardian didn't have the nickel alloy of the X-15, the titanium skin of the SR-71 Blackbird and XB-70 Valkyrie, or the thick ceramic tiles of the Space Shuttle. Instead, the aircraft used lightweight ceramic matrix composites. They were critical inside the scramjet and MHD core where temperatures exceeded 2,500 degrees Fahrenheit; and outside along leading edges. An SR-71 flying at Mach Three was blistering hot and had to be extensively cooled before the crew could safely exit after landing. With Guardian's skin, an SR-71 would have been cool to the touch by the time it taxied into its hangar. But even that advanced coating alone wouldn't protect Guardian from extended hypersonic cruise. Roger's team of engineers went beyond materials. They routed part of the ion drive itself to provide shielding.

Roger actuated the second mandatory manual control.

Generators sprayed a stream of ionized particles along the aircraft leading edges, creating a laminar flow at a much-reduced temperature. Farther back, microscopic ridges created wind-tunnel-perfected turbulence that reduced aerodynamic drag, like a shark's skin through the water. The high-velocity razor-sharp stream of ions cutting into the headwind, followed by the microturbulence, caused the high altitude air to sweep over the aircraft in a smooth flow. Guardian experienced less aerodynamic drag than the ancient and much slower needle-like F-104 Starfighter. An additional benefit: Instead of creating the typical dual thud-thud explosive sound of a supersonic shockwave, Guardian produced a gentler sound like distant thunder. No broken windows.

The Mach indicator and the altimeter readings climbed faster.

"Looks good, Roger; all indicators are green. You're free to kick it!" Justin smiled with satisfaction as nano-sensors all along the leading edge showed a clean, cool—relatively speaking, at over 572 degrees Fahrenheit—laminar flow over the aircraft's blended wing surfaces. "You should also have full I-A-C."

Weeks earlier than planned, Guardian was flying under full Ion Aerodynamic Control. The final beauty of the ion shield design was to morph the airflow by electronically adjusting the ion stream, hundreds of times per second, to control pitch, yaw, and roll. Larger control surfaces, necessary at takeoff and landing speeds all the way up to low supersonic speeds, remained locked once the IAC became fully active above Mach 5. The only remaining external physical movement was for the wingtips as they adjusted to maintain the optimal lifting body effect, allowing the craft to ride on its own shockwave. And, of course, the all-important tiny door that would slide open for a split-second to expel the rail gun's "slug."

"Looking good for Flight Level Nine Zero."

Roger was soaked in sweat, his heart beating wildly, and his hands shaking. There was just a momentary twitch of a smile as he imagined NORAD's reaction to Justin's comment. Guardian was approaching 90,000 feet. No one had ever maintained sustained, level flight at that altitude. About the time he finished that thought, Roger was there.

Although the sun was just setting on the Pacific Coast, it was dark around him. At his altitude, it would have been dark even in the middle of the day.

I've earned my Astronaut wings. Too bad I'll never have a chance to wear them.

He leveled the nose and finally got the gorilla off his chest. Roger and Justin watched as the Mach indicator immediately increased its climb past Six

Point Zero.

Massive power flowed through classified state-of-the-art graphene conductors.

"Colonel, I need vectors for the earliest intercept points at a beginning range of 300 nautical miles. I have three rail gun projectiles. I'll need to fire at ranges of 300, 150, and at eighty nautical miles. We're hoping for Mach Ten, but I'll push her as hard as she'll go, so I need figures between Mach Nine and Eleven."

Justin spoke up. "Roger, I've bypassed the test protocols. You're fully operational, including the rail gun. Shouldn't I be helping with vectors?" His question wasn't cocky. He was that good.

Roger's voice quivered so slightly that only Justin caught it. "We only bore sighted the gun to the ninth decimal place. I need a fallback option at fifty miles. I need you to set up Battle Short protocols for a fly-under and implosion."

Only Roger and Justin knew what all that meant. And even for them, it was hypothetical, something they'd kicked around with one of DPI's physicists during a coffee break on one of their many late nights during the early days of the program.

As for the best-of-the-best team at the Peterson Control Center, up to that point they had only understood some of the conversation between the two engineers. But that last exchange sounded ominous. They each returned their focus to telemetry, vectors, probability analyses, and everything else they could synthesize into the flight data that Guardian would need to make the intercept.

"Sir!" Colonel Draper looked over at the same Technical Sergeant who'd contacted Justin. The younger man was staring at his instrumentation in unbelief. "He's holding steady at Mach Ten! He's goin' like a bat outta hades!"

A new vector was tracking on their screen. It showed a green icon, sweeping from west to east, toward the red icon coming up from the south. Minutes earlier, no one in that room would have believed that a manned aircraft could travel as fast as they saw the green icon move, sweeping across entire states in minutes. Then again, no one would have believed an ICBM warhead would have come up from over the South Pole.

Roger desperately prayed that the intercept would succeed. So much could go wrong...

+ + +

"Come on, come on, come on..."

Anton Filipov was not a patient man. Patience is not what had earned him his position as the flight engineer of the highly specialized Ilyushin Il-96-400PU aircraft.

It had been a long day. Russia was such a huge country, any time President Viktor Savin needed to go anywhere, it normally had to be by aircraft. And each of his many trips meant a twenty to thirty-hour ordeal for the crew. Today was much closer to the thirty-hour mark, with at least six more to go.

They'll panic for a few moments and be dead within minutes.

The plan was simple. Diabolically so. As soon as he received the message on his secure maintenance net radio, he'd signal the co-pilot, who would take one of his breaks out of the cockpit. Only short breaks were allowed for the flight crew. Once both of them had donned portable oxygen bottles, Anton would rapidly depressurize the president's aircraft. Alarms would awaken anyone currently asleep at four a.m. Two seconds. Oxygen masks would automatically drop and cabin lights would illuminate to full brightness. Another second. Everyone would grab and put on his own mask—two more seconds; then help everyone else get theirs on— two more seconds. Total of seven seconds. Three more seconds to realize that the life-giving oxygen wasn't flowing, because Anton had set the valve to OFF during his pre-flight inspection. Ten seconds. They would panic, but in another five seconds, not a single person would have time to grab a stand-alone bottle. Not even the pilot. Fifteen seconds and they would all be unconscious.

The autopilot would react to the alarm by putting the plane into a controlled rapid descent. The co-pilot would simply walk back in the cockpit, take over manual control, and keep the plane near its current altitude of 40,000 feet. Within minutes, only two people in the aircraft would still be alive. By then Anton would have disabled all tracking beacons, they would drop below radar coverage, and then divert to their secret destination.

Anton impatiently awaited the call that would change Mother Russia. He knew it would come as soon as the very large explosion changed the United States of America forever. He expected it within the next fifteen minutes.

18. TARGET LOCK

The datalink streamed at maximum capacity. NORAD supercomputers crunched numbers with redundant teraflop precision. This was difficult because of the unexpected southern trajectory. The incoming arc was too high for the Robins Air Force Base backscatter radar, designed for closer-in and lower altitude SLBMs, to track accurately. So sketchy data from satellites and "best guess" probabilities continued to show wide paths instead of precise arcs. No one suspected the warhead to have terminal guidance. Fortunately, they were correct.

Gigabytes of data streamed to Guardian's Targeting and Flight Control Computer each second, but the aircraft system hardly broke a sweat. American ingenuity led the world in developing quantum computer technology, but even with the $1.2 billion allocated to Guardian's computer mainframe, quantum systems were still too risky. Instead, they chose a tristate "ternary" computer developed by Directed Paradigms, Inc. as a rugged, lower-risk solution with added benefits. Instead of simple binary ones and zeroes, the DPI-01Ternary Computer allowed states of positive, zero, and negative. The circuit board substrate materials, including graphene traces, allowed unheard-of packing of "Trisistors," which reduced electron travel times and enhanced clock speed. Shifting from bits and bytes to "trites" allowed for shorter words at the machine language level, faster bus speeds, and more efficient programming language. The suitcase-size TCS DPI-01 on Guardian easily kept up with the supercomputers at NORAD.

Roger turned on the interceptor's own Terminal Targeting System, its TTS. In a split second, its multi-frequency LIDAR—Light Detection and Ranging system—swept forward into space. The laser light wouldn't be distorted by the ion shield, nor would clouds be a concern at the planned intercept altitude. The design used multiple frequencies to mitigate intentional stealth coatings; a coating that could absorb visible light would reflect ultraviolet. Coatings that could absorb visible and UV would reflect infrared. Early self-driving cars used LIDARs with sixty-four lasers on turrets spinning at six hundred rpm. They generated over one and a half million voxels per second, mapping three dimensional space outward as far as a mile. In comparison, Guardian's LIDAR ranged outward to hundreds of nautical miles. The LIDAR Targeting System—LTS—was generating half a Gigavoxel per second.

"TTS on, LTS active," Roger reported. Guardian was now flying itself, following data feeds from NORAD. But it was also scanning thousands of cubic miles of space for the Doppler signature of a downward arcing object in a non-stable orbit: An incoming warhead.

"Copy. See that?" Justin directed Roger's attention back to NORAD's "best guess" arcs, which just tightened as the CEP could be better predicted.

"So, Florida and Georgia are clear. Looks like the earliest detonation would be a high altitude burst over North Carolina, and the furthest would fall short of Washington. Speculation, Colonel?"

Colonel Draper's team had been zooming in maps for both counter-force and counter-value targets. A high altitude burst over Fayetteville, North Carolina would be catastrophic to Fort Bragg, an Army base with a large Special Operations Command contingent. And there was Norfolk, Virginia with a very strong Navy presence. Like NAS Jacksonville, Naval Station Norfolk had recently taken on even more responsibilities, assuring its continuation as the world's largest naval station for decades to come.

"This is Draper. An air burst over Norfolk would destroy the base and cause collateral damage hundreds of miles out. A ground burst would have a smaller kill zone, but the fallout would be much greater and might spread up to Washington. Or it could go over to Roanoke, Virginia; or down to Fort Bragg in North Carolina depending on winds, which are right now..." A Navy ensign brought up a plot based on current weather, "...Southerly; twenty-five knots at 20,000 feet. And there's a huge storm over the entire region which could drop the fallout to the ground quickly in a high concentration."

"Any estimate of yield?" asked Roger.

The Colonel's voice lowered. "The White House reports from his Russian counterpart that those old birds carried a full megaton."

"God help us."

Roger's comment wasn't blasphemous. Justin knew that. His quiet "Amen" wasn't a blasphemy either. Nor, for once in his life, was Colonel Draper's.

"Roger!"

"I see it, Justin. Colonel, we have a positive lock. Back-feeding data to NORAD now."

All the way back in the '80s, Navy F-14 Tomcats received and sent radar information via an older Data Link 16. Guardian's LIDAR data link to NORAD now was incredible. Every two seconds, the massive display zooming in on the northeastern U.S. showed a progressively smaller oval for the CEP.

"Looks like you nailed it." After ten seconds of data from the aircraft, Roger and NORAD watched the oval decrease to an area sixty miles north and south of Norfolk, and just forty miles wide. Norfolk was at the center. Roger added, "Justin, can you see that?"

His resolution was lower due to the limitations of his 6G Multiphone's bandwidth, but it was enough.

"Got it. Colonel, Guardian's steady-state is Mach Ten Point One. Do you have vectors for his intercepts?"

Colonel Drake looked at Technical Sergeant Owens. "Ready to overlay, Sir." The Colonel nodded.

"This just might work." Roger's course tracked between Atlanta, Georgia and Charleston, South Carolina. Guardian automatically corrected a few degrees further south to optimize the intercept as far out over the Atlantic Ocean as possible.

"Charging capacitor bank." Roger initiated the third mandatory manual action, applying power to charge the super capacitor network that would fire the electromagnetic rail gun. Once operational, the aircraft would carry twelve ten-pound projectiles, or "slugs," to be fired in sets of two or three, for at least four intercepts. As targeting accuracy improved, an intercept might only take one or two shots. Each intercept would be as Roger described, giving adequate time for cooling, recalculating, and recharging the rail gun. For testing, Guardian only had three slugs. And he had one intercept. A two-inch diameter titanium-clad iron bullet, at over 9,000 miles per hour, had to intercept a warhead four to eight feet tall, with a base around three feet. The warhead would also be traveling thousands of miles per hour as it began its re-entry.

The system was only bore sighted to nine decimal places, not the ultimate ten. Guardian had two test shots to complete what should be at least eight shots over two test flights. With each shot, the TCS DPI-01 computer and Fire Control System would scream through teraflops of calculations, literally "on the fly," to recalibrate and increase accuracy. The final shot had to be dead on. Or…

"Justin, is my backup plan ready?" Roger asked.

After an uncharacteristic pause, Justin quietly replied, "Overrides ready." And to himself, *How I wish we could have used a laser instead of the rail gun.*

19. INTERCEPT

"Colonel, everything's 'go' for intercept. We expect the first two shots will miss. With each miss, the Fire Control System will recalibrate and increase accuracy by several orders of magnitude. The goal is for the final slug to pulverize the warhead. If it misses, the FCS won't let me ram it even if I could at this speed. So, here's Plan B. Justin, make it short. We've got less than a minute."

"Understood," Justin replied. "Colonel, Guardian's blowing conductive plasma out its tail at several thousand degrees. Inside, it's got a superconductive magnet and generator with enough juice to light up a small town. Roger and I speculate that if we over-ride safety interlocks and collapse that magnetic field, it should create a directional EMP back along that ionized gas tail, then on out into space. We expect an electronic kill radius of several miles."

"So, it wouldn't be area-wide like a NUDET?" asked the Colonel.

"That's the bad news. Guardian flies beneath the warhead, we collapse the field and produce an EMP, and a possible outcome of that much instantaneous power is that we set off the warhead ourselves. You'll have a high-altitude nuclear detonation—a NUDET—that could affect much of the central East Coast."

"But no casualties?"

"None, unless some airline flights are affected, or we get pile-ups on the interstate from fried ignition systems. Fortunately, this will be way off the coast. And you've got that bad storm going on."

Colonel Draper thought for a moment. "I need to contact Washington. This is above my pay grade."

Roger responded. "Negative, Colonel. No time. And not your decision. I just want someone there to notify authorities to be ready if stuff stops working. We have three shots. If they miss, Justin bypasses safety interlocks, and we hit the warhead with lightning. Literally. Total probability of success is sixty to eighty percent. But the consequences of failure are off the charts."

"If you have to do the Battle Short thing, what's the chance of your own survival?"

Justin quietly interjected. "Colonel, this was a one-way trip for Roger from the second Guardian launched over Texas."

Lord, help me to concentrate just a few more minutes. Roger's AFib was worsening. "NORAD, we're down to the critical final moments. I need exclusive communication with Justin." Without waiting for a response, he added, "All systems are green here. How's telemetry?"

Guardian required a two-person crew, and Justin was doing his best to remotely perform the back-seat role.

"Leading edge temperature's rising—you're really pushing it—but should stay within tolerance for the intercept."

"I don't have the TM steps memorized. Am I missing anything?"

Justin had the Technical Manual pulled up on another screen panel.

"Negative. Everything's nominal. FCS on Auto?"

"FCS on Auto."

Three shots. All automatic. Then only seconds to implode the drive if they miss.

Roger rubbed his elbows and flexed his fingers. His joints throbbed mercilessly. He'd never experienced the bends from SCUBA dives but knew exactly what was happening. Dissolved nitrogen slowly bubbled out into his bloodstream, starting in his joints. Pilots would never go to such an altitude without a pressure suit. Of course, they also wouldn't fly a high-performance aircraft without a G-suit to help with the high G-forces that almost ended Roger's mission before it began. The cabin was partially pressurized, or he'd already be dead. But eight psi was significantly less than fourteen-point-seven. At least he had an oxygen mask. The pure oxygen helped keep his thinking clear and slowly helped purge the nitrogen out of his bloodstream. But a pressure suit would have prevented the problem.

Doesn't matter. It's all over in minutes.

Justin's countdown to slug number one interrupted Roger's thoughts about joining his wife, their kids, and their Lord.

"...Three, two, one..."

No one knew how it would sound. A railgun launching a ten-pound projectile from an aircraft flying hypersonic at 90,000 feet? He heard a loud "whump" as the slug streaked out of the aircraft's nose. Within a second, it began glowing and leaving a tail. Muzzle velocity, as it exited the rail gun, was Mach Fifteen, and without the help of Guardian's ion shield the titanium outer shell began to ablate. On a clear night, a child might have thought it was a meteor and made a wish.

As expected, the first shot missed by several hundred meters. Now the

Trisistors in the TCS DPI-01 earned their pay, entering their teraflops burst mode as the seconds ticked away for launching the second slug.

"… Two, one…"

With another shudder and "whump," a second slug was on its way, within seconds lighting up the night sky.

"Three meters ahead of target," Justin reported.

"As soon as number three launches, I want you to bypass the interlocks. If we miss, the only thing I want on your mind is when to implode the drive." As an afterthought, Roger added: "Colonel, my legs are paralyzed and I won't be able to land this thing. But if General Alvarez wants I could try to ditch it, or put it down on a foamed runway. Justin, how's our count?"

"Stand by. If we miss, keep your heading and enter two degrees down elevation into the autopilot. Five seconds. Three… two… one."

"Number three is on the way. Initiate Battle Short!"

"Overrides initiated."

The warhead began re-entry and the burning ablative shield was now making it visible. Two bright streaks on a collision course…

"And we have a…Missed! Altering two degrees down. Justin, tell me when. Colonel, I guess the General doesn't get any of his plane back."

At that instant, he screamed below the streaking meteor that was the incoming warhead.

Roger had already seen the icon Justin added to his main touch screen. He held a shaking finger over the screen to force the implosion. His entire upper body ached from the bends. Mercifully, he couldn't feel anything below his waist.

There was nothing more to say. Only one more thing to do. Then he'd be with his family, his Lord, and His God. He was going home. *"Absent from the body…at home with the Lord…"*

"Now!" Justin shouted. Tears were streaming down his cheeks. "Goodbye, old friend."

And the comms went dead.

20. FALLOUT

The Secret Service agent received the terse, urgent text with mixed emotions. On the one hand, his country was safe—at least for now—from an extreme makeover akin to Stalin's Russia and Mao's China. Many lives were saved, including several key leaders who he had to admit, he had begun to like and even respect.

On the other hand, so many plans, such detail. All wasted. But Nathan Franks complied. That's what you do when you work for them. You obey, you're paid well; you disobey and the consequences…Nathan shuddered at the thought.

"Stand down."

A simple, short text. Nathan and everyone else who were also prepared to strike did exactly that. They stood down. And this night that was meant to end the United States of America as it had been for over two and a half centuries, became just another Saturday evening.

+ + +

Silence. No telemetry, and with the audio link through Guardian broken, Justin had also lost contact with NORAD.

He folded up his Multiphone and ran back to his living room.

He hardly noticed that Tamika had finished her glass of wine, the hors d'oeuvres on her plate, and left.

With a series of hand movements, he swiped the entertainment system screen away from the football wrap-up program—scores didn't matter now—and scanned through news channels. Major network channels. Weather channels. Stories of even more tensions with China. The latest sexting scandal from Washington. Continued rising poll numbers for President Garcia, despite, or perhaps because of, his strong conservative leadership, according to the commentator.

The Weather Channel had a comment about the Nor'easter pounding the East Coast from Virginia to the Carolinas. They mentioned an unusually bright flash accompanied much later with what sounded like a prolonged sonic boom.

Weather personnel speculated that it might have been an extremely rare occurrence of what they described as exploding ball lightning.

Justin sat in stunned silence.

Roger, you did it. You really did it.

+ + +

"Yes, Mr. President."

Twenty-four hours. He has an argument with his wife and realizes that short of a miracle, his marriage was history. He walks into the NORAD Command Center and finds that America is under nuclear attack. And now he's presenting his preliminary assessment to President Juan Garcia—America's first president of Hispanic descent—and his key staff.

Colonel Draper continued. "To summarize up front, there are thousands of ways this could have been worse, and few ways it could have been any better. What we know so far," Draper went into his briefing mode as he spoke to the video conference camera:

"First, the maximum yield of a nuclear device depends on a specific ignition sequence. In one design, for example, the precise ignition of a spherical high explosive shell creates a shock wave that implodes a plutonium core and triggers a fusion reaction. Guardian's EMP triggered an explosion, but it was not optimized. The yield may have been under a hundred kilotons, less than a tenth of what we feared.

"Second, the high-altitude detonation—roughly 90,000 feet—means no ground entered into a fireball to become radioactive fallout. Any radioactive material left from the warhead was vaporized. It was probably negligible and safely dispersed over a wide area by the storm.

"Third, the detonation occurred about 160 nautical miles east-southeast of Charleston, South Carolina. At that distance, altitude, and yield, there was only enough overpressure to rattle some windows.

"Fourth, the heavy Nor'easter covering the region blanketed northern Georgia and the Carolinas with clouds topping out at over 35,000 feet. Otherwise, a high-altitude detonation on a clear night would have blinded thousands, including pilots, drivers…there would have been significant collateral damage. As it was, reports are that it was no worse than a massive lightning flash and no thermal effects at all."

President Garcia interrupted. "What about EMP from the blast?"

"Sir, I can't explain this. It'll probably take a team of physicists with adequate security clearances to figure it out. Best we can tell, the EMP of the explosion somehow followed the ionized trail of Guardian. Rather than the expected omnidirectional spread, it apparently went along a straight line, above the earth and out into space to the east and west. We've had no reports of ground level EMP effects. We had one commercial satellite along that line to the east go dark, and one of our hardened GPS satellites to the west rebooted.

"Mr. President, it's like the first ever nuclear attack on the United States was a non-event."

+ + +

"It is appointed unto man once to die, and after that the judgment."

The Bible verse repeated as if on looped playback. Suddenly his entire body convulsed. His eyes flew open.

Impossible!

Roger knew from Scripture that there was no Purgatory. The Apostle Paul wrote that for believers, to be absent from the body is to be present with the Lord.

So... where was he?

Guardian!?

Again: *Impossible!*

Flat-screen displays blazed aircraft status in full high definition color. The aircraft was flying smooth, level, and subsonic. Outside, the sky appeared to be a strange semi-transparent light gray. He was in clouds but somehow saw through them, even at night. It reminded him of computer images, with "transparency" at eighty percent...

Night? He shook his head—actually, his whole body trembled—and looked back at the displays.

Time? The chronometer readings were gibberish, just random flashing numbers.

We should be vaporized.

Altitude? His radar altimeter flashed numbers between twenty and forty thousand feet, averaging around Flight Level Three Zero.

If the fireball didn't get us, the blast front should have ripped us apart.

Airspeed? Three hundred.

Even if Guardian survived, the gamma radiation from the NUDET should have already killed me. But...

He took a slow, deep breath.

He held out a hand. The trembling had stopped. His heart beat strong and steady; no AFib.

Course? The autopilot display indicated a faint orange ellipse, a track extending from 100 out to 150 nautical miles from the East Coast. Guardian was flying an elliptical track between Savannah, Georgia and Charleston, South Carolina. His current heading was down toward Savannah.

She's in a safe holding pattern, awaiting instructions...just like we programmed her.

Not only did Roger feel better than he had in years, but his joints weren't hurting. At the lower altitude, the cockpit air pressure was back up near fourteen point seven, he was still breathing pure oxygen, and he felt...he slowly shook his head.

I feel great!

Another quick survey assured Roger of adequate fuel for at least another hour for the turbojet engine, and that the ion drive and related systems had shut down. He could only imagine the severity of the buffeting when the ion shield collapsed, and the heat damage to leading edges before the aircraft slowed to subsonic.

What knocked me out? How long?

Something else caught Roger's attention. His legs were jerking. And...was it his imagination, or were they tingling?

Hmmm?

Roger checked his radio status and frequency. Still set to NORAD.

"NORAD, Guardian. NORAD, this is Guardian. Do you copy? Over."

Nothing.

After several more attempts, Roger scanned through other common aviation frequencies.

Silence.

Puzzled, he tried to datalink into the DPI network, trying to reverse the link Justin used. Nothing.

He checked his navigation again. *Ten Miles? This should be accurate to a few feet!* Checking his GPS screen, he saw he had no lock on any GPS satellite. Not a single one. Navigation was old fashioned, based on gyroscopes that hadn't been calibrated to fine precision due to the hurried airborne launch.

He had longed, ached to be reunited with his family. But the analytic engineer in him was overwhelmed with curiosity. This was a huge mystery, and he was in the data collection mode. What disabled communications while every other onboard system operated at one hundred percent? Except the clock.

With no outside help, he had to carefully consider his options while he still had a few.

Fact: Guardian was ultra-classified and must not simply be crashed at the nearest airport.

Fact: Unless he quickly reestablished communications, he would have to make his own decision, before fuel ran out within about one hour.

Fact: *What?!...* A sudden itching distracted him. First his scalp, then under his armpits. He tried to concentrate on his third fact, but his right knee was itching...His left foot twitched...he felt it!

A sense of awe swept over Roger. For the first time since the mid-air collision and crash-landing years earlier, the feeling was returning to his legs. He felt the relief as he scratched behind his right knee, then his left knee. The itching subsided as quickly as it had begun, replaced by a mild but bearable tingling sensation throughout his body. The feeling remained, and he could move his feet and legs! *Electric shock?* The strange calmness, and the healing of his paralysis; did he experience something like electro-shock therapy?

Lord, I don't understand...anything...but thank You!

For the first time since they strapped him into the aircraft high over Texas, he added the possibility of a safe landing to his list of options. And he removed one option he had seriously considered: A straight dive into a mountain or swamp to obliterate Guardian and its classified equipment.

At least for now.

21. JASON MATTHEWS

Jason Matthews is the Antichrist.

Well, perhaps not, but there had been speculation by the few who didn't come under his charismatic spell.

The man had been ruggedly handsome in his younger days and wasn't too bad for a man now in his mid-sixties. His dark complexion, dark eyes, and salt-and-pepper hair hinted at a Mediterranean heritage from at least one side of his family. His physical stature was not overwhelming at six feet tall, and a trim-and-fit 190 pounds. But his personality was another matter.

Jason was an avid student of personal power. Literally. Not as an undergraduate student, or while attaining his Doctor of Jurisprudence. Too obvious. Rather, Jason's study began years earlier growing up in Chicago, seeing his father cower to the respective powers of mob bosses, political bosses, and labor bosses. Jason hated seeing his father appear weak. And he despised the greater reality that his father was weak. He vowed that he would never be put in that position himself. He learned—and he learned exceptionally well—from his father's example of using subtle manipulation for survival. From that foundation Jason practiced and perfected what he learned at every opportunity; at home, at school, and in friendships and dating relationships.

There was the personal power of Attila the Hun: Brutal. No class. Hitler? Far better, using significant personal charisma and backing it up with violence as needed or desired. There were the examples that Jason was personally and painfully aware of, like the gang bosses and corrupt governors and mayors around the time and place of his upbringing. And he'd studied contemporary examples of presidential power and abuses thereof.

But in every case, and hundreds of others, they had one feature in common. Regardless of how brutal or how manipulative, Jason likened their form of power to world championship boxing. You had to win by being tougher, throwing more blows, and enduring more torment than your opponent. Not very elegant.

More to his liking, Jason studied and perfected the fine art and science of what he referred to as deep manipulation. He learned to exercise the enormous self-discipline of not showing his power. Ever. The greatest control over others, he learned, was when they didn't realize how much they were being controlled. Pretty amazing, actually.

<u>Rule One</u>: Always precede every important conversation with self-talk. State your objectives.

Quiet. Indirect; nothing anyone can pin on me. A reminder of expectations. Unmistakable expression of disappointment. Imply consequences.

All in a split second.

"Mr. Nesmith. Cliff, Cliff, Cliff. How could this happen?"

He waited an uncomfortable three seconds until Cliff made a stumbling comment, then immediately spoke over him in a slow monotone.

"You knew what we expected. You knew how much we've invested; what's at stake. A thousand variables had to be manipulated, hundreds of people at the right place at the right time. Even you; you were warm and cozy, ready for your place in our new arrangement while everyone believed you were on a cruise. How did you allow this to happen? When will we ever have such a perfect opportunity again?" Jason let out a long sigh. "Now talk."

This time, he let Cliff talk. It wasn't like Cliff to be nervous or confused. But Jason had that effect on people. Intentionally.

"Uh, I, uh, I told you the exact time it would be in transport, uh, unavailable. How was I to know a paraplegic engineer could fly it?"

"It didn't miss."

"Uh, yes sir, it did, actually. It really did. I don't know what they did. But…uh…it did miss. I made sure…"

Jason let the silence linger. Quietly, deadpan: "Where is it now?"

"Sir, it must have been vaporized. It couldn't have survived. No traces!"

"Good," Jason spat out, his tone making it clear that nothing about the entire situation was in any way "good." "We'll look for another opportunity. You won't let me down again. You won't let us down again."

Jason ended the call.

Quiet. Indirect. Nothing anyone can pin on me. Expectations. My disappointment. Consequences. Check.

Jason closed his eyes, took a long, slow breath, and committed every detail of the conversation to his eidetic memory. He always remembered what he said. And didn't say.

Jason had another call to make. Like the first, he used his front-line DARPA prototype phone. His part of the call could not be traced back to him, to the phone, or even recorded as having occurred.

"Mr. Premier." The translation was automatic, virtually instant, and as accurate as ninety-nine percent of native speakers. "We have a non-event. We'll make threats, back off negotiations for a while and wait for another opportunity."

"Understood. We're going dark for now. We'll await your next call."

Just like that, the call ended.

Jason helped himself to a tall shot of very expensive Scotch.

All his networks—"his," in his own mind; Jason would never slip up and say that out loud—were appalled when he had lost the election. His Hollywood friends and other supporters were inconsolable. Many wept bitterly, even threatening to move out of the United States. Jason had just shrugged it off. He had bigger plans. President of the United States memorabilia would be a nice-to-have addition to his I-love-me wall; especially since he would have been the last person to ever hold that office. But, who cares? The presidency, a delay in instigating the One World Peace Now takeover...

All just minor setbacks.

He poured himself a second shot. He never had over two shots per day.

Jason methodically planned his next move.

He smiled. And began his evening game.

+ + +

Cliff Nesmith was shaking, sweating, and swearing. His one consolation was that the discussion hadn't been face-to-face. He took the senator very seriously. He had heard rumors that Senator Matthews was responsible for a number of convenient "accidents" and "suicides." There was always the implied threat that Jason Matthews had to have his way. Or else.

He mixed himself a stiff drink. One thing he made sure of was that his shelter had a well-stocked bar.

How in the world did Roger and Justin pull this off? he marveled.

When no answer came to mind, his thoughts returned to Jason Matthews, and he scowled.

The "love-hate" relationship had gone too far in the wrong direction this time. Sure, Matthews drove the phenomenal success of DPI and, therefore, Cliff's personal wealth, many times beyond anything he ever imagined. But

Cliff had earned it. He would have become a multi-millionaire in his own right anyway. It just would have taken longer.

Would have. But he had seen the so-called writing on the wall. He knew enough from what little Jason had divulged, and from his own research, that a new order of things was coming. It was inevitable. The remaining variables were when, how, and what Cliff's role would be in that new world order. He knew his innovative manufacturing technology and other patents put him in a unique position to benefit personally. Jason had agreed. But continuing to work under Jason was like selling your soul.

"Okay, I'll play the game," he muttered. "I'll build your facility in Indiana. They've got cheap real estate and excellent access to transportation. But watch out, Mr. Senator...you may be the biggest game in town for now, but you're not the only one. And the right two or three can take you down, Big Man. I'll see to it."

He hated being bound to the senator. He despised the man almost as much as his Ex. Every month he watched thousands of dollars of his money get sucked up by her and her boy toy for their lavish lifestyle. Cliff knew they'd never marry. Why ruin a good thing and lose all that precious alimony?

How I wish that bomb had gone off as planned!

By a pleasant coincidence, his Ex lived almost exactly under the intended Ground Zero.

+ + +

A job, a quest, an obsession...as the years limped by, Skylar Brown became more determined to find Karen Lane, if it was his last task working for Senator Matthews. Now past-middle-age, the black man's knee continued to get worse. So was the harassment from the rest of Matthew's team. Never to his face; not yet. But it was always there on the down-low. Skylar was still stocky at five feet ten and 240 pounds, which he carried with very little body fat. Yet he had been dropped in seconds by a 150 pound woman, leaving a shattered knee that three surgeries still hadn't corrected. Worse, he faced a mandatory full knee replacement within the year, putting him back out of action for several more months. And that's when the younger men would make their collective moves to set up a new Alpha Male and team hierarchy.

But he would find her. That would keep him Number One. He could continue his search online during recovery as effectively as traveling the United States and abroad.

Patents. I need to tighten up research on patent applications!

Skylar took another narcotic painkiller.

Sometimes he got close to Karen, or Sally, or Joan, or Tammy, or whoever she pretended to be. Several times he missed her by less than a single day. Once his team broke into a small Swiss chalet she had rented for a year—paid in advance—to find her bath water still hot. But she was gone. And one time they did catch her. He lost two good men that night, and several others were compromised and had to be eliminated.

Untraceable, like a ghost. But in recent years, each time he discovered her current alias and researched what she'd been doing, he had found patent applications for her inventions. To the growing fury of his boss, the patents and royalties typically benefited various 501-C3 charitable organizations, most of which were Christian ministries. And all of her patents were significant, noteworthy accomplishments in some field that caught the world by surprise.

Karen continued to evade every facial recognition and every other biometric trick they'd used over the years. Even high-definition cameras and other means of scanning fingerprints were no longer any help. Since 2020, it was as if she had new prints with each alias; impossible even with enhanced DNA.

But behavior? I'll set up some web spiders to track how she operates. Worth a try.

Skylar sat back in his recliner in his modest one-bedroom apartment on the outskirts of Washington, still hating Matthews for moving his team inside the Beltway. He rubbed his knee while planning a new layer of cyber sniffing.

Matthews wanted her for more research. He needed her, but Skylar suspected that the not-so-good senator was also secretly afraid of her. Skylar knew all too well they had every reason to fear *the lady* as he often referred to her.

Yes, Jason, you'd better be afraid. If she ever gets tired of us chasing her…

Skylar shuddered at the thought as a new stab of pain reminded him of his own encounter.

Next time it'll be different. He would eventually capture her and hand her over for the research. He would also take great personal delight in contributing some significant data points of his own. Like, how long it would take for her enhanced DNA to recover from multiple broken bones. And worse. Much worse.

22. RECOVERY

A few taps on his fuel management display brought up Roger's remaining range as a circle, overlaying a map of airports within that area. Several Navy airfields were within range along the coast, but then he remembered a base in the middle of Georgia with an exceptionally long runway. He'd been told that the Boeing 747 that transported Space Shuttles back to Florida would occasionally rest overnight—RON—there, when weather kept them from flying down to Canaveral. It took the entire runway for the co-joined aircraft to takeoff, but they safely did so on several occasions.

Robins Air Force Base. That was it. They also once had bomber and tanker wings there, and he believed it now supported J-STARS, the Joint Surveillance Target Attack Radar System aircraft.

Adequate runway, large hangars, and security.

Roger disengaged the autopilot and directed the aircraft due west, straight and level.

Won't they be surprised!

Actually, the next surprise was his. Again, it centered on communication, or rather the lack thereof. As he re-entered U.S. airspace, he configured his radar display to show any planes above Flight Level Two Zero. Nothing. No radar images, no transponder readings.

Okay. No comms, no radar, no GPS, no transponders. Radar altimeter shaky. Am I a figment of my own imagination?

AM bands. FM bands. Crickets!

Roger looked outside. He was back over land now, and away from the storm, still somewhere around Flight Level Three Zero. But what should now be a clear night sky was more like the one time he'd seen a full solar eclipse. Dark, yes; and no colors. But a diffused light, like a strange colorless twilight or dawn. He saw the occasional small towns and interstate lighting. But…colorless, in stark contrast to the brilliant colors of his flat-screen displays, controls, warning labels, and everything else in his cockpit.

Roger debated on whether to set his transponder to the common General Aviation setting. Perhaps it would let authorities see him. He knew that would be a gamble. Guardian was untouchable with stealth cloaking and hypersonic drive at 90,000 feet in attack mode. But the anemic turbojet and mushy low-speed handling meant that it had the survivability of an overweight pigeon. An

F-35 with any questions would shoot first, ask questions later. He turned off the transponder.

Roger realized that he was flying VFR at an IFR altitude. If no one could see him, he'd better make sure he stayed out of everyone else's way. Warner Robins was a good ninety miles south of Atlanta's busy airport. But he still suspected there would be a large volume of air traffic, with much of it close to his altitude. For an extra margin of safety, he continued scanning the sky and began a slow decent as he followed I-16 east.

Roger continued scanning through various radio bands. Nothing. It made no sense. But neither did his survival or the strange phenomenon with the "unnight" sky and lights.

Then he saw the strange UFO. He could tell that it was coming straight at him because the craft became larger without moving left, right, up, or down. As it came closer, it looked dull gray and had an outline like a civilian airliner, but it moved impossibly slow. Yes, there were flashing lights on both sides, but they weren't the FAA-required colors for beacons, and their flash pattern was way too slow.

Amazed and confused, Roger simply lowered his nose to allow the slow craft to pass above him. It was…the outline was clear…a Boeing 787. It should fall out of the sky at that airspeed!

He scanned the surrounding airspace even more carefully and continued his slow descent. The aircraft passed through 20,000 feet, down to 15,000, then below 10,000 feet about the time he flew over Dublin, Georgia. Roger began a slow spiral descent around Robins Air Force Base while he still had the fuel and no intercept. It gave him a good look at the airfield and any ground or air activities to avoid.

Robins Air Force Base. Yes, the runway was substantial. He could have landed a Cessna just on a taxiway. There didn't appear to be much activity and none near the runway. He saw several J-STARS aircraft on a ramp off the north end of the runway, with a lot of open space around several hangars. That appeared to be a better choice than over in the maintenance area where several C-5 and C-130 aircraft were in various stages of depot maintenance.

Now under 3,000 feet, Roger went full manual. He had to get used to operating the rudder controls, even though in a formal sense Guardian had almost no rudder per se; most yaw functionality was built into its blended wing design.

Wow…I can operate the rudders! A distant object appeared to sweep side to side as he pushed in the left and then the right pedal. The tops of the rudder pedals pushed in as he tested his ability to apply brakes.

I just don't get it.

He lined up on runway three-three and pulled back power. The aircraft descended through 2,000, then 1,000 feet. Airspeed dropped to 200, then 180, 160, then 140 knots. He lowered the landing gear and verified three green lights, then set wing configuration to "land." That's all; no specific flaps. The wings re-configured to give the greatest lift, allowing him to slow to one-twenty. From there, all he had to do was keep the nose straight and control his descent by tweaking the throttle.

Touchdown. Smooth as glass, just past the numbers.

With plenty of runway ahead, Roger pulled the jet back to idle and rolled. He'd apply brakes once Security Police caught up with him. Otherwise, he'd roll toward the end, and turn off on a taxiway toward the J-STARS ramp.

No Security Police?!

Come to think of it, tower lights were on, ramp lights were on, and the base seemed normal except for the strange absence of color. But the runway lights were never turned on during his approach.

At the end of the runway, Roger increased the jet's throttle to a safe taxi setting and turned right, then right again toward the J-STARS ramp. He had planned to park on the tarmac, but he'd also expected a full security escort.

Is it really possible that no one can see me?

Roger double-checked that optical stealth was off and shrugged. He put aside the whys and wherefores and focused on facts as he knew them. Something happened when he collapsed Guardian's superconductive magnet and generated a directional EMP along the conductive ion trail as the warhead went through it. That probably ignited the warhead, generating a greater EMP followed by unimaginable electromagnetic radiation from gamma down to ultra-low frequency. Guardian was screaming away at over two miles per second, but still not fast enough to outrun the radiation or the fireball's overpressure.

But the aircraft survived. I survived. The nerves in my back are healed, and I can use my legs. We weren't vaporized. The radiation didn't kill me. The shock wave didn't pulverize us.

Roger slowed and turned off the taxiway onto the J-STARS ramp.

We're here. We're on the ground. Gravity's normal. But somehow, we're different.

He carefully rolled off the tarmac onto the grass between the taxiway and two hangars.

They may not see us, and I sure don't need a full-size J-STARS slamming into me as I try to figure out what's going on.

With all indicators showing normal, Roger transitioned the aircraft configuration to "Park" and shut down the engine. He opened the cockpit, extended the plane's ladder treads out from the fuselage, breathed in the cool fall air, and did something he never believed would be possible. He slowly, carefully climbed out of the aircraft.

I really feel good!

Giddy, he jumped the last couple of feet to the ground. And bounced.

23. A DIFFERENT REALITY

Roger thought he was beyond surprises. Until his feet hit the ground. Rather, they seemed to sink into the ground then rebounded, sending him several inches back into the air. Roger's knees began to tremble.

He quickly sat down, afraid he was about to collapse. But sitting on the hard ground was more like relaxing on a thick exercise mat. So, it wasn't a problem with his feet or legs. Something was different about the ground. Or about him?

What in the world?!!

Roger closed his eyes, lay down on the ground, and focused on long, slow, deep breaths. After a few moments, he slowly sat back up, then stood to his feet.

"Okay." Roger noted another anomaly. His voice. It sounded flat as if the natural harmonics were missing. And the volume was significantly less than what it should have been.

"I even sound different?" he asked to no one but the empty tarmac, raising and lowering both volume and pitch. *Yes, decidedly different.*

"All right," he continued out loud and paced around the aircraft. "Let's evaluate. I'm not dead, and I'm safe on the ground. Either I'm about to die, or not. If not, then I'll need water, shelter, and food. I have to figure out how to contact the rest of the world. Now, what's my first priority?"

A sudden urge reminded him it had been a long time since he'd relieved himself. Not that anyone might see him—apparently no one could, regardless—but out of a habit of modesty he walked behind a hangar.

Feeling better but unsteady on legs he had not used in years, he bent forward as he finished and pulled up his zipper. He placed a hand out to lean against the hangar wall and fell through. Roger literally went through the hangar wall, stumbled, then caught his balance. He was inside.

Lights were off, yet he saw clearly in shades of gray.

Incredible.

He shook his head and once again took several slow, deep breaths.

The implications didn't take long to sink in. He couldn't grasp anything. How would he drink? Eat? What other capabilities or limitations did he have? He looked around the hangar, empty for the moment of aircraft, but stocked with maintenance equipment, tools, and a case of water bottles in the corner. He walked toward them.

Two more observations: Matter, in the horizontal direction, seemed less substantial than matter and gravity in the vertical direction. Second was that vision thing again.

It's like I'm wearing night vision goggles.

He saw an unopened water bottle standing apart from the case. As expected, his hand went right through when he tried to grasp it. There was just the slightest resistance, like grasping an aerogel, or thick cotton candy.

OK, let's try something here.

Roger put his hand around the bottle, only allowing his fingers to go in about half an inch. He held his hand steady. Ever so slowly, the water bottle pushed his hand back out. After what seemed like a full minute, he firmly held the bottle.

So, some kind of transference going on?

Holding onto the water bottle, hoping to give it time to fully adapt to "his" reality—as he started calling it—Roger walked around the hangar. Sure enough, there was a break room with a refrigerator. He reached for the handle and again, held his hand just slightly inside the handle until the mass pushed his hand back out and he could grasp it. About two minutes, he guessed.

Roger was not one to steal, but to say his circumstances were unusual was like the classic "Doctor Livingston, I presume?" understatement of an earlier century. He grabbed—or rather, slowly grasped—a cup of yogurt. Between one and one-and-a-half minutes. He also picked up a plastic spoon; about thirty seconds.

All right, let's see if I can survive or not.

Roger twisted open the water bottle and took a sip. Water! Good old fashion H_2O. He finished the bottle and threw it in a trash can. It went halfway through the opposite side, then slowly backed into the center and fell in. He opened the blueberry yogurt, his favorite. After he finished it, he tossed the empty cup into the can. It, too, went part way through then plopped back into the center and fell in.

Roger started to walk out, then stopped and turned around. He reached for the refrigerator handle. His hand went right through it.

So… the transference is temporary?

Roger felt better now but noticed congestion building up in his sinuses and lungs. The famous Georgia allergies? That's how a "local" had described her sneezing and congestion the one springtime week Roger had visited the base many years ago. No, he'd never suffered from allergies. He'd only noticed this because he was in full analytical mode, trying to identify each variance from the expected, like a master forensic scientist. And it was well beyond allergy season.

He guessed he had been away from the aircraft about twenty minutes and decided to go after his next objective: Trying to communicate with "their world." He walked over to a wall that should put him close to Guardian and put his hand against it. There was a little resistance, and he panicked. Trapped inside? Was he transferring back to "their world?" The possibility encouraged him, but he knew from too many test failures over his long career, that sometimes you can push things too far, too fast. He resolutely leaned forward and walked through the wall.

Guardian looked as beautiful as ever. He walked around her, marveling at the clean leading edges. No evidence of charring. The aircraft must have transformed before the full impact of the hypersonic airstream damaged the surface when the implosion shut down the ion drive and shielding. And before the blast overpressure would have pulverized it.

"Now there's an interesting fact." Again, the quiet, flat voice, like standing in a large anechoic chamber. "How in the world were we even able to fly?!"

He compared transition times for the water bottle, refrigerator door, a cup of yogurt, and a plastic spoon. It occurred to him that he was breathing "their" air. *So…it's a function of density.* Air, almost instantaneous, but not so much to fry Guardian's skin. Liquids, a little longer. Solids, longer still. Presumably, there would be a direct correlation to the time of transition and the material's position on the Periodic Table. Fortunately, neither he nor Guardian needed plutonium or denser materials!

Roger looked at the landing gear. No, the tires had not sunk into the ground. Again, it seemed that matter behaved differently in the vertical dimension as defined by gravity. Could this add credence to gravity being trans-dimensional? *Hmm. Is that what I am now?*

But something else bothered him. Matter… light… sound… That was it. Sound. The graveyard shift work taking place across the field should have produced the distinct sound of diesel ground support equipment. But all Roger heard was something that sounded like deep moans; not like any internal combustion engine he'd ever heard. As he looked across the field, he noticed something even more astounding. He remembered from his General Aviation training that a military airport control tower beacon had a green beam and a split white beam. An observer would see the beacon flash white, white, a pause, then green. He'd already come to understand that what he observed in "their" reality would be shades of gray in his. But the timing? There should be around thirty flashes per minute. He regretted given up both his phone and watch when they put him into Guardian, though they would have both fried in the intense magnetic field anyway. So, his best guess...it looked like the flashes were at about a fourth of the expected rate.

Did he see infrared? Did he hear audio at several octaves lower than normal? Could "his reality" include a clock rate two, three, or even four times faster than "their reality?" Even that wouldn't account for all the anomalies...

The congestion became more noticeable, along with a slight wheezing. This could be serious. He leaned against Guardian's fuselage. Solid as a rock. Almost immediately the wheezing stopped. Within a few minutes the congestion cleared. There was something else strange...and it was the aircraft itself. Compared to shades of grey, the warning label near the recessed emergency canopy ejection handle door appeared bright yellow and red.

Roger gently ran his hand over the smooth surface of the aircraft. "Well, looks like we're inseparable for the foreseeable future."

Suddenly, he stumbled. He quickly half sat, half fell to the ground as his unsteady legs collapsed. In another moment he was flat on his back. His last seconds of consciousness swirled like a kaleidoscope of images and questions:

Who launched the nuke?

Airmen lowering him into Guardian.

Why? Will they launch again?

Dropping out of the C-17 and slamming into the headwind.

How will the U.S. respond?

Pulling out from the dive.

Why did the third slug miss?

Pressing the skull and crossbones icon that bypassed Guardian's safety protocols, collapsed the ion drive, and presumably triggered an EMP and destroying the warhead.

A name flashed through his mind; Karen Richardson. Then, the question Mordecai asked his niece in the Bible book of Esther, whether she had been placed in her unique position, "...for such a time as this?"

Karen...me...unique...

A prayer of Jesus the evening before his crucifixion... then everything faded to black.

Guardian – Altered Reality

24. NOT GOOD

Cindy Jacobs, the current alias of Karen Lane Richardson, was beside herself. She had worked out the biology and the math long ago and knew that the next doubling of her strength and intelligence would be far beyond her expected lifespan of "five score and ten" years. Her occasional dual streams of consciousness—like now—would likely not increase beyond the occasional couple of minutes here and there, even if she forced it. For all practical purposes, her genetic enhancement had finally maxed-out. That wasn't the problem.

She had two problems actually, and both streams were equally concerned.

Cindy had been fully focused on a plea for help from her long-time friend, Samantha Knowles. "Sam" was a regional director of the U.S. Department of Homeland Security and presented a compelling case to expect a brutal terrorist attack from an awaking sleeper cell, somewhere in the Southeast. Once again, she needed Cindy's—Karen's—help.

Sam only asked for assistance occasionally, knowing that each time Karen intervened, she put herself at extreme personal risk. Not just risk from the task itself, but risk of being tracked down and caught, or killed, by those who would do anything to make that happen. The threat was real. It had only been in the last few years that they could even communicate without both of them being in danger.

That request for help was the first problem. Cindy focused on it intently on that Saturday evening, November 21, 2025—as a Nor'easter pounded her current short-term home in Charleston, South Carolina.

A lot of lightning and thunder—normal. Heavy rainfall—normal. Then, a prolonged loud noise, like an extended sonic boom or thunderclap—not normal! Five seconds—ten—twenty—almost thirty seconds before it started to fade.

Definitely not normal. So, the second stream of consciousness ran through the possibilities, immediately eliminating a sonic boom or thunderclap because of the long duration. Even if she were in a valley surrounded by mountains, the echoes wouldn't have continued for that long.

Like a one-person engineering team conducting an analysis of alternatives, she brainstormed events like a railroad tanker car derailment and explosion; natural gas explosion in a very large building; explosion of a fueling truck, perhaps while it was pumping gasoline into service station tanks; construction demolition; and dozens of other possibilities.

Just as quickly, she eliminated non-players. A railroad derailment? Too far from tracks. Construction demolition? Not on a Saturday night in heavy thunderstorms. And so on. The exercise continued even as she scanned through news channels on television and the internet.

She didn't perceive any direct threat, so she would mentally add that to her "what in the world, now?" file for later clarification. Her full attention returned to the urgent plea from Sam.

There was no way she could know that the extended explosion was from a nuclear detonation—NUDET—160 miles east-southeast of Charleston, at an altitude of around 90,000 feet. Nor could she have known that her friend from 2006, Roger Brandon, was responsible for detonating it that high and that far out to sea, by creating a directed electromagnetic pulse. That EMP in turn focused the NUDET's EMP above the earth and out into space. Neither she nor anyone else would have imagined that the combined EMPs and the NUDET transformed Roger and the Top Secret hypersonic manned interceptor, Guardian—into, well, into an altered state of reality.

What she did know was that something very cruel, very evil was about to take place. If she could, she had to stop it. Cindy asked a few questions and Sam quickly responded in their ultra-secure chat session:

Sam: It could be any number of major cities. I personally suspect Charleston. Intel of some radical cell groups close by. There's a strong Christian heritage, and an old Jewish congregation, one of the largest in the continental United States. Also, one of the oldest Orthodox synagogues in the South. A target-rich location for jihadist attack. Wherever, we suspect the attack will be before Chanukah, which begins at sunset Monday, December 15th this year.

Cindy: Why me?

Sam: Not just you. But we're spread thin. Intel indicates a new low. They plan to rape, torture, and kill; then blow themselves up as soon as we can engage. It's lose-lose for us. People die horribly if we do nothing, and everyone dies if we try to do anything. Maybe you'd have a chance? We'll cover other cities and I'll leave Charleston for you. I'll have to put my neck and career on the line to exclude Charleston, but if the attack's there I believe you'll have a better chance than our forces would anywhere else. Anyway, I'm close to retirement. If I'm right and you succeed, I'll go out with my head high. If I'm wrong, we'll have more resources ready to respond at the other locations.

Cindy reflected a beat. Smart, strong, fast, and a woman—some Islamic terrorists believed they would automatically be damned if killed by a woman—maybe she could do something. She typed again.

Cindy: Any other intel? Likely targets? Combined attacks or just here? Anything?

Sam: Will send everything I've got, and anything more as soon as I get it. Karen, I'm really concerned about this one. We're overwhelmed—stretched too thin. Pray it isn't multiple attacks.

+ + +

"They are not of the world, even as I am not of the world." Those words of Jesus, from his prayer before his death, burial, and resurrection, were Roger's last thoughts before plummeting into a deep sleep. His last feeling was the dull ache of legs that had been paralyzed for years, suddenly functioning again. The ache, and a continued mild tingling sensation throughout his body.

He had air-launched Guardian out of a C-17 cargo aircraft, dove toward earth to get the supersonic shockwave into the intake to light the scramjet and ion drive, and was able to intercept the incoming nuclear warhead. His three slugs had all missed, so he and Justin had to implode the ion drives' super magnet to generate an EMP. They knew that it would destroy the warhead but feared that it might also detonate it. At least it would be high enough and far enough from land to prevent casualties. Except for him. But the warhead's EMP could affect millions along the eastern seaboard.

Apparently, something worked.

Roger and Guardian survived but were somehow different. Roger regained use of his legs, paralyzed since the mid-air collision and crash-landing years earlier that killed his family. Now, he and Guardian were apparently invisible to the "normal" world. He could walk through walls, and he could not communicate with anyone, by any means.

Transdimensional? He wondered as he suddenly collapsed, then thought of the words of Jesus just before he lost consciousness laying on the "soft" ground beside Guardian. It was impossible for Roger to know whether the deep sleep lasted for minutes or hours. But at some point, he dreamed.

The tingling; it's getting worse. But, I'm dreaming. Too intense for a dream. Aftereffects of electroshock?

He fidgeted, somewhere between sleep and wakefulness. Hi-def dreams, unlike anything he'd ever experienced, projected like an Imax movie. He caught glimpses of his career's countless System Requirements Reviews, Preliminary Design Reviews, Critical Design Reviews, and In-Process Reviews. He dreamt of endless Design Specifications, Performance Specifications, and Interface Control Specifications. There were the Critical Path Analyses, Pert and Gantt Charts, Risk Assessments, and Root Cause Analyses. The late nights, early mornings, and far too many all-nighters where the two became one. And excruciating "death by PowerPoint" meetings in the hundreds.

Black screen for a beat; then back to his days of courting Cindy in college. And her courting him! Their frequent teasing of each other, and how neither doubted that their feelings were mutual. Their almost unheard-of decision to save themselves for each other until marriage, and how God had blessed them for it. It was true. Their commitment to Him and to each other provided a foundation that held them together even through the turmoil of Roger's over-commitment to work and their daughter's years of destructive hedonism.

The birth and childhood of Frank, then Susan, and the crazy family vacations. The plane crash. Losing his family, but knowing he would never fully lose them, and would one day rejoin them with the Eternal One, as he liked to reverently refer to the Triune God.

Worse than a dream...it hurts!

Roger tossed and turned even more on the "soft" ground, feeling the emptiness as he finished the contract at his earlier job, dreading where life would take him next, and then the surprise call from Cliff to join Directed Paradigms, Incorporated—DPI. A vague reference to a concept that Roger had mentioned during a tour of a classified facility. He didn't need the money. Corporate lawyers of the company responsible for the UAV that caused the fatal crash begged him to take a lofty settlement after the accident. No, not the money. He battled depression daily. What he had needed was a purpose.

Fast forward.

Roger was given unprecedented—as far as anyone could remember—control over an ultra-secret program. As a contractor, Roger was empowered to act as both the Program Manager and Program Systems Engineer—always before a government position—and reported directly to Lieutenant General Rey Alvarez. In a sense, even his own boss, Clifford Nesmith, reported to him.

Roger was re-energized with the challenges, the unique manufacturing facility and techniques, the broad responsibilities without the typical "micromanagement."

As he slept and dreamed, a minor chord of discomfort returned as the strange playback in his mind recalled the occasional reports he and General Alvarez had to make to Senator Matthews. Roger got along with just about everyone, but Matthews made him very uncomfortable, way down deep. Roger was always guarded around Matthews. Always.

Another fast-forward, as the tingling increased.

It was the successful, uneventful test flight less than two days before. Loading Guardian into the C-17. The crisis, and his crazy plan to drop the hypersonic interceptor from the cargo aircraft, dive to go supersonic and light the ion drive, and attempt an intercept with a prototype that wasn't yet halfway through operational testing.

The tingling increased yet again, and the Imax movie took on a 3-D surround effect, with him in the cockpit.

He whimpered in his sleep at the crushing fear of being in a cockpit once again. He giggled at the absurdity of a crippled, overweight, retirement-age engineer trying to fly the beast. Then he lay still and quiet, as the dream played out; the slugs missed, the safety over-rides and ion drive implosion, and…the miraculous healing of his paralysis. Waking to an alternate reality. Stepping down from the aircraft into a different world; or the same world, but different?

Karen.

Roger half-jolted out of his dream state, into that strange world of a waking dream. He knew he was dreaming, but in a sense, he was consciously communicating with his dream.

Yes. Different. Like Karen.

The year was 2006, the one Sunday that Roger was asked to share from the pulpit when the pastor and associate pastor both had to be out of state. The one Sunday that Karen attended, after burying her husband.

She asked Roger and his wife if she could take them to lunch. The kids were with grandparents, Karen seemed genuine but troubled, and they agreed to go with the young woman. As they ate in a booth where they could talk privately, she handed her driver's license to Roger.

"This is no joke. No cosmetic procedures. No surgeries, other than to close up a bullet wound that should have killed me."

Roger and Cindy looked at the license. Karen Lane Richardson. Huntsville, Alabama address. Blonde, no glasses, five-feet-six-inches, born—Roger did the quick math and looked at the young lady sitting across from them. She looked like a high school senior, or at the most a college freshman. Long blonde hair, a little longer than in the picture on her license and wearing an attractive but modest black skirt and white blouse. Modest but expensive silver earrings hung just below her lobes from a single piercing, with no other visible piercings or tattoos. A small but elegant wedding ring. Little makeup, and none needed.

Karen Richardson was thirty-seven years old.

25. SLEEPLESS IN TITUSVILLE

Roger slept, and dreamed.

Justin Townsend did neither. Actually, he never went to bed. Why bother? After the bigger-than-life crisis of the previous evening, he doubted he'd be able to sleep for days.

At 5:00 a.m., he didn't have his pre-workout energy drink, then run along Titusville Beach like he always did on odd numbered days. Nor did he go to the gym like he did on even numbered days. Justin didn't even have his post-exercise breakfast. He didn't bother checking the forecast before choosing the bike instead of his car.

At 5:15 a.m., his hybrid Tesla Tiger touring motorcycle was all but silently clicking off the miles toward the Kennedy Space Center, and the re-purposed facility that was now the home of DPI.

The terror, the doubt, the crisis, and the climax of the previous night continued to play back and forth in his mind as it had nonstop for hours. A nuclear fireball didn't kill hundreds of thousands. The East Coast wasn't paralyzed by an EMP. Government and civilian infrastructures were still intact, with virtually the entire world unaware of how close they had come to World War III. Or how close it still might be.

From his bedroom, Justin had data-linked in and remotely served as Guardian's back-seater, as the classified prototype interceptor flown by a paraplegic engineer attempted a desperate suicide mission to intercept and destroy the incoming warhead.

Guardian's rail gun missed. Justin bypassed dozens of safety protocols so Roger could implode the superconductive magnet, hoping to destroy the warhead by releasing an EMP. It was all based on nothing more than speculation. Apparently, it had worked.

Roger, his boss and long-time friend, was dead.

Nine decimal places of accuracy. We needed ten. Two shots. Several orders of magnitude improvement from the first to the second. How did the third shot miss?

Justin's core competencies were programming and math. He led the programming team that developed the Ternary Operating System. In addition to electrical engineering and program management, Roger excelled in radar and LIDAR design and operation. He and Justin shared the lead on the LIDAR sensor. Cliff Nesmith himself, founder and president of DPI, oversaw the Terminal Targeting System.

We should have been within forty centimeters of center mass! Why did Roger insist on preparing the implosion? How could he have known?

"*Because I told him to.*"

It wasn't an audible voice, but it was clear and unmistakable. Its impact was profound.

A sense of calm and certainty flooded over Justin. He knew where it came from, although he'd never experienced it before.

Justin once asked Roger how he had handled a particularly difficult management confrontation without losing his temper. Roger explained about the still, quiet voice of peace, more like an impression, that had helped him in several pivotal situations over the years. Most recently, Roger said he'd experienced it after losing his family. And once more in the make-or-break meeting that had prompted Justin's question. A meeting which later lead to Cliff hiring him at DPI. Roger once told Justin that he was praying that the younger man would eventually experience and recognize the voice of the Eternal.

Like now.

Justin kept his eyes on the road. His augmented-vision helmet and visor tripled his view of the road ahead and enhanced his peripheral vision. Despite the moonless pre-dawn night, he clearly saw Florida deer well off the side of the road. They looked his way, but he hardly noticed. His heart was with his missing friend. And now, he felt in direct contact with the One his friend loved more than life itself.

You told him! You loved millions of us so much that you saved us from a direct nuclear attack. You gave us a fourth shot!

Again, not an audible voice. Nor a specific dream or vision. But a clear mind's-eye view of the elegant painting he had admired so many times on Roger's wall clearly appeared to Justin. He could see the details; the top of a mountain in a heavenly setting, with a regal Jesus dressed in white. His arms were bared and muscular, and he was confidently pulling on a strong rope that extended below the white clouds, and down through a terrible thunderstorm below. The end of the rope was secured to a mountain climber, struggling to climb up the treacherous mountain. To the side of Jesus were the words—clear in Justin's mind's eye: "All authority has been given to Me in heaven and on earth." To the side of the rope, above the clouds: "There is salvation in no one else." Also, beside the rope, but down below in the storm: "Believe in the Lord Jesus, and you will be saved." Finally, below the man struggling to climb the mountain, the words: "For man is born for trouble, as sparks fly upward."

Trouble. Believe. Authority. Salvation. A miraculous deliverance. Hundreds of thousands...maybe millions saved...

Justin realized that what happened last night was "a God thing."

He felt dirty. Ashamed of the years he'd denied God, made fun of Bible Bozos, as he'd called all Christians except Roger. He felt an overwhelming sadness that he'd rejected the Eternal for so long. And such love! Roger had given his life to save Americans. Now Justin felt a personal connection with Roger's Jesus, who had given his life to save everyone who would trust in him.

Justin wept.

Jesus. I believe you are the living God, who came in the flesh to die for my sins. Please forgive me, save me, receive me to yourself. Live in and through me as you did with Roger.

Justin saw an owl fly over the road ahead. The motorcycle's small, perfectly tuned gasoline engine started and reached its optimum rpm to help charge the batteries and continue powering the bike. Justin was surprised at a set of feelings...peace, and a sense of acceptance and purpose unlike any he'd ever experienced. He felt—he felt clean.

He also knew exactly which code subroutine he had to check when he got to his workstation at DPI.

"Thank you, Jesus," he prayed.

We should have been less than forty centimeters from center mass!

He didn't know why yet, but he was determined to find out.

In her alias as Cindy Jacobs, Karen slowed her pace on the Jacob's Ladder Exercise Machine for a five-minute cool-down after her one-hour workout. The machine had been eight years old when she bought it used and was the first she ever owned. The external frame she added increased the climbing angle from 40 degrees to a more-challenging 60 degrees and the extra weights helped get her heart rate up to a modest 160. This morning, she wore a 40-pound vest, two 20-pound ankle weights, and two 10-pound wrist weights. It was the best she could do. In years past she had sprinted up and down Pike's Peak in Colorado in the wee hours of the morning, but that was before the state added cameras. Same with running up and down stairs in skyscrapers the times she stayed in big cities like New York.

No, over the years far too many people had taken cell phone pictures and videos of the enigmatic young superwoman as she exercised, rescued people from wrecked cars or out of earthquake rubble, prevented jihadist attacks, and more.

There were dozens of web sites devoted to tracking the redhead, blonde, brunette, or whatever she was—or whoever they were, as some supposed. The times she was caught on surveillance cameras just added legitimacy to the speculations, and even led to a few TV programs.

So, she exercised inside. Even there she had to be careful, especially when lifting weights. Part of her routine was to gently lower weights to the floor. It would not bode well to drop a 500-pound barbell onto a third or fourth story apartment floor at 5:00 a.m. or so, which is when she typically exercised after her four-hour night's sleep. Not very neighborly.

Her cool-down ended about the same time as her audiobook, an up-to-date definitive analysis of Islamic terrorist organizations which she listened to at 5x speed. She had to tweak her multi-phone's app to go that fast, as she typically got bored listening at a slower speed.

26. SABOTAGE?

Roger awoke with Karen still on his mind, but he knew where he was. He realized that he had slept and was well, despite not being in direct physical contact with the aircraft. Also, he noted that he wasn't cold in spite of a light layer of frost on the ground, even though he was still just in his khakis and long sleeve cotton shirt.

He had no way to know the exact time until he got into Guardian, but then he questioned that assumption. What time would the aircraft's chronometer show? Would it show early Sunday morning, or would it still be gibberish as it was last night?

Okay, I guess I'm not in critical need of shelter from the cold. I can get water and snacks from the hangar, at least for a while. Time to figure out how to get in touch with someone.

The noise that awoke him grew louder, and he turned to face the runway.

"No…no, that's just wrong!" His mouth hung open and he slowly shook his head.

A Hercules C-130 was taking off, the four turboprops strangely quiet and at a lower pitch than he expected. But like the slow-moving UFO he saw the previous evening that turned out to be a Boeing 787, the venerable cargo aircraft appeared on the verge of a fatal stall.

"Nothing flies that slow!"

Well, okay, maybe an ultralight, a helicopter, a V-22, or Marine F-35B? But not a C-130! Not a Boeing 787! And the beacons are flashing slow…!

Roger was back in analysis mode.

If it were a matter of metabolism, like I'd converted to a hummingbird, I'd be moving around faster, but everything would still be solid. It's not.

He paced around the aircraft.

But an aircraft doesn't have metabolism, so something else is going on at the atomic level. Are we literally trans-dimensional?

He stopped. *It appears to be both. I don't see light differently; away from Guardian, I see different light, apparently infrared. I don't hear differently; away from Guardian, I hear different audio frequencies. And the audio has to travel from "their" air to "my" air, so that's another transition. Maybe that's why my voice sounds so strange and quiet since part of it goes out from "my" air to "their" air and then back to reach my ears.*

And there was something else.

"What kind of electrochemical shock healed the nerves in my spine?"

Roger leaned against the aircraft a moment, looking around, listening, and breathing in the strange air.

Let's see if we can get some answers.

His legs were sore as he slowly, carefully climbed up the retractable ladder rungs into the aircraft. *Haven't used them in four years*, he reminded himself.

Main power ON, computer systems ON, communications suite ON, glass panel displays ON.

Full computer boot-up complete in, what? About the usual five seconds. From his perspective. And the chronometer showed…flashing digits.

Still gibberish. *That's all right, young lady. It doesn't compute with me either.*

It occurred to him that, except for a few changes Justin made the night before, the aircraft software was still in test mode. He should be able to program in whatever changes he might need.

Roger climbed into the back seat and pulled down the touch screen monitor. As an electrical engineer, Roger had learned a respectable amount of software coding over the years. Guardian's unique Ternary Operating System had required more than a manager's oversight. He wasn't anywhere near Justin's level, but….

Frequency agile, software programmable radios. Roger smiled and began modifying code. *Let's start simple.*

Roger began with a stable, receive-only system. He wrote and executed a routine to re-tune GPS receivers, for both the L One and L Two GPS radio bands, by ten kilohertz at a time.

Reduce both L One and L Two frequencies by ten kilohertz. Pause for sync. No sync? Repeat.

Nothing.

Radios are tunable, but the antennas aren't. Did I go too far out of tolerance?

"You dummy! Use the frequency scanner."

He put the radio into the scanner mode and saw the spikes considerably lower on the scale than they should have been, almost like a huge red Doppler shift. Roger locked in the "new" GPS frequencies, lower than the nominal 1575.42 and 1227.60 megahertz settings.

Nothing.

What if...what if I also have to match data rates?

He programmed a routine to modify the data receive rate so the digital receiver would wait one thousandth of one percent longer than it normally would have before timing out. Pause for sync. No sync? Increment by another one thousandth of one percent, repeat.

One minute—two minutes? Solid. The data rate had to be slowed by a factor of...four! The GPS clock synced the aircraft chronometer, and Roger chose the setting for Eastern Standard Time. It was 5:30 a.m. *What, not even seven hours since intercept, implosion, and transition?*

Roger did the math to offset other radios' frequencies and data rates. He didn't bother with voice radios as he doubted anyone would be able to "hear" him with the auditory frequency offset.

Wonder if dogs can hear me. Maybe bats?

Soon, Roger could receive multiple signals across various bands. Because of antenna mismatches, readings were down by as much as ten decibels and would be similarly impacted during transmission. Fortunately, the aircraft was designed with superior receive sensitivity and transmit power.

He sat back and pondered. At least for now, he would put his main plan on hold. But he would have to reconsider it if he couldn't actually re-establish communications.

When the airmen had lowered Roger into the cockpit, Roger was certain he would die if:

One, he couldn't light the ion drive;

Two, he couldn't pull out of the dive;

Three, the ion shielding failed;

Four, there was any other major malfunction; or

Five, he tried to land the plane without the use of his legs.

Six, he didn't try to land, ran out of fuel, and crashed.

In other words, he knew he would be dead within an hour; two at the most.

But all three slugs missed. The only chance to stop the warhead would likely detonate it, which he assumed had happened. He had survived, but lost communications. Since he couldn't coordinate landing an aircraft so highly classified that fewer than 150 people knew it existed, he had figured he would nose it into one of the foothills of North Georgia or into the Okefenokee Swamp. Then he'd remembered the secure facilities at Robins Air Force Base.

But even now, he knew he could not allow Guardian to "convert back," not even near the runway of a military installation. The project was too sensitive, both militarily and politically, to suddenly "go public."

He couldn't think of any way, by himself, to refuel the aircraft. So, his plan was to launch and climb as high as he could over an unpopulated area around central Georgia with his remaining fuel. Then he would put the nose straight down. Conversion, time-shift, whatever; there shouldn't be enough left for anything except claims of a UFO crash and government cover-up.

If he couldn't re-establish communications.

+ + +

"Intense" didn't begin to describe Justin's concentration inside the Sensitive Compartmented Information Facility, or "SCIF" at DPI.

A programmer couldn't write the code necessary for Guardian to re-calibrate after each slug fired from the mini rail gun. Not without a very strong math background. And a mathematician would have to possess impressive programming skills. The program had to capture gigabytes of data at the exact instant a slug missed its target. It then had to do all the calculations to account for aircraft speed and heading, aim of the gun up to two degrees from centerline, projectile speed, and the speed and heading of the target. Factor in any output power anomalies of the coils, atmospheric drag, gravitational anomalies, and effects at that particular altitude above the earth, and "do the math." Then program the analysis and the resulting offset vectors into Guardian's unique Ternary Operating System. Finally: Do it all in seconds.

Cliff had both the programming and the math skills to make it all happen. So did Justin. And on his life-changing ride to DPI, Justin knew what segment of code to study.

In under four hours, he was convinced. At 9:00 a.m., Sunday morning, Justin would just about bet his life that the code was perfect. He then conducted simulations that added another standard of deviation to his confidence. Analysis of the specific telemetry reported from Guardian to Justin's workstation—then summarized and transmitted to his Multiphone during the intercept—verified that everything worked as intended. At least, between the first and second shots. But the recalibration segment of code didn't repeat between the second and third shots. It couldn't have.

There was no reason in the code he reviewed. The code that had been written, submitted to peer review, simulated, and loaded into Guardian; no reason that the subroutine wouldn't automatically execute after every shot. It was right there. And to make certain, Justin double-checked against the baselined code that had been stored "read-only," under strict configuration management once it was loaded into the aircraft. That software module had no engineering change requests pending. There were no engineering change proposals approved and applied. That module was secure, unchanged. Perfect.

Justin was more perplexed than ever.

+ + +

So was Roger. His radio recalibration programming had been interrupted by an almost painfully bright, deep orange colored light rising in the east.

Must be seeing in infrared. At least the sun has some color, even if it's weird.

After another hour or so of work—the chronometer showed only fifteen minutes had passed in "their" time—he climbed out of the aircraft and walked through the hangar wall as he had the night before. He helped himself to some more snacks, then took advantage of the indoor plumbing. Well, sort of. He didn't try to "convert" the toilet seat, he just squatted over it. He did convert the toilet paper, sink faucet, soap, and paper towels.

A loud, low roar caught his attention and he walked back through the wall, just as an F-15 Strike Eagle went vertical. It was performing a high-performance takeoff as part of its final test flight following depot maintenance. Noise from the twin engines in full afterburner should have been overwhelming. Yes, it was loud. But not that loud, and the pitch was low. So low that the earth should have been shaking. It wasn't. At least, not that Roger could feel.

Just before going back into the cockpit, he realized something else. The rising sun on that clear, cloudless morning cast long, distinct shadows of every structure, every tree, and each of the J-STARS aircraft on the tarmac.

There was no shadow associated with him. Or with Guardian.

Oh, great. So now I'm a vampire?

He painfully climbed back into the rear seat and continued programming.

27. CONTACT

Cindy Jacobs finished drying her short hair, put on a comfortable jogging suit—red with black stripes—and her favorite sneakers. She went to the kitchen and made her daily "super nutrition smoothie." She hadn't changed this SNS recipe much over the years except to take advantage of local organic produce when it was in-season. She poured peanuts, walnuts, and almonds into a blender along with raw fruits and vegetables and some yogurt. She ran the blender a few moments then poured her breakfast into a large sixteen-ounce insulated cup.

She stepped out onto the balcony of her third-floor apartment, closed her eyes, and savored the cool, clean air left behind by the previous day's Nor'easter.

Karen enjoyed being Cindy. This particular alias was one of her simpler ones. Her eyelash color and hair were close to her natural color, as well as she could remember. She liked the sportier, shorter hair style and enjoyed not using any dental appliances to alter her jaw structure. True, her eyes were brown rather than the natural hazel. After years of intentionally looking different, it was a good disguise to go back to near-normal. Of course, the whisper-thin graphene gloves were imprinted with unique fingerprints to match her current identity.

She tried not to dwell on the constant cat-and-mouse dynamic…too depressing. It was her life and had been for well over thirty years. Change locations at least once a year, or sooner if an alias was compromised. Move around the country. Around the world. Stay away from Jason Matthews. Live her genetically-enhanced life to the fullest, alone, since her husband was long dead.

She had made her mind up years earlier. She wouldn't intentionally attack Jason and his henchmen. But if it ever came down to it, she would fight to the death. Jason Matthews would deeply regret ever having touched her, or ever having tried to recapture her.

She began a shopping list to send to a long-time friend. Mick Thompson actually worked for her, although only the two of them knew it. To the outside world, Mick was the owner/operator of a modest but successful manufacturing facility in a rural, financially depressed HUB Zone part of Tennessee. There were only two other workers, and they all knew about the ultra-secure area they referred to as Level 2.

She sent the email, using the same ultra-secure protocols she developed to communicate with Sam.

"Mick, need four *Commando Flips*, eight *Incapacitators* and six *Blades* by Wednesday. Also, forty—make that sixty—*Video Spots*, and three *Pole Climbers*. One *Commando Suit*, gray, with helmet, for me; same measurements as before. Matching sneakers, same shoe size. *Vehicle Light and Sound Bar*. Send to the Charleston address where you sent the sets of gloves. Must be here Tuesday morning. And Mick—urgent—please pray!"

Sam and Mick both owed Karen their lives. She took the last "Five Score and Ten" dose—FSAT—to save them, believing that it would result in her own painful death. It didn't, and a determined Jason Matthews and his thugs relentlessly hunted her down to learn why. Other than Jason's people, only Sam, Mick, and Roger Brandon knew of her genetic transformation.

Karen continued to help Sam and Mick occasionally. And at times like this, Mick would help her. He and his team would put in some overtime in Level 2 and she'd have her highly proprietary and extremely lethal supplies, body armor, and intel gadgets within a few days.

What she heard from the audiobook matched what she'd followed on the news feeds and the behind-the-scenes snooping she'd done on her own. She hung her head and slowly shook it side to side.

Illegals came in, and we didn't secure the borders. Billions of dollars a year in drugs and crime, and we didn't secure the borders. Terrorists came in, and we didn't secure the borders. Now, we secured our boarders, and it's too late. California shootings…nightclub shootings…firebombs…no, if anything, Sam's really underestimated this one.

Before leaving DPI, Justin emailed Lieutenant General Alvarez over the classified network. He didn't go into any analysis or details, just a simple statement and question:

"General Alvarez,

No contact with Roger. Assume system is lost. Cliff is on a cruise with no secure contact possible. Anything you need from me before tomorrow? I'll leave here at 11 if I don't hear from you. You can always catch me by cell."

Moments later: "We'll talk tomorrow."

Time for some comfort food.

Ten minutes later Justin was back on his Tesla Tiger. The loss of his friend, no sleep, no breakfast; he was famished. He was also frustrated over the maddening quandary with the recalibration code. It was perfect! He knew he had to "disengage to re-engage," as Roger used to say. His ultra-lean, muscular body didn't handle fasting as well as Roger, who joked about "living off the fat of the land." So their occasional late nights often included a trip to a local always-open IHOP restaurant. Roger would get the Senior Omelet, and substitute in the Harvest Grain and Nut pancakes. Justin would go with the full Western Omelet. After that and a pot of coffee between them, they'd head back to work and often accomplish more in the next two hours than in the previous six.

Justin finished the final bite of his breakfast-anytime omelet and washed it down with the last of his third cup of coffee. He left his usual twenty percent tip; his mother raised two sons and a daughter as a single parent, working as a waitress. A server had to have a really bad attitude or do poorly for him to leave fifteen percent, and if it were worse than that? Justin would speak to the manager. Justin reconsidered and increased his tip to twenty-five percent. The elderly white lady who served him was as sweet as she could be.

He paid his bill and walked to his bike. The meal had indeed helped him to "re-engage." He was certain the code, as written and as stored under configuration management, was correct. And it wasn't possible that an earlier version of the code was loaded into the aircraft. That critical recalibration segment dated back so far that the plane would have been un-flyable with a software version that old.

And it worked; it just didn't re-execute after the second shot.

Somehow, someone must have changed one specific line, calling for the routine to be repeated OTO—one time only. And they had to have done that directly on the aircraft itself after the code was loaded. Three people at DPI could have done this. Maybe four? No more than five.

The most logical suspect was...Roger. Was there something about his Christian convictions that would cause him to fight for Guardian's success, but then undermine its ability to successfully intercept?

His Multiphone chirped. He absent-mindedly picked it up, continuing the disagreeable train of thought. *And then he had sacrificed himself to cover up what he'd done?*

It was an email from Roger.

Roger...?

"*Justin,*

Didn't know who to contact first. A lot to share but can't talk. Literally, can't. Well, I can, but no one can hear me.

Be careful. Third shot should have been perfect! There were no hardware problems. Check the code. Suspicious.

Send codec so we can communicate securely.

Urgent. I cannot communicate through any normal means.

Simple question: DID WE SUCCEED?"

Justin stared at his screen, a thousand emotions all caught in the same Atlanta-in-a-snowstorm traffic jam. The roar of a Boeing 787 flying overhead jolted him back to reality.

Roger!

He quickly sent his response:

"*Y!! Better than anything we hoped. Going back to the SCIF; will send codec. Start typing!!"*

In two hours, Justin was using the secure server in DPI's SCIF to uplink their private codec to Guardian, so they could "talk" by ultra-secure text and email when necessary. Justin couldn't understand what Roger meant about no one being able to hear him. Their Enigma codec was at least a generation—in current software terms, about five years—ahead of National Institute of Standards and Technology—NIST. Whatever they needed to discuss would be more secure than the best that NSA or the DOD offered, and it would even be private from DPI.

After he sent the codec software, he did something he never would have considered just one day before. He logged into the server as Administrator and deleted all evidence that the codec had been sent.

In ten minutes, he heard their unique ring tone he thought he'd never hear again; the short version, indicating an email.

If Justin was surprised outside IHOP on a cloudless November day on Florida's Space Coast, he was overwhelmed with all that Roger methodically reported in his message.

Once again, Justin had to kick himself into action. There was no time to consider consequences, or to analyze the aspects of trans-dimensional realities of walking through walls or seeing in infrared. His friend needed help.

He agreed with Roger's action points, starting with the Bottom Line Up Front: "BLUF: Believe you should contact Gen Alvarez. He needs to go through channels and let me taxi into a hangar. Will need food, water, etc. Post guards so nobody gets too close. No idea what the effects might be or how far they extend. I see dead insects around us!"

It was time to contact the general again and get him to his SCIF. He'd be able to find the J-STARS Commander and get a hangar open.

They may not see or hear it; wonder if they'll feel the jet blast as Roger taxis into the hangar? Better warn the general. This is just way too cool!

Then the thought struck him that for Roger, it wasn't cool at all. Roger was now, in a very real sense, the most isolated person alive.

28. RESPONSE AND SECURE

President Juan Garcia splashed cold water on his face and bowed his head in silent prayer. He would rejoin his crisis team in a couple of minutes, but he needed a few moments to himself.

Why? Why an unprovoked attack on the United States? The nuke could have quickly killed several hundred thousand. More than twice that number would have ultimately died from radiation and the breakdown of infrastructures and utilities, even without an all-out war. And the economic impact…

He slowly shook his head and prayed for discernment, for wisdom. The truth was that if the warhead had detonated at full design power, the economic impact on the U.S. economy—finally recovering from years of uncontrolled deficit spending and negative trade balances—would have been catastrophic.

Was that the plan?

President Garcia, his Joint Chiefs, his State Department, and every other available trusted advisor with adequate clearance, were exhausted. They had reviewed the what-ifs and what-nows countless times since the first meeting in the Situation Room the night before.

Uncharacteristically, the Russian President, Viktor Savin, had been going out of his way to reduce tensions. He called the President directly every six hours with updates on his investigation. His position was clear:

First, he emphatically denied knowledge of the missile which should have been decommissioned decades earlier;

Second, he was not aware of who gave the order, and he never would have ordered its unprovoked launch;

Third, he was not aware of any other such missile; and

Fourth, he was expending every legal—and some not so legal—effort to find those responsible for the unauthorized launch, and the existence of the Cold War relic.

Words; just words. But what impressed Garcia and some of his staff were the unusual ways Viktor backed up his words with action. Or rather, the absence of expected action.

While United States' missile and bomber crews had remained on high alert, the Russians did not. They even directed several deployed fleet ballistic missile submarines back to port, and "stood down" a major planned exercise of their Navy forces; something that never would have occurred under Putin. Savin confessed that he had used up every last ruble of political capital to stand down his forces for no apparent reason.

Juan shook his head, dried his face and hands.

None of it makes any sense. Almost like someone set this off as a catalyst, a provocation. Someone not acting as part of any official government. Who? Why?

The President re-entered his Situation Room and they continued their analysis and discussions.

The U.S. team did not breathe a word about Guardian and the nearly impossible intercept. In no way, Garcia emphasized, was the Kremlin to know of the hypersonic manned intercept capability the U.S. had developed, and that was destroyed to save Norfolk. As far as anyone knew, the warhead malfunctioned after its decades of secrecy. As for the bright flash of the exploding warhead, those satellites that did record it, along with the agencies represented, were led to believe it was an exploding meteor.

The much larger question: What should they share with the American public, and how? Had it not been for the massive Nor'easter, the entire East Coast would have known about the detonation. Had it not been for the unusual implosion or whatever they did with the interceptor, the EMP would also have given away the nuclear detonation. And had it been lower in the atmosphere, the blast wave would have done far more than just rattle a few windows.

To the chagrin of several hawks who wanted to act at once, to at least hit Siberia with a Minuteman ICBM, President Garcia chose to continue investigating, monitoring, and waiting. For now, key personnel like Colonel Draper and his team at Peterson were sworn to secrecy. Missile and bomber crews were brought down to only one notch above normal alert status, with a rumor of a satellite malfunction.

Garcia and his Russian counterpart would be given a little more time to avoid full-out nuclear war. The President directed that the U.S. response to the first-ever nuclear attack against the United States would be…wait.

After the rest of the staff was dismissed, Garcia and his Secretary of Defense called Senator Matthews back in. Together they conducted a secure teleconference with General Alvarez to learn how soon the second and third aircraft could be built and placed on alert.

Sunday afternoon, shortly after the teleconference ended, General Alvarez received an urgent email from Justin and was speaking to him from a SCIF within minutes. An incredulous Alvarez wanted to call the President back, or at least Senator Matthews. But he knew the correct military imperative was to first secure the asset. Too much depended on protecting Guardian and Roger. He'd break the news about the prototype once he had more facts.

For now, he'd secure System One and think through what he had to tell DPI tomorrow. They had to expedite the buildout and fielding of System Two, the first production plane. As far as he was concerned, as of last night the test program was complete except for an abbreviated set of characterization flights. Beyond the prototype, three production planes had been funded. The prototype was to become a trainer, leaving the other three so that at least one was on alert at all times, even if one or two were in maintenance. As of one hour ago, the schedule for System Two was moved to the left to just six months.

It had been a long weekend.

+ + +

Roger watched Air Force personnel rush to open the hangar furthest from the grass strip where he'd parked his aircraft. They raised the large door.

It was strangely comical. Clearly, they were attempting to hurry. But from Roger's perspective they moved like an animated slow-motion cartoon.

He was almost ecstatic to see them carry in food and water bottles. He'd been busy recalibrating communications and exchanging messages with Justin. From Justin's perspective, he'd hit "send" and would almost immediately get a reply. From Roger's perspective, Justin's replies took forever. The airmen drove back away from the empty hangar.

Showtime. This'll be interesting.

Back in the front seat, Roger fired up the turbojet. Fortunately, the third-generation lithium iron phosphate battery was extremely stable, lightweight, had ample capacity for multiple engine starts, and should last for a decade. Within thirty seconds, the turbojet was throttled up. Roger taxied the aircraft off the grass and onto the tarmac, then past the first and second hangars. Roger kept glancing over at the airmen, now a full hundred meters away from the open hangar.

Clueless. Incredible.

As he taxied, he folded up the wingtips. He turned into the third hangar. It was large enough that he could lock his left main brake and rotate the aircraft around to face back out...just in time to see an airman's flight cap blow off. In slow motion, the team looked around to determine the source of a blast of hot, Jet-A.

"Inside and secure. Lower and lock the door." Roger emailed to Justin and powered down the jet engine.

Justin relayed the message to the general, who relayed it to who-knows-who at Robins Air Force Base, who told the airmen, who closed the hangar door.

Roger exited the aircraft and headed for the groceries, again grateful that his request was granted. The airmen had opened the box of Meals Ready to Eat—MREs—and laid them out in a line, making it easier for him to "convert" one for his late lunch. Same with the water bottles.

Roger devoured one of the former and two of the latter. He was surprised at how hungry and thirsty he had become. He looked over at Guardian, sitting silently in what should have been a dark hangar.

The aircraft that didn't officially exist, and now couldn't be seen or heard, and which had just defeated the first attempted nuclear attack against the U.S., was secure. And suddenly, Roger again became very tired. Exhausted.

Circadian rhythm?

One more thing Roger hadn't thought through. If "his" reality was clocking four times faster than "their" reality, did that mean he'd need to sleep every four hours of "their" time? For two hours? He felt like he'd been awake for days. He woke that morning just before the late November sunrise...

A strange, low-pitched, melodic sound caught his attention. Very slow; it played for several minutes. Eventually, he realized it was the base "Giant Voice" speaker system, playing the National Anthem. So now, away from the aircraft's chronometer, he knew "their" time: 5:00 p.m.

His legs ached, he was exhausted, and there was no way he felt like climbing back up into the cockpit. But he suspected that if he changed the GPS-synched chronometer to read additional digits—hours, minutes, seconds, and tenths—he'd be able to see the tenths of seconds tick by. He put that on his mental to-do list, likely around 8:00 p.m. Eastern after he'd gotten a full "night's" sleep....

This will take getting used to.

Roger lay down on the soft concrete beside the aircraft nose wheel and fell fast asleep.

29. DARK REALITIES

Senator Jason Matthews was back in his condo after the grueling weekend meetings. The world was at the brink of nuclear war and only a few dozen people were even aware of it.

He was about to pour himself a drink when he received a call.

"Yes?" The call came in on his standard but unlisted personal Multiphone.

"Sir, it's Tamika. You told me to call you after I'd been at DPI a few months?"

"I'll call you right back."

Senator Matthews never discussed sensitive matters on any phone except his DARPA prototype. And no one had that number. Part of the phone's security is that the number was untraceable, so he always called back.

He stepped into the interior study of his condo, which he had scanned for "bugs" every month, for appearances only. What he really depended on was his own security sweeps for monitoring devices—again using the best available from DARPA, thanks to his Senate position over classified programs. The inside room prevented microwaves or lasers from collecting audio vibrations off his windows.

He was bone tired, but he never missed an opportunity to move his overall long-term plans forward, even after suffering a short-term defeat.

You're interested in her, her career. Encourage her loyalty. Remind her that she owes you.

Like a good customer service representative, he put a broad smile on his face to convey that level of friendliness in the conversation. He called her back.

"Miss Steward, how are you enjoying your internship? Is it sufficiently challenging for you?"

"Yes, sir. Thank you so much!" She gushed.

"Sure you wouldn't prefer to test metallurgical tabs on GE engines the rest of your career?" He chided. It hadn't been a bad job for her. Tamika's undergraduate degree in chemistry and her hard work had put her in an enviable position of managing quality control over materials used in General Electric's front-line unmanned bomber engines. But Jason had seen more than a competent quality engineer with a pretty face. He saw someone with places to go and things to do. Someone with a lot of potential. Most importantly, someone he could eventually manipulate. He had Cliff Nesmith give her a call...and a position.

"Oh, this'll do...for now," she said grinning. "And thanks for suggesting I get to know Justin. He certainly is interesting."

Play dumb. "Hmm? How so?"

"Well, we enjoy a lot of the same things. Motorcycles, extreme fitness and obstacle courses, even watching football. But, you know, the strangest thing...we were watching a game last night, he got a phone call, and he, well, zoned out."

"Zoned out?" he probed.

"He just, you know, went into his bedroom and forgot about everything. His big game, me, the special night we were having." She didn't elaborate.

"Did he, uh, did he stay in there, or did he come back out and send you home?"

"No, whatever it was, it was obviously very important to him. Sounded like he was talking to our program lead, Roger. Very intense. I waited around half an hour, then left."

"No idea what they were talking about?"

"Something was happening. Something right then. Big. I didn't hear much. A couple of technical things caught my attention because they were out of the ordinary. I heard the term 'Battle Short' and 'overrides.' No idea what any of that meant."

"Hmm."

"I thought I'd at least hear from him today with an explanation or apology, but I haven't heard a word." She suddenly caught herself. "Oh, sir, I'm so sorry. I'm just chattering and I know you're an incredibly busy man. Thanks again for this job. Uh...Is there anything I can do for you?"

"No, Tamika, nothing at all," he lied. "Just wanted you to call and let me know how it's going." He paused. "You know...there actually may be something you could do. I take my Senate position seriously and want to make sure we wisely invest every penny of the taxpayer's money in these perilous times. We're spending a lot of money at DPI. I get the formal reports, of course. But I'd appreciate hearing your take on everything. Like what the military describes as 'boots on the ground.'"

"Sir?"

"Yes. Just keep observing. Call me back every week about this time and give me an idea of what's going on from your perspective. And I'm curious whether Justin gives you an explanation for being so, well, rude to you."

"Sure, Senator. I'll let you know."

"Tamika, I knew I could trust you to be a great patriot there. I can see you going places, young lady. I helped you get a good start; the rest is up to you. I'm counting on you."

After he ended the call, Jason smiled and poured himself his first drink.

I'm interested in her, her career. I encouraged her loyalty and reminded her that she owes me. Check and check.

Jason mused to himself, "So Justin was a part of crushing my plans along with Roger. I've got him right where I can keep my eye on him."

Thoughts of the lovely, athletic Tamika Steward put him in the mood for a young Black girl tonight. He made that call and then began his evening game while he waited for his evening's entertainment to arrive.

+ + +

The tingling continued. As before, Roger slept hard. Then he started dreaming. Vibrant, 3-D dreams with surround sound. Like IMAX on steroids. Unlike anything he'd ever experienced before the conversion.

He and his wife were having lunch that Sunday afternoon with Karen in 2006. He could taste the sweet tea, then the after-dinner coffee. He smelled his favorite perfume that Cindy wore. He heard Karen explain that her husband died of pancreatic cancer, and there was nothing they had learned from their research into her genetic change that could save him.

"As he lay dying, he told me to keep seeking God, that He had something special for me, and to live my unique life to the fullest. Folks, that's why your message today about seeking strong foundations for our lives meant so much to me. That's why I wanted to meet you both and ask you to pray for me."

Roger awoke with a start. *Why am I dreaming about her?*

He slowly got up, his legs stiff and sore. He slowly paced inside the hangar around the aircraft.

Is it because we're both unique?

He thought of the special gift Karen sent to him when she learned that his wife and kids were killed in the accident. It meant a lot to him and motivated him to pray for her even more fervently. While Roger was still in rehabilitation, a package arrived for him. Inside the wrapped box was the unusual, elegant painting he later hung in his office at DPI. It was the one that Justin admired so much.

She had included a simple note:

Roger, so sorry for your loss. As you and your wonderful Cindy have prayed for me over the years, so I will be in prayer for you.

As I've said before, thanks for helping me focus on the foundations. I hope this little gift ministers to you and gives you hope that God is still in control, no matter how bleak our circumstances may appear.

I won't trouble you with more of my story, other than to say that when I learned of your loss, God used it to shock me back to reality. I had lost my focus and was heading down a very dangerous path.

As I prayed about the difficult circumstances you and I both face, this picture came to mind and I painted it as quickly as I could. May it bless you, as it has already blessed me.

Quietly in His love and service,

– Karen

Her thoughtfulness was overwhelming. He certainly needed that encouragement now.

I'm not getting any younger, he reflected, as he stopped pacing and rubbed his aching thighs.

Thinking of age brought on a wave of depression.

Good Lord! I'm sixty-four. If "my" reality is clocking four times faster than everyone else's, I'll be well over eighty-four in just five of "their" years!

As he had prayed so often over the years, especially after losing his wife and family, he said, "Return quickly, Lord Jesus."

Roger realized that he was famished. He slowly walked over to the table, "converted" and devoured another MRE and drank two bottles of water. It seemed to only take about half the time before he could firmly grasp them as it did previously. He did a quick estimate of how close the supplies were to Guardian. *Maybe they're close enough to start converting without me actually touching them?*

He also noticed a dead mouse near a trash can. He absent-mindedly kicked the mouse as he threw his containers into the can. His shoe made solid contact, and the dead animal skidded several feet away.

So…you were close enough to convert. And the conversion killed you.

Roger walked over to the mouse and stooped down for a closer look. He wasn't an expert on mice. But this one appeared to have died in agony.

A deepening darkness descended on Roger. He felt so isolated; so alone.

+ + +

"They call that intel?" Cindy shook her head and scowled. *Sam's got to be furious.* The email was short:

"Karen, here's what I've got:

World Islamic Caliphate—WIC—growing significantly in Iran, uniting many other terror cells and organizations as they see the possibility of a true Caliphate. Their financial resources are growing at an alarming rate, both from known terror supporters and a considerable amount from unknown sources. Their radical tactics, extreme by any other standard, are seen as moderate only when compared against what's left of ISIS.

ISIS continues to lose members and resources as they fail to consistently hold on to any land. No land, no legitimacy. Their desperate leadership is becoming even more extreme, more unpredictable, and more of a danger to Western countries. Most at risk is the United States, which they see as a major part of their downfall since Obama left office. They believe they can win the propaganda war and resume their role as the leader in global jihad, if they can successfully conduct serious attacks against the U.S. And, of course, against Israel."

Karen—Cindy—started typing.

"Sam, I went a lot deeper into the psychographics of their recent communications and activities. Some public, and, as you can imagine, I uncovered some that is not public knowledge. They're not looking at hard targets like industry or military. Not even soft targets like banking and commerce. I don't even think they're looking at infrastructure like utilities.

They want to really hurt the heart of the U.S. Since they have absolutely no respect for human life and are sexual predators, I'm afraid they'll go after kids, likely pubescent."

Cindy shuddered as she thought about the violent, heartless assaults she had suffered from Jason Matthews. Those occurred when she was an adult. She teared up thinking about the cruelty she anticipated with this attack, and possibly more attacks like them, against children.

Demonic. Absolutely demonic, from the pit of hell.

30. SIX MONTHS

Not your normal day at DPI. Not for Justin Townsend or for any of the rest of the team, many who had worked on Guardian for the previous four years.

General Alvarez chose to personally explain the heroic and successful intercept to the entire DPI team since each employee had the required compartmentalized, top secret clearance. The Twenty—they could no longer refer to themselves as "The Twenty-One"—were joined by the rest of the team. Eighty technicians, systems operators, material handlers, quality assurance personnel, and others brought the current total to one hundred. The entire team was crammed together for the "all-hands" announcement in the SCIF's conference room.

For once, he chose not to use the Telepresence robot, even though its security protocols allowed it to operate in the classified SCIF. He believed that, in this case, the multimedia system would be more proper and official, yet personal.

General Alvarez explained the truth as it was known at the time. The unexplainable launch of a single missile, and that it came from over the South Pole giving more time to respond. But there were no assets able to provide that response. None; except for their experimental hypersonic aircraft. Unusually, the plane was being transported "wet"—with enough fuel for both the turbojet and the scramjet/ion drive.

Alvarez explained how their Chief Engineer, Program Manager, and friend had devised a near-impossible plan to intercept the warhead. And with unfeigned admiration and respect, he praised Roger and Justin for devising a final way to intercept and destroy the warhead when the rail gun missed.

Alvarez told them that while there was a nuclear detonation, it was negligible due to the EMP circumventing the designed detonation sequence. What's more, somehow the ion drive and Guardian's EMP had strangely directed the warhead's EMP out into space. And he concluded, truthfully, that they would all miss seeing Roger and the craft they had worked on so tirelessly for so long. But they could each know that Roger and their efforts had saved the lives of hundreds of thousands, eventually even millions of Americans.

He reminded the team that what they had just learned, they would have to carry to their graves. And that due to a further worsening of international relations, Senator Matthews had strong-armed committee members to redirect funds and increase their budget to expedite production of System Two. They had six months.

There was no mistaking the urgency of the time schedule. "Cliff, go to two or three shift operations, work overtime, holidays; our nation needs this capability on alert, fully operational!"

In Justin's opinion, Clifford Nesmith was harder to read than ever. Back from his cruise, Cliff was as dead-pan as he'd ever seen him. The man looked over his DPI staff for a full half minute after the General signed off. When he spoke, he had a major surprise for Justin.

"Okay, team, you heard the man. We all depended on Roger for his wisdom, oversight, and leadership these years. He did well. You did well. He's out of the picture now. Justin, your programming is virtually done. You're our new Program Manager."

"Sir...?" Justin stammered. He'd expected Cliff would take the lead.

"Responsibility, raise, and long hours. And Tamika," he looked across the room at the intern, there by virtue of her interim security clearance. "I want you full time, as his deputy, or assistant, or what I suppose the military would describe as his Exec. Promotion for you also, and you can complete your master's at our expense once we meet schedule. Meet with your approval?"

Tamika only hesitated a second. "Uh, of course. Thank you, sir!"

Cliff continued. "Note to everyone. You know we do things a little differently around here. We won this interceptor away from the SR-78 project when my third-generation additive manufacturing and other patents made typical facilities and manufacturing techniques obsolete.

"We're going to do this a little different as well. Justin will need...*I* am going to need...someone who's smart, capable, and energetic to help him fill Roger's shoes. She's been studying Advanced Production Management, and that's what we'll need around here." He gazed directly at Justin yet seemed to look beyond him. "Justin, I know you and Tamika have some chemistry going on. And I'm notifying everyone that I approve. I don't care if they, or any of the rest of you, work together and sleep together. You do whatever it takes to get this job done."

The HR team was surprised, but just looked at each other and shrugged. Tamika's lovely dark complexion deepened. Justin just raised his eyebrows and said nothing.

"Make it happen, Justin." And Cliff left the room.

All eyes turned to Justin. Tamika's were accompanied by a slight smile and her own raised eyebrows.

Justin felt completely overwhelmed. For the first time in his life, he silently, sincerely prayed, "Why me, Lord?" He knew the team well. But to lead? *Dude, I'm a programmer!*

"Okay," he began. "Alright. Let's scrub all remaining tasks for System One. It's not coming back." *And no one could see it if it did.* "Team Leads, re-baseline everything for System Two as far to the left as you can. Figure out what it'll take to transition to full-rate production. For each Level Two task, I need to know what the best operations schedule will be. Do we go to six ten-hour days? Two shifts? Three shifts? We'll likely need a hybrid schedule combining several plans. How will we coordinate? For now, Team Leads will meet with Tamika and me twice each day this week at nine and at three. Questions?"

Sandra, in Quality, spoke up. "Justin, I mean, are we going to do anything for Roger's family? Will there be a memorial service or something?"

Justin was thoughtful. "He lost his family in that plane accident in 2020. I know he was close to the folks at his church. But his parents passed and he didn't have any other extended family. I'll check with General Alvarez and see what the official story will be, and let you know."

Sandra nodded slowly. "Just saying, this guy was a hero. I mean, it's incredible what he did—and what you did." Tamika continued her slight smile and knowing nod; she now understood what had happened. "Could we, maybe, have a memorial service here?"

Justin hadn't thought about it. He, Cliff, and the general knew that Roger was still alive, sort of. He didn't know whether even Senator Matthews had been read in on the surprising transformation.

"I think that's a great idea. We'll talk it over for the next day or so and let's plan for something Friday afternoon. Anything else? All right, like the man said, let's make this happen."

The DPI team was more than just co-workers. The requirement for significant expertise in at least two disciplines meant that each person was important, but nobody was indispensable. Still, Roger…

On their way back to their work stations, many folks came up to congratulate Justin. Finally, he was face-to-face with Tamika.

Wow! Justin was amazed. It wasn't that the lovely Tamika Stewart, eight years his junior, was now under his direct supervision, and that she apparently was most pleased with the arrangement. *What has happened to me?!* In fact, totally out of character since his pre-puberty first girlfriend, he found himself not seeing her as a fling, a "Lady de jour," a partner for a year or so. But she was a…*a person who Jesus died for?!*

"Justin? Hey, are you okay?"

"Uh…sorry, Tamika. I guess I'm so overwhelmed by everything."

That's an understatement. And you don't know the half of it.

But there was something more. More than his huge increase in responsibilities. More than the massive challenge of compressing an eighteen-month schedule into six. More than having an imminently lovely, capable, and available young woman as his assistant. There was a strange nagging feeling that there was something he needed to be careful about. Very careful.

+ + +

With everyone busy on their new assignments, Justin stepped into Roger's office. He looked around for the thousandth time at Roger's pleasant but functional blond oak furniture. In all the years he had known the man, that described everything about Roger; pleasant but functional. His home, his wheelchair-friendly vehicle, his clothes, his office. Roger lived in stark contrast to the elaborate, expensive and over-the-top solid mahogany furniture that adorned Cliff Nesmith's office as President of DPI.

Roger scanned the twenty-by-thirty-foot room. It was the second largest in the company, by reason of both Roger's position and his handicap. There was plenty of room for Roger to wheel from his desk to his small conference table to his several bookshelves, each low enough so he could reach books from his chair. Roger was comfortable with tech but still liked referring to classic engineering volumes in print. The room was the only office with tile floors, easier to navigate a wheelchair over than carpet.

The view out the large windows was spectacular, a back-to-nature look toward the Atlantic. Roger wasn't one to over-decorate, and the truth is that too much would have detracted from the view. So, the walls only held a few certificates, his cherished painting, and a few underwater scenes from his SCUBA days. On his desk, a few family pictures; camping, basketball games, pageants...

Justin took a deep breath as memories of their years of friendship and joint, hard work flooded over him. He had to admit that he wanted to one day occupy that office. But now was not the time. He decided to stay where he was and leave Roger's office as it was, for now. Except...

There was no one to claim Roger's personal effects, and the painting on Roger's wall now meant more to the young man than anyone could imagine. Justin carefully took the painting down and walked back to his office.

Roger, your prayers for me were finally answered. I'd sure like to have us a long, private face-to-face.

31. ALIVE?!

Cliff had lied about being on a cruise during "the incident." He felt it best to be incommunicado during what he expected to be the fall of the United States of America. He sequestered himself in his well-stocked survival shelter. Matthews knew where to find him for the Reconstruction, during which his technology would be a key factor. He would never lack for anything again.

"The Incident." A monumental non-event, thanks to his "friend," Roger Brandon.

At least Roger was no longer an issue. He and Guardian System One were history. Vaporized. That's what he'd told Senator Matthews.

An hour before General Alvarez addressed the team at DPI, he had called Cliff to a private video conference in the SCIF. That's when Cliff learned that Roger had inconveniently invalidated several so-called "laws" of physics.

He and the general would have a classified private conference with the esteemed senator later that afternoon, as soon as Senator Matthews could break away to a secure facility. Already, he'd experienced the veiled but unmistakable wrath of Jason Matthews, along with the certainty of serious consequences if he "failed again." Then, there was the strongly worded "suggestion" that Justin take over the program, with Tamika assigned as his assistant.

What in the world will happen when he learns that Roger's alive?

Back in his office, he dreaded each call that Stacey took at her receptionist's desk. She was a huge asset to the company. Others at DPI might have multiple degrees, certifications, professional memberships, and lists of patents and accomplishments that would guarantee recognition in *Who's Who*. But Stacey? She'd be Number One if there were ever a publication, "Who's Not but Should Be." No degree, no certifications, no patents. But the standing joke was that she had a black belt in common sense and a doctorate in diplomacy. The grandmother stood barely an inch above five feet, weighed no more than a hundred and twenty, and her once brunette hair was now more salt than pepper. She was close to retirement but had as much spunk as any of the team thirty years younger. She seemed to keep track of the very heartbeat of the company; who was doing what, who was where, what didn't make sense, and whether an important document or email should be reworded.

Pretty good for a non-engineer, Cliff thought. *And always so pleasant, so respectful. Hiring her was one of my best decisions. And one of the few I've been able to make without "input" from the good senator.* At that thought his scowl returned and his gut tightened.

He had so looked forward to all their plans moving ahead. He would finally get the worldwide recognition he deserved, which was currently hidden by Matthews for the sake of the classified program. Cliff's manufacturing capabilities would spread from DPI to the general purpose facility he was planning near Chicago with the senator's blessing. Better yet, they would also spread to the one in South America that even the senator didn't know about. Those would later be augmented with facilities in China, Russia, throughout Europe; at least one in each of the One World Peace Now—OWPN nation-states. And he'd live like a king.

No more alimony. That was the other part he had looked forward to, that Annette and her live-in leech would both be vaporized under "Ground Zero." The blast would do what the court hadn't done; end her nagging, her manipulation, and her sucking off his success all these miserable years! But Roger...

The phone rang again. Stacey answered, motioned to Cliff, pointed toward the SCIF, and held up four fingers. *Be ready for your classified call in four minutes.*

Cliff let out a long sigh and resolutely headed down the hall.

"Gentlemen! That's the best news I've heard since the successful intercept! How I wish we could have a parade for him. What a hero!"

Cliff remained expressionless. The 4K ultra-high-definition wide-angle teleconference video would betray even the slightest twitch of an eye. It would be bad enough if the good general suspected anything, but Cliff believed deep in his gut that it could be fatal if the not-so-good senator did. *Just go along with him, like you've done for years.* He once again marveled at Jason's ability to lie so convincingly.

"General, you make sure Roger has everything, I mean anything and everything he might need. You need more budget, you let me know. See how soon we can do more testing with this marvel and let's see what she can do now. Cliff, congratulations to you and your team. Incredible. Just incredible! And how soon will System Two be operational?"

They talked programmatics, budgets, schedules, and a plausible story to share with Roger's church that would paint his "passing" in a positive but unclassified light. General Alvarez had already "talked"—he was getting used to using that term for their email chat sessions—with Roger about needing a cover story. Roger suggested telling the truth, but not fill in the details: While supervising the test of a classified system, Roger had intervened to prevent a serious loss of life at the loss of his own. And his body could not be recovered. As Alvarez shared Roger's recommendation, Senator Matthews seemed overcome with emotion. He strongly endorsed the story and promised to get the proper death certificate and paperwork to lock it down.

After ten minutes, the video conference was over.

Cliff remained in place, staring at the video screens' unnecessary but beautiful screen saver that Roger had installed; an underwater coral reef off Marathon, Florida. The beauty was wasted on Cliff, who fully expected a private, scathing follow-up from the senator. When it didn't come after twenty minutes, he went back to his office. He picked up his coat and walked to his car. The setting sun sprayed a kaleidoscope of purples, reds, oranges, and yellows across the scattered clouds to the west. That, too, was unnoticed by the man. Cliff's thoughts were more in tune with the dark and foreboding thunderstorm building up over the east coast.

Roger's alive. He might be on alert soon if the plane can still perform intercepts in its altered state. He may eventually find the software I changed. System Two will be operational in six months. Jason says there aren't any more clandestine "Soviet" missiles that can be launched. What can we use now to kick off the Fall and Reconstruction?

Cliff wasn't paid to have all the answers. But he knew that to hold his position and build his business empire under Premiere Jason Matthews—or whatever title he would choose—he needed to show he could be counted on as a team player. At least, until others knocked Matthews off his pedestal.

A possible plan developed. He'd need to know what Roger and System One were capable of in their altered state. He'd work with the general, Justin, and Roger to set up an abbreviated test plan; maybe just two launches.

System Two…Not an attack from Russia to the United States, but one that could be construed as a retaliatory attack against Russia from the U.S.?

Cliff continued thinking through the various ramifications of every known fact of the situation. He mulled over how each one might be used to his personal advantage. He had to come up with a plan to assure he'd be in Jason's good graces once the fecal matter hit the air ventilation system.

Cliff wasn't a dumb man. He fully believed that his 3D additive manufacturing processes were an order-of-magnitude superior to anything anyone else was doing anywhere. Not only did his system make most large manufacturing facilities obsolete; it had also cut typical manufacturing times by eighty percent while using far fewer people. And process control improved with tighter tolerances, less rework, and much less scrap.

Nor was Cliff unaware of opportunities. His play to Senator Matthews years earlier had resulted in the technology remaining highly classified, but just as personally profitable. DPI was born, Cliff was fully funded, and the course of his life changed forever.

But Cliff was a student of the international scene. He had figured out the goals and at least part of the OWPN organization.

As Cliff approached his exclusive private community, the gate sensed his community-specific extended range radio frequency identification chip—SERRFIC—and swung the gate open. Arriving at his high six-figure condominium, he felt better.

His door opened as he approached, the lights turned on, and his bar opened out from its cabinet. It was a good night for Scotch, Cliff decided. And Drambuie. He mixed the Rusty Nail and thought of maximum one-way ranges and possible recovery points. After ten minutes, he mixed another Rusty Nail and began planning. Twenty minutes later, Cliff was in a much better mood and mixed himself a third. Unlike Senator Matthews, Cliff didn't have a strict two-drink limit. Or any limit, for that matter.

Matthews.

Cliff relished knowing that Jason wasn't the only game in town. Or in the United States, for that matter. OWPN might have their plans for six or seven leaders, and Jason might want the entire hemisphere for himself. But Cliff believed that if Jason got knocked down a notch or two, there were three other key OWPN players who would likely split the hemisphere into four countries. He carefully studied the geopolitical scene and the rising stars. His expectation was that one would take Canada and Alaska and a second would take most of the continental United States. Texas, New Mexico, and Arizona would join with Mexico and Central America under a third leader, and the fourth leader would take South America.

Four nations in this hemisphere. That's what made sense to Cliff. And he personally knew two of those other three players. He poured another drink, reclined his chair all the way back, and smiled.

32. CINDY AND TAYLOR AL-AMRIKI

"Maybe just once?"

Cindy wheeled into her parking spot at her apartment and shut off the Chevy Ultra Volt. It was her practice to always buy a well-maintained used car, typically several years old, then when she had to leave, she would send the keys, the title, and arrange for a charity to pick it up. That would be whenever her current alias was compromised, when she suspected that Jason Matthews' team was getting too close, or at the end of her self-imposed limit of one year in any location, whichever came first.

I'd really love to get the latest and greatest; wonder how a new one would perform? Haven't had this much fun driving in years!

She picked up two bags of groceries from the back seat, locked the spunky hybrid—bright red, which was a color she normally shied away from—and walked toward her building.

A girl's gotta have some fun in life. Maybe even a convertible?

As she approached her stairway, the bottom right apartment door opened and the young, first-time mother who lived there stepped out, pushing her baby in a stroller.

"Hi. Going for your walk?"

"Yeah, it's so pleasant this evening. Supposed to turn cold tomorrow. Just got another ten pounds to get off!"

"Oh, she's so cute!" Cindy gushed, as she leaned over the crib. "Six weeks?"

"Seven this Friday."

"Be safe."

"Bye."

Cindy walked up the stairs carrying her bags as the young mother pushed her baby stroller down the sidewalk. The sun was setting; soon the LED street lights would come on.

God bless her and her little family. Keep them safe, she prayed silently. And she choked back a sob.

Ed, how I miss you! How I wish we could have had kids. How I wish I could have a normal life.

Her late husband would have been sixty-eight, had cancer not taken his life at forty-nine. Cindy...Karen Lane Richardson...was fifty-seven. She looked no more than thirty-two. And she could never have children.

"Hi, may I help you with your bags?" Her upstairs neighbor, Taylor, startled her as he stepped around the corner.

"Uh, sure. Thanks." Cindy handed him the bags, retrieved her keys, and opened her door.

"Anytime." He handed the bags back to her and without another word, turned and walked down the steps.

Pleasant. But strange. Hmm.

She carried her bags inside, set them on her kitchen counter, walked back to the door and locked it.

+ + +

Cindy's fingers flew across the keyboard.

"Sam—No time for a doctoral thesis with footnotes. Make sure your team knows these facts. Most were suspected since late '90s ... better documented and verified over last decade. Validated by several terrorist defectors.

Disclaimer: Still true that many Muslims are so by culture and tradition. However, they all follow the same *Quran*, so whether they are a peaceful neighbor or a violent extremist is how they interpret that book.

Therefore, any group of Moslems that does not specifically and emphatically denounce—not just words, but actually take actions against—radical extremists, is suspect. They may be endorsing, supporting, or even preparing to participate in those actions.

Some Imams have personally taken a firm stand against extremism and have worked with authorities to help identify terrorist cells. I'll include a list; they should be contacted. Perhaps they can provide some help or information. Just be aware that they put their own lives at risk by doing so.

Next, your team must understand that regardless of any politically correct rhetoric they've heard in the past, there are two significant issues with Islam.

First, some hard liners believe that *taqiyya*, *kitman*, *tawriya*, *murana*, and similar terms discussed in the *Quran* permit Muslims to intentionally lie, deceive, create false impressions, break vows, and more. These teachers approve and even encourage these practices against "infidels" for the so-called higher purpose of advancing Islam. You must understand that those who hold this view will violate their oaths of office, allegiance to the Constitution, and anything else. There have been examples from Muhammad in Mecca to Saddam Hussein to U.S. military officers and others more recently.

Second, Muhammed ruled that if a latter Surah contradicted a previous Surah, then the newer Surah was the true word of Allah. That means—make sure your team understands—the early writings from the relatively peaceful days of Muhammad's long stay in Medina, can thus be over-ruled by writings during his shorter and more violent time in Mecca.

Bottom line: Be prepared! While some Muslims will be allies when you prepare to identify and defeat this and other attacks, it will be exceptionally hard to know which ones to trust. Your greatest confidence will be in those who have paid a price. Like the list of Imams I'll send you, they have stood against radicals even at great personal risk. Otherwise—Watch out!"

Cindy finished, hit send, and took a long, deep breath. As deceptive as political soundbites had become, they paled into insignificance against the intentional lies of so many radicals. She had learned to speak several languages over the years and could understand even more. With her internet skills—exceeding most NSA analysts—she often heard so-called Islamic Peace Council—IPC—members say one thing on U.S. Sunday morning news shows, then invalidate those comments in Arabic later the same day.

She looked up to the ceiling, closed her eyes, and prayed. "Please, Lord God. Reveal truth and lead us to it. Expose deception and deliver us from it. Compel even the media to tell the truth."

Then she lowered her head and slowly shook it back and forth. "I'm so tired of all the deception." She shuddered as she thought of how the impending attack would likely play out.

+ + +

"Soon it will all be over."

Taylor al-Amriki looked at himself in the mirror, wearing only his gym shorts. His still-damp blonde hair was cut in the fashion…or lack thereof…of the gang he joined in his late teens. His arms were adorned with tats from the motorcycle gang he was a part of for the few short years before his drug dealing sent him to prison.

The haircut also helped cover the scar above his left ear, left there by his

Dad's big diamond ring. He remembered a lot of hits in general before his Dad left home when he was ten. But that was the one that required stitches. It also left him with a concussion. He remembered that hit very well.

"Dad, may you rot in hell!"

He turned away from the bathroom mirror and stepped into his Spartan bedroom. Box spring and mattress on the floor, used dresser from the Salvation Army, same with various ill-fitting clothes, floor lamp, and an old TV blaring the local Wednesday morning news show.

Demon Dad, or DD he called him. He remembered being dragged away to Reading Rooms, Temples, and Assembly Halls. He remembered DD lecturing him about all the things he had to do, and all the other things he would be damned for if he ever did them. He remembered the fury toward him and his mother. He remembered the night DD left, never seen by him or his mother again.

Rumor was that he went off to some commune or something.

Sixteen years ago.

Taylor put on a pair of his better-fitting jeans and a collared pull-over shirt, white socks, and sneakers. Nothing ostentatious; that wouldn't do for this meeting! He brushed his hand through his hair to smooth it down, made sure his light beard was trimmed but not too neat, and headed past the mostly empty living room to his old car.

Neither DD nor anyone else had to tell Taylor that his heart was cold, hard. Yes, he had acted out in school and ended up in alternate schools for troubled youth, while his mother worked two jobs to keep food on the table and a roof over their heads. She still needed food stamps, and they lived in government subsidized housing.

That's how he ended up in his gang. From there, the motorcycle and the "big leagues." He still didn't feel like he belonged.

Drugs, then dealing, then prison; and some things there he especially wasn't proud of. Especially after he found the father figure and the brotherhood he longed for under his Imam and the Islamic faith. But he also knew that the homosexual longings he struggled with would be quickly and brutally fatal if he were found out. He informally changed his given name, Jonathan Taylor, to Taylor al-Amriki; Taylor, the American. He made the change legal once he was released from jail.

Taylor shook his head and sighed, as anger, shame, loneliness, but also resolve slammed against him like a paintball war run amok. He imagined himself being hit relentlessly with different colors of paint at close range, each hit leaving a painful, massive bruise on unprotected flesh. But there was more. The paint was oil based, and DD appeared from off to the side, screaming that Taylor wasn't good enough, would never be good enough, as he lit an oily rag and threw it at his son.

Taylor had to brake hard to keep from rear-ending a line of cars at an intersection. The anti-lock brakes didn't work—no surprise with the old clunker—and the car screeched to a stop just inches behind a school bus. The kids looked down at him and pointed their fingers at him, like "you bad man."

"If only you knew," he muttered.

The burning rag ignited the oil-based paint that covered Taylor, and he was engulfed in flames, screaming, crying, dying.

Taylor wasn't imagining. He was remembering the nightmare he had at least once a week, one of several that would wake him up in a cold sweat, his sheets soaked.

Not good enough; never good enough.

"Soon, I will be."

That's the way his Imam explained the passages in the *Quran*. That's how he, Bassam al-Jabbar, Salim al Mahir, and Umar al-Muntaqim were going to assure themselves of heaven. For the others, there was also the ISIS reward that would go to their survivors. There was no one to receive a reward for Taylor's act of faith. His mom died of cirrhosis of the liver while he was in prison. She had coped with DD's abuse, desertion, and the flagrant rebellion of her only child by climbing in a bottle.

So, for Taylor, it was simply to leave the pain of this world and assure his peace and comfort in the world to come. He looked at the boys and girls in the rear of the bus as it drove away, taking them to middle school. A wicked grin crept across his face. *Maybe Allah will reward me with a little pleasure with some infidels as I move away from this world to the next.*

That afternoon, Cindy picked up the boxes Mick had shipped her and transported them to her apartment. Phil, a muscled-up young neighbor who she knew to be a firefighter, offered to carry them up her steps, but she politely refused, saying they were mostly empty and she needed the exercise. In reality, she didn't want to embarrass him, as each was likely more than he could lift and carry even one flight of stairs.

Within the hour she had the boxes open, inventoried the contents, checked the fit of her armor suit and armored sneakers, and completed functional checkouts to the extent that she could on the various equipment.

By morning, she would be ready.

33. RELOCATE

Roger finished his pre-flight about the same time the hangar door opened. He stepped to the back wall inside the hangar and watched as an airman drove the fuel truck into what appeared to be an empty hangar. Randy Holmes carefully followed the thick chalk marks Roger had drawn on the floor with a marker he had found in the hangar supplies and had "converted." The lines allowed the truck to come close—but not too close—to the aircraft that couldn't be seen. The driver stopped the truck with the front tires on the double chalk line as ordered.

Continuing to follow orders that made no sense, Randy set the brake, jumped out, and partially lowered the hangar door, leaving a ventilation gap of three feet. He then jogged back a hundred yards to join the security team, guarding an empty hangar.

Roger had no idea how long it would take the truck to "convert," or whether it would need to. Could the nozzle and part of the hose convert enough to connect to Guardian while the rest remained in "their" world? The fuel itself had a low molecular density, so it should quickly convert even as it traveled through the hose.

Roger would wait awhile and then find out. To simplify matters, since his upcoming flight would be subsonic, there was no need to worry about fueling the scramjet/ion drive.

He wasn't a fueling technician, but the general had the information sent to Justin, who then forwarded it to Roger using ordinary but classified email. As long as possible, Justin and Roger would keep the Enigma codec as their personal off-line communication link. And Justin already decided that he wouldn't surrender his Multiphone unless ordered to. Something didn't seem right, and he needed to maintain that direct, private line to Roger.

After thirty of "his" minutes, Roger held his hand against the fueling nozzle. It finished "converting" in just a few more minutes.

Okay. Now let's see what happens when I pull it away from the truck.

As he did so, it was much heavier than he had expected, like he was pulling a large fire hose. But eventually he was able to drag it over to the aircraft and insert it into the main tank.

"Good Lord!" Roger exclaimed. His sudden realization of what might have happened sent a cold chill down his spine. Instead of a gradual, linear conversion between "realities"—what felt to him like a very heavy hose—

what if the hose had broken, spilling fuel and filling the hangar? With the fuel truck running!?

Both our realities would have gone up in flames!

Roger breathed a long sigh of relief and made a strong commitment to think things through better in the future. With 20-20 hindsight, he realized he should have first experimented with a garden hose and water.

After a silent prayer of thanks, he began filling the main tank.

So...at least inanimate objects can transition smoothly.

He had already positioned aircraft transfer valves to "Open," so auxiliary tanks would gravity-fill off the main tank as long as he was patient. Weight and balance weren't issues as he had no electronics warfare officer—EWO— and also didn't have any slugs for the rail gun. But he still needed every drop of fuel to get where he needed to go. He couldn't just rest overnight—RON— at some convenient base if he got tired or ran low on fuel.

After he was certain the main tank was full and no more could be fed to the auxiliary tanks, Roger returned the nozzle to the truck. Stepping to the control power panel he "converted" the main power switch and turned off the transfer pump. Similarly, he reached inside the open window, "converted" the key, and switched off the engine.

Another MRE, more water, and a final trip to the bathroom. It was far enough from the aircraft that he could still walk through the door.

Soon we'll be gone, leaving a fuel truck much lighter than when it came in. Somebody's gonna have to figure out who left all the empty MREs and water containers.

Roger stowed a few of the remaining MREs and water bottles in the only airplane compartment available. He took a final, quick walk-around making sure he could safely clear the fuel truck and walked to the hangar door control switch.

Glad the old legs are working, but good grief they're sore!

"Here we go!" Airman Holmes was the first to see the hangar door start opening. His maintenance chief had told him to remain with the security team, that he would either come get him or he'd be able to drive the fuel truck after the hangar was cleared. "But...there's nothing in the hangar," he'd responded to his boss. "Just stay with the security team. And under no circumstances are any of you to approach that hangar without orders!"

Randy and the four security personnel all turned back to the hangar. From the last rays of the setting sun, they could barely make out the fuel truck, right where it had been—and what still appeared to be an empty hangar.

A few moments later they experienced a silent but unmistakable hot blast and distinct scent of jet exhaust. Then it was gone.

Captain Jasmine Brown understood her orders and was emphatically briefed not to deviate an inch unless ordered to do so. And she was given the single name of the only officer who had that authority. She was to fly her F-15 Eagle as a lead plane for a highly classified cloaked drone that had lost significant FAA-required communications, and, therefore, couldn't safely navigate back to Grand Forks, North Dakota. Something like that. Never mind that a cargo aircraft didn't come to Warner Robins to pick up the drone, or why it needed to go to Grand Forks.

So, the whispered speculation concerning the strange events at the J-STARS ramp at Robins Air Force Base was that a highly classified, ultra-stealthy drone landed one night and departed a couple of nights later. But Randy Holmes always wondered how a drone was able to refuel itself, open the hangar door, and eat MREs...

Captain Brown received her clearance and throttled forward into a standard takeoff, not a take-it-to-the-limit high-performance, straight-up climb and flight checkout she performed at the end of depot maintenance before the aircraft was returned to its unit.

Roger didn't even taxi to the runway. He throttled Guardian up while still on the taxiway and followed the F-15's climb, staying a thousand feet behind and several hundred feet below to avoid any wake turbulence. The twin aircraft formation, one seen and the other following like the reflection of a shadow, slowly climbed to the selected altitude of just 25,000 feet.

The low altitude was based on prevailing winds aloft, to maximize Guardian's range with the turbojet. Even with a full load of JP-8, Roger wouldn't make it fighting against the higher altitude jet stream. The flight was point-to-point and skies were clear, another reason for the quick turn-around. A large storm system was entering western Kansas, and a single day's delay would have meant at least another week in middle Georgia.

Roger could certainly fly around bad weather, but any diversion around storms would put Grand Forks beyond his fuel range, and aerial refueling was not an option. Literally. To minimize weight and reduce cost and complexity, air refueling hadn't been designed into the plane. For long trips, the interceptor's wingtips neatly folded up for transport in a C-17. Also, once Guardian became hypersonic at the edge of space, its range was calculated in thousands of miles, not hundreds.

But what did they know about low altitude jet operation? From the limited test flight data, Roger calculated a range of around 1,200 nautical miles. With a Great Circle distance of 1,112 nautical miles between the two points, taking into account the curvature of the earth, that was less than a ten percent reserve factor. And even that involved considerable speculation.

Fortunately, at 25,000 feet and well ahead of the storm, the jet stream would not be as much of an issue as it would be in another twenty-four hours. But he would still have a long flight. He calculated that his maximum range would be at a ground speed of just 400 knots. Captain Brown would have a pleasant flight with plenty of sightseeing for just under three hours. For Roger, in "his" time frame, he had to stay awake and alert for almost twelve. He was glad he remembered to bring an empty water bottle!

With little else to do, Roger thought back through some of what he'd learned.

One: My reality is "clocking" four times faster.

Two: There's also a dimensional shift of some kind...I can walk through walls.

Three: The transition even affects sound and electromagnetic radiation, or at least what I'm able to perceive of those frequencies.

Four: Even with the faster clock rate, my lower frequencies of sound and light should be discernible to others....

Five: But they aren't....

Six: So, my sound and electromagnetic frequencies not only shift, but also transition between dimensions to such an extent that they are further attenuated, or cloaked, or whatever....

The flight seemed to go on forever. Eventually, emotional darkness began to descend.

I'll never again have any direct contact with another living person...

A deep ache welled up in his chest. Not only the perpetual emptiness after the loss of his family, but now also the profound loneliness of his unique condition. At least a prisoner in solitary confinement could hold onto the hope of one day again being with other people.

Roger wanted to close his eyes one last time, push the stick forward, and nose into the countryside. He took a deep breath and thanked God for the assurance that no matter how he felt, he knew that he would never truly be alone. Whatever time he had left...

Time? That train of thought prompted Roger to glance at the chronometer and instruments.

He stared at his fuel indicator. Then at his course plot. He ran the numbers and checked his fuel indicator again. Yes, the reading was decrementing—the indicator was working—but very slowly.

Either he had a hurricane for a tailwind, or he was burning fuel at half the expected rate.

He shifted to "engineer mode."

So...maybe the air converts as it enters the zone around Guardian, the Bernoulli effect provides lift, then converts back as it leaves the zone behind us—and reduces drag?

"What in the world would this baby do with the ion drive at full altitude, wide open!?" he exclaimed out loud, to himself.

Would it even work?

34. ON STATION

After the uneventful flight to Grand Forks, an exhausted Roger Brandon was glad to taxi into the waiting hangar. As at Robins, Grand Forks Air Force Base had once hosted huge aircraft like strategic B-52 bombers and KC-135 tankers. It still had hangars. Very large hangars. It also had a robust drone mission. But Roger taxied to a much smaller assigned hangar. He was just able to lock a wheel and do a "one-eighty" inside to face the aircraft nose back toward the entrance. He powered down, walked to the hangar door, and "hovered" his finger against the "CLOSE" button until he could push it and secure the facility.

The closed door just accentuated his feeling of isolation.

Roger knew his earthly time was limited, if for no other reason than his age. But there was more. The sudden pandemonium of the EMP and NUDET had somehow healed the damage to his spinal cord. And it seemed that his heart rate was steadier; he couldn't remember any episode of A-Fib since the transformation. But there was something else. The occasional twinge in his side reminded him of his ailing gall bladder. Now in his isolation, those or countless other health problems could quickly become fatal. No doctor would ever see him again. *Nor will anyone else.*

His crushing emptiness went beyond even the health concerns. He was more than ready to join his Lord, his family, and other loved ones who had gone before. He'd experienced a deep sense of anticipation as he was lowered and strapped into Guardian just a few nights earlier. It was a matter of both humility and honor to follow his Lord in giving his own life to save many.

Now, he couldn't even have fellowship and corporate worship with other Christians. Nor would he be able to join his church prayer meetings. He and many others had made it a priority to meet and wrestle in prayer over marriages, families, and continuing cultural degradation in America and around the world. They began seeing some remarkable breakthroughs.

After a long sigh, he willed himself to refocus.

"Let's check out the accommodations," he said as he walked over to the side.

To his delight, the pantry was well-stocked.

Back in the cockpit, Roger sent a quick email to announce his successful arrival. He painfully climbed back down, had a quick meal, and then collapsed exhausted on the "soft" concrete floor.

Eight months early, Guardian System One was on base.

He was fast asleep in moments. This time, he remembered no dreams. He awoke rested and grateful that the soreness in his legs was less intense. Curious of the time, he climbed up enough to look into the cockpit. He had only slept two hours! *A circadian rhythm completely separate from "their" twenty-four-hour schedule.*

He took a moment to assess the big picture. Since System Two wouldn't be ready for months, and the international scene continued to degrade, General Alvarez needed to know how soon Roger could go on alert.

Yes, Roger, a "senior citizen" civilian, was the only one able to fly or even see System One. So he would be on alert at "Center Field," in striking distance to protect either coast, as well as attacks over the North Pole, or up from "down under" if there were another FOBS missile.

Time for my punch list.

Years of engineering had taught Roger to organize an outline first, then fill in the details later. For now:

One: Personal needs
- Clothes, socks, shoes
- A jacket and gloves? NOTE: Walk outside; see if I'm impervious to North Dakota cold like at Warner Robins
- Toiletries
- Data drive from home – Bible study, pictures, etcetera
- Comfortable recliner
- Supplements; make list
- Medicine, such as:
- Low dose aspirin
- Meds for occasional A-Fib
- Meds for gall bladder, for what little good they've done

Two: Food and fixings
- Table and microwave, stocked refrigerator, pantry goods; everything on wheels so I can roll it near rear of the aircraft to convert, but not in the way of an alert
- Wish list of food, beverages, snacks, condiments

Three: Alert
- Pressure and G-suit to fit me, and a better-fitting helmet
- Supplies and maintenance instructions:
- Oxygen generator

- Lubricants
- Fuel for scramjet/ion drive
- JP-8
- Slugs for the rail gun
- Tools
- Maintenance instructions from DPI

SRBs and a trailer I can operate to raise and secure them in place

He paused after the last. He needed a test run. But he strongly suspected that with the unexpected low drag, Guardian could use the lower thrust "flight test" SRBs, cutting several more months off the alert schedule.

As soon as the supplies arrive, he'd conduct his own test flight. He began a new list:

- Optimal climb angle with "flight test" SRBs?
- Will ion drive work in the "new reality?"
- How?
- Range?
- Speed?
- Altitude?
- Will the now off-frequency LIDAR work?
- The rail gun: Will it work? Accuracy? Lethality?

Again, he paused. Roger checked the time. One a.m. Eastern. He'd wait till Justin was at work in another six hours, then send him an email using Enigma. It was time to check the recalibration routine. And he'd need to download final "non-test" operational software into the aircraft, with Justin's modifications to allow him to fly without a back-seater.

Software. He'd need Justin to program alert notifications. Since "his" reality couldn't accommodate him having a cell phone, he depended on Guardian for communications. And, so, began another list:

- Need cockpit to remain "hot" at all times to receive comms and alerts
- Therefore, need ground power cart with quick disconnect
- Because of weird sleep schedule, need important alerts to wake me:
    - I'll sleep in front of Guardian
    - Flash landing lights if urgent message
    - Flash landing lights fast and auto-start engine upon order to launch

The discipline of writing lists and organizing his thoughts brought something else to mind. *I'll be operating up to four times faster than NORAD. Somebody's got to figure out how I'm going to fly through this airspace.* Air Traffic Control didn't need to see him, even if they could. His exorbitant speeds would cause Air Traffic Control to casually dismiss any transponder pings as equipment malfunctions and complain to service personnel to fix perfectly functioning equipment. But he needed to avoid other aircraft during slower, lower altitude launch and recovery.

There was more. *I can't be reading emails while flying. We'll have to use speech recognition.*

The challenges just went on and on. Like timing. Guardian was designed to be on "warm alert," ready to be airborne in under five minutes at the first sign of a potential hostile launch. This meant having a crew suited up, in the hangar, and the first crewmember in the aircraft within two minutes of alert, starting the engine and opening the hangar. The second crewmember had exactly one more minute. Wheels-up in under five, hypersonic in another two, and ready to engage a warhead as it began re-entry. An inertial kill with the ten-pound slug at a combined speed of several thousand miles an hour...well, modeling showed that all known and foreseen weapon designs would be destroyed. Any explosion would be non-nuclear, and most of the warhead would vaporize as the pieces re-entered without the protection of an intact heat shield.

How in the world can a single person stay on alert indefinitely? How fast can I respond, even at my enhanced speed?

Another more compelling thought occurred. Time for...what? With his new circadian rhythm, there was no such thing as breakfast, lunch, or dinner according to a set time of day. He decided to keep it simple:

Time to eat.

About the time Roger had his MRE in his new Grand Forks, North Dakota home, Cindy was half-way through her drive around Charleston, South Carolina. Her itinerary had her scheduled to travel over 120 miles, stopping for several minutes at each of over three dozen locations. She used the reusable Pole Climbers to position Video Spots on trees or poles. The Video Spots would secure in-place and "borrow" cellular service to link up. She'd retrieve the Pole Climber and move on to the next location.

It was 3:00 a.m. when she finally returned to her apartment and organized all the feeds. The forty cameras came up live on her multitablet. She then streamed their feeds to her large flat screen TV and adjusted the feed to run as a slide show. She set eight feeds for each screen, for a total of five screens. Each screen displayed for twelve seconds at a time. She named the feeds by location, organized the sets based on those locations, and set up background recording on her eight-terabyte solid state drive.

Cindy sat back and watched as the screen morphed from eight video feeds from the north, then from the east, then south, west, and center, each displayed for twelve seconds and repeated every minute. The clarity was full HD. And that was with IR at night.

She took a long, deep breath, lay back in her couch, and shut her eyes for a quick two-hour nap. She would be up by six, shower, and have her morning smoothie breakfast. She would then wait for pandemonium to break loose sometime in the next few weeks.

35. MAKE THEM SUFFER

Taylor al-Amriki drove in silence. Every minute or so, he would wipe his sweaty hands on his shirt, despite his windows being down on that cool afternoon. Daylight Savings Time had ended weeks earlier, and at 4:00 p.m. it was already late afternoon. The traffic was heavier than normal for a Wednesday, but he had left early to make sure he wasn't late. He would park and sit until it was time to move.

He silently gave thanks to Allah for smiling upon their holy mission with cold weather. Their long winter coats were entirely appropriate. They were also perfect for hiding weapons and their vests.

Six heavily armed men were on their way to an appointment with destiny, each driving a separate car and traveling a different route. The Great Satan would be knocked to its knees more brutally than at any time since September 11, 2001. And he would be a part of it. On earth, soldiers of the True Jihad would remember and honor his name forever. Eternally, he would receive his reward and be welcomed by the merciful Allah. His Imam assured him that this was the most noble, courageous, sacrificial act he could possibly accomplish in his few years on earth.

A lot of Americans are about to die.

Sure, he was an American, too. But he was no longer an infidel. He thought his citizenship would help them get weapons and ammo, but the truth was that firearms laws on the books for decades, were finally being enforced. Any investigation would quickly set off alarms that would affect the whole cell group. So, he helped get firearms, explosives, and everything else the old-fashioned way; the black market. In just a few weeks they had all they could possibly need. He couldn't help but smile at the thought that a few weapons might have come back across the border years before during "Operation Fast and Furious".

Now if only Demon Dad was in the line of fire! I'd pull the trigger myself.

+ + +

Cindy's heart sank as she read the secure email from Sam.

"Lord help us, we were wrong! Are you watching the news?"

Cindy quickly re-configured her TV to compress the live video streams to just the top half, and then scanned through local and national news sources on the bottom half. In moments she heard a report from a blonde, thirty-something newswoman sitting behind a desk at a local station. The news anchor reported breathlessly:

"A deadly attack has apparently just occurred in Mt. Pleasant. We have unconfirmed reports of at least a dozen casualties, and possibly hundreds of injuries. No word from officials yet, and it's too early to speculate, but one woman on the scene has described it as a terrorist attack. This is a developing story and still a potentially dangerous situation. If you are in the area, please stay indoors.

"Our Trevor Wright is over at the Union Terminal, and we go now to him live. Trevor, what do we know?"

"Susan, we were here at Union Terminal doing a story on a new Carnival cruise, when what appears to be a planned attack occurred. This is what we know so far. At about 4:20 p.m., there was an explosion at the Wando Welch Terminal in Mt. Pleasant. According to my source at the South Carolina Port Authority, a device, possibly a remote-control submarine, exploded between two container ships. Waves from the blast apparently nearly capsized some smaller vessels on Wando River, and we could hear the blast all the way over here at Union Pier.

"No other damage from this initial blast has been reported. But I just spoke to one official who said it appears the initial explosion was simply to attract attention and draw people outside. We have reports that a few minutes after the initial blast, an unauthorized unmanned aerial vehicle, or UAV, flew in to the area at somewhere around 100 feet above the ground, possibly lower. We have some cell phone footage. It's grainy, but you can see it appears to be towing something. It looks like maybe a dirigible, you know, like a smaller version of the Hindenburg—I'm guessing maybe fourteen to twenty-foot-long..."

"Jason, I'm sorry to interrupt. I am on the phone with an eyewitness. Ma'am? Can you describe what you saw?"

Cindy listened as the voice of an obviously distraught woman filled in more details.

"We—me and my husband—we were outside when we heard this explosion down at the terminal. At first, we thought there had been a terrible accident. Then we saw this drone thing. It was almost like a small helicopter towing a long balloon or something. Of course, a lot of people were heading over to the explosion to see what happened and if they could help. We help each other around here. And then...and then..."

The woman broke down in tears, and Cindy had to wipe tears from her own eyes.

"Ma'am?" intoned the news anchor's voice.

"I'm sorry. It's just so horrible. We were still at a distance, but it was like everyone had the same idea at the same time, that this might be an attack. Everyone started to run away. But it was too late. The drone copter and the balloon thing started sinking to the ground. Then it exploded..."

Cindy clenched her fists. *Hydrogen for lift, then they released a canister of oxygen and ignited it. Like a mini-MOAB!*

The newswoman continued:

"Thank you, ma'am. I know that must have been a horrific thing to witness. We are starting to get reports of at least twelve casualties, and many additional injuries, possibly hundreds, from shrapnel that apparently blew from the dirigible out to several hundred feet..."

Cindy muted the audio. "No! We couldn't have been that wrong!"

She quickly maximized her live video feeds and minimized the news story, scanning hard as she donned her Commando Suit and armored sneakers. She slipped into her dual consciousness mode.

Cindy #1 turned the audio back up and listened to the news audio, even as she continued searching on her multitablet for more information from official channels. Not what they shared with the public; what she was able to hack in and intercept.

Cindy #2 watched her own live camera feeds even more intently, while also considering possible traffic backups around the city in case she needed to get somewhere fast. She quickly reviewed her pre-departure checklist:

Her Chevy Ultra Volt was fully charged and loaded. She could secure the Vehicle Light Bar in seconds.

She had disabled the vehicle's data reporting functions and GPS; she didn't need to alert officials if she had to bend or break some traffic rules.

She was suited up and could grab her helmet on the way out.

The reconstitution kit was securely pre-positioned, and there was nothing left in the apartment she would need to come back for. She just had to make sure to take her multitablet with her.

Check, and check. She could be on her way in less than ninety seconds.

There was nothing of immediate concern on the news feeds or live video feeds. The twin streams of consciousness rejoined and Cindy quickly went to the bathroom.

Could be a long time before I get another potty break, she thought. *If ever.*

+ + +

It was time. Taylor started the car and drove the last mile to his destination.

Normal extracurricular school activities like extended band practice had to be over by 6:00 pm. All faculty, staff, students, and teachers were cleared out by 6:30 and the gates locked. Only janitorial services were allowed in and out after that, except for scheduled sports and other activities where the school board brought in extra armed guards. Security was far more visible and intense than anyone could have imagined at the turn of the century.

"It won't be enough." Taylor said to himself, as he gripped the steering wheel, gritted his teeth, and glanced again at the meticulously packed duffel bag in his passenger seat. "Definitely won't be enough."

+ + +

"What...?" Cindy exclaimed, and expanded the video feed from Camera Ten. Four cars were driving quickly toward the main entrance of a school, and three pulled up to the front with no effort to park normally. The fourth car appeared to be going behind the complex. Men quickly got out of the cars carrying large bags. Cindy quickly took control of that camera, panned, and zoomed in closer...

"Lord, God, help us!" she prayed.

Her fingers flew over the keyboard:

"Sam, all a diversion! Attack in progress at Charleston County School of the Arts. Four men, full length coats, beards, carrying duffel bags. On my way."

In seventy-five seconds, her Chevy Ultra Volt was power-sliding out of her apartment complex near the Citadel. The Vehicle Light Bar was emphatically illegal for a "civilian"—and would be the envy of any police cruiser that happened to get near her. Its Micro Acoustic Hailer screamed out a warning that could be heard half a mile away.

In two more minutes, she was on I-26.

Her multitablet was streaming police bands to the Bluetooth 6.0 headset in her helmet. As she drove through rush-hour traffic at speeds up to 100 miles per hour, she monitored the feeds for any calls to try to intercept or block her. From what she heard, she probably would not even see a police cruiser.

"They planned well," she said sadly. The overall attack, so far, was in four layers. First, the attention-getting unmanned submarine explosion. Then the aerial explosion that killed or maimed dozens. All available emergency workers converged on the scene.

Exactly twenty minutes later, a rental truck crossing the Arthur Ravenel Jr. Bridge on U.S. 17 slammed into the median and ignited what appeared to be barrels of fuel oil and created a chain reaction pile-up involving several dozen other vehicles. The westbound lanes were completely blocked, along with two eastbound lanes.

At the same time, another rental truck suddenly stopped in the middle of the westbound lanes of I-526, creating another pile-up, and ignited more fuel oil, kerosene, or some combination. The eastbound traffic was spared from direct impact and fire, but the prevailing winds carried the smoke across to that side and caused numerous accidents and pile-ups anyway.

Cindy's eyes welled with tears. *It'll take hours for police to get back across to the school. The terrorists are making sure they have all the time in the world to do everything they want with these children...*

The fourth attack, the one in progress, was against the teenagers involved in extracurricular activities at the School of the Arts.

How sadistic! They attack anything decent, beautiful, or meaningful...and spread violence, hatred, and perversion. Demonic!

36. FINAL REWARD

Bassam al-Jabbar drove around behind the school, off the asphalt and directly up against the rear door blocking any exit. He stepped out and lay his weapons on the hood. If any kids tried to come out the windows, he would pick them off one-by-one. If anyone tried to rescue them from the back, he would fight them off as long as he could. He was the only one who didn't have a vest. Instead, he bought the best black-market body armor a lot of money could buy. He had his choice of weapons, and he decided to start with a 12-gauge semi-automatic shotgun firing slugs. If he needed more range, he'd use a 30-06 with a scope. If the diversions worked and they had enough time to carry out the Imam's mission, Salim al Mahir would call him in for his pick of the girls before they detonated their vests.

Taylor, Salim, and Umar stormed through the front door and down the hallways, shooting every adult in sight. If there were any armed guards, they either died before drawing weapons or weren't in that part of the facility. One reason they chose Charleston, South Carolina was that unlike several other states, South Carolina did not permit any teachers to carry concealed firearms.

Within moments the men were outside the band room door. By drawing lots, they determined that Umar would remain outside in the hallway and shoot anything that moved. The other men tried to open the steel doors but found them locked. While they duct-taped a stick of dynamite to the latch mechanism, lit the fuse, and ran back several dozen yards, they could hear Bassam firing round after round from his shotgun as students and faculty tried to escape out of other doors in adjacent buildings.

A deafening explosion brought them back to their mission and a mangled door. The acid stench of the explosive burned Taylor's nostrils as he ran through the opening and faced the terrified faces and screams from sixty teenagers, ages thirteen and up. A teacher, a woman in her thirties, started to speak. Salim fired two 9mm rounds at her, center-mass. He didn't miss.

Several kids passed out. Others threw up. They all had backed as far away against a back corner as they could get.

Five more shotgun blasts came from outside, and six from Umar's long gun in the hallway, firing two at a time.

"Are any of you Muslim? Step forward now!" shouted Salim.

The kids looked at each other, and one young woman shakily stepped forward. Her hair was jet black, her complexion and eyes were dark. She was an attractive sixteen or seventeen, slender, wearing sandals, a short blue skirt, and a collared blouse of a lighter shade of blue. The top two buttons were open, revealing cleavage and just a glimpse of a stylish red bra.

"You dare call yourself Muslim and defame Allah by dressing as an Infidel?" Salim's long coat was now open. He quickly drew a sword and, in a flash, decapitated the young woman.

Taylor felt sick. This wasn't glorious; it was brutal, vicious. Did this really honor Allah?

Salim was again bellowing orders. "Line up against the wall, now!"

The youth scurried to comply, except for the two who had passed out. Stained pants and other clothing revealed that several young men and women had lost bladder control or soiled themselves.

"Choose quickly! We have a lot to do."

Taylor glanced over the girls. Several were extremely attractive, and the thought of being with them appealed to him—maybe he was bisexual? But he didn't know if he could even rape them under such tension if he wanted to. Could he perform? If he couldn't, would Salim turn on him? Would Allah be offended, and condemn him to hell?

"You first," he stalled, dropping his duffel bag and opening it up. He quickly laid out long spikes and a mallet to crucify as many as they had time to. He would start with the dead teacher, dragging her over to a wooden instrument case.

Several more shots were fired from down the hallway. More slugs were fired outside from the 12-gauge. No sirens.

+ + +

Cindy turned off the Micro Acoustic Hailer once she got off of I-26 onto East Montague Avenue and prayed that there wasn't a train at the crossing. There wasn't. She turned off the light bar and slowed to turn into a subdivision without squealing tires. But there was no time to be elegant; after she turned left onto Luella Avenue, she made another quick left onto Lester Street, then drove across an open grassy area leading up to the Rose Maree Myers Theater. She parked right up against the building and jumped from the car.

She looked somewhat like an Olympic snow skier, except that she wore sneakers instead of ski boots, no gloves, and she had strange devices conformally fitted to her gray armor suit. Her tinted visor was down, with just a slight glint from the setting sun.

Another shot rang out from the 12-gauge, hitting Cindy square in the chest as she ran around the corner into Bassam's sights. The impact of the slug literally knocked her off her feet and backward several yards.

Bassam smiled and turned back to the other direction as he had for minutes; left, forward, right and back, sweeping the back of the buildings every two to three seconds, firing at anything that moved.

When he again glanced back where he shot Cindy, she wasn't there. She was less than twenty yards away, running faster than anyone he'd ever seen. His last conscious thought was how silly it was that she would throw something at him!

The Incapacitator slammed into his armored chest plate and immediately released a conductive gas, followed in a split second by the equivalent of several Tasers firing simultaneously. The effect was instant and could in some cases be fatal. In Bassam's case it wasn't, but the effect of the Blade was. Cindy returned her specially-designed throwing and close-in fighting knife to its sheath; she might need it again.

"*Lord, give me wisdom,*" she prayed silently. She assumed there were three men left. Any or all of them would likely have explosive vests, which they would set off the moment they believed they could not fight off an attacker. That would be a far more merciful death than what the men obviously had in mind. Cindy didn't know how many had already died, but she only wanted three more, and if possible, she wanted them to know they were defeated and killed by a woman.

Commando Flips. Incapacitators. Blades. Plus a 12-gauge shotgun and a rifle; looks like a 30-06 with a scope. Okay, this might hurt.

Shouting from a man inside, crying, hammering all helped hide her next moves. Cindy faced the side of the sedan, bent down, placed her hands under the frame, and lifted. She brought it up enough to roll it onto its side, clearing a door at the rear of the building. She tried the door handle; locked. Cindy quickly extracted a locksmith set and was able to turn the handle within seconds.

Cindy opened the door and casually walked in, hands empty.

Students had their faces against the wall, except for several terrified girls in their early teens who were in various stages of undress as one man watched them, like he was making up his mind. Another man was struggling to hold a dead woman against wooden shelving, and had driven a spike into one hand, just above the wrist.

At the sight of the five-foot-six; 150-pound woman in strange gray body armor and helmet, everyone froze. Then Salim raised his weapon.

Good! thought Cindy.

She extracted a Commando Flip. The Flip was about the size of a paperback novel. It hinged in the middle. She opened it like she was reading half-way through. It locked into place, and the bottom half formed a grip and trigger. Salim began emptying his 9mm pistol against her armor at point blank range. She aimed the Flip just below his chin to avoid any vest he might be wearing, and pulled the trigger.

A momentary swoosh. And Salim was slammed back against a wall, breaking the sheetrock.

The other man had dropped the dead woman and reached for a handgun. He fired at Cindy's head. The helmet's visor deflected the round as she leaned against the impact and squeezed off a second shot.

A powerful spring in the next chamber released a projectile out of its barrel. Once it was three feet from the gun, solid rocket propellant ignited and increased velocity to just under the speed of sound. The spinning projectile could travel straight and true for hundreds of yards. The front of the projectile was a penetrator that could go through plate steel. The back had a small amount of softer mass, and as the front began to slow, the middle of the projectile mushroomed out. So, unlike a hollow point bullet that would expand upon impact, the Flip would penetrate—almost anything—and then expand. The projectile was about the size of a .270 Winchester bullet. There was no case, as the entire projectile burst through the thick foil cover on the Flip's front face, with less recoil than a high velocity .22. The Flip carried eight projectiles, each in its own non-reloadable chamber, and had three times the impact of the 12-gauge slugs Bassam had been shooting.

The projectile knocked Taylor off his feet. His dead body slid backward across the floor and slammed into the opposite wall. Cindy had again shot just above his vest. She motioned for the youth to go out the back door. Several of the nerdier-looking boys left last, helping two of the girls who had fainted.

Cindy faced the mangled door to the hallway, just as a man swung into view and leveled his assault rifle. Before he could pull the trigger, Cindy launched a third projectile from her Flip. This time, center mass. The hallway exploded. What was left of the steel door caught some of the blast, but the residual force still knocked Cindy all the way to the back wall. She stumbled to her feet, folded her Flip and secured it to her suit. She glanced around the room. All the students were outside, safe. The sight of the teacher hanging on the wall was revolting.

Sprinklers began to spray water to douse the fire spreading from the hallway into the room. She quickly ran through the fire and carnage and down the hallway to a restroom, removed the armor suit, weapons, and helmet, and placed all of them into a collapsible bag she pulled out of a pouch in her suit. The modest but tight-fitting clothing she had worn under her armor made her look the exactly like a young-thirties mother on her way to pick up her kids.

As she walked through the school away from the area now in shambles, she heard the increasing noise, confusion, shouts, crying, and other pandemonium, and even a few sirens as police finally arrived from other areas not blocked by traffic jams. For days she had memorized every traffic route to every school, every school layout inside and out, and knew exactly how to get back to her car. She quickly put her bag in the back seat along with the vehicle light bar.

Within minutes she was on the interstate, heading toward her reconstitution point. She would go through her routine of changing aliases again, and Cindy Jacobs would never again be seen in Charleston, South Carolina. All her belongings and the car—this time she really hated letting it go—would go to a worthwhile charity she had already selected within a few weeks of arriving almost a year earlier. The crew from the charity would no doubt marvel at the modified exercise equipment and weights they would find.

The school survivors would need a lot of love and counsel. On the one hand, they would have incredible, unbelievable stories of how a single woman had prevented what was meant to be a brutal bloodbath against America's youth. The ISIS attack on Charleston that had been so successful up to a point, completely lost credibility when its primary objective was foiled by a single person—a woman.

On the other hand, the youth, their parents, and the world once again had to comprehend how anyone could be so cruel, so vicious and brutal.

The twilight was fading. Cindy took a long, slow breath. "Thank you, Lord Jesus. I don't have to die to prove anything to you or anyone else. You came and died for me."

She thought of the children, and again felt a tug at her heart that she could never have her own. Nor could she adopt and put children at risk as she constantly had to avoid Matthews and, at times like these, put her own life in jeopardy.

+ + +

Cindy made her plans to leave South Carolina—and possibly leave the United States.

Roger made his plans to conduct a test flight with the altered Guardian hypersonic manned interceptor. He actually looked forward to seeing what it could do in its new trans-dimensional state.

Justin's plans centered on how to build, test, and field Guardian System Two within six months, and what his relationship with Tamika should be now that he was a Christian.

Taylor al-Amriki? In a fraction of a second after Cindy pulled the trigger that ended his life, he realized that he had been wrong. Very wrong. About everything. So had Bassam al-Jabbar (one who smiles / the irresistible), Salim al Mahir (peaceful / skillful), and Umar al-Muntaqim (name of one of the first caliphs / the vindictive, or avenger). It was the same for Demon Dad who had died several years earlier. He had also instantly realized that his legalism and religions had been very wrong.

They had no plans. Not for that day, the next ten days, or six months, or ever. They also had no hope.

Their reward was certainly not what they had expected.

Guardian – System Two

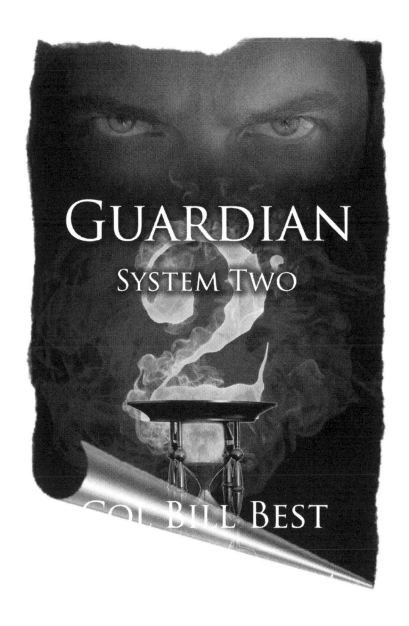

37. THE GAME

Senator Jason Matthews walked slowly into his study and collapsed onto a plush, over-stuffed leather recliner. He leaned his head back and put soothing eye drops into his bloodshot, twitching eyes.

Jason was exhausted from another long week of closed, secure meetings. Regular attendees could be counted on one hand, excluding the thumb. Only President Garcia, his Secretary of State, the Secretary of Defense, and, in his position as Chairman of the Senate Armed Services Committee, Senator Matthews were there every day. Individual members of the Joint Chiefs and others were called in as required.

The issue at hand? How to respond to an intentional direct attack on the United States, an event that should have been catastrophic. It wasn't, thanks to Roger, Justin, and Guardian. Few Americans were even aware that anything had happened, other than a massive storm and what appeared to be an unusual lightning event or exploding meteor. As key national advisors continued to meet, no one suspected that it was in fact Jason who planned the exact timing of the attack. Nor did anyone suspect his increasing frustration that Garcia was still President, and that Jason wasn't at the helm of a new world order as the Joint Americas' Premier.

So, the discussions continued, and Jason played along.

The Russians and their newly regained Ukrainian state? Unknown. By all appearances, Russian President Viktor Savin was sincere in his efforts to determine what happened and how—how what seemed to be a throwback to the Cold War could have remained operational after so many decades. How it could have been launched the long way around—over the South Pole—to attack the United States with a nuclear warhead.

The United States and Russian relations were at their lowest since before the Reagan/Gorbachev thaw of the Cold War. Russia continued to support Iran and Syria and other countries that championed terror attacks against U.S. and its Western allies. Most serious pundits judged relations with Russia as only marginally better than those between the U.S. and China. The Communist Party's government in Beijing continued to support North Korea, which incessantly threatened a preemptive nuclear attack against South Korea and the U.S. Now that North Korea had successfully completed space launches that could also deliver nuclear warheads, many took that threat seriously.

Frankly, the United States didn't have very good relations with some former friends either.

Doesn't matter. A whole new world order is just months away.

Jason Matthews relaxed in his exclusive penthouse condominium, engulfed in his overstuffed chair, and smiled.

Perhaps just one drink tonight.

He began his game.

His multiphone App selected the date and time of July 22, 2022, 10:00 p.m. As his calendar entry opened for that block of time, Jason's smile grew wider.

Oh, yes. I remember this very well!

No one had ever heard or read of Senator Matthew's SORDAMN philosophy. No one ever would. It wasn't as if Jason would one day write a book, "How to Control Everyone at All Times." His greatest weapon was the absolute secrecy that he even had such a philosophy and how he employed it.

SORDAMN:

Self-Control. In all things, at all times.

Offense. Play several moves ahead. Readily lose visible battles to win invisible wars.

Remember: Who said what, verbatim; what they meant by what they said; and use either their actual words *or* their implied meaning back against them, as appropriate.

There were the other planks of Jason's SORDAMN philosophy: **D**eceive (whenever appropriate), **A**void (anything that would limit or weaken his ultimate goals), **M**anipulate (always, toward his ultimate goals). And finally, **N**ever (never regret, or waste energy on remorse).

His nightly game, which he relished for the sheer challenge of its difficulty, focused on Goal Three: Remember. And Jason excelled at remembering. Over the years, he had honed his skills by randomly selecting a past conversation and recalling all the details.

From a brief note in his multiphone calendar, he could remember who he talked with and what they had discussed. More importantly, he recalled significant details about that person, all key points of the conversation, and what the other person actually meant by what he said—or didn't say.

The discipline made him like the only shipwreck survivor with a flashlight, or food, or water, or any of countless other critical items. But even better, nobody—not Chicago gangs, bosses, politicians—not Washington, or the press, or anyone else—could take that away from him.

July 22, 2022

"We need you to run for President."

No prelude, no chit-chat. Right to the point.

"You've positioned yourself well. We've built the infrastructure and have the finances. The transition is almost complete. We need you in the White House."

Not only did Jason fully agree, it was part of his own plan. But as always, he needed it to be "forced" on him, so he could humbly acquiesce to the will of the people.

Stan Bishop, the reclusive billionaire, continued.

"We have the usual media in our pocket, and we'll attack the alternate media with everything we've got. They'll be too busy fending off audits, lawsuits, and innuendos to focus on being 'fair and balanced' or to mounting an effective analysis."

"Lawsuits?" Jason asked.

"Since Obama, we've quietly continued weaponized the IRS, CIA, Justice Department, part of the DOD—just about everything. We're subtler now, of course. He pushed things ahead much faster than we intended, and ultimately, that led to Trump. He really set us back. That's why we need you in the seat now. We'll keep the other side busy while we complete our agenda."

Jason remembered the conversation well. He and Stan went through the list of inside media and government personnel who could assist with the needed astroturfing. The process should go smoothly, as Jason had already established himself as a maverick—a trusted short-term statesman in sharp contrast to the proverbial Washington career insider.

They had continued talking about the progressive plans, including what they privately called the Balaam Initiatives; get people to support the very decisions that would bring about their own downfall. They were like the plans of Saul Alinsky that the Clintons, the Obamas, and hundreds of others had followed since the seventies—but on steroids. And they were working.

It had all gone so well. Recalling the compliments from his "angel," Jason smiled. Even the younger billionaire hadn't suspected how effectively he was being played. Oh yes, SORDAMN worked.

Usually.

One time, one man, one debate. And Jason Matthews lost the presidency.

I hate Christians.

He didn't hate the lukewarm, country-club, so-called Christians who checked the block every Sunday morning. Or the ones who went to church another once or twice each week for extra credit. Not them. No, Jason loved them, because they were easy to manipulate. Make them think they're doing something good for the downtrodden, and they'll do just about anything without even basic fact-checking. Totally unaware of second and third order consequences until it was too late. They never seem to learn that the very effects of those consequences were often the motives behind the actions in the first place.

Mindless puppets.

Not them. It was the ones who actually believed John 3:16, that Jesus was serious when He told a religious leader that he must be "born again." These were the hardest to manipulate. And occasionally, like with Juan Garcia, it was as if they could see right through the very best façade. Even Jason's.

Jason had never lost a debate. He excelled in high school and collegiate competitions, relishing his keen ability to verbally shred his opponents—sometimes literally to tears. His first few presidential debates were perfectly scripted. He was asked all the right questions, in the right order, with precise lead-ins so he could attack his opponents. With great elegance, he mercilessly ripped the contenders to pieces one by one. But that last debate!

Jason had finally argued Juan to the brink of launching an emotional attack that would allow him to deal a brutal counterattack, a final death blow to the conservative. The particular issue was unimportant. His strategy was. He carefully twisted facts, sprinkled in innuendo, and added a generous dash of character assassination. Then he pulled out a famous Obama line, "We're better than that," meaning his plan might benefit one percent at the expense of ninety-nine percent. It was the perfect setup. Juan fell right into the trap. Then suddenly, in mid-sentence, the man paused ever so slightly, cocked his head to one side, and looked intently at Jason. Calmly, slowly, almost sadly, Juan said eight simple words. Words that at any other time, in any other context, would have been ignored. But that night, they were words that all the analysts said cost Jason the presidency.

"Jason. Do you really believe what you're saying?"

That was all. No further argument. No back-and-forth. When Juan was asked questions, he'd state facts, present his appraisal and the best path forward. He would describe how his plan would uphold the U.S. Constitution and personal freedoms. He'd also provide a quick assessment of the pros and cons of his approach, how he would mitigate any cons, and sometimes even name who should draft the required legislation. On one occasion, he even recommended his opponent, Senator Jason Matthews, as his preferred point-man.

Not even the carefully planted moderators could recover enough to feed Jason the questions that would allow him to regain the upper hand. There was no leverage, no traction left. Nothing.

Overnight, Jason's ratings dropped six points. Juan's skyrocketed eight points. One month later, Juan won the election.

"God, I hate that man!" Jason exclaimed, alone in his living room sanctuary.

The irony was that Jason did, in fact, believe in the existence of God. And he hated Him even more than he hated Juan.

Jason decided he would have that second drink.

Doesn't matter. I'll have the White House within two years. Might even move my capital to Chicago.

He may have lost the election, but his consolation prize was unheard of in modern history. Jason had only been a senator for one term before running for president and was already serving as the Chairman of the Senate Armed Services Committee. Among his many responsibilities, this position allowed him to oversee all the classified "black" DOD programs. Then after losing the Presidency, for the first time since 1949, the Senate's President Pro Tem was not the senior senator. By a clear majority, the Senate selected the junior senator from Illinois...Jason Matthews.

So simple; third in succession to the Presidency. Everything had been in place to take out the President, Madame Vice President, and the Speaker of the House just a few days earlier.

It'll take a while to set everything up again and then stage the terrorist attacks. We'll make it happen. I'll make it happen.

Normally his "game" didn't bring up so much baggage.

Jason took a long, deep breath. He clasped his hands behind his head, leaned back in his plush leather chair, looked up at the cathedral ceiling in his opulent penthouse study, and smiled.

38. PAST, PRESENT, AND PURPOSE

You're going to die tonight.

You may prevent World War III for another year or two. But you're going to die.

All three shots missed. If Battle Short doesn't work, you're still going to die, and hundreds of thousands more.

You're alive, but nobody can see you. No one can hear you. No one can touch you. Not now, not ever.

So much had occurred in the past several weeks. Roger was more depressed than any time he could remember. For the first time since the difficult years following the loss of his family, he wept.

He sat on the "soft" concrete floor of the Grand Forks hangar; his back against the firm side of Guardian's left main landing gear and wept uncontrollably.

There would again come a time when he would quote Romans 8:28–29, the Twenty-Third Psalm, and many other Bible verses he had committed to memory and had meditated on regularly.

He would again rejoice that his prayer for Justin's salvation had been answered, literally while Justin rode his motorcycle to Directed Paradigms, Incorporated—DPI—to check on the software issue.

But at the moment, he understood Elijah's deep depression after confronting the false prophets of Baal and experiencing incredible miracles from God. Not that he considered himself a prophet, or even anyone special. But the "fiery darts" of Satan made him feel like a lone rabbit trapped above ground, downfield at a sniper training range. His mood was dark, foreboding. The crushing loneliness and isolation? Overwhelming.

Eventually, Roger would also be able to meditate on the "full armor of God" described in Ephesians, chapter 6. But for now, the loneliness was crushing. He also felt a twinge in his side signaling the onset of another gallbladder attack. In emotional, physical, and spiritual exhaustion, he lay down beside the aircraft and eventually fell into a restless sleep. Dreams returned. Strange, ultra-high definition 4K, immersive 3-D dreams.

Am I awake and dreaming? Is this part of what healed my paralysis? Electroshock? EMP? What in the world?

He had accepted Cliff Nesmith's job offer to work at PDI on the hypersonic manned interceptor. General Alvarez said he had four years, which took him to his planned retirement. He had moved to the Space Coast, found a suitable condo to accommodate his paraplegia, and joined Community Church. So much else occurred over those first years, including the tornado that destroyed most of the church, then the beloved pastor's sudden fatal heart attack.

Roger woke up and was even more depressed as he answered the call of nature and walked to the bathroom. In the dismal gray light that matched his mood, he walked through the bathroom door, took care of business, and walked back through the wall toward the aircraft.

Wonder if I'd die quietly in my sleep if I just lay down right here away from the aircraft? Nah. Probably wake up coughing so hard I'd crack a rib.

He walked back to the aircraft, his critical lifeline to the strange, new interdimensional reality, and lay down.

He was exhausted, but he just tossed and turned for what seemed like hours. Eventually, he drifted off to sleep and began to dream again.

The much smaller church, under its new pastor, began a series of studies that were designed not to know more about God, but to more personally experience a relationship with God. They studied 'Experiencing God' by Henry Blackaby, 'Secrets of the Vine' by Bruce Wilkinson, and more.

In his strange, waking dream, Roger saw and heard himself sharing about an unusual, personal experience with God.

Like an outsider looking in, he relived his telling of his daughter's struggles as a young adult and the tough consequences of her terrible lifestyle. He shared how she eventually connected the dots and realized her need to know Jesus. But then, the very next day on their flight back to Savannah, he described the terrible crash that killed his family and left him paralyzed.

"You might think, 'That's not much of a deal. You trust in Christ, then get killed in a freak accident!' I personally believe that God had prolonged Susan's days to give her that one last opportunity to accept or reject him forever. And I know she's with him today."

"I've never told this to anyone before. It's the most spectacular miracle I've ever witnessed.

"Susan and I were in the same hospital before a blood clot took her life. After they did all they could to save her, they wheeled me in to see her. My heart broke. My wife had died instantly, and my son died before they got him to the hospital. Now Susan. A thousand questions overwhelmed me.

Suddenly—at that precise moment—an afternoon thunderstorm ended. A tiny opening appeared in a sky full of heavy clouds, and a sunbeam lasered through the hospital room's window. The light spotlighted Susan's face. Just her face. And I saw an angelic look of peace. I hadn't seen her so peaceful since she was a child. I already knew and believed she was with Jesus. But that miracle was just there, just then, just for me, so I could see even more clearly that my family was in the presence of the living Light of the World."

The strange dream-state fast-forwarded as Roger saw the church grow and lives change. At PDI, Guardian came together as computer-aided designs, then models, then actual constructs using PDIs—Cliff's—proprietary and highly classified 3-D additive manufacturing processes. Test flights began. It was time for the next series at Groom Dry Lake just north of Las Vegas, to finally allow the Guardian prototype to use its classified scram jet and magneto-hydrodynamic ion drive.

Then, he remembered the last message he heard his pastor share, the Sunday before Roger flew out to Groom Dry Lake. It was a message about building one's life on a solid foundation.

Roger awoke with a start. He remembered! Pastor Andy's words were almost identical to what he had shared years earlier at his former church when he filled in for Pastor Hicks; the message that had such an impact on Karen Richardson. After Brother Andy's message, Roger had rolled his wheelchair forward and prayed with the pastor. He recommitted his remaining years to serving God. He asked the Holy Spirit to enable him for whatever purpose God had for him.

That was less than two weeks ago. Yes, it was the Sunday before his flight in Guardian that saved countless lives around Virginia!

Roger bowed his head in sincere reverence. "Thank You, Lord God Almighty."

God's got me here for a reason. He's chosen me for something and even healed my paralysis. As He gives me strength, I will serve Him, even as the loneliest man alive…

His sadness remained, but the deep, dark depression gave way to rest. Roger slept. This time, there were no dreams.

39. ALIAS

One purpose in life. That's all that was left. Many would consider such a narrow focus as morbid, depressing. For Skylar Brown, it was enough.

There she is!

The fifty-eight-year-old African American was instantly alert. In moments, he executed "Plan Alpha" around Charleston, South Carolina. He gave no thought whatsoever to the dozens who had been killed or injured by the terrorists' diversionary attack at the shipyard. He had no concern at all about the others who died or were seriously hurt by the next set of diversions on the major bridges twenty minutes later. And the faculty and staff killed at the main target, the school? Or what the terrorists might have planned for the teenagers? Not important.

But eyewitness accounts from some of the youth, that a lone woman had quickly overcome and killed four heavily armed and highly trained terrorists? In minutes? Priceless!

Plan Alpha meant that in minutes, police would be deployed to train and bus terminals to take pictures of all females over eighteen who were around five feet six and between 130 to 160 pounds and note their destinations. Airports already had sufficient cameras, so he'd just use Senator Matthews' credentials to authorize tapping in. "The lady," as he referred to Karen Richardson, never purchased a vehicle on-the-spot, always waiting till she reached her destination. He hoped that would still be the case. But he would send investigators to review the driver's licenses for any one-way rentals of any women who fit those general physical characteristics.

That was the legal, legitimate side of Alpha. Law enforcement personnel would meticulously follow orders and do honest work, based on phony information Skylar had already prepared for just such an opportunity.

In the meantime, his team would deploy. Well, he couldn't really describe it as his team anymore. He was no longer officially part of the primary team. Even with the full knee replacement, his age and permanent reliance on a cane had put him on the sidelines. Still, Matthews paid him well to hunt for "the lady." Skylar was the one person who wanted Karen Lane Richardson—dead or alive—almost as much as Jason Matthews. Preferably, alive. He had a score to settle with the superwoman who caused him many years of excruciating pain, followed by embarrassing rehab to break free from addiction to the painkillers, and worse.

Sure, she could have killed him back in 2020, but she chose instead to spare his life. He would gladly return the favor and leave her some things to remember for the rest of her life. Rumor had it that she might live to 110 or longer.

The rest of Matthew's personal team—meaning, those who weren't paid by or known by the government personnel responsible for protecting the senator—would converge on Charleston within hours.

He closed up his notebook workstation, grabbed the prepacked bag he always had at the ready, put on his coat, and turned out the lights. Cane or not, Skylar Brown wasn't about to sit this one out.

+ + +

How many times had it been? How many years?

Ellen O'Brien sighed, closed her eyes, and hung her head. How many aliases had she hidden under? How many times had she moved, both in the U.S. and abroad? Somewhere around thirty-six times over what, thirty-plus years?

She breathed in the cool, crisp mid-day sea breeze, and for the first time in years enjoyed what was for her both a luxury and a necessity—a week-long ocean cruise. She lay in a padded lounge chair near the cruise ship's stern, snacking on fruit cocktail and staring at the mesmerizing wake trailing aft.

Ellen—Karen Lane Richardson—needed to break out of her routine. Not for "R and R," although she desperately needed both rest and relaxation. No, she literally needed to break out of her routine, to escape.

This time, there had been no cameras to capture her defeat of the vicious ISIS attack against the youth at the Charleston school. The students were in such extreme danger that none of them had an opportunity to capture her on video or in pictures. Even if they had, her armor suit, helmet, and visor hid her identity.

But Jason Matthews and his team would know it was her. One woman, defeating a team of well-armed, trained, and suicidal terrorists?

Yes, they knew. They also would expect her to immediately head to the nearest bus station, or rent a car and drive at least 800 miles, stopping only to fill the tank, grab some snacks, and use the bathroom. Out of Charleston? Maybe they'd look for her to catch a north or southbound Amtrak train.

One of those options. That's what she always did.

So, it was time to take a cruise. She would leave, relax, return, and then relocate. They would look for her everywhere, except right where she had been: Charleston, South Carolina. With a new identity, of course. Now a green-eyed redhead, wearing glasses, and a dental appliance that artificially rounded her lower jaw. Of course, a new set of transparent, whisper-thin graphene gloves with fingerprints identifying her as…Ellen O'Brien.

Thirty-eight. Yes, thirty-eight different aliases, not including the ones she and her deceased husband used together during their years on the run.

She had shipped everything back to Mick Thompson before getting her ticket for the cruise; the Commando Flips, the remaining Incapacitators and Blades, the Pole Climbers, her Commando Suit, and her helmet and armored sneakers. She sent the destruct code to each of the Video Spots. Even if and when they were discovered and taken down from the poles and trees near Charleston's schools, the insides were fused solid. No reverse-engineering possible.

A winter cruise. Great food, some entertainment, and a chance to run some research through the new genetic modeling algorithms she had developed. A strange thought had occurred to her the night she prepared the video feeds to monitor Charleston schools for an expected attack. While placing a camera at one school, she looked at its playground and had grieved over her inability to ever have children. She would never know that special intimate bonding of a mother with her child. That level of oxytocin.

Oxytocin. Which is also very high with other forms of human bonding. Like when she risked her life in the early nineties to save Dr. Richardson, who later became her husband. And Mick and Sam. Oxytocin…

40. SHE'S ALL THAT

"There it is!"

Roger Brandon couldn't believe it was so simple. One character. A line of code beginning with "D" for "Documentation," used in Guardian's ternary code to automatically generate documentation for the code's Software Design Description.

The line of code that should have repeated the recalibration of the Terminal Targeting System each time the rail gun fired was preceded by a "D," making the instruction non-executable.

"How in the world did we miss that?" Roger asked himself.

Or did we?

Roger emailed his finding to Justin Townsend, who insisted that he'd already checked for exactly that possibility the Sunday morning he rode to DPI after the "incident." But at Roger's recommendation, he checked out the configured software code again…and verified that the "D" was there.

"I guess I somehow missed it," Justin replied in his email.

Moments later, through their "back door" communications link using their secure Enigma codec: "Roger, that's exactly what I looked for that next morning. I KNOW I checked that code. Someone made that change to the aircraft software, then changed the repository's configured copy of the code after that Sunday!"

A gnawing uneasiness settled on Roger.

After the fact. Only Justin, Cliff, or I…maybe two or three others at DPI…could have intentionally made that change and then covered it up in configuration management.

Roger's dark musings were interrupted by another message from Justin, this time back on the normal link. "How soon can you be ready to launch? We're being pushed to see what capabilities she still has. What do you need?"

"A co-pilot?" Roger teased.

They compared notes and schedules. "Next Wednesday," Roger finally responded. "You set the time and the tests."

Knowing they could now fully calibrate the gun, and with Guardian arguably the ultimate stealth aircraft, Roger asked if Justin had considered the possibility of ground and sea attack. Justin's reply answered in the affirmative: "Got some software I'd like you to try. You know I moved more of the controls up front so you can operate better alone. I've also wondered if we could modify the weather radar for surface attacks. I'd like to try it."

Roger nodded thoughtfully. The weather radar didn't have any traditional target acquisition functionality, nor did it have any countermeasures to use against enemy jamming. But, with the timing and frequency changes provided by the strange trans-dimensional shift, it just might work. Plus, it would allow look-down target acquisition in all weather conditions.

+ + +

Wednesday, 0600

Roger awoke from a good "night's" sleep, all two hours of it, and ate a great breakfast. He suited up in his new flight suit, tailored specifically for him and designed to protect him from both high-G maneuvers and during high altitude flight. He put on the test pilot's helmet he used for his previous flight, grateful for the new insert that more comfortably conformed it to his own head. After rechecking all the suit and helmet adjustments, he climbed aboard his fully fueled aircraft. Solid rocket boosters—SRBs—hung under the fuselage like sleek air-to-air missiles. Inside, the rail gun's cartridge contained a full complement of twelve "slugs." He attached audio and oxygen feeds to his helmet, turned on the aircraft avionics, and ran through system self-tests.

Tests complete, Roger started the turbojet, remotely opened the hangar doors, and taxied out.

Communications would be verbal, in a synthetic sense. Roger couldn't operate and monitor the aircraft's performance while typing and reading emails. So, he and Justin had optimized popular commercial, off-the-shelf voice recognition and speech synthesis software to their specific voices and technical vocabulary. Their "hands-free" communication was hitting over ninety-nine percent accuracy. Of course, from Roger's perspective, there were long pauses between sending a message and getting a response back from Justin. From Justin's perspective, he would receive a response almost as soon as he said the word "send."

Most communications would take place between the two of them with General Alvarez and Cliff Nesmith monitoring. NORAD was not even aware of the test—or even of the aircraft's existence—as they still believed that

Guardian and Roger were vaporized in the blast weeks earlier.

Roger lined up on the runway and completed his preflight checklist. The new satellite data link to the National Air Traffic Control network showed clear airspace all around and above as planned.

While he waited for superconductivity, he visually verified the aircraft control surfaces worked. Effectors smoothly curved sections of the wing that only vaguely resembled traditional ailerons and were only used for maneuvering at subsonic and low supersonic speeds.

"Clear to go. Have fun," Justin sent.

"This time I will. Send." Roger responded. No gut-wrenching drop out of the back of a cargo plane, slamming into the slipstream. No neck-snapping pullout just seconds before creating a giant crater. No threat of blacking out as he climbed out of a brutal dive or of getting the bends from not having a pressure suit.

Magnets sixty percent to superconductivity. Roger began his takeoff roll. At 3,500 feet down the runway he smoothly pulled up and retracted the landing gear. As he continued a gentle 1,000 feet-per-minute climb, the magnets went superconductive. Roger slammed the large Main Charge circuit breaker to ON. In moments, the first LED bar segment illuminated to a bright green as the magnets for the magneto-hydrodynamic ion drive began charging.

Roger appreciated the colors inside the aircraft. Everything outside, even the cloudless sunrise over North Dakota's cool, crisp, snow-covered landscape was just shades of gray.

The next LED segment illuminated as he continued climbing through 6,000 feet.

Roger narrated the status one item at a time.

"Charged to forty percent. Send."

"Charged to sixty percent. Send."

"Charged to eighty percent. Ready to bring MHD online. Send."

"One hundred percent. MHD now online. Firing SRBs. Send."

"SRBs ignited. Increasing rate of climb; passing 10,000 feet; started at zero-point-four Mach. Send."

"Altitude 20,000; Speed is zero-point-eight Mach. Send."

"Passing 26,000; zero-point-nine-five Mach. Send."

Mach One, and the ion drive screamed online, quickly followed by the scramjet. The acceleration slammed him back into his seat. The spent SRBs dropped off over open fields and parachuted down...

What in the world?!

"Justin... Uh...wow. The figures aren't making sense." He struggled to catch his breath. "Uh...okay, I'm fighting off four-point-eight Gs. Incredible acceleration. Send."

He was climbing through 60,000 feet and already close to Mach Three! Leading edge heat sensors were turning from green to yellow. Roger quickly engaged the ion shielding and Ion Aerodynamic Control System. Before the transformation, Guardian's sonic boom was subdued by the ion shielding. Now, after the transformation? Maybe a few distinct animals or carefully tuned instruments could detect it; people could not.

"Alright, everything's going faster than expected, even given my 4-X perspective. I just brought the shielding and the IAC online. Had some thermal sensors go yellow, one went red...they're all green now. I'm throttling back a little till I catch up with what's going on. Already at Flight Level Seven Zero and Mach Seven. Send."

Not only does everything still work, everything's working better! Just how fast can she go now?

Per the plan, Roger was heading due west. At a steady Mach Seven at 70,000 feet, he tested the IAC at increasing levels of bank, and to two Gs in each direction. *Smooth as silk.* He already knew—all too painfully well—that Guardian could pull more positive Gs than he could endure, although the new flight suit and working legs should help him handle one or two more. But he had no interest in finding out. Finally, he performed some minor dives to minus one G.

After each test, he reported the results to Justin.

Now it's show time.

"Charging capacitor bank. Send." Roger initiated the third mandatory manual action, charging the super capacitor network that would power the electromagnetic rail gun.

He pushed the throttle forward.

"Throttling up again. Acceleration at four-point-eight Gs. Send."

"Mach Eight...Nine...Ten...Justin, I've got Mach Eleven! Send."

Roger didn't announce that the aircraft actually reached a steady-state level flight speed of Mach Twelve-point-Five. He felt compelled to reserve that factoid for a private Enigma message to Justin later.

Surprisingly, even at that speed the leading-edge temperatures were within tolerance. He throttled way back to Mach Three to conserve fuel, and flew wide, lazy S's so he wouldn't overshoot the West Coast. At his altitude, he didn't bother with the ATC overlay. Virgin Galactic didn't have any scheduled flights, and currently no Google Wireless Balloons were aloft within a thousand miles.

"Got a target for me? Send."

Now General Alvarez responded. "De-orbiting now. You should be able to acquire within eight minutes."

A classified low-orbit satellite had intentionally been left in space beyond its primary mission, as an eventual test target for Guardian once other scheduled flight tests were completed. Months ahead of that schedule, today was the day. The first phase of Roger's test flight was timed to be completed as the satellite came into position.

"De-orbit burn confirmed. Target should begin re-entry 250 nautical miles west of Vandenberg Air Force Base, California. Monitoring systems online."

If the engagement succeeded, monitoring stations would simply report that the classified satellite burned up upon re-entry out over the ocean. Roger entered the parameters into the Terminal Targeting System, selected Auto Engage, and took his hands off the controls.

All right. Let's see what you've got.

"Acceleration of two Gs. She's climbing at 1,000 feet-per-minute. LIDAR is scanning. Send."

Justin, who'd been quiet while Roger was hands-on, now responded. "Any magnetic anomalies?"

"Negative. Send," Roger said. "The LIDAR works; target acquired. Send."

"Fuel status?"

"Sixty percent remaining. More than twice what I need to get home. Send."

"Engagement points?"

"Three automatically set at one-hundred-twenty, at eighty, and at forty nautical miles; speed now Mach Eight. Level at 80,000 feet. Send."

At precisely 120 nautical miles from the unseen target, the first slug fired. The scream of Guardian's ion drive and scram jet was more subdued and yet more ominous since the trans-dimensional shift. The "whomp" of the rail gun had also taken on a lower but more sinister sound.

Strange. I don't see the slug's trail.

"Miss. Huge miss. And I didn't see the ablative glow from the slug. Send."

He saw a faint trail from the satellite as it heated up and its shield began ablating.

Eighty miles. The gun fired again.

"Second slug away...and...a miss. First slug was one kilometer ahead of the target. Second was one hundred meters ahead. Still not seeing the slugs or their trails. I'm guessing they're not encountering the expected drag and are going a lot faster. Wonder if they'll go right through the target? Send."

He needn't have worried.

The satellite was constructed to resemble a warhead upon re-entry. If Roger used the aircraft optics for a close-up, he would have seen a five-foot-long cone as it streaked down into the upper atmosphere. At a range of forty miles, the rail gun fired again, and a split second later the satellite exploded in a blinding flash. Roger's helmet visor instantly darkened to shield his eyes, or he would have been temporarily blinded. Perhaps worse.

"Hit! What kind of explosives were in that target? Send."

General Alvarez responded after a longer delay, as he had to type: "None! Ground stations confirm a massive explosion. Speculation?"

During the time it had taken the General to type and send his response, Roger had already considered dozens of possible explanations. His speculation brought an increased sense of awe and the certainty that Guardian was now the United States' most incredible clandestine weapon. He also speculated that what they'd just experienced was nothing compared to what was coming.

"I'll need to think it through. Recommend we proceed to next phase. Do you approve? Do you have target parameters? Send."

While he awaited the slow response, Roger confirmed that the non-combat autopilot had re-taken control of the aircraft after the Auto Engage tasking was complete. The aircraft gently descended to 60,000 feet and slowed to Mach Three. If Roger didn't intervene in five minutes, it would alert him. If he still didn't intervene, the aircraft would descend further and go into a subsonic orbit track, just as it had the night of the "incident."

"Proceed. Visual and GPS coordinates attached."

This should be very interesting!

Roger copied and pasted the coordinates into the special Surface Attack program Justin had written. A picture of the target appeared on-screen; an offshore barge that had been towed sixty miles west of the California peninsula jutting out below Vandenberg Air Force Base. The team agreed that Roger should make a positive visual verification before engaging, as this attack mode had never been tested. Clear weather and the aircraft's superior digital optics would make that possible.

Roger set the attack speed and engaged Justin's new Surface Attack Auto Engage option. They hadn't thoroughly characterized Guardian's propulsion system and ion shield performance in the denser air of lower altitudes. They finally agreed that Mach Two should be a safe speed. At the envisioned altitude for a surface attack, that would still put him at over 1,300 miles-per-hour.

"Speed and altitude dropping. Slowly turning back toward the east. Send."

"40,000 and steady at Mach Two. Send."

"30,000. Target area bracketed on HUD and magnifying…magnifying…okay, verified. Justin, the Weather Radar seems to be tracking. Looks like we could do this IFR if we had to. Surface Attack mode fully engaged. Attack points set at forty, twenty-five, and ten nautical miles. Descending at 2,000 feet per minute. Send."

The first slug fired. Again, invisible.

"Number one is away. And… overshot by 500 meters. Send."

Yep. Just what I thought.

"Number two's away. And…overshot by 80 meters. Send."

Good thing they made sure the waters are clear!

Satellite and surveillance aircraft had verified there were no boats in the vicinity.

Time for the fireworks. I'd bet a steak dinner that…

The rail gun fired a third time as Roger yanked down his helmet sun shield for an extra measure of protection.

In Solvang, Lompoc, and at Vandenberg Air Force Base, anyone looking west saw a brief flash of light, followed later…much later…by a sound like distant thunder. They would have been amazed to know that what they saw and heard was from a barge blown 100 feet out of the water, over sixty miles offshore. The explosion was so powerful that minor blips were recorded on several California seismographs. Fortunately, the test was conducted away from any populated beachfront property. No one reported the surprisingly high wave that hit minutes later.

Roger took manual control of the aircraft as soon as the third slug fired and began a rapid climb—just in case. Was it his imagination, or did he feel a brief shudder from the blast? He raised the sun shield and let out a long, slow breath.

Yep. No way any of us could have expected this.

41. FOX

Many words had been used over the years. Some were complimentary. Others? Not so much. *Babe, Knock-out, Smoking Hot,* and *Fox* were just a few that had been thrown Tamika's way at different times and in different places. She had heard them all. Now, as she stood in Justin's doorway, she knew she would have fit any of those words, at any age, in anyone's opinion.

Justin gulped and looked as if he were trying not to appear overwhelmed.

He failed.

Tamika smiled.

It was just over a full month since the "incident," at six o'clock on another Saturday night. She was absolutely stunning. And she knew it.

Everyone at DPI dressed for comfort, mobility, and long hours. Basically, it was Casual Friday every day. Tamika had also put aside the business suits she had worn as an intern. She fit right in as Justin's "Exec," wearing sneakers, comfortable jeans, and casual, almost-modest tops.

But now, on a January evening that was warm even by Melbourne standards, she stood there in a summer-like minidress with matching handbag, heels, and tasteful but expensive jewelry.

"So, it's a beautiful evening and we *could* stay out on your porch," she teased, smiling at his apparent approval.

Justin stammered. "Okay, got me. Tamika, you look like you came right out of a fashion magazine."

Her smile broadened as she slipped past him into his apartment. She lightly brushed up against him and felt him flinch, if ever so slightly.

"I just had to get out of the work clothes and get my girl on again," Tamika said as she did a graceful half twirl. "So, Boss, you approve?" She playfully bit her lip and raised her eyebrows.

"Hmmm. I think my Porterhouse steaks should have been chateaubriand downtown with an evening of dancing. And I'm definitely underdressed." Sandals, jeans, collared pullover; Justin looked sharp, but he was clearly outclassed.

"We can dance here," she teased.

"Well, at least I didn't cook hamburgers. Wine?"

"Of course."

He poured two glasses, left his on the table, and handed her the other.

"Medium well, as I recall?" he asked, as he walked to his balcony.

"Perfect. Anything I can help with?"

Tamika knew that Justin had grown to sincerely admire, respect, and appreciate her. He told her that often. They worked well together through their seventy hour weeks, coordinating the multiple teams working various shifts, carrying out the General's mandate to have System Two operational in six months. Justin really depended on her as his Exec, and she had no doubt that the entire company appreciated her strong work ethic and encouragement. While she helped hold everyone accountable, she was no one's boss and everyone's assistant.

"Hey. We're off the clock. I'm not your boss here," Justin said over his shoulder as he turned over the steaks.

Tamika picked up his wine glass in her other hand and walked out to join him.

"What you see is what you get. I am what I am. All that sappy stuff. No clock. How can I help?"

Justin took his glass from her and raised it for a toast.

"To the classiest lady I've ever met, the most competent co-worker, and one of the best things that has ever happened to me."

"Thank you. So...I'm not THE best thing? Well, I like a challenge."

She left no doubt about her intentions for the evening as she pressed up against him and gently, sensuously kissed him. Then she slowly backed away and sipped her wine, never looking away from his eyes.

"Put the salads on the table?" Justin said. She could feel his admiring eyes on her as she turned and walked toward the kitchen.

An hour later, Tamika admitted to herself that she was impressed. Justin was handsome, athletic, intelligent, a terrific boss, and now she could add that he was also an outstanding cook. The dinner would have placed as one of the premium menu selections at any of the top ten steak restaurants along the Space Coast.

Their conversation was light, pleasant, and flirty. It was a welcome change as she bantered back and forth with Justin about being overwhelmed by their job. They had progressed—or perhaps digressed—from the classic "sipping from a fire hydrant," to "trying to keep my head above water," to "trying to stay within snorkeling depth." Justin added that he was so deep he "needed another SCUBA tank." And they joked about getting a patent for developing "unobtainium" and getting bonuses for delivering massive quantities of "imposibilitite," all ahead of schedule.

Justin tried to get her to sit and enjoy her third glass of wine, but she insisted on helping load the dishwasher and putting leftovers in the fridge.

Justin told the audio to play their favorite music, Soft Techno New Age, and told the lights to dim down to fifty percent, sunset. The surround music quietly engulfed them and the light softened to a pleasant reddish glow. Tamika sat beside him on the couch; they snuggled, sipped their wine, and were comfortably quiet for several moments. Finally, Justin took a deep breath.

"Tamika, I need to share some important stuff with you. It's about us, it's about work, and it's about some things that are so big I can't comprehend them."

She leaned back and looked at him quizzically. *Not like any line I've ever heard.*

"I don't know where to start. And nobody at work would believe any of this. But you need to know."

"You're...not into women?"

Justin laughed. "Oh, believe me, there are a number of..." he lowered his head and paused. "There are some women who would testify that's not the case. But never again. I mean, look, okay, it's always been mutual, you know? No commitment, have fun, and move on. Well, that's over. The game's over. It's over right now."

Tamika sat up and moved slightly away from him, so she could better see his face and read his body language.

He got up from the couch and faced his bedroom. Then he looked back at her.

"My life changed starting the last time you were here. I went into that bedroom during that call from Roger. When I went in I was solid, a player, the guy who had it all together. Tamika, I came out as a hero but broken, small. I realized how insignificant I really am. I've been doing a lot of research...well, as much as I can while clocking seventy hours a week. And I believe...I know for an absolute fact that the world as we know it is about to change big time.

"I don't know where you are spiritually. I was an avowed atheist through college and right up till that night. Roger had shared with me, not pressuring, but the dude really cared, and suddenly it started making sense. I became a Christian early the next morning. Maybe that's a showstopper for you. I know it would have been for me with any dating interest. But there's more.

"I need you to know that I don't have everything figured out like I used to think I did. And I see a lot of stuff that's scary. I mean, really scary. Terrifying. I believe that someone at DPI tampered with the code. If Roger hadn't thought of his workaround, the entire East Coast would be crippled and we'd probably be standing in the smoldering leftovers of the start of World War III."

He sat back down, facing her.

"You are smart, wise, motivated, and I believe somewhat idealistic. I am too. And very patriotic. There are a lot of things going on in America that I believe are tearing us apart from the inside-out. And I think something's going down that's even bigger. Somehow it includes DPI. Somehow it involves us."

Tamika shifted. Not away, but not toward him either.

"Well, you sure have a way of killing a romantic evening. But I know you're not a fluff ball or a wacko. I'm listening."

And what you tell me will go directly to Senator Matthews.

42. ENEMIES, OR...?

"Lord God, in heaven's name, what would you have me do?"

It was the sincere and common prayer of Juan Garcia, the forty-sixth President of the United States. And one he repeated silently or out loud many times each day as he faced overwhelming pressure from an America in transition...good or bad...and from an increasingly complex and hostile world.

The prayer was not flippant. When he had the time to unpack it, his meditation went something like this:

Lord: My master, redeemer, savior, and the sovereign over all the affairs of man, who alone knows the end from the beginning.

God: The most-high; creator of heaven and earth; our provider, healer, shepherd and our peace.

In heaven's name: That your kingdom may come and your will be done on earth as it is in heaven.

What would you have me to do? This question was a simple, humble act of seeking wisdom, guidance, and empowerment from on high. He was reporting for duty to his own Commander and Chief.

"What would you have me to do?" he asked again.

Juan was amazed that so few of his colleagues knew of the hundreds of specific, miraculous interventions that led to the formation of the United States as a country, and then as a world power. Calls for fasting and prayer to the almighty were answered by unimaginable victories during the War for Independence. At the Constitutional Convention, the challenge by Benjamin Franklin to again seek the aid of the sovereign God broke through a hopeless impasse and led to a Constitution and government unlike anything the world had ever witnessed. Juan's homeschooling exposed him to a side of American history almost completely ignored in public school textbooks. Even worse, revisionists over the decades had not only eliminated references to God but had done everything possible to marginalize those who had called upon his name.

No one was perfect. Not Columbus, not Washington, not Lincoln, not Reagan, and certainly not Garcia. Juan knew that better than his fiercest enemies, and he had many.

Certainly, no country was perfect. Yes, America was founded upon Judeo-

Christian principles. In previous years, even secular scholars, Supreme Court justices, and social commentators had referred to the United States as a Christian nation. No more.

The United States was awash in moral anarchy, as if the nation itself was schizophrenic. As many expected following the Supreme Court ruling on same-sex marriage in 2015, there were now demands for marriage rights for siblings, threesomes, and even for a young man to marry his stepmother. The country desperately needed to return to God for a measure of sanity. But even as president, Juan doubted he could call the country to prayer without locking horns with a hostile Supreme Court and Congress.

Juan never wanted to be president. Never even considered it. But he agonized over the pathetically dysfunctional branches of government. Legislation was enacted by the Oval Office through Executive Orders. Social agendas that couldn't pass any other way were forced upon the states by Supreme Court rulings. An impotent Congress never impeached judges for anything, no matter how unconstitutional. Finally, there was the ever-growing fourth branch of government; an entrenched bureaucracy of unelected federal employees who grew more powerful and less accountable, regardless of the party in power. Trump and others referred to them as the "deep state" and was only marginally successful in identifying and bringing a few to justice for treasonous actions.

Juan believed he had been called to run for the presidency by the will of God: *What would you have me to do?* "Run for president."

To everyone's amazement, especially his, eighteen months later he and Priscilla changed their address to 1600 Pennsylvania Avenue.

Then there was his Russian counterpart. Viktor Savin's rise to power in Russia was just as unlikely. He didn't share Juan's background as a nationally renowned endocrinologist and senior medical administrator. Nor did he match Juan's success as a key consultant who helped Congress overhaul the failed Obamacare program, the miracle that put Juan's name on the political map.

No, what was so unusual about Viktor was his expertise as an academician. He'd never served in the Russian military, but he was an expert on Sun Tzu's "The Art of War." He wasn't a part of any Russian secret service, but he had written extensively on the proper roles of the Federal Security Service of the Russian Federation and the Foreign Intelligence Service. Victor wasn't a reformer per se, but his writings, blogs, and speeches on economic and social reform were credited with increasing the overall Russian standard of living.

His ideas were slowly rebuilding the country's economy following the excesses of Putin.

Viktor Savin had basically been pushed into office by the Russian people.

And now...now he had clandestinely contacted the president of the United States. The note was as succinct as it was urgent:

"Mr. President, we are both in danger. I not trust normal channels of communication. This one American reporter, I believe she we can trust. She interview me again in two week. give her message for me. I accept to any reasonable back door communication you choose. Pardon bad English. Don't trust interpreting. Viktor."

The Russian president had signed and dated it, so Juan verified it was from him, at least as well as he could without calling in a handwriting expert.

Lord, what would you have me to do?

Juan not only had the disciplined, analytical mind of a medical doctor. He also was sensitive to personal interaction and perceptions. He was an outsider who could work with insiders. But he knew he had to be careful. He knew of Sybil Blalock as the culture correspondent with Fox News, and her presence at his wife's "Responsible Now!" kickoff was not a surprise. Nor was Juan surprised that she would also have recently seen Victor Savin, as some of his reforms in Russia were not unlike those the First Lady was trying to foster in the U.S..

Might she become a go-between? If Juan spent too much time with the young, attractive blonde, the rumor mill would kick into overdrive. On the one hand, the digital telephotos of the news paparazzi would document even the most discrete handover of a small envelope in minute detail, down to the exchange of glances or tightening of neck muscles. On the other hand, avoiding the press with multiple private meetings was equally unthinkable and impossible.

Viktor would be even more vulnerable. He was not known for entertaining media, even within his own country. Seeing a young forty-something American, while his own wife was struggling with cancer? And neither president could conceal private meetings from their own staff.

Culture. Responsibility. Perhaps in that capacity? Bridge the two cultures, emphasizing freedom and responsibility? Could it work?

Juan only had moments before his next crisis. His time in office had taught him to expect at least one crisis before lunch. And while he didn't micromanage, neither did he live on the golf course or go on multiple vacations at taxpayer expense, then deny knowledge of major executive branch meltdowns.

Juan made sure that each member of his staff knew three things about their particular jobs:

Here are the areas where you make the decisions and don't bother telling me.

Here are the areas where you make the decisions but be sure to inform me. Juan would give them examples of whether to tell him within the day, the week, or at the next scheduled staff meeting.

And finally, *here are the specific areas of crisis that I'm to be made aware of immediately, which I'll handle personally.*

All part of Total Quality Management, which he'd implemented as a senior hospital administrator, then demanded at the White House.

Not surprisingly, he usually had an unscheduled "Hey, Boss" several times a day. So, he quickly formulated a plan. He didn't always agree with Fox News. But while their personnel and analysts were tough, they had also been respectful. And he knew that given the pressure their personnel received from the "other" news organizations, he suspected that anyone working there for awhile must have a tough skin and a lot of integrity.

He'd talk to Priscilla tonight.

Might eventually send her to Moscow. She loves to travel, and wouldn't that blow everybody's minds? Clandestine communications in plain sight while making the world a better place.

Juan took a deep breath and let it out slowly. He was always amazed how subtle, how simple, and how profound God's answers could be. *Like using Queen Esther to save the Jewish race and lineage of the Messiah.*

"Thank you, Lord," he quietly whispered.

And his phone chirped.

OK. What now?

43. A PAWN IS LOST

Juan's humble attitude was in stark contrast to that displayed by his former political opponent that evening.

As he disconnected from Tamika's weekly call, Jason's practiced calm, quiet composure quickly morphed into fury and then overwhelming rage. He wished, for the first time in his life, that he had a puppy, or even a kitten. How he would have loved to take the filthy creature, hold it at arm's length and look deep into its sad little eyes. He would slowly choke the life out of it then slam it into the far wall of his condominium.

Jason hated animals. He hated God. And he hated Christians.

And Tamika had just told him that Justin had become a...a Christian!

"So damn unpredictable!" He shouted in his soundproof condo. *And so hard to manipulate,* he thought.

She said that Justin had even turned down a night in bed with her! That he cared for her so much, he wanted them to date and wait until their wedding night if their relationship continued to grow!

What's with that trash? They should be living together by now! How pathetic.

And...was there a touch, ever so slight, of waiver in Tamika's loyalty? Did she somehow actually respect the profound idiot for turning down her availability?

An outside observer would marvel at Jason's sudden transformation over what seemed so trivial. But all the thoughts of losing the presidency to the Christian Juan Garcia slammed over him like an avalanche. His meticulous self-control in public shattered in the privacy of his condo, as he realized he had just lost one of his key pawns.

Why did it even matter? Jason always played many steps ahead. He didn't have a plan. He never had a plan. He always had dozens! Jason would have laughed at the grandiose schemes Cliff was formulating for Guardian System Two, had Jason known them. He was already several steps beyond what Cliff still hadn't fully worked out in his own mind. And frankly, Jason was already well beyond Cliff. The man would soon end up as the victim of an unexplainable accident once he moved beyond his usefulness.

But no. This was an overwhelming anger that possessed Jason like an obsession. Uncharacteristically, he had even cut the call short with Tamika, failing to complete his typical objectives when talking to his sources: *Encourage her loyalty. Remind her she owes you.*

Furious, he cursed loudly. How could he have missed something so simple, so standard?

If an outsider really knew Jason well—and nobody did—and if that person also knew about his SORDAMN philosophy, they may have told the senator that he was slipping a little. Specifically, his "self-control in all things at all times" plank was picking up a few splinters. But if that person really did know Jason well? He also would have known better than to say a word. Especially right now.

Jason poured his first drink and brooded over it. He considered the options within his power. And his power extended very far indeed.

I can send some thugs to threaten him and beat him within an inch of his life.

I can shut down DPI.

I can kidnap Tamika and demand Justin reprogram Guardian if he ever wants to see her alive again.

Jason wasn't thinking clearly. He knew it. He poured his second drink.

He had planned to manipulate Justin to program Guardian System One, the trans-dimensional one or whatever they called it, for remote control. It would take off without Roger and trigger the start of the one world reorganization, since the ICBM had failed. Roger would painfully die away from the aircraft. That thought alone delighted the senator. It was a shame the plane couldn't land itself. It would have been an excellent asset for One World Peace Now, even better than Jason's original plan for the "unconverted" Guardian aircraft. Still, after the incredible results from a single ten-pound slug slamming into a satellite or barge, he could just imagine the entire multi-ton aircraft slamming into Moscow…! Everyone would suspect a nuke. Best of all, no radioactive fallout. Easy for the new Russian Premier to rebuild.

Cliff had faithfully reported Roger's speculation about the slug's impact. It was a reasonable theory; it made sense. An unknown amount of energy was absorbed in the trans-dimensional conversion of Guardian. That energy was then transferred to gasses, liquids, and solids as Roger had learned after landing. The time it took for the transformation depended on the substances' density. Conversely, the transformation back would take longer for a high-density solid. Normally. But if all that latent energy of transformation was instantly released, as when a high-density slug impacted another solid object at hypersonic speeds...

Calm slowly returned as Jason got out of the moment and planned forward.

"We will win this thing. We will be in power!" He started to pour a third drink, just this once, then stopped himself. "*I* will be in power!"

He told his multimedia system to play "normal." His seven-channel, high-def multimedia surround system responded with loud acid rock and a kaleidoscope of flashes, explosions, lightning, and chaos.

He sat back in his recliner, taking it all in. The tension slowly melted away.

Well, if I can't manipulate Justin to program System One, I'll just have the hangar torn down with the plane and Roger in it. Make sure Roger doesn't pull some more heroics and get in my way again. I'll send my errand boy Cliff out in System Two to stir up trouble as soon as it's ready. Not as spectacular, but it should work.

If only "Five Score and Ten" had worked out. I'd have another forty-five years to do everything I want to get done. Hmm. We will find her. I will get that formula.

Jason checked his Multiphone calendar. He didn't have any urgent plans for the morning. He could afford to stay up late.

Time to enjoy some of the finer things in life.

He muted his multimedia system and called a special number from his untraceable phone. He identified himself by a secure code.

"Yes, Sir? What's your pleasure tonight?" a personable female voice responded.

"Female. Fifteen or sixteen. Hmm...don't care about the race. At my place in an hour; pick her up at 9 a.m."

It was time to play. The sex slave would be delighted to give him anything he desired, as often as he desired, for another hit of the designer narcotic the team had addicted her to. With his special access code, he could even take out some of his anger on her, no questions asked. He'd call back and ask for a "cleanup crew" instead of the pickup.

No one would miss her. There were plenty more where she came from, and there will be even more, at least for him, when he becomes America's Premier.

Jason turned the noise back up, even louder.

Who knows? Maybe this time we'll even get our hands back on Karen.

+ + +

Ellen's cruise was nothing short of divine. Was it somehow too good to be true?

She carefully—but discretely—checked all her surroundings as she disembarked from the cruise ship, fully expecting uniformed police or plainclothes personnel to be waiting for her. Or for that matter, a fully deployed SWAT team. Or even worse, some of Jason's henchmen, who wouldn't care about who they injured or how many, so long as they captured her. Or recovered her body.

It was mid-morning. A cold, damp wind threatened rain from low, heavy clouds. Ellen followed the crowd, careful to stay close and tight, and not to draw any undue attention. Within thirty minutes, she was through customs, outside the cruise facility, and in a cab.

Just like that.

"Mornin', Ma'am. Where to?" the driver asked.

Ellen had considered calling for an Uber pickup, or maybe trying one of the new fully automated cabs, but instead she chose to simply hail a traditional taxi and quickly be on her way.

"Tanger Outlet, please."

Another twenty minutes and she was there.

A quick lunch and short walk, and she was at her intended destination; a sports center she'd looked up on the internet. One that had a good selection of motorcycles.

Ellen really enjoyed the Chevy Ultra Volt and hated that she had to give it up with her latest change of identities. It had served her especially well in her unplanned assignment to get across town through heavy traffic in time to stop the vulgar terrorist attack against the school. So…? Ellen would further break all old patterns. She really wanted a new hybrid touring cycle, but she settled for a 2020 Yamaha V Star 1300.

By five o'clock that afternoon, Ellen, her new helmet, gloves, riding gear, and her ever-present backpack were at a Hampton Inn on the outskirts of Columbia, South Carolina. More specifically, she was in a hot tub of water in a comfortable room, grateful for a pleasant and surprisingly uneventful week.

She wouldn't keep the motorcycle long; it was too much of an attention-getter. But that was the exact motive for the moment; leave Charleston using the most unlikely mode possible.

Ellen O'Brien had to admit, it sure was fun!

44. A DEEPENING DARKNESS

Roger awoke to a sudden pain and pressure in his upper right abdomen. As he stood to his feet, a wave of nausea swept over him and he threw up.

Great. America's ultimate secret weapon, piloted by an old man with a bad gallbladder.

He steadied himself against the landing gear strut. He knew from experience that the pain would likely last several hours, followed by a mild ache for a day.

Depression gnawed at him again. It was more than just the loneliness. Several things hung heavily over him.

For one thing, Roger wasn't a warrior. Sure, he would defend the United States to save American lives as he'd already done. But his recent test flight showed that his unique trans-dimensional aircraft could carry out devastating offensive attacks. He had already done the math and realized that he was able to wipe out any dam in the world with two, or at the most, three slugs. Entire cities could be destroyed. Hundreds of thousands killed within minutes. And no one could stop him, or even prove who did it or how. The ultimate counter-value targeting. Would he be willing to do so if ordered? He trusted President Garcia; he was the first person Roger ever campaigned for. But who would be the next Commander-in-Chief?

And there was the bad gallbladder. The attacks were getting worse. Strange. His once-paralyzed legs were now completely functional. But his gallbladder was giving him fits. The Atrial Fibrillation came and went as before, neither better nor worse.

And how long would he and the aircraft be trans-dimensional? He had taken up the habit of measuring the "deadline," how close flies, rodents, cockroaches, and other unfortunates would get to the aircraft before dying. He couldn't tell that they were able to get any closer or that they were dying farther away. Nor could he discern any change in the time it took for various substances, like his water and food, to convert so he could hold on to it. But would the effect last forever? It didn't seem to be extending out farther; that was good. His existence in the hangar didn't appear to be putting anyone at Grand Fork Air Force Base at risk.

Not yet. But what about when he died? Would the hangar become the world's most secret and dangerous superfund site? Would they have to encase the whole thing in concrete, like the ten nuclear reactors that had melted down over the years?

Roger thought about how close he'd come to ending it all before choosing to land at Robins Air Force Base. He'd had every intention of nosing the aircraft into the Okefenokee Swamp in southern Georgia, or into a foothill in the northern part of the state. A chill ran through him and he shuddered. If a ten-pound slug had impacted a barge with such transformational force that it registered on seismometers, the instant conversion of a nineteen-ton aircraft would be like, what? A small nuke? All the energy that had gone into converting Guardian and Roger would be instantly released...

Roger feared that every time he flew over land, he put cities at risk. If he ditched over water, he could set off a massive tsunami that would also kill thousands.

Good grief. Would I even set off a reaction with a hard landing?!

So many questions. So many risks.

The dark thoughts swirled. Nevada? Arizona? Alaska? Sahara Desert? Would he be asked to make that final flight after Systems Two and Three were on alert? Or should he go ahead and do it on his own?

And where in the world did that warhead come from? Just how close are we to World War III?

In a mass attack, what could he do? Twelve "slugs" meant up to twelve intercepts if the recent test had completed the gun's boresighting for "one shot, one kill" accuracy. How many more warheads would he *not* be able to stop while he returned, reloaded, refueled, and mounted two fresh SRBs? The interceptor program was meant to protect the country from rogues like North Korea and Iran. It wasn't designed to counter a full-scale nuclear attack.

Roger slowly got up and gingerly walked to the bathroom to relieve himself, then back to the table where "converted" water and paper towels were there for his convenience. He grabbed several towels and cleaned up his vomit. About the time he threw the towels away he became sick again.

No food today.

It was great seeing Justin the day before, but even that was depressing. Justin had flown to Grand Forks to bring Roger a few personal belongings from his apartment. He stepped into the hangar from a side door, turned on the lights, and just stared into what must have appeared to be a hangar with tables to the side of...nothing. Justin was careful not come closer than the duct tape

Roger had placed on the hangar floor. Roger could tell that the young man was tearing up and trying to communicate, but to no avail. Justin's words...too slow to lip read, even if he knew how...were subsonic to Roger. Likewise, Roger's words would be ultrasonic to Justin, and delivered at a micro-burst rate much faster than he could comprehend.

Roger longed to reach out to his friend, and now his new brother in Christ, and hug him. But he was not about to put the young man at risk. Matter could transform back and forth, but not even so-called nuclear-survivable roaches could get closer than five yards and live.

After what to Roger was several minutes, Justin brought in the cases, set them down, waved into the empty hangar, turned out the lights, and left. Roger stood there for several more minutes, overwhelmed by crushing loneliness, before slowly walking over to retrieve his few belongings.

Yesterday. Roger sighed. He looked again at what Justin had brought. To protect his secret existence, Roger didn't want any pictures or items that would disclose his identity if he had to abandon them. So, most of what Justin brought were books. The greatest treasure was the brand new, non-magnetic solid state, ten terabyte memory drive with a full dump off his home computer. Roger would be able to plug it into Guardian and enjoy his family videos, pictures, favorite music, and everything else he'd electronically collected over the decades.

For that, Roger was grateful. But he just didn't feel up to climbing into the cockpit until his gallbladder attack subsided.

As if on cue, another wave of nausea hit. Almost as painful, Roger suddenly remembered that tornados were not unheard of in North Dakota. Just a year earlier, a massive EF-4 tornado had leveled a fracking facility in the western part of the state, with winds over 180 miles per hour. Roger shuddered again, both from the physical pain and from the realization that destruction could come not only from Guardian slamming into something solid. It could also occur from something solid slamming into the aircraft. All of Grand Forks Air Force Base could become a crater, dozens of feet deep.

Well, at least we're still a few months away from tornado season. I hope...

There was a small, ragged cardboard box he'd asked Justin to bring out of his garage. It had some of his old favorite books. Roger found it in the second crate he opened. He removed the Bubble Wrap packing material and stood speechless, staring at the last thing he imaged he would ever see again.

A chameleon lizard, brown to match the cardboard color, scurried out of the box and onto the table. Apparently, the stowaway from the warmer central

Florida climate didn't realize it was supposed to be dead.

45. *A TIME TO REMEMBER*

"It's time."

The impression was as clear as if she'd audibly heard the voice. Startled, she rose out of bed and looked at the clock. Two a.m. The voice, or impression, or prompting of the Holy Spirit, didn't come again. It didn't have to. Ellen O'Brien had suspected from that first meeting in 2006 that somehow her life would again intersect the lives of Roger and Cindy Brandon. She intentionally stayed away, not wanting to put them in any danger from Jason and his team. He had proved too often that he would do anything, use anyone, to get to her. Over the years, she and Roger and Cindy made sure that even emails were carefully encrypted.

When she learned of Roger's accident and his loss of Cindy and the kids, her heart broke for him. While he was still recovering in the rehab center, she sent him a painting she had made for him. It portrayed a muscular Jesus, on top of a heavenly mountain, confidently pulling on a rope that extended down below white clouds and through a terrible thunderstorm. The end of the rope was secured to a mountain climber, struggling to climb up the treacherous earthly mountain.

Even now, years later, she prayed for Roger daily.

Ellen was wide awake now. She walked into the bathroom and checked her hair before showering. Good; no roots showing. As she showered, she went through her mental checklist. Her one-year lease had just started, and as always, was paid in full. She never stayed anywhere longer than a year. She would leave with her "short list" of belongings and send the key and a note for everything else to be donated to the local charity she'd already chosen. It was all so routine.

She dried off from her shower. Before touching anything other than the washcloth—which she used to turn the faucets on and off and to handle her shampoo and soap containers—she put on her gloves. The 3-D printed graphene gloves with her "Ellen O'Brien" set of fingerprints and fingernails fit seamlessly over her hands and closely manicured nails. This was one of the several technologies she didn't patent and didn't share with anyone. The gloves stayed on twenty-four/seven, except when she carefully showered. The unique, durable, breathable material with integral fingernails would fool even an expert. They would, and had, even held up under a police fingerprinting scanner one time.

Now, the most important thing. She kept it in the washing machine, of all places, suspecting that would be one of the last places an intruder would look. She opened the lockbox and spread out her credentials.

Ellen O'Brien. Red hair, green eyes, glasses, thirty-two. The next passport was for a Kim Brandon. Okay, she did kind of like that last name. Black hair, dark brown eyes, thirty-two. There were other sets of passports, Social Security cards, and driver's licenses. Various colored contact lenses, fingerprint gloves, and more. Various sets of glasses meticulously designed to foil facial recognition cameras, even the newest multi-spectral systems used in airports.

Ellen didn't like to deceive. It was against her nature. But she also didn't like being a lab rat… and worse. Desperate men would do desperate things to acquire what she had. Already, many had lost their lives. Very painfully.

So, Ellen had learned how to work the system. Or systems. All of them. Her high IQ, memory, attention to detail, decades of study, and years of practice had made her an expert on many things—including the various dental devices she had designed. They could give the appearance of higher cheekbones, a narrower or broader chin, or puffier cheeks. She was familiar with all current facial recognition cameras and had access to the world's best facial recognition software. She regularly made sure that each of her aliases could not trace her back to any of the others.

The lady knew all the tricks. After Matthews' team found her again four years after the death of her husband, she had to.

Ellen opened an envelope in the lockbox to look at the original. Strawberry blonde, five feet six inches, weight 150, hazel eyes. A full-length picture would have shown her as a beautiful thirty-two-year-old woman, who could easily be an athlete or physical trainer. Jennifer Karen Lane Richardson. Actual age? Fifty-six. Ellen sighed and put everything back in the box and then placed it in her backpack.

She took a last quick peek at herself in the mirror to make sure she hadn't missed anything.

A sudden realization hit her so hard she almost collapsed. She grabbed the countertop to steady her shaking knees. For the first time in years, in spite of her incredible health, she felt faint.

"My God!" she exclaimed, in reverence and awe.

Like the scales that fell from the eyes of Saul of Tarsus, who later became the great Apostle Paul, Karen's mind was suddenly opened. And she remembered. She sat down hard on the sofa as she did the math. Thirty-five years had passed.

Karen fell off the couch and onto her knees.

"My God!" she exclaimed again.

She had a decision to make. How different might her life have been? How much heartache could she have avoided? Would she have ever come to Christ any other way? Would her life have ever had the influence and purpose she'd experienced all these years? She never would have met her late husband and would have missed those short but precious years together. Yet…to have had a normal life?

She fast-forwarded through the difficult decades of her adult life, since being turned inside-out and upside-down by what had happened early one morning those thirty-five years ago. And she knew what she had to do. What she would do. What she had already done.

Years of intense Bible memorization and study flashed through her mind. Her study of Scripture was just one of her many academic pursuits. But it was the most special, intense, and precious. It was out of love and relationship, not out of simple interest or curiosity. It was to build a strong foundation for her life, as Roger had admonished that fateful Sunday morning so many years ago.

She knew there was no Biblical precedent or even a general principle for what was about to take place. But she firmly believed that all things are possible with the Great I Am, the true and living God of eternity. And she also knew that what had already happened to her through FSAT was without precedent.

Does even this capability date all the way back to Genesis? An ability God created in us, that we lost during the Fall?

Kneeling against her couch cushion as a makeshift altar, she quietly began to pray. "Father, you know the end from the beginning. You are the self-existing God, who created time. I humbly ask you to do what I believe you have already done. Because I believe that your will is perfect. And that you have a plan and are still carrying it out. Father, I wait on you."

In her imagination, her mind's eye—like a waking dream, although much clearer than that—Karen thought of a particular phone number. Strange that she remembered it after all these years. She saw and heard herself calling it, and it was answered on the third ring.

She said to a young woman, "We need to talk. You have a book due in a week. You have no idea where to start or what to write. I have a story to tell you that I promise will change your life. I know your favorite coffee and the pastry you only allow yourself to enjoy once a month. I'll bring them to your apartment in half an hour." And she did.

As the strange—what was it, a dream, a vision? As whatever it was continued, she met with the twenty-two-year-old college graduate, and they talked for hours. The young woman was skeptical—of course—but couldn't seem to drag herself away, as if the story itself compelled her to listen to the end. Karen reflected with shame on how self-centered and shallow the young woman seemed.

Then it was over.

"Father, then and now, Thy will be done."

She glanced at the clock. Only minutes had passed. Ellen—Karen—rose from her knees and looked again in the mirror at the red hair, the comfortable but attractive pantsuit, and the matching flats and handbag.

She remembered everything from that strange event those thirty-four years ago. She was staring at the very same thirty-two-year-old-looking woman who brought her a tall cup of her favorite coffee and that to-die-for-pastry, in what was somehow more than a dream one early morning. It was a dream that changed her life forever, yet until now it was a dream which had been forgotten almost exactly seven days later. Apparently, the memory of that encounter was the one thing she lost when she slammed her head against a pipe and suffered a mild concussion while fleeing for her life. But she had remembered long enough during those few days to write her story as a fiction novel. She had raced to deliver it on time, got off the elevator on the wrong floor, and witnessed an execution over the formula for Five Score and Ten— FSAT. A formula funded by Jason Matthews. An execution ordered by Jason Matthews. All of that led to her meeting Mick, Samantha, and Dr. Andy Richardson, who helped lead her to Christ, and later led her to the altar.

So much had happened in those fateful few weeks so many years ago. She came to realize how shallow and worthless her life was. Then she began to fear for her life. That condition remained to the current day, although tempered and focused into actionable precautions. Finally, she saw her new friends in imminent danger of torture and death. And by the grace of God, she did the three things she never imagined doing. First, she became a Christian. Second, she took the last existing dose of FSAT, expecting it to slowly and painfully kill her. And third, with the superhuman physical strength it gave her, she overpowered the guards and freed her friends. But the altercation left her mortally wounded, assured that either the bullet or FSAT would quickly end her young life.

Yet she lived.

The lovely woman smiled at herself in the mirror and raised her eyebrows.

"Jennifer Karen Lane, have you ever got a wild ride ahead of you, young lady!"

She glanced at the weight set over in the corner and smiled. She always wondered about the reaction of the charity workers coming to receive her donation. A bed, miscellaneous furnishings, appliances, some linen…oh, and over a thousand pounds of free weights and an extremely heavy-duty weight bench! She couldn't afford the attention she would receive going to a local gym and out-lifting even Olympic weightlifters, so she did her serious exercising at home.

"Yes, young lady, a wild ride indeed."

46. A TIME TO FORGET?

Ellen placed her limited possessions in her car, an old 2015 Ford Taurus, and drove down the street to gas up. That done, but before she got back in the car, she heard a collision. Even as the wreck continued, she immediately discerned what happened…and it was bad. A city van had swerved to avoid a car that ran a red light at an intersection fifty yards from Ellen. The van glanced off a parked car, hit a curb at an angle, partially rolled on its side, and hit a light pole. A pedestrian was trapped under the van. She knew this particular van ran on liquid petroleum gas—LPG—and the tank was right where the van was leaning against the light pole.

Her evaluation: If the LPG tank ruptured, the heavier-than-air gas could suffocate the pedestrian, at the very least. Worse, it would ignite from any suitable source of heat, like a lit cigarette. Rare, yes. But after years of decline and problems with vaping, pipes had started becoming popular again.

Ellen sprinted toward the scene and was there as the driver pulled himself out of the van. She avoided high heels, choosing rather to wear shoes and clothing that, while attractive, allowed her to move quickly. Over the decades, she had needed that ability all too often.

Her fears were confirmed. She heard the hissing and smelled the odor of leaking LPG. The tank, placed up high for safety in the event of more likely collisions, had been ruptured by the unusual tip-over against the light pole.

Under the van, the pedestrian, a middle-aged man of about five feet ten inches and around 190 pounds, was clearly in pain. His left leg was trapped between the van's rear tire and the curb, but he was not in immediate danger from that. The real danger to him and the gathering crowd was the leaking LPG that could suffocate or explode.

Ellen made direct eye contact with a thirtyish man with close-cropped hair who appeared to be a body builder. He was moving forward through the crowd with a clear intent to help.

Ellen carefully modulated her voice to be directive but not to offend the man's ego and create a battle of wills. It was a psychological balancing act she had honed but only used in emergencies such as this. She directed him to grab the man's shoulders and prepare to pull.

The man dropped to his knees, grabbed the man's shoulders, and braced himself. What happened next caught everyone by surprise. Without asking for any assistance, Ellen placed her back to the van. She squatted down, grabbed the underside of the van just in front of the rear tire, lifted it a full foot off the ground, and yelled "Pull! Now!"

The body builder pulled the pedestrian free and Ellen dropped the van. Then she did use her "fully directive" voice: "Everyone back! This gas is going to explode!" And in the confusion, she quickly returned to her vehicle and left.

She knew her current identity was blown. Multiphone pictures and videos would be posted all over social media within minutes. More pictures and video would be extracted from traffic cameras and plastered over the news networks within the hour. Commentators would call in experts to evaluate the superhuman strength of a young woman deadlifting at least 1,000 pounds to a height of a foot for five seconds. Pictures and videos from documentaries that had been produced about "her" or "them" over the years would be brought up, new documentaries produced, web sites updated; the list went on and on.

But the real concern was that Matthew's team would instantly know it was her and would be there within hours. Legitimate police would be on the lookout even sooner.

Ellen knew all that before she took her first step to help. But she understood that her special abilities were God-given, and she was committed to use them when necessary to honor God and to help others. That's why she had so many aliases and was so adept at changing from one to the other.

Ellen drove around for fifteen minutes to make sure she wasn't being followed, then parked at the opposite end of her apartment complex. She grabbed her backpack, and quickly walked back toward her apartment and to the motorcycle she had not yet disposed of.

Once again, Jason Matthew's team would be checking airports, bus stations, train stations, car rental agencies, and traffic cameras. She was sure someone would have captured her car's license tag. So, she again did the unexpected.

She took her riding gear out of the sidebags and went back into her apartment. Five minutes later, a young woman with different glasses, different colored contacts, different denture appliances, darker red hair, and different fingerprints exited the apartment. If anyone happened to see her enter and exit the apartment, they wouldn't know the difference; she left wearing leather from neck-to-boots, with a full-face helmet and a dark visor.

The morning in Asheville, North Carolina was cold, but there was no snow or ice in town or on surrounding mountain roads, so she took the scenic route and leisurely rode through the Great Smoky Mountains, thus avoiding cameras along interstates. By evening she was in Helen, Georgia.

+ + +

Three days later, Stacey looked up from her receptionist's desk at DPI. The young-thirties redhead standing before her in a classy red blouse, black business suit, black pumps, and modest jewelry would turn heads in any venue, but she was clearly overdressed for DPI.

There was something else about her. On the one hand, Karen seemed to have the confidence and self-assurance of a much older woman. On the other hand, she seemed, well, lost.

She had introduced herself as Karen Lane Richardson, an acquaintance of Roger Brandon's since before he lost his family.

"Ms. Richardson, I'm so sorry you hadn't heard. Roger was killed back in November during a flight test of one of our systems. I'm not even allowed to give you any details, other than that he put himself in jeopardy to save others. There are a lot of folks here who loved him very much, and there are many who owe him their lives."

Karen just stood there, bewildered.

Stacey's legendary perception was at maximum. "You know, Justin Townsend was one of Roger's closest friends and took over Roger's responsibilities after the accident. Let me see if he has a moment…"

A few minutes later, she ushered Karen into Justin's office.

"Please sit down, Ms. Richardson. Is it Karen Richardson? Your name sounds familiar."

Karen just stood there, staring over his shoulder. Justin followed her gaze to the picture on his wall. The one that had hung in Roger's office.

"Karen Richardson…"

Justin sat down, hard.

Karen lowered her head. "I…I guess…so it's true then? Roger's gone…" she said dejectedly and plopped down into a chair.

After a few moments, Justin regained his composure. "Karen, you're a Christian, aren't you?"

"Yes. And Christ used Roger at a very critical point in my life. A crisis."

"And He used you at a very critical point in my life. That picture you painted for Roger? I looked at it daily as we'd talk in his office. After the…accident…I couldn't get it out of my head. This painting. The Scriptures. I asked Jesus to forgive me and be my Savior and Lord. Thank you."

Karen looked at him long and hard. Justin became uncomfortable under the gaze. Finally, she took a long deep breath and reached into her purse.

"Justin, I'm going to show you something you won't believe. But it's true. I showed this to Roger and Cindy back in 2006. God brought me here for a reason, so it must be to let you know this. I don't understand why. I thought I was to come here to meet up with Roger, and God was somehow going to use us in some special way to serve Him. Now I understand he's dead. You will be one of very few people who know about me. All but two are mortal enemies. I am not exaggerating to say that this can put my life in extreme danger, so I trust you to keep my secret."

She handed him the old driver's license, which listed her correct birthdate.

Justin studied the license and did the math. Now it was Justin's turn to take a long, hard look at her.

"Roger only spoke of you a few times. Always with deep respect. Karen…." He let out a sigh. "Give me a moment."

Justin reached for his Multiphone, pulled up the Enigma App, and sent a quick message to Roger. Almost as soon as he hit "Send," Roger responded.

Justin stared at the message for a full minute. Then he rose from his chair, stepped to his office door and opened it. "Stacey, we'll be in the SCIF."

Karen silently followed him into the company's Sensitive Compartmented Information Facility.

+ + +

"That's terrible!" Karen exclaimed.

"There's so much we don't know. The dude's safe for now, at least, except for a bad gallbladder. He's having attacks, like, about once a week. But…how do you operate on a ghost?"

"Hmm. So, all this is a dark program for the Department of Defense?"

"Yes. DPI's founder, Cliff Nesmith, invented and perfected a transformational technology for additive manufacturing—most people think of 3D printing—that puts us light-years ahead of competitors. He caught the attention of Senator Matthews—"

"*Jason* Matthews?" she exclaimed.

Karen shuddered and turned pale. Her body stiffened.

"You know him? Why…what's wrong?"

Karen stood and turned, walked several steps away. She faced back to Justin. A wave of fury rose up and turned her face from pale to red. Her pleasant countenance hardened, and she clenched her fists. She paused a beat before answering.

"Okay, everything on the table. That man has blood on his hands. And he'd kill many more to get those hands back on me again. I'd die first."

"Karen…?"

"Long story. Short version: Yes, I'm fifty-six. A team of scientists, paid by Jason Matthews before he got into politics and whatever else he's doing covertly, found a longevity breakthrough. It likely goes all the way back to the time of Genesis and somehow survived the flood. The scientists called it FSAT; Five Score and Ten. Early modeling indicated that it should increase lifespans to a healthy 110 years. But it was stolen while still being tested. It reportedly imbued the subject with a remarkable increase in strength and intelligence…but only for a few days. A lot has changed on the earth since the Garden of Eden days, and thousands of years of genetic degradation has also changed us. The product painfully killed everyone who took it. Except me. When the formula was lost, I was the only link. Jason and his people, they tracked me down, kidnaped me, and tested me mercilessly until I finally escaped. I've been running ever since. Don't trust Jason Matthews. And be careful about trusting anyone who's really close to him."

"Like Cliff…" Justin said thoughtfully.

"Pardon?"

"Karen, somebody changed the aircraft's attack software. Only a few of us could have done that and hidden the trace. Roger, Cliff, me, and maybe a few others. If the software hadn't been altered, the intercept would have worked and Roger and the aircraft wouldn't have changed. It was almost like somebody wanted to make sure the aircraft couldn't accomplish its primary mission. Hmm…"

"What?"

"I never thought about it before, but the nuke launched precisely when Guardian should have been NMC…Non-Mission Capable, inside a cargo aircraft being transported back here. Even the test pilot wasn't on board. But Roger found a way—"

"And the two of you saved hundreds of thousands, even when the gun missed."

"And Cliff. He's been acting really strange since the accident. He says he's working on another advance in additive manufacturing, but the rest of us work seventy-hour weeks or more, and he just drops in every week or so…"

47. TRUTH

"Sybil Blalock. It's so good to see you again."

"It's good to see you, too, Mrs. Garcia," the former Fox News culture reporter said.

"Please have a seat. Would you like something to drink? Tea, coffee, water…?" Priscilla Garcia and the young woman both sat down in the First Lady's private office.

"Thank you, I would love some coffee. The anti-jetlag medicines may work for some, but it's just not there for me, if you know what I mean."

Priscilla pressed Intercom on her desk phone and asked her assistant for hot tea for her, and a coffee serving for her guest.

"Will your husband be joining us?" Sybil asked.

"He's pretty much left this project up to us, but he'll drop in from time to time as we meet. Did your trip go well?"

"Yes, Ma'am. I really appreciate the opportunity you've given me. And I have these notes and papers for you and President Garcia."

Sybil handed a folder to the First Lady. Inside was a personal note from Viktor Savin.

The beverages were brought in, including a small insulated carafe, cream, and various sweeteners, much to Sybil's delight. The ladies spent the next half an hour going over how the two countries could learn from each other's attempts to implement economic and social reforms, within the frameworks of their individual cultures and constitutions.

+ + +

Two hours later, President Garcia was alone, reading the letter.

"Mr. President, I spent several year study English. Regret that I speak and read much better than write.

"You and I are in danger. We were allowed to presidency. Secret organizations. Skull and Bones, Illuminati, Club of Rome—not enemy. They are just for recruiting. Real enemy more subtle. Think they call themselves

One World Peace Now. Ten or so rulers over earth, one currency, possibly one religion.

"Nuclear missile was not Cold War! Modern, but I nor my people can find who or how it was made. Was stored and launched from an abandoned Soviet silo in Ukraine. Very few I trust, but one man was able to persuade a captured guard to talk. Unpleasant.

"Appears OWPN is trying to bring our countries to brink of war, then eliminate elected leaders and use crisis to take over. Old plan. Never waste a good crisis. If one is not available, make one! Martial law. Eliminate Bill of Rights in your country, personal freedoms left in mine.

"Watch out for false provocations. Do not have all your key people be vulnerable in same place. Find out who would take over and expect a traitor. Find him, her fast. Possibly many, but one key leader."

You must know that my control and influence, limited. Particularly over military. Will do all I can.

Be safe,

Viktor"

For a moment, a stunned President Garcia sat motionless. Then, he considered the most obvious question. Did the note truly come from Viktor? Priscilla Garcia had a good read on people, and she had interviewed Sybil Blalock extensively before recruiting her as their clandestine go-between. She believed Sybil passed it directly from one leader to the other.

Second question: Was Viktor telling the truth? If not, what could he gain from it, unless his goal was to mislead a naïve "non-politician" president? For what purpose? Viktor was himself a non-politician president; the first Russian President without roots in the KGB.

Juan knew of the Bible prophecies foretelling the general arrangement of world power that Viktor was describing. But he also knew that nowhere did the Bible suggest that he should lie down and passively wait for the apocalypse. No, not on his watch. It would happen in God's time regardless. But Juan Garcia would fight to keep the Church Age open as long as possible. He understood God was holding off judgment because He was "…not willing that any should perish, but that all should be saved."

"Lord God, in heaven's name, what would You have me do?"

He trusted Vice President Linda Manfrida and Speaker of the House Charles Zucker. He counted both of them as friends, as patriots, and as great

Americans. And he respected that they had each taken difficult stands on critical issues despite brutal, unrelenting, personal attacks by the press against them, their families, and their credibility. They had taken the heat without flinching. Unlike so many in Washington, they actually believed in the Constitution, the separation of powers, and the concept of personal freedoms matched with personal responsibilities. No free lunches. A hand up, always. But no handouts.

Jason Matthews.

Juan's blood ran cold as he remembered the grueling debates against Jason. For the thousandth time, he reflected in amazement over the final debate. He knew it was the Spirit of God who pulled aside Jason's mask just enough for Juan to see that the man was a master of graphite statistics and doublespeak. There, on national television, Juan asked the one completely unexpected question that caught Jason off guard. The one question he had no perfectly manicured response for. And he asked it in such a humble, non-confrontational manner that he blew the tires right out from under Jason's bandwagon: "Jason. Do you really believe what you're saying?"

Of course, Washington—and the rest of the country—has a poor memory. Also, multi-million-dollar ad campaigns based on extensive focus-group-tested sound bites make sure that overworked, over-materialized Americans quickly forgot. Jason easily returned to the Senate and even to a position that put him fourth in line for the Presidency.

What were the other three of us doing the night the nuke was launched?

Juan quickly checked his calendar.

A conservative off-site to work out a detailed, structured plan for tax reform. All three of us were there!

Unlike some previous Presidents, Juan trusted, respected, and appreciated his Secret Service team. He believed that most or all would give their lives to protect him. But thinking back to that venue, he had to admit that it was vulnerable to attack from another nation or a Jihadist bombing. And a successful attack on that night would have provided the additional benefit of eliminating a significant number of remaining pro-capitalists and conservatives from influence in the Beltway.

Also troubling, if a secret organization was bent on taking over the world, they would certainly try to infiltrate the bodyguards tasked to protect the world's key leaders.

He had been spirited away to an underground bunker, along with the Vice President. Was an assassin down there with them? What about the others? Did they make it to their shelter in time, with someone there to take them out as well?

So...what now?

As usual, Juan knew he might only have minutes before he'd be pulled away from his reverie by another crisis. He also knew that this was not an issue that he wanted any written or electronic copy of. He quickly wrote notes to help him visualize the situation. He would chop-shred them along with Viktor's note before leaving the room:

- Viktor's analysis seems reasonable and must be taken seriously.
- Jason is the likely point-man; probably many others through news media, academia, politics, possibly military.
- Passive options?
    o Do nothing, rely on Secret Service protection.
    o Warn Secret Service, Vice, and Speaker.
    o Avoid any venue that puts all three of us together.
- Active options?
    o Investigate Jason.
    o Find a way to match mine and Viktor's schedules; increase security when we're both most vulnerable. Try to flush out the enemy.

Next, Juan went through the list to eliminate options that were non-players. Doing nothing was the first to go. He would notify the VP Linda Manfrida and Speaker of the House Charles Zucker; that made sense. They needed to be aware of their personal danger and be ready to step in if an attack were partially successful. But should he tell the Secret Service? If even one of them might be a mole, the risk would be unacceptable. Anyone there he could trust?

For active options, Juan knew that any attempt to launch an investigation of Jason would be practically futile and politically devastating. The man was too slick, too powerful, with too many connections. He was able to make Teflon look like course sandpaper.

Should he warn other world leaders? While he and Viktor certainly weren't the only key leaders, it was possible that some of the others might already be part of One World Peace Now, especially China. Again, too risky to alert them. But it might be wise to watch for a time when several of them would be simultaneously vulnerable to attack. Juan knew that any request from the president immediately generated assumptions and speculations. Even asking an aide to look at the schedules of key leaders could be on social media today, in the news tomorrow, and on talk shows the day after.

Priscilla.

Another task for the one person he trusted the most; his eminently capable wife.

It wasn't like he and Viktor could share their calendars online so they could watch out for events where they'd both be vulnerable. On the other hand?

A plan began to form. Juan took his faith very seriously. His marriage and family and his responsibilities were all extremely important. But he didn't take himself seriously. He was just a servant, whether as a doctor, an administrator, or as president in the White House.

President Garcia had his answer.

48. YOU NEED TO KNOW

Tamika was wrapping up her long shift, looking forward to getting some much needed and well deserved sleep, then spending an hour at the gym for her heavy workout. In the evening, she'd make her next call to the senator.

She couldn't remember feeling more alive, more excited, more of an up-and-comer since Professor Jacobs secretly recruited her to collect social media information on rival faculty members in his department. Tamika had felt so alone going to the university, leaving the welfare and entitlement mentality of her family and everyone she'd grown up with in the housing project. She worked hard for scholarships and grants, then still had to work almost full-time hours to make it through college. It took her five long years instead of four, plus five more years to pay off her academic loans. College for her provided little time for friends or relationships. She worked hard for her high GPA, and Professor Jacobs saw that she had potential.

Senator Matthews also made her feel important. She was honored to serve her country in these difficult times. The man was always so keenly attuned to her ambitions, her dreams, and even to her frustration that Justin wouldn't let their relationship get physical. Although, as she expressed to Senator Matthews, it was nice to be appreciated for more than just her body.

"Yes, Tamika, certainly. But you are a lovely, young, healthy woman, and you have needs. And it's so natural that you would want to share those needs with each other and be intimate," he said the last time they talked.

Tamika began collecting and organizing information for her weekly report.

There wasn't much to discuss this time. The various DPI teams had reached an efficient plateau to carry them through the final stages to deploy System Two by the six month deadline. With few exceptions, they now worked two twelve-hour shifts, Monday through Saturday, and took Sundays off. One shift worked from 7:00 a.m. to 7:00 p.m.; the other from 9:00 p.m. to 9:00 a.m. That allowed for a two-hour morning overlap to meet and plan, which "The New Twenty-One," with the addition of Tamika, did daily. The two-hour evening break gave Maintenance a chance to service and recalibrate machines and equipment. Maintenance personnel split their shifts between the other two, but several of them were always on call in case something broke between times.

Justin was currently with the day crew and Tamika was on the night crew. They hadn't had time for much social interaction, aside from casual Sunday afternoon dates after he had gone to church and she'd gotten some rest.

Tamika looked over her notes. No unusual purchases, problems, or issues. The only visitor they'd had in several weeks was some woman named Karen L. Richardson. Everything was on schedule. Her full report shouldn't take more than a couple of minutes of the senator's time, once he called her back on his private phone as he did every time.

"Tamika, got a minute?"

She jumped. "Justin! You startled me." She slid the note in with other papers and rose to her feet, giving him a hug.

"Always have time for you, Boss," she teased.

It was six in the morning, so Justin had come in an hour early.

"Let me get some coffee and let's go to the SCIF."

They walked to the snack area together, kidding and teasing, with more than a little PDA between them; although technically there was no public to witness their genuine displays of affection at the time.

Once inside the SCIF though, Justin sat down and became strangely thoughtful. Tamika remembered the evening in his apartment when he fed her a gourmet meal and surprised her about his conversion to Christianity, along with his serious concerns for America. She had shared the first with Jason; for some reason, she hadn't felt compelled to share the second.

"Tamika," Justin started. "Have you ever felt you were part of something big, I mean really big, and you were only able to see some very small part of it?"

"Well, I guess that just about covers everything here at DPI, doesn't it?" she responded.

"What if I told you that I believe this is just the tip of a very large iceberg?"

Tamika cocked her head to one side. He'd gotten her interest.

"And, you know how sometimes a person you most trust, you later find out was just using you?"

Does he know about my calls to the senator?

"Okay...something really big, and an issue of trust?" she raised her eyebrows.

Justin stood and began pacing.

"Honey, I can't get it out of my mind that we were not supposed to be able to intercept that warhead back in November. It was launched just a few months before Guardian was operational, while it was being transported, without the test pilot, and I already told you about the targeting software issue. It took miracles to pull off what we did."

Yep. Just like the night at his apartment.

"I'm about to let you in on something that less than ten people know about. Then after our morning meeting, I want you to meet somebody."

He turned to face her and took a deep breath.

"Roger is alive."

She dropped into the nearest chair, mouth agape.

Over the next thirty minutes, Justin brought her up to date on the transformation, the secret alert facility at Grand Forks, and the incredible test results. Tamika went with Justin to the morning meeting with her head spinning.

Man, do I have some information to share with Senator Matthews now!

As soon as the thought came, she dismissed it. He'd known all along. And if she told him that she now knew one of the best-kept secrets in the United States, she'd put Justin's security clearance and position at risk. She was impressed and more than a little surprised at the risk Justin had taken to share everything with her.

Why?

After the meeting, she and Justin drove to a parking area on the beach. It was a beautiful Tuesday morning on Florida's East Coast. The low surf, a few puffy clouds, and the sound of seagulls as they lazily circled looking for food; it's what postcards were made of. More than once she dozed during the morning drive.

A few moments after they parked, a rental minivan pulled up driven by an attractive redhead. Justin smiled at Tamika as he got out of his car and walked around to open her door.

"Honey, if you were shocked at what I told you before, this'll absolutely blow your mind!"

After he had made the introductions, they entered the van, Tamika in the front passenger seat and Justin in the seat directly behind Karen. Karen asked them to put any electronic devices into a small metal box which she then shut. Then she entered a code on the top of the box, and three LEDs turned from red to green.

"Are you CIA?" Tamika asked.

"Wish it was that simple. Believe me, I do," Karen responded with a smile.

She let that sink in for a few moments as she backed out and drove off.

"Tamika, you'll see me do a lot of cloak-and-dagger stuff that won't make much sense, but my life depends on it. And in just a few moments, it will also depend on Justin's perception of you as someone I…we…can trust.

"For example…" She turned down a dead-end street, drove to a cul-de-sac with lots for sale, and parked. Turning to face Tamika: "Here's a location without any cameras. Cameras at shopping centers, convenience stores, traffic lights, interstates, and such are good enough now that experts can read lips from hundreds of yards away. And this box not only shields RF going in or out of phones, but also GPS tracking and any common surveillance bugs within thirty meters of us."

"Okay…" Tamika looked back and forth between Karen in the front seat, and Justin sitting behind Karen in the back seat.

Justin spoke up. "Honey, there are some things you should know about our sponsor, and what appears to be going on around us. Did you know that Cliff spends hours most Sundays in the Flight Simulator? And only an hour or two the entire rest of the week at DPI? And while the rest of us work seventy-plus hour weeks, he travels a lot. I'm not sure where he's going, but I don't think he's going on vacations."

Karen's voice became more intense. "Tamika, I understand that Senator Matthews had something to do with your internship at DPI. You need to know that he is the exact reason I have to take all of these precautions. I personally know of ten people he had killed, and he almost killed me. And…" she shuddered, "…there were other things he did to me I still don't want to talk about. I'm not exaggerating to tell you, that man is drenched in blood."

+ + +

Skylar was deeply, profoundly grateful that he'd learned his lesson. He no longer reported the "good news" to Jason Matthews every time he had a strong lead on "the lady." Over the years there had been too many false alarms, too many callbacks where he had to report that Karen had again escaped.

Asheville was turning up dry. She had once again, apparently, completely disappeared off the face of the earth.

Is she also a ghost? He wondered.

Jason had called a few months earlier about the Charleston, South Carolina incident. There was no way Jason could have missed that, as it was the lead story on all news media for days. Jason initiated that call, and Skylar was delighted to tell the senator that he'd already initiated Plan Alpha almost a full day earlier. Still, he had to report back a week later that all attempts to track her had failed.

The Asheville incident? A woman lifting the side of a van was certainly newsworthy, but with all the riots and cultural meltdowns fanned by media for ratings, it didn't qualify as a lead story on most networks. Jason likely missed it. He hadn't called, and Skylar kept it quiet. He just kept looking. He continued to scour through video surveillance feeds, check driver's licenses at rental agencies, and anything else he could think of.

Skylar Brown thought long and hard about calling one of his former suppliers for some pills. Just this once.

49. DILEMMA

Karen took a deep breath and regained her composure. It also gave Tamika a moment to feel the weight of Karen's hatred, distrust, and hurt toward the man who had been Tamika's benefactor. Or, who appeared to be…

Karen continued. "Now, there are some things you should know about me.

"First, I'm almost twice as old as you might think I am. I'm not immortal, but scientists—all dead thanks to Jason Matthews—believed the DNA reboot I took back in the early 90's should keep me in full health till around 110. Right now, I'm fifty-six."

She gave Tamika a few moments to process all that. The young African American looked back and forth between the stranger and Justin. He somberly nodded his agreement, that he'd already verified her story.

"Now, and I say this as a simple fact, not to boast. The transformation has brought me to where by now, I probably have the highest IQ of anyone alive today. I had to stop taking the tests because Jason used the last one I took to track me down. I barely escaped. But the reality is that while I've had to stay on the run and relocate at least once a year, I've completed dozens of doctorate-level online classes. I've studied everything from molecular biochemistry to quantum physics. Justin told me about the ternary computer in your aircraft. I've already drafted plans for a five-state computer. It will likely be an order of magnitude faster, use less power, and be more reliable than your computer or any quantum computers now under development.

"Third, I'm not just a Christian. I've become a scholar of the Old Testament, New Testament, and especially of prophecy.

"Here's the bottom line. Take my word for now, but I hope you'll study for yourself like Justin's been doing since the trans-dimensional shift took place…and Justin, Roger's right. The fact that the trans-dimensional effects differentiate based on planar vice gravitational axes? I believe that proves that gravity is also trans-dimensional. Which not only does away with a need for hypothetical dark matter and dark energy but also provides one more proof against a 'Big Bang' origin."

She caught herself, smiled and shook her head. "Sorry. I get carried away. Not ADHD; more like multi-core brain functioning. Tamika, hundreds of prophecies over a period of thousands of years have been fulfilled in precise, minute detail. The Bible tells Christians to be aware and to expect what's called the 'Blessed Hope,' the return of Christ for His Church. But we are not told to climb a mountain, suck our collective thumbs, and wait for the world to end.

"I'd like to tell you about the most important decision you can ever make, and why it's urgent that you make it quickly. About why I believe what I believe, and how you can receive God's gift of eternal life through Christ.

"But right now, I need to warn you about things you personally need to watch out for. Please believe that I have learned to check my sources very, very carefully."

Two hours later, Justin had taken Tamika back to her car at DPI and she was on her way home to rest. Not that she'd be able to sleep a wink. The senator expected her call early that evening. Tamika's stomach was in knots. She knew the man was powerful. She never expected that he might be dangerous. But according to Karen, he was more than any of that; he was diabolical.

As she sifted through everything Karen had shared, she had to admit that beyond his smooth facade, Jason did always seem to have a hidden motive. Then she remembered something else. She remembered what eventually happened to Professor Jacobs back at the college. His unethical tactics against fellow college staff members were discovered. He was unceremoniously fired. Additional investigations led to his conviction of attempted extortion against several faculty members. Like being back-handed by her alcoholic father or drug-addicted mother, it suddenly struck Tamika just how close she must have been to being drawn into the professor's scandal. How was it that her involvement wasn't discovered? That her own activities weren't brought before the College Board or into the courtroom?

"Thank God!" she said.

Realizing how devastating such a revelation would have been to her future, she sincerely meant it.

She also had felt a change in her feelings for Justin. Tamika had avoided boys in high school. Most were shallow jerks. Then she left Section Eight public housing, went to college, and didn't have time for dating. But since she graduated, well, she was probably as much of a player as Justin had admitted to. But the change in him was starting to affect her as well. She was being treated with respect as an equal. Even cherished?

Now both her thoughts and emotions were in turmoil.

+ + +

Eight hours later, it was far worse. Tamika shook uncontrollably. She had to hold her wine glass with both hands.

Through the sleepless day, she carefully reviewed, analyzed, and evaluated everything she heard that morning. She devised an amazingly simple test.

With each call, Senator Matthews seemed to start the conversation with sincere personal interest in her, her career ambitions, and her relationship with Justin. If it were true that he was only manipulating her to be his eyes and ears, it would likely lead to increasingly compromising or illegal assignments in the future. Maybe she could discern his motives if she didn't play along with his little game. From what Karen shared, if he did react out of character, it would be subtle. Jason was a master at subterfuge, so Tamika made sure her radar was at maximum as she made her call.

As always, Jason called her back from his private, secure phone a few moments later. As if he were following a script, she perceived the same line of discussion as before. Why hadn't she noticed it? He began by expressing his interest in her and her career. She stayed on that subject awhile, and even went back to it when he asked questions about her and Justin. Then again when he asked about operations at DPI.

After a few moments, Jason interrupted and encouraged her loyalty, but seemed a little more pointed and agitated. He asked again about DPI, and she briefly skimmed over some general information, conveniently omitting the visit by one Karen Richardson. Then she asked about the possibility of future work for her as a staffer for him in Washington.

It was subtle, so subtle, but she could sense even more agitation, followed by a fleeting reminder that she owed him. She continued her lighthearted chat about her future aspirations a few moments more, and it happened. Like a plate glass window slammed shut so hard that it shattered into a thousand shards, he interrupted. "Tamika, don't tell me you've been listening to his

Christianity crap? Look, I have to go. Call me next week, and you'd better have something to report."

And he ended the call.

Most people would attribute his response to a bad day, or to the overwhelming pressures and demands of his position.

Tamika wasn't most people. Especially after the earful she received that morning by a young-looking older woman who would fight for her life rather than fall back into that man's hands. And his anger toward Christianity? Not Buddhism, or Islam, or any of a hundred of other religions or philosophies. This was real, and personal, and visceral—and Jason Matthews was eternally on the opposite side of that fence.

Tamika was frightened. Her hands continued shaking as she poured another glass of wine. She wasn't sipping tonight.

Unbeknownst to her, Karen and Justin had both been earnestly praying for her all day.

Thoughts swirled.

A fifty-six-year-old woman who appeared to be thirty-two, and who could live in full health to 110 or beyond.

A hypersonic manned interceptor and its pilot—if the mid-sixties engineer could be called a fighter pilot—now both trans-dimensional. *Guess he does qualify, as he flew the plane and saved the country from a nuclear attack.*

Her love interest becomes a Christian, and he and this strange lady tell her about fulfilled prophecy.

Her benefactor, the man responsible for her job and who she'd been confiding in, is a cold-hearted, blood-thirsty killer; and one of the most powerful people in the United States.

What in the world is really going on around here?

Tamika was not a weak woman. You don't make it to adulthood growing up in the projects, then get out of there and make it through college by being weak. She wasn't weepy either. But she desperately wanted to be in Justin's arms and for him to hold her tight and tell her everything would be alright. She wanted him to be a strong but tender and caring man in her life, what neither she nor her own mother had ever known.

For at least for the next few days, she urgently needed everything else to go away.

She could not even begin to imagine the extent that her entire life was about to change...forever.

Guardian – The Reckoning

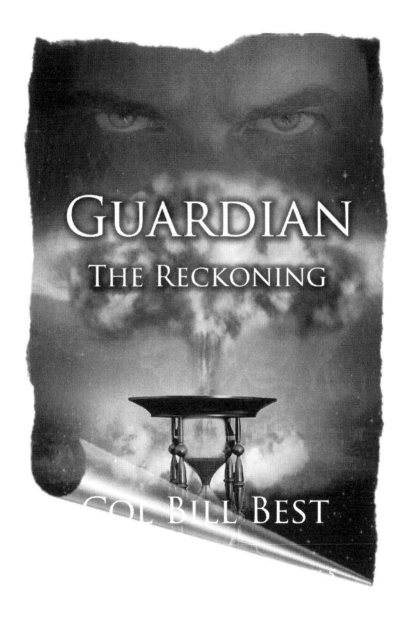

50. SUNDAY

As usual, Sunday was quiet at Directed Paradigms, Incorporated—DPI. Once the Saturday night crew left Sunday morning, the parking lot in front of the facility was typically vacant until the Monday morning shift arrived.

Justin drove up and parked. He and Tamika stepped out of his car as Karen pulled up in her rental. The three of them walked into the company's Sensitive Compartmented Information Facility—SKIF.

Tamika had taken time off from DPI after her meeting with Justin and Karen, and her conversation with Jason. Also uncharacteristically—though it would not have surprised anyone at DPI—she had spent those nights at Justin's apartment. So had Karen, once she made sure she could enter without being seen by security cameras.

The three of them, and the two ladies while Justin was at work, spent hours evaluating the news stories. They looked over Bible prophecies and discussed events at DPI both before and since the "transformation" of Roger and System One.

Karen had brought more small electronic packages with her, and she assured them that they could talk securely while her RF jammer and sweeping audio noise cloak were on. She would also daily scan around the apartment for eavesdropping devices. Before they would discuss anything that could put them in jeopardy, they put their electronic devices in her metal case. Like clockwork, they would sequester them for just under twenty minutes, then they would all check for missed calls or messages to prevent suspicious gaps in their electronic availability.

To Roger's immense delight on alert in Grand Forks, North Dakota, he was kept in the loop. Karen would tether her TEMPEST-proof Bluetooth keyboard to Justin's Multiphone and use the Enigma codec, sending and receiving messages at lightning speed. Justin speculated that her typing speed was well over 100 words per minute; so fast she nearly communicated with Roger in real time despite his trans-dimensional shift.

By the time Justin came in from work on Saturday night, they had made several significant discoveries.

First, they determined that the nuclear attack against the United States had to have been planned as a catalyst, an event that would quickly start a chain reaction of other events. The attack's failure prevented those other events from occurring, at least for the time being. The precise timing of the attack indicated a high probability that a person in the planning knew that Guardian System One would have soon been operational. The attack was apparently expedited to occur before that milestone. It may have even been planned at the precise time when the aircraft should not have been flyable; being transported back across the U.S. in the back of a C-17 cargo aircraft. As a final precaution, someone sabotaged Guardian's targeting software. Finally, Karen was adamant that 1960s Soviet technology would not have remained operational after so many years. The ICBM must have been a recent, ultra-secret build to have possessed the treaty-prohibited FOBS capability.

All that meant a well-connected, powerful, and secretive group of international players. A group that was immensely well-funded. It all fit right in line with Biblical predictions. It seemed pretty clear that Jason Matthews was positioned to become one of the top world leaders. It wasn't difficult for them to learn that with key conservative U.S. government officials meeting off-site that night, and more vulnerable to attack, Jason would have been next in line to the Presidency. As for Cliff Nesmith, he was one of Jason's underlings—likely just a pawn—feeding him information and doing his bidding.

So, the next questions were: What next, and when? And how did Justin, Tamika, and Karen fit in?

What, now, for Roger? A retirement-age engineer who launched Guardian out the back of the Globemaster III cargo plane, intercepted a nuclear warhead, and destroyed it with an EMP? What of Roger and Guardian, now somehow trans-dimensional from the combined EMPs from the aircraft and the exploding nuke? The loneliest man on earth, on secret alert in Grand Forks in what appears to be an empty hangar.

Something else occurred on that Saturday. Tamika's agitation and fear had escalated into a full-blown panic attack.

"It's all bogus! Nothing I've believed is true, everything I've doubted is. I'm scared and worried and…and I just feel the whole world's dirty, even me. I've washed my hands dozens of times today, and I'm not even OCD! And all this stuff I'm reading from thousands of years ago? It's in today's news!" She was shaking and fighting back tears.

Karen reached out and took the younger woman's hands in hers and looked tenderly into her eyes.

"Honey, the world is dirty. You're dirty. The Bible calls it sin and says we've all sinned and come short of the glory of God. And we can't save ourselves from it. That's why all the religions of the world fail. Man can't be good enough to get to God. So, Christ died for us, the sinless for the sinful, so that anyone who will believe in Him will not perish but have eternal life. He, himself is the bridge we can cross over to get to God. We can be saved...clean before God...adopted as children into his forever family. Not by any works of righteousness we do, but by his grace He saves us. We receive it by faith."

Tears ran down Tamika's cheeks.

"Everything is so...so...evil! They're willing to kill hundreds of thousands...millions..."

"Over 100 million died last century in world wars brought about by communism, socialism, and Jihadist attacks. Millions of innocent Jews and others died in the Holocaust, and millions more Russians and Chinese died in their own countries. Babies have died by the millions in their mothers' wombs. Elderly and infirm are being euthanized.

"It's a very evil world. Jesus told us it would be like in the days of Noah, where everyone was so wicked that he destroyed them all except Noah and his family. Or like the days of Lot, when the wickedness of Sodom and Gomorrah was so horrible that he rained down fire, saving only Lot and his daughters. And they weren't all that great, either! We're warned that while God still offers salvation, very soon his judgment will fall on this evil, unbelieving world. He'll literally allow all hell to break loose."

She hugged the younger woman as Tamika sobbed.

"Tamika, don't you want peace? Don't you want to be above all this? For your life to count for something good?"

When Justin came in that evening, he was surprised by a gourmet meal rivaling his own best efforts, and two women greeting him with smiles and giggles like schoolgirls with a secret. He looked deep into Tamika's eyes, saw the peace that had been missing for days, and knew that she had chosen Jesus.

Much had occurred in the past few days as they tried to put the pieces of the puzzle together. One final piece was Justin and Roger's decision to formalize the bond that had formed between the four of them. That was the purpose of the visit to DPI on Sunday morning.

In one of the top secret safes in the SKIF, Justin removed an encrypted external solid state drive. He connected it to a tablet workstation, then one at a time, he connected Karen's and Tamika's Multiphones, loaded in the Enigma App and their personal digital keys. He spent an hour setting up Tamika's phone and explaining the App to her while Karen skimmed through hundreds of screens of Guardian documentation on an engineering workstation. She looked at interface diagrams, 3-D CAD drawings, flowcharts, and technical specifications as casually as if she were glancing over vacation pictures.

How things have changed, Justin thought as he gave her access to the very core of the aircraft's ultra-classified data. In days' past, he would have reported the security compromise on his phone and turned it in for destruction. And he *never* would have allowed a person without adequate security clearance and need-to-know to have access to even Confidential information. Certainly, he wouldn't have given access to information well above Top Secret. But studying the software code the morning after the intercept had quickly convinced Justin that the entire project was already compromised, far more than just the data. All the events since then further confirmed his suspicions. He, Karen, and Tamika were the only ones he believed might be able to unravel the truth and possibly protect the program...and somehow, the country. She definitely had a need-to-know.

He finished with Tamika's phone about the time Karen closed the last engineering document. Justin just looked at her and shook his head. Even more disconcerting, she smiled and went through all the set-up on her own phone, duplicating what Justin did for Tamika in a fraction of the time. Had she really just followed his every step while simultaneously looking over highly technical documentation that would have taken seasoned professionals weeks to absorb? Justin again shook his head in bewilderment.

After half an hour of instruction, testing, and ensuring the codec couldn't be discovered, they were confident that The Four were ready to tackle the world.

Justin opened the SKIF door for the two women, just as Cliff Nesmith was reaching for the handle.

"Mr. Nesmith!" blurted Tamika.

"Cliff..." A startled Justin and Tamika stared like deer in the headlights, while Cliff looked hard at an unknown redhead just walking out of a...out of *his*...top secret SKIF on a Sunday afternoon.

Karen smiled sweetly and extended her hand. "Mr. Nesmith? A pleasure. I'm Sandra Taylor. Telepresence robots and the security requirements of a SKIF don't usually play well together."

She reached into her purse and pulled out a business card, "Sandra Taylor, Telepresence Security Consulting." She handed the card to Cliff.

"It's possible to not only support secure telepresence, which, of course, you already do now. But you can also maintain gigabit throughput and seamless audio-video integration without the artifacts, buffering, and dropouts that end up defeating the purpose of telepresence."

She stepped back so she could look at Cliff, Tamika, and Justin.

"Thank you again for bringing me here on a Sunday so I wouldn't conflict with your operation and security protocols. Please let me know if I can evaluate upgrading your current OS-12V4 system, or if you'd be interested in a quote on our VOX-37B."

Justin was stunned. She knew exactly what she was talking about, and he vaguely remembered that it was indeed someone named Sandra who developed the popular VOX series of telepresence robots. He had been intrigued with the leading-edge technology he'd read about in one of his tech magazines a few years earlier. He played along.

"Sandra, like I said, we often use the capability, and I think the new system would significantly help our coordination with our customer. Right now, though, we need to focus on an important deadline. Maybe we'll be able to get back to you in a couple of months."

In a few more moments, they were on their way to their cars and Cliff had entered the SKIF. Justin wondered to what extent Cliff had accepted Karen's…Sandra's…stellar performance.

He's wondering what we're doing here, and I'll bet he's going into the Simulator.

Justin cast a sideways glance at Karen.

How incredibly believable! I hadn't even noticed that the OS-12V4 was in there today. She not only saw it, but recognized it, and on-the-fly recommended a better state-of-the-art solution; one that she apparently invented herself!

He marveled that she could remain incognito yet still research, invent, and even launch new companies, and then just move on.

What else has she been responsible for?

Justin took a long, slow breath as he remote-started his hybrid car and unlocked the doors.

Karen Richardson most likely really is the smartest person on earth.

51. MONDAY: All-Hands-on-Deck

The months of twelve-hour shifts at DPI were over. Discussions during the previous Friday morning meeting confirmed that Guardian System Two should be ready for transport the following Friday. The final night shift had ended Sunday morning. That was the day Justin, Tamika, and Karen ran into Cliff at DPI. On Monday, the company began full team shifts of seven-to-seven…or later.

It would be five full days of double- and triple-checking everything. Teams reviewed engineering documents, retested systems and subsystems, and identified and addressed any anomalies. Test review boards developed an abbreviated acceptance test plan that would take System Two through flight testing to Fully Mission Capable.

In other words, more of the same. A lot more, in a lot less time. "One test can invalidate a thousand studies," stated a sign at DPI. A significant breakthrough in Cliff's additive manufacturing again proved its worth. The design-and-build process automatically included built-in-testing as an integral component of each subsystem. Tests weren't just performed on completed equipment; testing was completed literally during the build-up. No external Automated Test Equipment—ATE—required; all testing could be completed and reported by the aircraft itself.

System Two appeared ready.

The team finalized plans to covertly transport the aircraft to the nearby airfield, where it would be loaded into a C-17 for a flight to Nevada. Monday afternoon, Justin told General Alvarez that they would be ready for transport Friday morning.

General Alvarez passed that information on to Senator Matthews as part of his weekly report.

+ + +

In Grand Forks, Roger suspected that he'd lost over ten pounds during the winter and spring. The good news was that he looked slimmer than he had in six years. The bad news was that the gall bladder attacks were occurring almost daily and were lasting longer. His communications with Karen had been considerable since she acquired the Enigma codec, and she asked many questions about his condition. Roger told her how many months he had suffered from the attacks, what meds he had tried, what his diet consisted of, his symptoms, and more. He discussed the electro-shock phenomenon that apparently healed his paralysis, had a temporary calming effect on him, and also seemed to increase and intensify his dreams during the few hours he slept.

The two would also discuss the "transition effect" as she called it, and how the lizard was doing. Roger would leave food and water out for the creature. It tried to go outside the "boundary" a few times but quickly returned. It seemed to realize that it had to stay within the area Roger had taped off around the aircraft. Roger also reported that the lizard moved in "Roger's" time, not in slow motion.

They would discuss how a lizard could adapt, but rodents and bugs could not. They would speculate about the physics of the trans-dimensional shift. And Karen would chase rabbits, speculating on the time shift in terms of the space-time-matter/energy fabric of the known universe.

More than once, Roger would ask how she came to be an expert on everything from physiology to physics.

"I read a lot."

"Well, it's giving me a brain cramp trying to keep up!"

+ + +

"Tamika...?!"

"I need to sit down!"

Tamika sat, trembling. She leaned over and grabbed her knees and rocked as Justin knelt beside her and put his arm around her shoulder.

"Who called?" he asked.

"Jason Matthews. He called from that secret phone of his. I never know it's him; it just shows up as 'Unlisted.'"

She sat up, leaned back, closed her eyes, and took several long, slow breaths. Then she looked at Justin.

"Supposedly, he was just checking status since our regular weekly call. But I feel so uncomfortable talking to him now. And he's always...well, usually…so polite, so controlled. Yet, I don't know, it's like, since that call where I tested him, it's like there's a hidden agenda and a veiled threat. One thing he did say is that he's adamant that he's going to be in Nevada this weekend for the first test flight. He said that not even a presidential recall would keep him away."

"Hmm…"

"OK, I've seen that look. What are you thinking?" she asked, somewhat calmer.

Justin stood and walked around the room for a few moments.

"It just might be possible…"

He suddenly turned and faced her.

"His phone. He always calls you from some kind of special phone?"

"Always. Even when I call him first, he calls me right back from that other phone of his. We never discuss anything on a regular line."

Justin knelt down in front of her, put his hands on her knees, and looked intently into her eyes.

"Tamika, have you ever seen this phone? This is very important!"

"Well…" she paused thoughtfully. "Yes. Yes, one time I did. We were talking, back when I met him and before I came to DPI. Somebody called on his regular Multiphone, and he did the same thing he does with me. He said he'd call right back. He hung up, excused himself, and pulled an odd phone out of his coat as he walked away. Why?"

"An odd phone," Justin repeated. "What makes you say that?"

Tamika placed her hands on top of Justin's hands, leaned forward inches from his face.

"Because, my dear, it looked like one of those old-style flip phones. But it was really strange; it was all flat black, with a red border. Really tacky."

She leaned back as Justin startled her by jumping to his feet and pumping the air.

"Yes!!!!"

Tamika hadn't seen him so excited in months.

"I gotta tell Roger!" he exclaimed, grabbed his phone and began dictating.

"Roger, he's got one of our phones! One of the ones we sent to DARPA, with our codec installed! The dude let the program die so he could use the technology himself!"

Roger's reply came back: "You can open the 'Compromised' protocol and set it to 'Track.' We'll know exactly where he is!"

Justin responded: "Got it. I'll also turn on 'Report' and we can know who he's been contacting on that phone for the past few months!"

"Good idea. One more step. He may have both of the phones and alternate between them. Or, he could have given one to another key person. You should assume they're both compromised and set them both to Track and Report."

There was a pause. Then another message from Roger arrived.

Justin frowned.

"What is it, Justin?" asked Tamika.

"Another message from Roger." He read it to her: "Justin, you and the others may have to go this alone soon. I'm really bad. I'm dying. You and the ladies get together and pray for me. See if God reveals anything to you. Otherwise, I need you and Karen to help me plan the best exit strategy. I think I need to launch while I still can, then try to set down in northern Alaska. I believe that'll have the least potential impact on populations and the ecology."

Tamika put her hand on Justin's shoulder. "Justin, I'm..."

Another message appeared from Roger: "Justin. Hurry, my friend. I don't think I can last more than another few days."

+ + +

"Yes, Justin?"

"General Alvarez, are you alone?"

"I am. Is there a problem with our schedule?"

"No, Sir. It's actually more critical than that. Much more. I believe you've met Tamika?"

Justin and Tamika were both in the SKIF speaking to the General, who was coming to them over the telepresence 'bot.

"Yes. Hello, Tamika. Thank you for helping compress this schedule for us. Wish it wasn't such a national emergency, but we have to get a bird on alert."

"Sir, that's part of what we need to talk to you about," said Justin. "First, you may be about to lose your first one, and second, we may know why America came under attack."

"Tamika…?"

"Yes, General, she knows about Roger. And there's a lot more we both know, and that we believe we need to share with someone in authority. You're it, and there's not much time. And please be very careful about where all this goes from here. I believe we'll all be in personal danger."

"Go on."

+ + +

Jason didn't often allow himself to gloat, even in private. But he'd finished his nightly game and his first drink, and now laughed out loud as the cacophony he called "music" engulfed him. He enjoyed his second drink, and even more, he enjoyed thinking about how he was going to clear up the loose ends. All of them.

I hate loose ends.

First, Justin and Tamika. DPI could now run without them, and Guardian wouldn't be all that important in the new world order anyway. He laughed again. This is one he'd order himself, and he already knew how he wanted to see it done. He hated Christians like Justin and by now, probably Tamika as well. This would be sweet.

Second, Roger. It was time to send him and Guardian System One all the way into their new dimension. He'd have the hangar bulldozed down over them. "I can do that," he shouted out loud. No one would even ask why. At least, no one who mattered. And if it set off a...well, an unpleasant little explosion? As president, he'd just add that to the list of "attacks" justifying emergency martial law.

Third, Juan. President Juan Garcia. *What in the world was he thinking?* This Saturday night, virtually all conservatives in the Beltway, along with him, Vice, and the Speaker; they'll all be together! They'll be in one venue that Jason can easily take out. That call from his Secret Service informant had made his day.

Tamika had assured him that everything was "go" for System Two. His Russian counterpart confirmed that the first operational exercise of Russian Tupolev PAK-DA strategic bombers was on schedule. And his puppet Cliff Nesmith was ready to suit up and change the world.

Guess I'll keep Cliff around. At least for now. Still working on that facility...

Jason had tasked Cliff to manufacture micro-RFID implantable chips and build additional DPI-01 supercomputers—the same suitcase-size ternary computers that powered the flight and targeting routines in Guardian. One in each region, networked together, and One World Peace Now—OWPN—could quickly transition the world to a cashless society.

And track every person on the planet! Yeah, Cliff stays for another year or two.

The transition plan was nowhere near as elegant as the original planned NUDET over the East Coast, but it would work.

The good general was another matter. Jason had coordinated a trip for Alvarez to brief the Senate Armed Services Committee on Friday afternoon, and he made sure the general was invited to the conservative off-site on Saturday. "Anything for a friend," Jason chuckled. He'd be glad to add Lieutenant General Alvarez to the impending carnage. Nothing like a good clean sweep. Rey was too much of an old-school patriot; therefore, difficult to control. Worse, Jason had seen him bow his head before a meal one evening, setting off his "Christian" detector.

Everyone else was so easy to manipulate. All the other world religions? Just help them earn what they want. Promise them Nirvana, or seventy-two virgins. Tell them they could become one of 144,000 or an eternal god over their own world. Encourage them to become one with Mother Earth, or to follow the *do's and don'ts* of whatever holy book someone wrote under some worldly or other-worldly influence. Even atheists. Just overwhelm them with philosophics. They all had their hot buttons. So easy to distract. So easy to lead like sheep to a slaughter.

But not Christians. Not the real ones.

Matthews took a deep breath.

No. I will succeed. This will go my way. I will be the most powerful being this world has ever seen!

Senator Jason Matthews turned the noise up louder and twirled like a little kid in the center of his room, sipping his drink, and laughing at all the little people under his command.

Maybe a young boy tonight?

52. GOODBYE

Wednesday, 1500 EST:
Kim Brandon made her last phone call. After five minutes, she was as sure as humanly possible that all the equipment would arrive early Friday morning. Each of the cases, from several locations, would be at her motel in time for her final trip. She would load them into a rented van and head for the base. She had already arranged for suitable credentials to guarantee that neither she nor her cargo would be subject to inspection. It wouldn't do for anyone to look at her ultra-specialized equipment, or at the strange suit quickly manufactured per specifications she had memorized during her trip to DPI.

Kim was more excited than she'd been in years. It was like the first time she'd left home to go to college, or even her honeymoon. She wasn't at all bothered by the knowledge that it was a one-way trip.

She carefully packed her passports and IDs and put on the makeup to match her current hair color. Then she picked up the dental devices and glasses. She already had on the correct finger print gloves.

Should be the last time I'll ever need any of this.

She carefully looked at herself in the mirror. Then Kim—Karen Lane Richardson—took all her belongings and headed for the airport.

Wednesday, 1700 EST:
"Are you sure, Mr. President?"

Chet Rowland was a short, stocky, retired Marine—some say once a Marine, always a Marine—and addressed President Garcia with both respect and sincere concern.

"Chet, what's going to happen is going to happen. But only when the very last person is led to salvation during the Church Age, this age of grace. If that door closes this Saturday, so be it. But if not, I'm going to serve my country and my God every day I can." He paused and grinned. "Hmm. Sounds kind of hokey doesn't it."

"Not at all, Sir," the younger man replied. "Guess that's why I'm where I am as well."

The President smiled. "Yes. Yes, you're right."

While Chet was high up the food chain, he was not the chief of the Secret

Service. He was, however, the one man who Juan and Priscilla had decided they could confide in. As usual, Priscilla took the lead. The salt-and-pepper-haired Hispanic was smart, elegant, and had a pleasantly disarming personality that allowed her to fit in with just about anyone, anywhere. She had simply engaged the different senior security personnel in casual conversations, chatting with them over the course of several weeks. Among many topics, she'd drop in a question about their favorite wines. Not that drinking disqualified a person from consideration, but all too many of the agents gave such detailed answers that it appeared they drank to excess.

She also asked what they would do if they won a lottery. She immediately took a liking to Chet, who answered that he didn't gamble. He did say, though, that if he suddenly came into a large amount of money, he would tithe and give an additional amount of money to several key ministries he and his wife supported. Then he'd pay off their mortgage and save the rest for some things the two of them had wanted to do for years.

Priscilla was impressed. "Hmm. 'In all your ways acknowledge him…' "

" '…and He will make your paths straight,' " Chet had finished without skipping a beat.

So, Juan and Priscilla discretely invited him to an informal chat, which turned out to be so much more.

"Sir, I guess I'd look for those who have paid a price."

"Paid a price? Paid a price. Hmm." the President had repeated. *Like the Vice and the Speaker. That's why I trust them.* "Yes. Jesus said to count the cost."

"I know some Marines and a few Sailors I'd trust with my life. Some of our detail, actually most of them, as well. I'm not saying someone has to be a Christian to be trusted, and I'm sure we both know a lot of folks claiming to be Christians who I wouldn't trust to pick up my mail. Like I say, Sir, if it came down to it, I'd look for men and women who've been willing to put it on the line."

That had certainly been the case during an earlier administration where Christians in uniform, especially senior officers, were intentionally passed over for promotions. One officer, just to test the system, quoted verbatim a prayer from General George Washington at an official function. The result? She was threatened with an Article 15. Garcia also thought of one of his generals who had been held back because of his convictions, until Juan became president and promoted him.

"Mr. President?"

"Sorry, Chet. Just thinking about all we've been through the past weeks. Yes, I'm sure. And thank you. Thanks for your witness, friendship, counsel, prayers, and concern. I'm proud to be in this with you."

The younger man blushed. "Thank you, Sir," was all he could say.

+ + +

Friday, 0730 EST:
"Okay, that's it. Time's up."

No more discussions, no more waiting. Roger knew it was time to go. Like that Saturday evening many months—it seemed like years—ago, when he was lowered into Guardian to try an impossible intercept, he knew he was going home. It was time to make sure that he and the aircraft would never be a menace to others while he still was able to make that call.

Roger crawled toward the aircraft. No pressure suit needed for this one last flight. He looked around. No, nothing else he needed to take with him either. Once the aircraft cleared the hangar, everything else would eventually "change back"—much to the confusion and consternation of many. Probably be a TV show made about it one day, with experts speculating that Grand Forks had housed aliens.

Sweat poured from his forehead. He wiped his eyes and rolled onto his back, exhausted. Just a few feet to go. *And at Mach Ten, less than an hour.*

Another wave of pain engulfed him. He rolled to his side, pulled into a fetal position and passed out.

After what seemed an eternity, Roger awoke, feeling somewhat revived. The pain wasn't quite as bad, and the cold sweat had ended, although his jumpsuit was soaked.

He crawled the rest of the way to the fuselage, grabbed the extended ladder rungs resolutely, and climbed up. Power on, retract ladder, close canopy, and start the engine. The datalink connection installed in the hangar door engaged and the door opened.

Roger took a few moments to send one last message on the secure link to Justin, Tamika, and Karen:

"Friends, I love you all. I'm looking forward to seeing my wife and kids soon, and each of you again one day. I'm leaving the telemetry link active so

Justin can know our final location and respond accordingly, whatever that would be. I'll try to set down easy so I don't cause a catastrophe. I'll go as far as I can into the wilderness in case I go in rough and set off what Karen calls a 'transitional event.' I'm trying to fly clear of populated areas and won't go near any large bodies of water where I could set off a tsunami if I crash."

He gunned the engine and rolled out the open door, onto the taxiway toward the end of the runway.

"Sorry I couldn't hold out any longer. But I don't want to be responsible for thousands of deaths. So that's it. Now I've got to try to stay conscious and fly this thing. I'm out. Maranatha! Send."

The aircraft cleared the runway with fully two-thirds left to go. Roger raised the gear, pointed the nose up at forty-five degrees, and lit the SRBs. The thrust slammed him back in his seat as the aircraft streaked into the clear, cold morning air. The magnets were sixty percent towards superconductive...

+ + +

<u>Friday, 0850 EST</u>:

Justin and Tamika, along with PDI's test pilot Tim Cason, watched as Guardian System Two was carefully rolled into the C-17 and secured. It was quite an event. The ultra-classified aircraft was completely covered in tarps and transported by a wide-load semitrailer truck. At the air base, the semi backed up to an open hangar. Crews removed the tarps and rolled the aircraft down a ramp into the hangar. The semi drove off, and in its place, a C-17 backed up to the hangar, whereupon crews rolled System Two up into its cargo bay.

The transfer had been meticulously orchestrated so no overhead satellites could get a glimpse of the aircraft. With even commercial satellites now able to read license plates from low orbit, neither DPI nor the government was taking any chances. Flight testing would be another matter, but the aircraft's ultra-stealth radar coatings and active optical camouflage would be operational at that point.

+ + +

Friday, 0920 EST:
Woods everywhere.

He had tried. God knows, he had tried. Roger had screamed across Saskatchewan, the top of Alberta, continued across the Northwest and Yukon Territories, then into Alaska's airspace. His goal was to gently set down into the Brooks Range, but the shakiness, tunnel vision, pain and profound weakness screamed that he'd never make it.

It's better to set down here in one piece than to make a crater trying to go farther.

He had already pulled back on the throttle and dropped down to 30,000 feet. As his speed dropped below Mach One, the scramjet flamed out and the ion drive disengaged. At 10,000 feet and 400 knots, he began lazy S-turns, throttled back the turbojet, and began looking for a suitable clearing in the trees.

At least I'm well clear of villages and towns.

At 5,000 feet, he chose the most promising real estate and pulled the turbojet down to idle while slowly circling and losing more altitude.

If I can just set down without initiating the transition effect, I'll open the canopy. Should freeze to death within minutes, even with my strange metabolism.

Tears welled in his eyes, and he had to wipe them to keep his vision clear. They were tears of joy.

He shouted. "Finally...finally, I'm going home. Jesus, Cindy, Frank, Susan; I'm coming home!"

He was mostly at peace, but not quite. One final, critical task lay before him. He turned from base to his final approach, dropping below 1,000 feet and steady at 140 knots. His heart dropped as he realized that the clearing he was aiming for was anything but! Yes, it was the only area clear of trees, and there was still enough snow to do a gear-up landing. But then he saw the boulders everywhere rising out of the snow. He was physically too far gone to climb out and try to find a frozen stream somewhere to slide in on.

In the end, the lack of a decent landing option was moot. The tightness that gripped his abdomen instantly turned into another massive cramp. He doubled over in the most intense agony he'd ever experienced. He felt the plane yaw and bank, and there was nothing he could do about it. Absolutely nothing.

+ + +

Friday, 1145 EST:

Justin and Tamika each shook Tim Cason's hand and wished him well. They were exhausted from their six-month marathon to bring the second Guardian hypersonic interceptor to this final stage. Tim's hours had been much more bearable, as his priorities were to continue studying and spending time in the Simulator. Now, Justin and Tamika were looking forward to a break in their schedule, while the retired Navy aviator would be the one pulling sixteen to eighteen-hour days.

Tim entered the cargo aircraft, the ramp was raised, and ground support equipment pulled the massive aircraft out onto the tarmac.

"Well, there goes my baby," said Justin as he again wiped his brow.

"Getting nostalgic? I think the next line is, 'there she goes now,' " Tamika quipped.

They hugged, sighed, and held each other for a full minute. Justin gently stroked her hair.

"Well, we've done all we can at this point. You hungry?" he asked. The noon summer sun and humidity had them looking forward to sweet tea and air conditioning.

"Starved!" She grinned.

+ + +

Friday, 1530 EST:

It was a beautiful Space Coast day for a drive to the beach and some fresh seafood, and Justin thoroughly enjoyed every air-conditioned minute of it. He remarked to Tamika how nice it was to have a "real" server bring their food—fresh grouper and a basket of shrimp—rather than grabbing something from the customary digital kiosk at a deli.

Pleasantly full, he drove her to the beach for a mandatory barefoot walk in the fine, white sand along the waterline. The two of them laughed like children as together they chased and then ran away from the endless waves. Justin inhaled the warm salt air and marveled at how such a simple act of enjoying a piece of God's creation could restore the soul. Then he surprised her with a quick drive to an area with several blocks of novelty shops that she thoroughly enjoyed browsing through. Mid-afternoon they cooled down with some frozen yogurt—and time seemed to stand still.

Finally, they headed back to his apartment. Justin glanced at the lovely young lady beside him in his open convertible. The afternoon had been perfect, and all the tension and stress of the previous months and recent days had been replaced with a sense of peace. All Justin was thinking about now was the world-class steak he was going to prepare for dinner.

Justin smiled. *A great start to a few days off.*

While Cliff had been strangely aloof during construction of System Two, he insisted on taking over the test phase out west. He also instructed Justin and Tamika to take some well-earned and much needed time off. They didn't argue.

The Friday afternoon traffic on I-95 wasn't too heavy yet, but Justin knew he and Tamika still had a lot to discuss. He engaged Auto-Drive and set the exit number on the car's touchscreen. The car automatically navigated to the far-left AD Lane, data-linking with other Auto-Drive vehicles and increasing the speed to ten miles per hour beyond what "manually driven" cars were allowed. For the next twenty minutes or so, Jason relaxed and devoted his full attention to the lovely woman beside him. A woman he was falling more and more in love with each and every day.

Their conversation was light but purposeful, planning what they would do over the next week. Justin's ulterior motive was to figure out how to get her over to her favorite jewelry store. He already had his short speech memorized, but—

An unusual alarm sounded, screaming urgency. Justin looked at the touchscreen. A skull-and-crossbones icon indicated an active, hostile cyber attack. Instinctively, Justin disengaged Auto-Drive. At first, the system appeared to refuse to disengage. Then the Auto-Drive light blinked off and the car lurched violently to the right. They were fortunate that no car was in the lane next to them. Justin quickly pulled all the way over to the far right-hand lane.

"What's that?" Tamika asked.

"See that column there to the right?" he pointed to the pop-up window on the right side of the screen, then turned his attention back to the road. "Read everything you see."

"Okay... 'Attack unknown. Source unknown. Systems at risk: Speed, steering, brakes. Severity: forty percent. Wait, fifty percent...sixty... Recommended action: Power down. Urgent!'"

Justin was already taking the next exit ramp, going well above the posted speed limit. After a quick glance to the left, he ran the stop sign and turned right. He wheeled into the nearest service station, then cut the ignition and removed the key.

He wiped the beads of sweat from his forehead, even as his entire body shivered. Staring in disbelief at the steering wheel, he let out a long, slow breath.

"What in the world just happened?" Tamika asked quietly. "I'm not up on all the latest technology, but I don't think that particular antivirus routine—or whatever that was—comes standard with Auto-Drive. Not even as Beta...?"

"My love, someone just tried to kill us."

"What do you mean?" She held his arm and smiled. But her smile quickly vanished when she saw the expression on his face. "Wait, that wasn't a bug, or some random hack?"

"Tamika...I'm serious. Someone just deliberately tried to kill us. I've overlaid my car's software with NSA-level security. More mundane stuff and we wouldn't have even been notified of an attack. This was, like, spy-level stuff. If I hadn't been able to disengage Auto-Drive..."

"Matthews."

"Yep."

53. FRIDAY EVENING

Friday, 1600 EST:

"You're...you're all here!"

"Hi, Sweetheart." the beautiful redhead gushed, looking a healthy thirty-three.

"Dad!" smiled two other adults, each also looking a healthy thirty-three. The man had light brown hair and brown eyes, and a darker complexion like Roger's. The woman's hair was strawberry blonde, and her lighter complexion matched that of her mother, standing beside her.

Their garments were wispy robes that shimmered all the colors of a rainbow, and somehow more.

"You're here..." Roger stammered again and immediately knew where "here" was.

There was no clear up, down, left, or right. They seemed to be firmly suspended in white nothingness, although he could see figures in the distance, and knew that he was near some kind of destination.

The four of them hugged, and immense joy and peace overwhelmed Roger. And rest. After what seemed minutes with no words being said, or needing to be said, Cindy pulled away, smiled, and looked deep into Roger's eyes.

"Sweetheart, we all owe so much to you. And we're so excited that you'll be joining us..."

Frank continued without a beat: "...but Dad, it's not time yet. You are unique among billions of people, and God's purpose for your life is not complete."

Susan said, "Dad, thank you so much for everything! Now, live, Dad!"

The light was getting brighter.

Roger heard Cindy say, "And we mean, truly live, Roger. There's no marriage here; the least relationship here is infinitely better than the best relationship there. You have a fantastic future in store, my love. It won't be easy, but you won't be alone. And we all fully approve!"

The light was now blinding, painful.

Roger was looking at a bright light shining into his left eye, then his right.

A beautiful angelic face, framed in short, pretty red hair, was looking down at him. Her complexion was perfect from her face, down her neck, to the top of a bright green medical gown. Certainly, she didn't have a speck of makeup, yet she couldn't have been prettier if Hollywood's finest had spent half a day with her. She looked to be somewhere in her early thirties, and somehow, she looked familiar…

"Roger? You with me, friend?"

He blinked. If he was in heaven, why would he be lying on a table looking up at her? But she couldn't be in his altered world; he could hear her, see her, and feel the warm touch of her hand on his arm. And they certainly weren't in Alaska.

"Hello? Anyone home?" she smiled.

The…the hangar? On a table?

Roger tried to get up.

"Ow!"

"Not yet. Maybe five or ten more minutes."

He took a deep breath and slowly let it out.

"Welcome back. I was tempted to use tele-surgery on you, but I suspected you were too far gone. I was right. You were in pretty bad shape. Hallucinations and everything. Looked like you were trying to crawl to the aircraft."

Roger looked around the hangar and at the strange equipment over to his left. It looked ominous, and he thought he recognized it from a science and technology show he'd seen.

The lady followed his glance and smiled. "Makes Da Vinci 6.0 look like surgery with a Swiss Army Knife, if I do say so myself. But, there are times when one still needs the personal touch."

Roger looked back into her beautiful hazel eyes.

"Who… how…" he stammered.

"Over the years, I've been known by many names. You will remember me by my real, married…or at least, widowed name." Her smile broadened and his whole world brightened. "Hello, Roger. I'm Karen Lane Richardson."

His mouth dropped open. She continued smiling and gently stroked his cheek.

He reached up and touched her arm, her shoulder, her face. She held his hand to her face.

"You're here…?"

"I'm here. I've converted. Guardian has a co-pilot."

+ + +

<u>Friday, 1830 EST</u>:
"*I really think Hawaii would be a cool place to see. Would not want to go there tomorrow though. Some weird airplanes going there. Showing off or something. Probably unarmed. Could not stop them. I would rather have lunch inside and play safe with friends."*

The text was stilted due to the automatic translation of the social media website, ostensibly between two young teens, and because it was meant to be vague. Since Snowden, some social media sites, like the one President Garcia had set up through Sybil Blalock to communicate with Viktor, were more secure. Some even rivaled NSA and World Bank sites. Still, the two world leaders had to be careful.

"Something going on around lunchtime tomorrow in Hawaii? Planes that don't belong there? Probably unarmed?" President Garcia was clearly perplexed.

Priscilla had finished her lunch. She opened her Multiphone and did some quick calculations.

"Juan...noon in Hawaii is six p.m. here. You told him to be careful around that time."

The President looked at his wife thoughtfully for several seconds. They weren't always able to have a private dinner due to affairs of state, and even when they did something often came up. Like today.

"What are the other leaders doing?" he asked.

"Actually, not much. And I've been thinking. It's hard to control too many variables at one time, honey. Maybe they're just trying to take out the two main players, apart from China, and stir up the possibility of a nuclear war to bring in their peacemaker."

"The man of peace, who will be anything but that. And like Viktor says, never waste a good crisis, right?" Juan smiled.

"And if there isn't a convenient one coming along, create one."

He looked again at the message, then back at his wife of over forty-two years, his best friend, a world-class academician and analyst in her own right. She was also the proud mother of their three children and the grandmother to six, with number seven on the way.

"I guess the social media link is working for now. I've got a call to make about this thing in Hawaii tomorrow. And I do want you to go to that concert tomorrow evening."

Priscilla's attendance at an international cultural event allowed Juan to diplomatically request that his head of security lead her security detail. That allowed Juan to make sure that Chet Rowland and the personnel he recommended were the key part of the primary detail to watch over him at the conservative off-site. The site of the meeting was the Gaylord National Resort & Convention Center in National Harbor, Maryland. If there was trouble, he wanted the most important person in his life to be far from it.

+ + +

Friday, 2045 EST:

"I expected a lot more pain from the carbon dioxide in your laparoscopy," Roger stated quizzically, as he walked back from the latrine.

Karen smiled. "If you can do your work quickly, you can use different gasses. I use a mixture of carbon dioxide along with nitrogen, nitrous oxide, a little helium, and even some good old-fashioned air. The body tolerates it very well and absorbs it quickly. Less pain, faster recovery."

Her phone alerted. It was Tamika. She read the message to Roger.

"How's Roger? A couple of hours ago, someone tried to commandeer Justin's car's software while we were on I-95. He parked it in time and we abandoned it. Took a taxi to his apartment. Suspect Matthews."

Karen responded immediately. "Leave now! Only take what you absolutely can't live without. No more than a carry-on bag. His motorcycle should be safe. Tamika, do NOT go to your place. Immediately go to an ATM and each of you get out as much cash as you can. If your accounts aren't already frozen, they soon will be. Everything by cash until I set you up with new IDs and accounts. Don't worry; you'll each have over 100,000 dollars available within a week. Just get out of there. Your lives as you knew them are over. Take this seriously. You are both in extreme, imminent danger. Send."

"Karen?"

"Yes, Roger?"

"How in the world did you get a Multiphone to link up in this Transdimensional state?"

Karen smiled.

54. DEEPENING DARKNESS

Friday, 2050 EST:
"Justin!" Tamika called.
"Just a moment," he replied from his bedroom, about the same instant they heard a car horn sound and tires screech. A moment later they heard several car doors slam.

"We've gotta get out of here now! Karen says we're still in danger!"

They heard heavy footsteps on the stairs and coming up the walkway.

"The glass door!" Justin said, but she was already there. Six flights up and only small balconies; no one in sight. Whoever was after them apparently didn't think they would or could try to escape out the back. Justin did have a small bag packed, having reached the same conclusion as Karen. He tossed it down to the ground. He and Tamika swung and jumped from balcony to balcony like Cirque du Soleil acrobats. Thanks to their mutual love of extreme workouts and pars course training, they were safely down on the ground within seconds.

Justin grabbed his bag in time to hear his heavy steel apartment door blown out of its frame. They quickly dodged around a corner so they couldn't be seen from the sliding glass door. Justin was grateful that he thought to close it. That might buy another five or ten seconds while the intruders searched the empty apartment. They quickly worked their way to the garage.

Justin looked around carefully to make sure nobody was watching for them. The path looked clear, although he suspected that the intruders would be hacking into the security cameras within seconds.

Those few seconds were all he and Tamika needed. He switched his hybrid motorcycle to silent full-electric mode, and they quietly rode out of the garage at a normal speed so as not to attract attention. Justin had a thought. He knew they would be coming after them and that it would be critical to get his next move just right. He signaled and casually turned south onto the main road. A few minutes later, he stopped at a local gas station to fill up the tank and purchase some snacks and a few other items. He continued south and drove to the next available ATM as Karen had advised. Both he and Tamika withdrew as much cash as the ATM would allow. Then Justin continued south for a few more minutes, passing through numerous traffic lights. He turned into a rundown shopping plaza.

Justin drove around to the back of the building, then turned onto a side street. He then turned around and headed back north on a long, circuitous route through little-used back roads. Knowing that security cameras would lock down the locations and times of the gas station and ATM transactions...and maybe traffic cameras through some of the traffic lights...Justin hoped their pursuers would keep heading south. After they had driven well north of his apartment, he pulled over briefly.

Justin pulled out one of the purchases from the gas station, a roll of lowly duct tape. Karen had told them that police car cameras were now able to read license plates of vehicles traveling even seventy miles an hour in the opposite direction, in the dark. To remove or cover a license plate would be an automatic traffic stop, but if he just covered part of one letter, he would likely escape notice for a few days. Unless an officer pulled directly up behind him. He applied the duct tape quickly and they started off on the road again.

Karen assured them in subsequent messages that she would teach them how to alter their appearances to fool facial recognition software and that she would be able to teach them how to travel undetected.

"Who IS this woman?!" Tamika commented.

"Exactly who she said she is, and let's be glad that she's on our side," Justin responded. He switched to full-hybrid mode, gunned the motorcycle, and they headed north up US 1 along with the evening traffic. He carefully kept his speed right at the posted limit. Soon, he turned west on 46 toward Sanford, Florida.

Looks like the proposal will have to wait, Justin lamented, as he wondered what, exactly, the future might hold for him and his beautiful passenger.

+ + +

Friday, 2100 EST (1800 Pacific):

Cliff smiled as he watched Guardian off-loaded from the C-17 that had been backed to a hangar. The scene was eerily illuminated by the fading twilight of the stark Nevada landscape.

He knew that crews would work through the night preparing for the early afternoon test flight. The accelerated test schedule was to commence immediately. After a lengthy pre-flight in the hangar, Tim Cason would engage visual cloaking, perform a standard take-off, and fly System Two subsonically for two hours. If everything checked out, he would light the SRBs and go low-supersonic until the SRBs burned out, then land. After a successful review of telemetry, he'd be cleared for his second test flight a few days later. He would launch, fire SRBs, and go supersonic. This time, he'd light the ion drive and accelerate to Mach Five. After another successful review, he'd be cleared for test flight three. He'd repeat the second test with the addition of the scramjet and an extended Mach Eight high altitude flight. The final planned test was to achieve maximum Mach and engage a re-entering satellite target to finish boresighting the rail gun. The test flights were tentatively scheduled three days apart, assuming no serious anomalies were noted. It was more testing than they originally planned, but they were being thorough.

Cliff looked over at his test pilot. He knew the cocky Tim Cason couldn't wait to get into the aircraft, light the SRBs, and finally get to full hypersonic speeds. He never had that chance with System One.

Too bad he'll never have the chance with this one either.

+ + +

Friday, 2130 EST (1930 Grand Forks):

"Karen...what's happening to me?" Roger asked in astonishment. He felt completely healed, only a few hours after having his gall bladder removed. But there was something else going on...

They had just finished eating and were walking around the aircraft.

"How do you feel?" she asked.

"Well...younger? Strong?"

Karen smiled, turned toward the "older" man, put both of her hands on his shoulders, and looked straight into his eyes.

"Roger, I'm now one of two. So are you. This is going to take a while to explain."

He instinctively put his hands on her waist for a moment, then quickly removed them and blushed. Karen's gentle smile was reassuring. She firmly squeezed his shoulders then lowered her hands to her side.

"Shall we retire to your living room?" she asked playfully as she walked toward the couch near a table to one side in the hangar.

+ + +

Friday, 2145 EST:

"How sweet!" Tamika exclaimed as they walked up the porch steps, under the slowly-turning ceiling fans, and into the 19th century Higgins House.

The quaint Victorian bed-and-breakfast in Sanford was a perfect hideaway, not being a national chain hotel. And Justin had paid cash.

"Why, thank you kindly, Sir!" She slipped past him as he held the door open for her to the Cedar Room. She felt a little better. While they were riding, Karen had sent several more messages about where to safely shop for essentials—like a change of clothes, toiletries, and food. She also made recommendations on lodging—hence, the bed-and-breakfast.

The rustic but comfortable décor also helped reduce the tension. She tossed her new backpack on the couch. Justin did likewise with his small bag, and they fell into each other's arms. After a few moments, he gently pushed her out to arms' length, looked deep into her eyes.

"Tamika Stewart, I had some really great plans for what I wanted to do and how I wanted to do it. But it looks like all that is OBE; overcome by events. Bottom line is, I can't believe all that's happened in the past seven months, and I can't imagine what's ahead now with folks out to kill us. But whatever happens, however long we have here," he took her hands in his and dropped to one knee. He continued looking into her deep, moist eyes; "I want to spend all of it…the rest of my life…with you. Will you marry me?"

+ + +

Friday, 2200 EST:

"I'll call you back."

Within thirty seconds, Senator Matthews had Skylar on his DARPA prototype.

"Mission accomplished?" he asked.

After a brief pause, "Not yet, Sir. Some level of anti-spyware in his car I've never seen before, and they abandoned it just moments before I could break through. I got a team together and went to his apartment, but I guess they're into obstacle courses or something. They climbed down the back from six flights up before we could get through the front door…"

Skylar was sweating. He paced around his SUV, leaning hard on his cane. This was tech stuff, right down the middle of his lane. It's what he had extensively studied and worked with when his bad knee took him out of the more physically demanding side of working for Jason. And he'd blown it.

Jason let the silence linger.

"Uh, they got away on his motorcycle. One of those electric hybrid types; couldn't even hear them leave. Bought some gas and stuff from a convenience store and took out as much cash as they could from an ATM. They were heading south, but we're monitoring the turnpike and interstates. I've got my police contacts alerted. We'll find them, sir."

"See that you do." And with that, Jason hung up. *Nothing more to say. He knows he screwed up. And he knows I won't tolerate screw-ups. Not again.*

Skylar stopped his pacing. With a string of profanity, he leaned over and rubbed his bum knee. Good as the replacement was, it hadn't been designed for quickly climbing up and down six flights of stairs or running around Justin's apartment complex.

He had no intention of letting Matthews down. He'd worked with the man for decades, long before Jason became a public figure. He was even an understudy of Jason's previous "fix-it" man, Louis "Bull" Thatcher, before the older man took that FSAT stuff and went crazy.

Skylar knew that one of the main reasons Jason kept him around was that he was as tenacious as Matthews about recapturing Karen Lane even after all these years. Matthews wanted to continue his experiments. Skylar just wanted to inflict enough suffering to avenge his shattered knee from the morning she escaped back in 2020. Then he could retire, or more likely continue as a security consultant for Jason. Skylar speculated that staying involved would be the safer position, as he questioned whether any of Jason's private "security" team ever actually retired. Especially ones like himself who knew where the bodies were buried, so to speak.

His team had positively identified her in Asheville, North Carolina weeks ago, and in Charleston, South Carolina a few months before that. He had well-paid people going over surveillance videos 24-7. He would find her.

Right now, his main focus was on quickly finding and eliminating a young Black couple who had the audacity to escape him. Twice. That made it personal.

55. REVELATIONS

Saturday, 0300 EST (0100 Grand Forks):

Karen shared with Roger until fatigue overwhelmed them both. In spite of her heroic high-tech intervention, the truth was that he had been in and out of death's door and had undergone major surgery just hours earlier. She had almost died as well. The "transition effect" had rocked her, literally, all the way down to the atomic level. When Roger asked her what it was like, she didn't go into a lot of details. Maybe later. But truthfully, she knew that no one else could have survived. She also knew that she could never go back. And the pain…!

After what seemed like days of sleep punctuated by vivid, sometimes troubling dreams, Karen awoke.

What?

The unfamiliar sensation was one she hadn't experienced in, what? Nineteen years since her husband died?

Roger was sitting on the couch beside her, gently stroking her face and hair. She looked up, startled.

"I owe you my life. And not just for the surgery."

She rubbed her eyes and smiled. "Now Roger, you know it's not uncommon for a patient to develop feelings for a doctor of the opposite sex," she quipped.

"Hush. You're not really a doctor."

"Okay, point taken. Go on."

He stroked her face and returned her smile.

"I'm very, very grateful you're here."

"Me, too." She sat up. "You know, this is the first time in many years that I haven't had to worry about Jason and his goons?"

He stood. "That, too. But I think you have some more explaining to do."

Karen nodded. "Let's eat. And you're right. I brought you right up to after I converted and found you unconscious on the floor. Now you need to know what else I did to you yesterday."

An hour later in "their time," Roger looked at her in silence with his mouth hanging open.

"That's right. My husband was correct. At least, partially. Of course, we live in a different world now. And we're carrying the baggage of several thousand years of significant genetic degradation. I've personally verified what's been reported in peer-reviewed journals, that the human genome is not mutating to the good. It's being corrupted, up to three percent per generation. I also believe that our average IQ has been dropping about one point per generation, at least for the past several hundred years."

His scientific mind kicked back in, at least for the moment.

"So, the reason more children are unhealthy is more than environmental?"

"Both nature and nurture, actually. But yes, diabetes, autoimmune diseases, eyesight problems, and hundreds of other common disorders are increasing due to genomic degradation. One reason I believe Christ's return is imminent is that my studies show we're within just a few more generations of reaching significant infant mortality rates."

"So...FSAT doesn't always work?"

She gently placed her hand on his knee as they sat together on the couch. It seemed to Roger that her eyes were tearing up.

"Roger, FSAT *never* works. At least, not for long." She took a long, deep breath. "The only time that it hasn't killed the recipient is when they—you and me—are already within moments of death."

She shuddered, remembering the agony of her transition the previous day, coming through just in time to see Roger take his last breath. There had been no time to set up the surgical equipment. She had grabbed him like he was a young toddler—she hadn't yet fully explained the superhuman strength benefit of FSAT—and tossed him on a table. She fought to keep him alive long enough to do what she'd never done to anyone before. Only then, after it began to take effect, was she able to operate. Roger's heart had literally stopped several times.

Roger put his hand on hers.

"There's something else, isn't there?"

Now a tear did roll down her cheek.

"Roger, it's the hardest thing of all. Even after all these years I haven't broken it down completely. Of course, since I'm the only carrier now, the recipient's blood type has to match mine. Yours does. Another requirement is that the body must be in extreme stress, under the influence of either natural or synthetic adrenalin. So, that one's also easy. I'd just been shot, and you appeared to be fighting with your last breath to launch and get away from civilization. Pure oxygen, compliments of Guardian. Then there are other hormonal requirements, most of which can be met synthetically." She paused.

"Karen...!"

"OK. Here's the deal. The advanced biological modeling I just completed a month ago, shows that it can only work correctly if one other hormone is present soon after the transformation begins. It's oxytocin, the so-called love hormone. And it has to be natural; none of the synthetics will work. That happened to me, and that's where Matthews' team failed time and time again. I don't think any of them have an ounce of love for anyone, except for themselves."

Visibly nervous, she blushed. "And I was afraid you might fail, too. The person has to have a desire to live, to love, to bond. You didn't have any of that. I knew you didn't. I could tell by our emails. You wanted...well, you were clearly ready to go. You longed to be back with your family and to finally be with the Lord. But I believed God was impressing on me that I had to try, and that...somehow..." her voice trailed off. She was arguably the most intelligent, most learned person on earth, and she felt like an embarrassed adolescent with a crush.

Tears rolled down her cheeks.

Roger looked at the beautiful woman who appeared to be exactly half of his sixty-four years but was actually only a few years younger than himself. She had clearly put her own life at risk to save his, to painfully enter into his seclusion, and then to remain alone there herself, taking his place, if she couldn't save him.

What a sacrifice!

Roger reached up and gently wiped tears from her cheeks. His eyes were starting to tear up as well. A wave of hope, of possibilities, even euphoria, swept over him.

"So, let me get this straight," he said. "The greatest effects take place in the first several years? So, if we're still around in 2035, I might look like I'm in my early fifties, and you'll look like you're in your mid-forties?"

"Uh, something like that. Of course, in those ten years we may be close to 100 years of age because of the trans-dimensional effect. I just won't know until we study it for a while."

Roger smiled, pulled her close to his chest, and whispered in her ear. "Karen Lane, let's spend the rest of our lives together." He started to let her go, not wanting to seem inappropriate, but she responded by holding him tightly and burying her head into his shoulder. It seemed to Roger that she was shaking slightly, even trembling.

They both laughed. And cried. And held each other close for a very long time. If anyone were to analyze blood samples at that precise moment, they would have seen several key chemical markers rise to very high levels in Roger's sample. And in hers. Higher than either had experienced in many, many years.

+ + +

Saturday, 0900 EST:
Finishing their breakfast, Justin and Tamika were also laughing. They were young, healthy, deeply in love, and engaged. With the recently liberalized Florida laws, they would get married first thing Monday morning, then be on their way before they could be caught when the documents identified them and their location to Matthews' henchmen.

They'd also enjoyed a good night of rest and a terrific breakfast. And they were taking the mysterious Karen Lane Richardson at her word, knowing that that they would financially lack for nothing.

+ + +

On the other side of the world, it was already in the early hours of Sunday morning. Two flight crews of Russian Tupolev PAK-DA strategic bombers were completing the pre-flight mission briefing in a secure room at the Petropavlovsk-Yelizovo airfield. Major Dmitry Orlov Shimko was grateful to be chosen to command the first operational flights of the first two production aircraft. He and his hand-picked crew were about to fly in formation with the second aircraft, and accompanied by a tanker for at least part of the way. They were taking a route that was rare for Russian bombers. True, Russian military aircraft had increasingly extended their flights further out from the mainland since 2014. As in the Cold War days, they had been testing and challenging the airspace, detection, and defenses of other nations.

Why in the world would we fly to Hawaii?
More perplexing were the orders both crews received.
The pre-flight briefing details continued; weather aloft, contingency

fields—which were basically non-existent over the ocean. They discussed refueling details with the third crew, which would fly an IL-78M tanker aircraft with them out to a distance of 1,000 nautical miles. Out there, the tanker would refuel both bombers and then orbit, awaiting their return to top them off and follow them back.

The stealthy bombers would be virtually invisible to radar as they approached Hawaii, and current weather conditions indicated they could fly at 40,000 feet without leaving contrails. That also meant that once they broke from the tanker, they could accelerate to their full cruise speed of Mach Zero-point-Eight-Five.

The briefing finally ended, and they were transported out to pre-flight the three aircraft.

Wheels up in three hours.

+ + +

Saturday, 1200 EST (1000 Grand Forks):

"Not again!"

Brent Knowles was furious. As if it wasn't bad enough that he was two weeks behind on his home renovation—his wife was reminding him each day—but now he was called in to tear down a hangar. On a Saturday! No apparent reason; just one of the hangars had to be flattened today. No time to study, no time to plan the best and safest way, just get the heaviest equipment over there and knock it down.

It's not even safe to do something like that alone! The whole thing could come down on top of me.

Then he remembered that this particular hangar was small and also low. His largest 'dozer might just be able to do it by pushing in from each of the four corners, with the scoop up as high as possible. Still...

His team for this particular weekend, including himself, was exactly...one. No one else was available to help within 200 miles. Military off on a Prime Beef exercise. One Civil Service worker out-of-state for his daughter's wedding. Well, there was Jeff; sure, bring him in two days after his major back surgery.

Brent cursed. The call came at 0830. Hangar needed to be rubble by 1600; clean-up would be taken care of in the next few weeks. He arrived at 1000.

The only 'dozer with a chance of doing any real damage had a dead battery. And it didn't just need a jump; it was stone cold dead.

"I'm getting too old for this. Way too old."

Years in Civil Engineering, pouring concrete and asphalt, digging trenches, scraping ice and snow; the fifty-five-year-old Civil Service employee was counting the years until retirement. "Fishing in the summer, hunting in the winter, and honey-dos when I have to," is what he'd been telling people for the past five years.

The old-style lead acid battery was heavy. Exorbitantly heavy. He finally got it out, found a dolly he could use to get it to his truck, then wasted half an hour at the motor pool. Nothing even close. Back in his truck and a trip to a truck supply company back in East Grand Forks. Twenty miles each way. The speeding ticket didn't help his schedule, and certainly not his disposition.

Roll the huge battery back to the 'dozer, fight to get it in, get it connected, fire up the diesel.

"Who used this last!?" More choice profanity. Near empty. Just enough to get to the pumps. Fill it up...

"Gonna be a long day."

56. ATTACK!

Saturday, 1400 EST:
Chet Rowland finished his walk-around.
I hate off-sites!

Eight miles south of Washington DC on the banks of the Potomac River, The Gaylord National Resort & Convention Center was a huge facility. Chet expected sore feet by the end of the evening. Many security items had been completed days before, such as background checks on all personnel. Others were put in place yesterday, to include sequestering the convention center part of the complex and maintaining positive control over everyone and everything that entered and exited.

He stood outside in front of the Riverview Ballroom, a popular addition that was completed in 2017. To his left stood the main convention center. To his right, the Potomac. During the off-site, the ballroom would be closed.

Soon they would establish the no-fly zone over the venue, and finally they would visibly station armed personnel and snipers around the facility. The Gaylord featured a stunning nineteen-story glass atrium that overlooked the Potomac. Chet wasn't as concerned about the giant open space as he was about the river. He made sure that two of his most trusted personnel manned the two radar-assisted fifty-caliber machine guns—the fifty Cals—set up in portable bunkers 150 yards on either side of the dock. Additional security and firepower would be provided by two Coast Guard cutters. They would maintain a "no boating" zone from Rosilie Island at the base of the I-495 Capital Beltway Bridge, most of the way across the Potomac, and out just as far along the south bank. Still, with current laser and computer augmented sniper rifles, Chet mandated that drapes would remain closed at all times.

What could we have missed?

+ + +

Saturday, 1730 EST (1430 Nevada):
"Justin!"

Why in the world would Tim Cason be calling? Something wrong with System Two?!

"Tim, what's up?"

Tim's cocky, self-assured bravado was gone.

"System Two just launched! I was heading to the lab to get suited up. I heard the turbojet wind up, ran around the building, and saw it clear the runway and fire the SRBs! And the optical cloaking isn't on; it's as clear as day!"

Justin glanced at Tamika, wide-eyed, and put Tim on speakerphone just as he spoke again.

"Wait... there it goes! The SRBs are spent, and I hear the ion drive kicking in!"

"Can you tell what direction it's going?" Justin asked.

"West!"

"Does Cliff know?"

"Don't know where he is, and he doesn't answer!"

+ + +

No rest for the weary. Or for General Officers.

It was Justin.

"General, we have an emergency. Can you talk?"

"I'm private, between meetings. Go ahead."

"Sir, Tamika and I had two attempts on our lives yesterday. We can't prove who's behind it, but you know who we suspect."

"Are you both alright?" he asked.

"We're in seclusion. We don't dare go back to DPI, or anywhere else where we could be recognized. But here's the emergency. Our test pilot, Tim Cason, just called from Groom Lake. Someone just launched System Two! It had to be Cliff. He had almost nothing to do with the production of System Two, but he's spent many Sundays in the Simulator. I did a run-time check, and he's got almost half as many seat hours in there as Tim!"

"Hmm. And Senator Matthews is out in Nevada as well."

"In Nevada? Just a moment." Justin checked his tracking App.

"No Sir. It's a long story, but we can track him. He's in Washington, and he called Cliff...uh...less than an hour ago."

"Okay. There's even more that isn't adding up. System Two...did Cason say anything more about how it was flying or which direction it was going?"

"Full mission profile, except he didn't turn on the optical stealth. It's completely visible. And he lit the drive. He's heading west!"

The General's mind was whirling. "Justin, I can't reveal my source, but I just learned there's reason to believe some new front line Russian long-range bombers are flying toward Hawaii; should be there around noon Hawaii time. Could there be a connection?"

"Hold on," Justin told the general. He turned to Tamika and asked, "How far from Groom Lake to Hawaii? Nautical miles?"

She had the answer in moments. "It converts to 2,317 nautical miles."

"What time is it there now?" Justin asked as he did some quick math. "General, here's the deal. If he's heading to Hawaii, he could be there in about an hour, given time to climb and ramp up to full speed. I don't think he'd do that in an aircraft that's never been flown, though. And if he doesn't have a pressure suit, he won't go up to max altitude where he could go wide open. So, if he flies lower at a more reasonable Mach Four, it'll take him about ninety minutes."

"Can Roger intercept?"

Tamika spoke up. "It's 10:30 a.m. in Hawaii, so Cliff would be there sometime shortly after 12 noon. And I already checked. It's 3,267 nautical miles from Grand Forks..."

"General... he can go even faster than you're aware of. He may be able to make it."

Saturday, 1740 EST (1540 Grand Forks):

"What's that?" Karen asked, startled.

A low, throbbing rumble was getting louder, coming from the back of the hangar. Slowly, part of the rear corner wall caved in to expose a huge bulldozer.

At the same instant, Guardian's landing lights came on, along with an alarm. The engine ignited and began to spin up. The hangar door started opening automatically.

"We're on alert, and somebody's trying to tear down the hangar around us. We've gotta get out of here!"

Roger was climbing into his pressure suit. Karen ran to another of her cases, quickly opened it, and to his amazement she pulled out her own pressure suit and slipped it on over the scrubs she had been wearing. She smiled before putting on a helmet she also pulled out of the case.

"Didn't think I'd come to the party unprepared, did you?" she smiled.

Good grief, it's even tailored! Roger tore his eyes back to the task at hand just in time to keep from tripping over a heavy toolbox. He kicked it out of the way and marveled that it didn't just slide a foot or two; it skidded over twenty feet away.

The bulldozer stopped momentarily. If Roger had looked back, he would have seen a stunned Brent Knowles looking into the empty hangar with a mixture of consternation and confusion. No doubt he was feeling the unmistakable hot blast of Jet-A hitting him from…from nothing! With no sound, even when he shut off the diesel of his 'dozer.

Karen grabbed her phone and a few other things and put them into a small case.

"No!" Roger yelled over the noise. "Magnetic!"

"Yes," she hollered back and held up the case, smiling. "Shielded!" She stuffed the case inside the one small compartment beside the steps that was reserved for future avionics and climbed the ladder into the back seat.

Roger was only seconds behind her, and he paused long enough at the top of the ladder to make sure she knew how to buckle in and attach her helmet, mask, and headset. She was already secure and connected! He jumped into the front seat. Before he could actuate his switch to retract the ladder into the fuselage, she had already hit hers and was also lowering the canopy.

"Comm check?" he asked into his mic.

"Loud and clear, 'Commander.' Let's light this thing off."

She never ceases to amaze.

The text reader started speaking.

"From Justin. Roger, Cliff has taken off in System Two. General Alvarez also has word that two Russian strategic bombers are heading toward Hawaii. We suspect that this may be like the missile attack, designed to increase tensions and lead to government overthrows. We don't know if the bombers are armed or not, but we suspect that Cliff is going to attack them. He's flying without optical stealth. Probably less than full speed for several reasons. If he

goes around Mach Four, he should be there in 80 minutes. Can that baby hold Mach Twelve-point-Five?"

"From General Alvarez: Justin's message confirmed. Launch and try to intercept System Two. Destroy it if it takes unprovoked hostile actions against Russians. Suspect bombers are unarmed. Repeat, not armed."

"Well? Can it?" Karen asked, as Roger lined up on the runway and gunned the turbojet. In seconds, they'd cleared the runway and the wheels were retracted.

"Maybe Twelve-point-Six with you here; better weight distribution. Hold on!" Roger said and lit the SRBs.

"Wow! I could get used to this!" she squealed as the thrust slammed them back in their seats.

Roger ignored her for the moment.

"Message to Justin and General Alvarez: 'If he's going to attack, he'll have to drop to a lower altitude and slow down. I assume the bombers are stealth against radar, but his LIDAR should still work if the weather's clear. Any clouds? Send."

"Karen, I doubt that our weather radar will work against System Two. We'll have to use our LIDAR as well."

The magnets were superconductive.

57. REACTION

Saturday, 1730 EST (Sunday, 0130 Moscow):
Two more hours back to Moscow. Another long day.
Maybe they'll get everything right this time.

As he had over six months ago, Anton was awaiting his call over the secure maintenance net radio. The co-pilot was also waiting for his signal. Virtually everyone on board was asleep, and no one would think anything of the flight engineer going down into the lower compartment. Just routine checks.

Altitude of 40,000 feet, enough fuel to divert once all but the co-pilot and Anton were dead, and the world restructuring would begin. As soon as they confirmed the American president and key leaders were dead, he'd be notified and key leadership in Russia would be eliminated as well. Same plan. Decompress the aircraft, and everyone would grab for oxygen masks. But no oxygen would flow, because Anton had turned off the supply valves. Only he and the copilot, who would have slipped out of the cockpit to use the latrine, would have on portable oxygen bottles. Within minutes President Viktor Savin and his staff would be corpses. Take the plane off autopilot and drop below radar coverage.

Some kind of international crisis would be kindled, apparently through an aircraft attack. New American and Russian leadership would step forward with a lot of saber-rattling, then stand down and look like heroes. Imams would turn loose imbedded Jihadists, thinking they were doing the work of Allah, to launch massive attacks in the United States, Russia, throughout Europe, and, of course, against Israel. Nations would clamp down and initiate martial law. The entire world would change—forever—in just a few days.

Anton wasn't privy to all the details. Didn't want to be. He had his orders, his very considerable compensation, and he was already promised a key position as flight engineer for the Russian Premier—or whatever he chose to call himself.

After miserable decades of long hours and poor pay, which was often weeks late at that, Anton and his family would never lack for anything again.

He expected the call within another hour or so.

+ + +

Saturday, 1800 EST:
President Garcia approached the podium, and the crowd grew subdued. As he often did in such venues, he dressed "business casual" and expected the same from everyone else.

"Please. Keep enjoying the food and conversations. As you finish up, if you'll start working toward your tables, I'd like us to get started by 6:15."

In typical President Garcia style, he didn't have an emcee, moderator, or facilitator to host his events. He was a worker, a leader. This was his meeting, and he was going to run it.

"I sincerely thank you all for being here. We still have a lot to do, but I wanted each of your teams to present the recommendations you've been working on over the past six months."

The Baltimore Conference Rooms were set up in "classroom" style. Attendees had ample room to bring their hors d'oeuvres and beverages to their tables, then spread their materials out and also take notes on their handouts during the upcoming presentations.

As he stepped back down to his own table, Vice President Manfrida picked up her purse and walked out as if to go to the bathroom. Within five minutes, Chet had personally escorted her to one of the farthest rooms from the convention, on the lowest floor of the hotel side of the complex.

As Juan Garcia again stepped to the podium, he looked around and spotted Charles, the Speaker of the House. As planned, he was seated at a table at the rear of the conference room, near an exit. *Good.*

Juan felt comfortable leaving the Presidency in either of their ethical and highly capable hands. If anything was going to happen tonight, he'd go out knowing he'd done everything he could to ensure the constitutional republic would continue. And if some bad guys needed a lightning rod, well, here he was.

Chet walked back to the convention center, listening carefully to the random roll-call. Rather than set times where potential enemies could plan attacks between call-ins, the roll-calls were computerized and voice-monitored, conducted between three and seven minutes apart. Once begun, if an agent couldn't answer when polled, he or she would be skipped and then randomly polled again. If they didn't respond at that time, two back-ups would dispatch to their last known location. The low frequency, spread spectrum radios were extremely difficult to jam and were also able to travel through most walls, floors, and roofs.

Chet responded to his call-sign and continued walking. Suddenly the roll-call was interrupted.

"What the... We're under attack from the harbor!" It was one of Chet's men on a fifty Cal. "A small ship, smaller than the Coast Guard cutters, just torpedoed them. Blew them both out of the water! It's coming toward us like a speed boat!" The sound of his fifty Cal drowned out anything else he might have said.

"Evacuate everyone to Zone One now! All backup personnel, head to the riverfront!" Chet ordered. He was already in the auditorium and quickly moved to the microphone. President Garcia stepped aside.

"Everyone, follow me! We're under attack. We're going to put some extra walls between them and us."

With that he quickly led the group toward the front of the center further away from the shore, but not too close to the front in case there might be a coordinated attack launched from that direction.

Both Fifty Cal guns along the shoreline were silent. Ominous, thick plumes of smoke billowed up from their temporary embankments.

Approaching at over thirty miles per hour, the stealth gunship's sensors had quickly neutralized them. From the bank, security personnel pummeled the craft with small arms fire and sniper rifle bullets, which simply bounced off the angular metal hull and heavy canopy of the never-fielded prototype. Matthews had held onto the small, high-speed stealth ship for years, with his OWPN-trusted personnel continuing to upgrade sensors, software, and weaponry. The large, red Russian star on the side were a last-minute addition. Never mind that the small vessel couldn't have traveled all the way across the ocean, nor entered into North American territorial waters even if the Russians had intended to do so.

Ports opened on the top, and in quick succession three small missiles launched in an upward arc which would lead them to impact directly down on the center of the convention side of the complex. Any single missile would likely have killed all intended targets. Matthews was taking no chances. The first two were armed with penetrating high-explosive warheads to open up the roof and gut out the building. The third one, and then a final fourth, would deliver overpressure detonations that would kill any survivors inside and reduce the building to a very deep crater.

\+ + +

Saturday, 1820 EST:
Beautiful. Absolutely beautiful.

The unearthly scream of Guardian System Two was accompanied many octaves lower by a deep-throated roar like massive afterburners, or multiple seven-liter V-8 engines screaming around the track at the Daytona Speedway. Around him was the dark of space above, the blue sky below, and the ocean far below that. Cliff was presented with a kaleidoscope of feelings he had never expected. He had been so tempted to have a drink or two before climbing into the unguarded aircraft. He was so glad that he had not.

A sense of euphoria spread over him. He really wasn't much of a pilot. But then he didn't have to be to operate the highly-automated aircraft. Basically, he just had to run the programs, actuate a few switches at the appropriate time, and land. Sure, there were a few more minor details. He had to buzz the Russian stealth bombers and make sure they got a good look at his aircraft. They needed to radio back that they were under attack. Then, he would fire his slugs into the bombers until they either crashed or he ran out. In the ultimate scheme of things, it really didn't matter which. Then he'd head back to the planned reconstitution point in California, above Los Angeles.

That was the plan according to Matthews. And of course, Cliff would execute it perfectly. After all the turmoil settled down and Matthews was Premier over the North American Kingdom, Cliff was to fly the aircraft to one of the Reconstitution Centers he had been developing over the previous year.

Now, that was the part of the plan that Cliff had no intention of executing. At least, not the way Matthews envisioned it. From Cliff's perspective, there were three higher bidders, and Matthew's plan for ten kingdoms was most likely going to be thirteen by the time all the smoke and dust cleared. Cliff would be very pleased to be safely out from under the senator.

He scanned all the readouts. Everything was optimal. His unique additive manufacturing, unprecedented improvements involving built-in testing, and test-as-you-build methodologies were once more proving their value.

Based on time-to-rendezvous and his fuel consumption, he was cruising at a comfortable Mach Three-point-Six.

He began to gradually reduce speed and altitude. He had to be much lower and slower, in much denser atmosphere, to meet up with the bombers. He planned to buzz them, then attack them at Mach Two.

+ + +

Saturday, 1830 EST:

Senator Jason Matthews was at another Washington, D.C. off-site, having a small strategy session of his own. He was with his senior liberal, progressive, and socialist partners in Congress, planning counter-attacks against what they expected President Garcia's working group would try to implement. They didn't know it yet, but many of the attendees would be part of Matthews' hand-picked transition team. Most others were simply puppets following a party and feathering their own nests. He might allow them to serve as enforcers, since they had already proven their ability to blindly follow directions without thinking through—or perhaps, without caring about—the consequences.

As usual, Matthews' small gathering had over three times the number of news personnel as Garcia's much larger working session.

Jason glanced at his watch. He expected the first of several reports within about half an hour. It was going to be an exciting night. The dawn of a new age.

+ + +

Saturday, 1835 EST:

"I don't see anything but shades of gray!"

"That's about it, outside of light from Guardian or our own 'transformed' sources," Roger replied. "It's like even the photon spins and frequencies are off."

"Hmm. That's going to take a while to digest."

Roger had already learned that such a comment from Karen likely meant that a world-class Einstein-like theory would soon emerge. But he was just grateful that she would include him in on it and ask his opinion. He wondered if he would ever reach her level. Strangely, he could already detect a mental clearing and ability to focus as the FSAT transition continued. The surgery scar was almost completely healed and he also felt more energetic. Of course, much of that could be attributed to being rid of his diseased gall bladder.

"Sure glad you didn't use pure CO_2." He commented as he glanced at the altimeter.

"Yep, at this altitude, even with the suit and pure oxygen, you'd be in a world of hurt."

The aircraft screamed forward at Mach Twelve-point-Six, Flight Level Eight Five.

58. CONFRONTATION

The first missile had reached its apogee and was descending down to the convention center. Suddenly a stream of metal projectiles intersected its arc and split it in two, igniting its warhead in a blinding flash and deafening explosion. The stream of projectiles quickly swept down to intercept the next two missiles with similar results, one after the other. At the very moment the fourth and final missile launched, before it was even five yards above the deck of the strange Ghost craft, the stream of projectiles slammed into it. The concussion shattered the bulletproof canopy of the watercraft, and the overpressure blew out the deck plating of the stealth craft. A split second later, secondary ignitions of its remaining ordinance and fuel reduced the craft to a fireball greater than both of the destroyed Coast Guard cutters combined. Many window panes in the convention center and hotel shattered from all the blasts; all the glass around the ballroom was destroyed.

Close to shore, right in front of the convention center, a small Navy SEALs submarine continued to scan the river and overhead for any further attacks. The SEALs team commander was a man who Chet had served with in combat and, fortunately, was one of the men he trusted with his life. In coordination with Chet, the commander had scheduled a covert "tactical exercise" for that evening. His hand-picked team had been monitoring the river using a low-profile periscope. Even Chet's gunners hadn't seen it. The small sub carried a big punch, including four torpedoes and a miniature version of the Phalanx radar-guided gun. The gun system had effectively neutralized four missiles; the torpedoes had not been necessary.

"Mr. President, the threat has been eliminated," Chet reported moments later, smiling.

Nathan Franks quickly glanced around to make sure there were no other Secret Service agents close by, then drew his sidearm. He was under orders that if anything interfered with the success of Plan A, he was to take out as many of the key personnel as possible, then take his own life. He had lived a very lucrative lifestyle since being recruited by OWPN, but they also had the means to demand ultimate, unconditional loyalty. He had hoped it would never come to that. He wanted that key position in the New World Order. But he also loved his family. He knew if he didn't obey his orders he was as good as dead anyway, as well as his wife and kids. He also understood that none of them would be allowed to die quickly or painlessly.

Nathan wasn't sure where Madame Vice was; he had not been a part of that plan. But he had stayed close to Juan and was careful to keep the house speaker in view, though the speaker had stayed frustratingly as far from the president as possible. He took aim at the president for a clean head shot above the protection of his concealed vest.

When Nathan had looked around for other Secret Service agents, he had not taken notice of a very no-nonsense Lieutenant General off to his right, dressed "business casual" rather than in uniform. General Alvarez flew into the agent, simultaneously jerking the gun down to the man's side as it discharged into the floor. He wrapped his other arm around Nathan's neck as the two men hit the floor...hard.

Before Nathan could react, Chet was on top of him, his knee on Nathan's gun hand and his own weapon drawn and firmly planted against the man's temple. Chet barked out orders for other agents to surround the president and speaker, facing outward against any other threats.

Juan Garcia watched as General Alvarez slowly stood to his feet—not quite as young as he was in his Infantry days. Juan gave him a nod and a knowing smile. He knew his call to Rey the day before had been a good choice. He also knew that the two of them would be spending a lot of time together during the remainder of his presidency. Juan was especially grateful that soon after his inauguration, he'd made sure that the man and other officers like him were given the promotions they deserved. They had been passed over because they refused to support social policies they knew were destructive to military readiness.

Juan recalled Chet's wise advice: *Look for those who have paid the price of their convictions.* He said a quick prayer of thanks to the Lord for placing such good people around him.

Major Shimko, in the lead PAK-DA bomber, began his descent. The flight plan, which he was ordered to follow precisely, was to pass over Hickam Field at an altitude of 20,000 feet. The stealth nature of the bombers meant that they would not be detected until heard. Eventually, they would be seen and F-22s would scramble to intercept. By then the bombers would already be returning to Russia, hopefully well beyond the territorial waters of the United States. A "significant" international incident would be reported.

Those were the orders. And he instructed his navigator to watch radar—not that they would detect approaching stealth F-22 Raptors—while he and his co-pilot scanned the skies.

As Major Shimko's bomber dropped below 25,000 feet, his engineer hollered and pointed straight ahead. By the time Shimko followed his gesture, the small point approaching them had become a strange aircraft that streaked past and between the two bombers. They expected a sonic boom from the clearly supersonic craft. Instead, they only heard a strange "swoosh," a sound like a high-pitched woman's scream, and a roar as if from multiple engines on full afterburner.

Instinctively, but too late to have made any difference, both pilots had turned away, spreading their two-ship formation farther apart.

"Maintain course!" he barked to the other ship. "I'm calling Ops!"

As he initiated the call via satellite, the strange delta-shaped craft circled around and streaked across in front of them, from left to right.

Inside that delta-shaped craft, Cliff had turned on the Terminal Targeting System and the LIDAR and applied power to charge the rail gun's capacitor bank. He flew a large arc and lined up several miles behind the bombers. Radar would have been useless, but the TTS had no problem seeing the aircraft on the cloudless day.

"Piece of cake," said Cliff as the first slug fired. Cliff climbed to pass the bombers above and to the right.

The slug would have missed a warhead, at only several feet in diameter. The Russian bombers were hundreds of times larger. The slug slammed into the bomber on the right, ripping a hole through the bat-shaped wing two-thirds of the way toward the wing tip. Fuel spilled from the ruptured wing tank.

"We're hit!" exclaimed Captain Volkov.

"Abort! Back to Russia. Evade!" ordered Shimko. "What's the damage?"

"Controls are good, but we're losing fuel from the right wing. We'll transfer remaining fuel from both wing tanks to center, but we'll need the tanker sooner. What *is* that thing?"

Cliff's long arc took him many miles out as he continued supersonic, then brought him back facing the bombers as they began to turn back to Russia. He fired his second round.

The TTS boresight compensation routine put the hypersonic slug directly through the center of the crippled bomber and splattered through the fuselage, as the slug converted to molten metal and plasma. What was left of the slug blew a huge hole out the rear. Before Captain Volkov could radio updated status, the aircraft exploded.

The flash drew the attention of Roger and Karen as they were reducing speed and dropping altitude.

"There! Three o'clock and low!" Karen exclaimed.

"I see it. Looks like Cliff went in for a kill," Roger responded. He continued his descent and pulled back to Mach Four. Karen directed their TTS and optics to concentrate on the area around the explosion. Roger charged the capacitor bank.

"What do you make out?" he asked.

"Large bat-wing aircraft—the bomber—and…there it is! System Two! He's coming around; we've only got a few seconds!"

"Lock?"

"Got him!"

"Fire quick; if we hit him too close to the bomber, it'll take it out, too."

Cliff, you should have left your optical stealth on.

Major Shimko saw a flash of light around him, from an explosion that took place miles behind his aircraft. Several seconds later, he heard a deafening explosion. Moments later, he and his crew also experienced several seconds of severe buffeting.

In Honolulu, anyone looking in a particular direction saw a bright flash off in the distance, high in the sky. Then about two minutes later, they heard the muted sound of a distant, but very large explosion.

The remaining PAK-DA bomber set a return course for Russia and climbed to best cruise altitude, while the crewmembers continued to scan the skies for the mysterious aircraft that had downed their twin. The never saw the strange aircraft again.

For more reasons than one, they never saw its remaining twin either.

+ + +

Dinner was over, and Jason Matthews was officially greeting his attendees and the press. He was in rare form, actually looking "presidential," as one of the reporters tweeted.

An aide quickly approached him and held out a hand-scribbled note.

"Sir, excuse me...important...the president and everyone at the convention center..."

Before he could finish, Senator Matthews took the note, glanced quickly at it, and somberly scanned the faces of the assembled crowd. As he did, Multiphones began to vibrate throughout the room.

"My friends, my fellow Americans, I've just been notified of a terrible tragedy," he said deliberately. "As you know, this great nation has many adversaries. It appears that one has just attacked the convention center where our president, vice president, speaker of the house, and hundreds of our colleagues and friends were gathered."

He paused dramatically for effect, but silently he was frustrated that many were getting the same information from texts and emails over their phones.

"I'm afraid there were no survivors," he stated sadly. He even conjured a bit of mist in his eyes. *An Oscar-worthy performance*, he thought. He had done it. He had successfully launched the coup.

"Sir?" the aide spoke up from off to the side. He looked distressed.

"Senator Matthews?" said one of the network reporters. "The attack was defeated."

A female newspaper reporter spoke up. "Two agents were killed, and two Coast Guard cutters were sunk, but a submarine destroyed the attacking boat," she said.

Just as he was on the night he lost the debate and the election, Senator Matthews was suddenly flustered and speechless.

"A submarine?" he blurted. "A submarine?!"

He looked at the note he'd been given, then at the crowd that had suddenly become strangely silent.

"I... I, uh... well, this is indeed good news! I thought..."

"Just what did you think, Senator?" asked a respected elderly reporter, a man in his seventies. He wasn't smiling.

59. RESOLUTION

"So, where do we make our home now?" Karen asked as they flew east at 75,000 feet, and a leisurely Mach Three. Those were the parameters she calculated would give them the maximum range.

"Should we try to return to Grand Forks?"

"Just checked. Hangar's gone."

"You...just checked?"

"Satellite feed. Pretty secure, but not for Guardian's processing. And I hack for entertainment. Have to, to stay ahead of Matthews and his goons."

"Hmm. Okay, well, let's catch up on what's going on and see if anyone else has any suggestions."

They quickly informed General Alvarez, Justin, and Tamika that Cliff had destroyed one Russian bomber, and that System Two was destroyed before it could attack the second aircraft. Since the attacks involved stealth aircraft and took place well out to sea, there was no evidence that Hickam was even aware of the confrontation. They didn't see any interceptors scrambled.

General Alvarez quickly summarized the failed attack on the president and other personnel, humbly leaving out his heroic role in saving President Garcia. Unknown to them at the time was the viral explosion of news feeds and social media over the senator's gaffe. It seemed that Jason may have implicated himself in foreknowledge of the attack against national leadership. Even liberals were demanding a full investigation.

They discussed a new home for Roger, Karen, and the aircraft. The General now knew about her conversion and suggested a return to Robins Air Force Base until a more permanent arrangement could be secured.

Roger programmed Warner Robins, Georgia into the autopilot and relaxed.

"I like that. It's not too far from a place I have in mind for us."

"Really?" Roger responded.

"Yes, actually a small farm I own under one of my other names. It used to be a small airfield, with a hangar for crop dusters and a suitable runway. Justin and Tamika could stay in the house. It's pretty much off the grid, so to speak. I have some things stored there. It'd be perfect to bring the team together."

"The team?"

"Do you want to have hangars bulldozed down around us? I think we need a place of our own. It seems that General Alvarez is trustworthy. He can keep us informed and send us on alert when necessary. I've done a full background investigation on him."

"You hacked DOD records as well? You're scary," he quipped.

"I've had to protect myself. I thought many times of going on the offensive, of taking out Matthews and his people. At one time, it actually became an obsession. I've planned dozens of attacks and I know I could do it. I just came to realize that's not what God wants me to do."

"So, you stay on the defensive?"

"For now. But I won't hesitate to defend myself. Never again."

"But…hacking?"

"I had to know my enemy to protect myself from him. Who do you think was behind the deep web?"

"Really? And Bitcoin?"

"Nope. Can't take credit for that one. And definitely not the dark web. But like I said, I have to stay sharp and know what the other side is up to."

"So, you hack instead of playing word games?"

"How else did you think I looked over all your medical records? You didn't think I just walked into your doctor's office and asked for your charts? Of course, I now know more about you than their charts would show."

"Okay…tell me, how's my prostate?" He chuckled.

Karen smiled and didn't say a word.

"You're kidding. Tell me you're kidding!"

She laughed pleasantly. "Your prostate's fine, and you have no other cancer either. And I know that by the blood work I did, not the old-fashioned way."

"I'll say it again. You're scary!"

"I'm alive. And I'm absolutely certain that I wouldn't be if I hadn't learned to be careful. The world should be very, very grateful that Matthews didn't succeed with FSAT."

"Oh?"

"The transition tends to enhance whatever motivations or personality characteristics we already have, even if they're latent. I saw some really, really ugly examples of that with a few of Matthews' experiments."

"So…we're not like any kind of new race or anything?"

"Not even close. The Bible describes Christ as the Second Adam, of course, and he's the last one. No sin of his own, so he could die sacrificially as a sin-bearer for us. And the FSAT transition made me sterile, destroying my ova. I'm the end of the line; like somehow God wanted just one of me. I'm even 'one-deep.' I developed the serum to transition you, but that's as far as it goes. Your blood and DNA can't be used to help anyone else. And even I can only pass it on under extremely controlled conditions. Like I said, you're Number Two."

"And, of course, you and I are double-unique."

"Yep, you're stuck with me, old guy. Get used to it. I'm even looking forward to letting my hair return to its natural color. So now we're a team, and you're the leader."

"Leader?"

"Correct. You're it. Sorry, I took the vote while you were recovering from surgery. You were volunteered. Leadership has never been my strong suit. Neither is organization, and I think Tamika would be perfect for that."

"Why do I somehow get the feeling that I've been railroaded? You're the smartest person on the planet, and you want a tired old engineer to be a leader?!"

The playful banter continued as they streaked toward Robins Air Force Base, with not even a sonic boom giving away their leisurely supersonic cruise.

"Hey, just 'cause I got a few years' head start, don't think you won't catch up fast. You had a higher IQ to begin with, a whole lifetime of using it to the max, and you're an obvious leader or we wouldn't be flying in your aircraft right now. You know Justin thinks the world of you."

"So... exactly what am I the reluctant leader of?"

"What we just did. The way I see it, we need to be making a difference for Christ however we can, while we still can. Things are already far worse than anyone could have imagined at the turn of the century. Once the Church is removed, all hell will break loose, literally. We know the Tribulation, especially the last half, will be unimaginably horrible. So, while we can, we need to support good ministries, meet humanitarian needs, protect our country; whatever. As Jesus said, we need to work while it's light because a time of darkness is coming when no one can work."

"So would I be correct to presume that a lot of otherwise unexplainable good things over the past several years could be attributed to a lovely redhead, or whatever color it was at the time?"

"Let's just say, God has given me some unique opportunities and His grace has led to some interesting outcomes."

"Do tell...?"

"Plenty of time for that. You'll be in for some interesting surprises yourself."

"How so?"

"Well, factoring in our advanced time frame, your recovery from the surgery, the rate of genetic alterations…Roger, if we went to a gym right now, I suspect there's currently only one person alive today who could out-lift you. And within another week, you will be able to out-lift me as well. Same thing with running, jumping, and endurance. Think 'Samson.' Really! Just that you won't have to wear your hair long."

"Then I'm not just feeling good because we stopped the attack?"

"When you look at yourself in a mirror, you'll already see a huge difference. And your occasional A-Fib should already be history. I wouldn't be at all surprised if you have a regenerated, fully healthy gallbladder within a few weeks."

"So…you won't be stuck with an old man?"

She chuckled. "Oh, no my friend. Pretty soon I'll be the one struggling to keep up with you. Like I said before, we're stuck with each other."

"And we're stuck with the aircraft."

"Yes, but we can go out for maybe a day at a time."

"Really? I started going into respiratory distress in less than half an hour."

"I've done the math. We can carry a backpack with a couple of slugs, or some other dense converted object, and go out for a while. Kind of a *ghost patrol*."

"Hmm. Like reflections of a shadow. That could certainly weird some people out."

"Gotta admit, it makes me think again about going after Matthews and his team for all the years they made my life such a nightmare." She took a deep breath then continued. "But on a positive note, you'll be glad to know that Guardian is stable for at least fifty years, or until it slams into a mountain, whichever occurs first. More good news, the explosive transition effect can only occur if an impact occurs at hypersonic speeds. It has to be severe enough to create a plasma, not just a crash, or fire, or even a normal explosion. Tearing down the hangar wouldn't have caused it, nor would a tornado. I'm estimating at least Mach Six, which is why the slugs are so effective at speeds well above Mach Ten."

"That's a relief! I've been terrified of doing more damage than what Justin and I prevented."

They were both quiet for a beat. When she spoke again, she was more reflective. "I have no idea what all the Lord has for us. We are absolutely unique in the history of this world. And the timing which has brought us together, and how we are now both double-unique? It's a 'God thing,' as they say. But I'm convinced that he means for us to occupy till he returns."

"I agree. I'm amazed and humbled, and...well, a little scared. 'From everyone who has been given much, much will be required.' I'm just so grateful that you chose to come to me and were able to."

"I prayed hard and long. When you told me a chameleon somehow survived, I had peace that I could too. A chameleon is known for its ability to adapt and to regenerate lost tails. I don't have a tail in that sense, but I guess I have the best ability to adapt and otherwise regenerate of any person alive until you joined me as Number Two."

Roger changed the subject after looking at his navigation display.

"Hmm. Well, we should be at our new home in less than half an hour. You'll love the decor; early 1980's hangar, wall-to-wall painted concrete floor, and high ceilings. *Really* high ceilings. And the food...! All the latest MREs and the very best of discount store bottled water. All the comforts of home."

There was a long, relaxed pause as they were each lost in their own thoughts.

For his part, Roger engaged in one of his eight-second odysseys, considering the future and the possibilities. It was very pleasant.

Finally, Karen spoke up again.

"Roger?" she asked quietly.

"Hmm?"

"The answer is yes," she said softly. The non-magnetic transducers flawlessly transferred every vocal nuance from her microphone to Roger's noise-cancelling headset. His now-years-younger ears heard perfectly, even though what she had said was just above a whisper.

He didn't answer immediately.

"Do I know the question?" His voice was also uncharacteristically quiet. His strong, healthy heart was racing.

"I think you do. And the answer is yes."

Roger smiled. He really was feeling younger—decades younger—and he was certain it couldn't be entirely attributed to the effects of FSAT.

Guardian was back over the continental United States. It streaked across state after state at Flight Level Seven Five, at a comfortable cruise speed of Mach Three. About the same altitude and speed of the SR-71 Blackbird spy plane, retired decades earlier.

Below was Texas, where it all began. *Just over six months ago,* Roger reflected.

I knew I was going to die, whether the intercept succeeded or not. I couldn't land the aircraft. Karen...Jennifer back then... expected to die when she took FSAT. It was the only way to save her friends.

He didn't know about it yet, but that was the sacrificial attitude of the President of the United States. Juan had made himself vulnerable to try to flush out a lethal traitor. And Chet, willing to put his life on the line to protect that President and his administration. There was a more to be known about a certain no-nonsense General who took his oath of office seriously. And, a young couple whose lives had just recently changed forever.

So much Roger and Karen didn't know. Yet.

We've been through so much, Roger pondered. *Wonder what's next?*

Probably for the best, he couldn't imagine.

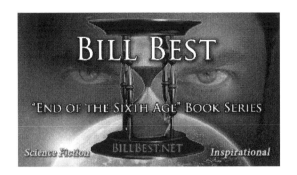

Unusual circumstances bring together an unlikely team, who risk everything to hold off the ultimate, prophesied evil as long as possible.

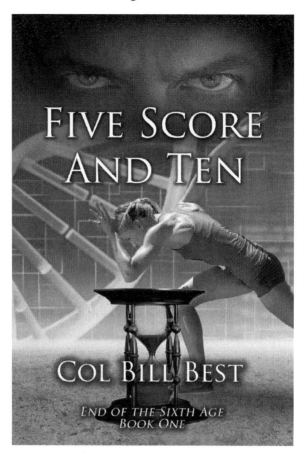

Book One, "*Five Score and Ten,*" tells the story of the first member of this team. Jennifer Karen Lane is a flighty, narcissistic college grad. Follow the gut-wrenching, overwhelming tragedies that crush and transform her into the world's strongest, most intelligent human being. She's a beautiful but troubled woman relentlessly pursued by the evil Jason Matthews.

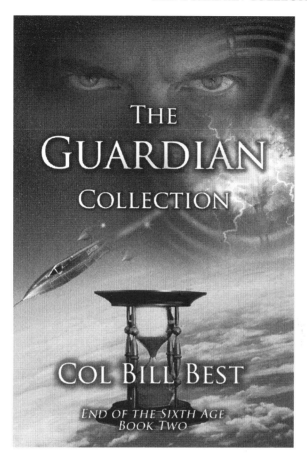

Book Two, "*The Guardian Collection*," brings us up-to-date on Karen's struggles in 2020, and the One World Peace Now countdown for world dominance by the mid-2020's. It all comes together in the "Guardian" novellas, as more lives are changed forever. Will the planet be destroyed by World War III, or will every country be crushed by an authoritarian one-world government? Will there be any time left for each person to make decisions with eternal consequences?

Next? Book Three: "**Reflections of a Shadow**." Now in the late 2020s, the unique team fight the growing forces of darkness, hell-bent on ushering in a one world government, the Antichrist, and the "End of the Sixth Age!"

Want More?

- How did Karen and Roger meet?
- How did Roger lose his family, and the use of his legs in 2020?
- Why did he choose to join DPI and become the driving force behind the Guardian hypersonic manned interceptor?
- Finally, were the events in Roger's life a specific answer to prayer? Was he uniquely positioned, "…for such a time as this?"

Free eBook Novelette at **BillBest.Net/Free**

ABOUT THE AUTHOR

Colonel Bill Best (B.S., MBA; USAF, Retired) began writing as a culmination of many interests and careers.

Bill read every Science Fiction book in his school libraries.

After college, he served as an Active Duty Air Force officer for nine years. He continued an additional twenty-one years as a Reservist while serving at AM and FM Christian radio ministries around Warner Robins, Georgia.

As a broadcaster, Bill interviewed hundreds of Christian leaders such as the late Dr. D. James Kennedy (Coral Ridge Ministries) and Dr. Duane Gish (Institute for Creation Research). He also interviewed Joni Eareckson Tada, Herb Shreve (founder of Christian Motorcyclist Association) and Dr. Tim LaHaye (co-author of the incredible Left Behind series)!

 Bill's interest in computers and Science Fiction; his military background, experience as a Program Manager for a Department of

Defense Contractor, and years in a Christian radio ministry have led to a unique writing "voice" and perspective.

His "End of the Sixth Age" series combines today's headlines with tomorrow's technology, as the world inevitably moves to the prophesied One World Government and Tribulation.

Bill and his wife Barbara live in Middle Georgia. They have two daughters and – currently – four grandchildren.

Follow Bill at **BillBest.net**.

Made in the USA
Columbia, SC
14 September 2020